THE
HAUNTER
OF THE
RING

AND OTHER STORIES

THE HAUNTER OF THE RING

AND OTHER STORIES

ROBERT E. HOWARD

This edition published in 2021 by Arcturus Publishing Limited
26/27 Bickels Yard, 151–153 Bermondsey Street,
London SE1 3HA

Cover design: Peter Ridley
Cover illustration: Peter Gray

AD008447US

Printed in the UK

CONTENTS

INTRODUCTION

Robert Ervin Howard (1906–1936) was one of the founders of the sword and sorcery genre, a prolific short story writer and one of the most influential figures in fantasy fiction. He created a range of iconic characters including Conan the Barbarian, the somber Solomon Kane, and the lovable Sailor Steve Costigan. Yet he was an accomplished horror writer and a close confidante of H. P. Lovecraft. His stories have enthralled and chilled readers for generations.

Robert E. Howard was born in Peaster, Texas. His father was a traveling physician. The oil boom had begun just a few years earlier, and with the rise of several boom towns, his services were always in demand. Much of Howard's childhood was therefore spent traveling through the small towns of Texas and absorbing the culture of a growing, loosely regulated, society not far removed from the chaos of the frontier period.

Everywhere around him he saw violence and hatred in the rough-and-ready boom towns and the lesson he learned from these experiences was the importance of strength and power. He became fascinated by boxing and, in particular, by those boxers whose feats of stamina and endurance led them to victory. Meanwhile, his mother carefully nurtured his love of poetry, literature, and history as she sought to shield him from the violent realities of the world outside.

At the age of eight, he first attended school but, with his eidetic memory and brilliant mind, he found the experience dull and soon became embroiled in schoolyard fights and fending off bullies. By the time he was nine, he had already begun writing stories, which included vivid descriptions of Viking and Arab warriors in battle. The family finally settled down in the small quiet town of Cross Plains in 1919, and while it at first seemed to provide a respite from the hectic world they had previously lived in, the discovery of an oil spout a year later brought with it everything they had tried to escape.

Howard, still only 14, turned his attention to writing. He began submitting his stories to the pulp magazines, and it was around this time that he created many of his most beloved characters—including Solomon Kane, Bran Mak Morn, and El Borak—but initially he found little appreciation for his work. His first stories, "Golden Hope Christmas" and "West is West" were published in 1922 in his high school newspaper, *The Tattler.*

Two years later his literary career began in earnest, when *Weird Tales* published "Spear and Fang." It was the beginning of a relationship that would last for the rest of his life. His first story to be featured on the cover of the magazine was "Wolfshead," a disconcerting werewolf tale. Several more successes followed, including "The Shadow Kingdom" in 1927, which introduced Kull of Atlantis to the reading public and proved a cornerstone of the sword and sorcery genre. Howard was nonetheless very pragmatic about his work. He explained: "Literature is a business to me... My sole desire in writing is to make a reasonable living."

He also conducted an extensive literary correspondence with H. P. Lovecraft. The two writers met in 1930, and they discussed everything from the history of Celtic Britain to the virtues and vices of barbarism and civilization. The two came from almost diametrically opposite backgrounds and often fiercely disagreed. Nonetheless, they had great respect for each other, and when Howard read "The Rats in the Walls" he was deeply impressed. He developed a great interest in the Cthulhu Mythos and even contributed a few of his own stories, including "Skull-Face," "The Thing on the Roof," and "The Fire of Asshurbanipal."

In 1932 he came up with his most compelling creation yet—Conan of Cimmeria. The first tale, "The Phoenix of the Sword," was an instant success, and a flurry of stories followed, and it seemed that nothing could stop his literary ascent.

Then, in June 1936, without warning his mother fell ill from tuberculosis and slipped into a coma from which she would not awaken. Howard, who had struggled with mental health issues throughout his life, killed himself just a day before his mother died.

Howard's era-defining stories ranged from the Wild West to medieval France to the fantastical setting of Hyperborea. There are few writers who could claim to have had a greater impact on the fantasy landscape.

IN THE FOREST OF VILLEFÈRE

The sun had set. The great shadows came striding over the forest. In the weird twilight of a late summer day, I saw the path ahead glide on among the mighty trees and disappear. And I shuddered and glanced fearfully over my shoulder. Miles behind lay the nearest village—miles ahead the next.

I looked to left and to right as I strode on, and anon I looked behind me. And anon I stopped short, grasping my rapier, as a breaking twig betokened the going of some small beast. Or was it a beast?

But the path led on and I followed, because, forsooth, I had naught else to do.

As I went I bethought me, "My own thoughts will rout me, if I be not aware. What is there in this forest, except perhaps the creatures that roam it, deer and the like? Tush, the foolish legends of those villagers!"

And so I went and the twilight faded into dusk. Stars began to blink and the leaves of the trees murmured in the faint breeze. And then I stopped short, my sword leaping to my hand, for just ahead, around a curve of the path, someone was singing. The words I could not distinguish, but the accent was strange, almost barbaric.

I stepped behind a great tree, and the cold sweat beaded my forehead. Then the singer came in sight, a tall, thin man, vague in the twilight. I shrugged my shoulders. A *man* I did not fear. I sprang out, my point raised.

"Stand!"

He showed no surprise. "I prithee, handle thy blade with care, friend," he said.

Somewhat ashamed, I lowered my sword.

"I am new to this forest," I quoth, apologetically. "I heard talk of bandits. I crave pardon. Where lies the road to Villefère?"

"*Corbleu,* you've missed it," he answered. "You should have branched off to the right some distance back. I am going there myself. If you may abide my company, I will direct you."

I hesitated. Yet why should I hesitate?

"Why, certainly. My name is de Montour, of Normandy."

"And I am Carolus le Loup."

"No!" I started back.

He looked at me in astonishment.

"Pardon," said I; "the name is strange. Does not *loup* mean wolf?"

"My family were always great hunters," he answered. He did not offer his hand.

"You will pardon my staring," said I as we walked down the path, "but I can hardly see your face in the dusk."

I sensed that he was laughing, though he made no sound.

"It is little to look upon," he answered.

I stepped closer and then leaped away, my hair bristling.

"A mask!" I exclaimed. "Why do you wear a mask, *m'sieu*?"

"It is a vow," he exclaimed. "In fleeing a pack of hounds I vowed that if I escaped I would wear a mask for a certain time."

"Hounds, *m'sieu*?"

"Wolves," he answered quickly; "I said wolves."

We walked in silence for awhile and then my companion said, "I am surprised that you walk these woods by night. Few people come these ways even in the day."

"I am in haste to reach the border," I answered. "A treaty has been signed with the English, and the Duke of Burgundy should know of it. The people at the village sought to dissuade me. They spoke of—a wolf that was purported to roam these woods."

"Here the path branches to Villefère," said he, and I saw a narrow, crooked path that I had not seen when I passed it before. It led in amid the darkness of the trees. I shuddered.

"You wish to return to the village?"

"No!" I exclaimed. "No, no! Lead on."

So narrow was the path that we walked single file, he leading. I looked well at him. He was taller, much taller than I, and thin, wiry. He was dressed in a costume that smacked of Spain. A long rapier swung at his hip. He walked with long easy strides, noiselessly.

Then he began to talk of travel and adventure. He spoke of many lands and seas he had seen and many strange things. So we talked and went farther and farther into the forest.

I presumed that he was French, and yet he had a very strange accent, that was neither French nor Spanish nor English, not like any language I had ever heard. Some words he slurred strangely and some he could not pronounce at all.

"This path is often used, is it?" I asked.

"Not by many," he answered and laughed silently. I shuddered. It was very dark and the leaves whispered together among the branches.

"A fiend haunts this forest," I said.

"So the peasants say," he answered, "but I have roamed it oft and have never seen his face."

Then he began to speak of strange creatures of darkness, and the moon rose and shadows glided among the trees. He looked up at the moon.

"Haste!" said he. "We must reach our destination before the moon reaches her zenith."

We hurried along the trail.

"They say," said I, "that a werewolf haunts these woodlands."

"It might be," said he, and we argued much upon the subject.

"The old women say," said he, "that if a werewolf is slain while a wolf, then he is slain, but if he is slain as a man, then his half-soul will haunt his slayer forever. But haste thee, the moon nears her zenith."

We came into a small moonlit glade and the stranger stopped.

"Let us pause a while," said he.

"Nay, let us be gone," I urged; "I like not this place."

He laughed without sound. "Why," said he, "This is a fair glade. As good as a banquet hall it is, and many times have I feasted here. Ha, ha, ha! Look ye, I will show you a dance." And he began bounding here and there, anon flinging back his head and laughing silently. Thought I, the man is mad.

As he danced his weird dance I looked about me. *The trail went not on but stopped in the glade.*

"Come," said I "we must on. Do you not smell the rank, hairy scent that hovers about the glade? Wolves den here. Perhaps they are about us and are gliding upon us even now."

He dropped upon all fours, bounded higher than my head, and came toward me with a strange slinking motion.

"That dance is called the Dance of the Wolf," said he, and my hair bristled.

"Keep off!" I stepped back, and with a screech that set the echoes shuddering he leaped for me, and though a sword hung at his belt he did not draw it. My rapier was half out when he grasped my arm and flung me headlong. I dragged him with me and we struck the ground together. Wrenching a hand free I jerked off the mask. A shriek of horror broke from my lips. Beast eyes glittered beneath that mask, white fangs flashed in the moonlight. *The face was that of a wolf.*

In an instant those fangs were at my throat. Taloned hands tore the sword from my grasp. I beat at that horrible face with my clenched fists, but his jaws were fastened on my shoulders, his talons tore at my throat. Then I was on my back. The world was fading. Blindly I struck out. My hand dropped, then closed automatically about the hilt of my dagger, which I had been unable to get at. I drew and stabbed. A terrible, half-bestial bellowing screech. Then I reeled to my feet, free. At my feet lay the werewolf.

I stooped, raised the dagger, then paused, looked up. The moon hovered close to her zenith. *If I slew the thing as a man its frightful spirit would haunt me forever.* I sat down waiting. The *thing* watched me with flaming wolf eyes. The long wiry limbs seemed to shrink, to crook; hair seemed to grow upon them. Fearing madness, I snatched up the *thing's* own sword and hacked it to pieces. Then I flung the sword away and fled.

WOLFSHEAD

Fear? Your pardon, *Messieurs*, but the meaning of fear you do not know. No, I hold to my statement. You are soldiers, adventurers. You have known the charges of regiments of dragoons, the frenzy of wind-lashed seas. But fear, real hair-raising, horror-crawling fear, you have not known. I myself have known such fear; but until the legions of darkness swirl from hell's gate and the world flames to ruin, will never such fear again be known to men.

Hark, I will tell you the tale; for it was many years ago and half across the world; and none of you will ever see the man of whom I tell you, or seeing, know.

Return, then, with me across the years to a day when I, a reckless young cavalier, stepped from the small boat that had landed me from the ship floating in the harbor, cursed the mud that littered the crude wharf, and strode up the landing toward the castle, in answer to the invitation of an old friend, Dom Vincente da Lusto.

Dom Vincente was a strange, far-sighted man—a strong man, one who saw visions beyond the ken of his time. In his veins, perhaps, ran the blood of those old Phoenicians who, the priests tell us, ruled the seas and built cities in far lands, in the dim ages. His plan of fortune was strange and yet successful; few men would have thought of it; fewer could have succeeded. For his estate was upon the western coast of that dark, mystic continent, that baffler of explorers—Africa.

There by a small bay had he cleared away the sullen jungle, built his castle and his storehouses, and with ruthless hand had he wrested the riches of the land. Four ships he had: three smaller craft and one great galleon. These plied between his domains and the cities of Spain, Portugal, France, and even England, laden with rare woods, ivory, slaves; the thousand strange riches that Dom Vincente had gained by trade and by conquest.

Aye, a wild venture, a wilder commerce. And yet might he have shaped an empire from the dark land, had it not been for the rat-faced Carlos, his nephew—but I run ahead of my tale.

Look, *Messieurs*, I draw a map on the table, thus, with finger dipped in wine. Here lay the small, shallow harbor, and here the wide wharves. A landing ran thus, up the slight slope with hutlike warehouses on each side, and here it stopped at a wide, shallow moat. Over it went a narrow drawbridge and then one was confronted with a high palisade of logs set in the ground. This extended entirely around the castle. The castle itself was built on the model of another, earlier age; being more for strength than beauty. Built of stone brought from a great distance; years of labor and a thousand Negroes toiling beneath the lash had reared its walls, and now, completed, it offered an almost impregnable appearance. Such was the—intention of its builders, for Barbary pirates ranged the coasts, and the horror of a native uprising lurked ever near.

A space of about a half-mile on every side of the castle was kept cleared away and roads had been built through the marshy land. All this had required an immense amount of labor, but manpower was plentiful. A present to a chief, and he furnished all that was needed. And Portuguese know how to make men work!

Less than three hundred yards to the east of the castle ran a wide, shallow river, which emptied into the harbor. The name has entirely slipped my mind. It was a heathenish title and I could never lay my tongue to it.

I found that I was not the only friend invited to the castle. It seems that once a year or some such matter, Dom Vincente brought a host of jolly companions to his lonely estate and made merry for some weeks, to make up for the work and solitude of the rest of the year.

In fact, it was nearly night, and a great banquet was in progress when I entered. I was acclaimed with great delight, greeted boisterously by friends and introduced to such strangers as were there.

Entirely too weary to take much part in the revelry, I ate, drank quietly, listened to the toasts and songs, and studied the feasters.

Dom Vincente, of course, I knew, as I had been intimate with him for years; also his pretty niece, Ysabel, who was one reason I had accepted his invitation to come to that stinking wilderness. Her second cousin, Carlos, I knew and disliked—a sly, mincing fellow with a face like a mink's. Then there was my old friend, Luigi Verenza, an Italian; and his flirt of a sister, Marcita, making eyes at the men as usual. Then there was a short, stocky German who called himself Baron von Schiller; and Jean Desmarte, an out-at-the-elbows nobleman of Gascony; and Don Florenzo de Seville, a lean, dark, silent man, who called himself a Spaniard and wore a rapier nearly as long as himself.

There were others, men and women, but it was long ago and all their names and faces I do not remember.

But there was one man whose face somehow drew my gaze as an alchemist's magnet draws steel. He was a leanly built man of slightly more than medium height, dressed plainly, almost austerely, and he wore a sword almost as long as the Spaniard's.

But it was neither his clothes nor his sword which attracted my attention. It was his face. A refined, high-bred face, it was furrowed deep with lines that gave it a weary, haggard expression. Tiny scars flecked jaw and forehead as if torn by savage claws; I could have sworn the narrow gray eyes had a fleeting, haunted look in their expression at times.

I leaned over to that flirt, Marcita, and asked the name of the man, as it had slipped my mind that we had been introduced.

"De Montour, from Normandy," she answered. "A strange man. I don't think I like him."

"Then he resists your snares, my little enchantress?" I murmured; long friendship making me as immune from her anger as from her wiles. But she chose not to be angry and answered coyly, glancing from under demurely lowered lashes.

I watched de Montour much, feeling somehow a strange

fascination. He ate lightly, drank much, seldom spoke, and then only to answer questions.

Presently, toasts making the rounds, I noticed his companions urging him to rise and give a health. At first he refused, then rose, upon their repeated urgings, and stood silent for a moment, goblet raised. He seemed to dominate, to overawe the group of revelers. Then with a mocking, savage laugh, he lifted the goblet above his head.

"To Solomon," he exclaimed, "who bound all devils! And thrice cursed be he for that some escaped!"

A toast and a curse in one! It was drunk silently, and with many sidelong, doubting glances.

That night I retired early, weary of the long sea voyage and my head spinning from the strength of the wine,—of which Dom Vincente kept such great stores.

My room was near the top of the castle and looked out toward the forests of the south and the river. The room was furnished in crude, barbaric splendor, as was all the rest of the castle.

Going to the window, I gazed out at the arquebusier pacing the castle grounds just inside the palisade; at the cleared space lying unsightly and barren in the moonlight; at the forest beyond; at the silent river.

From the native quarters close to the river bank came the weird twanging of some rude lute, sounding a barbaric melody.

In the dark shadows of the forest some uncanny nightbird lifted a mocking voice. A thousand minor notes sounded—birds, and beasts, and the devil knows what else! Some great jungle cat began a hair-lifting yowling. I shrugged my shoulders and turned from the windows. Surely devils lurked in those somber depths.

There came a knock at my door and I opened it, to admit de Montour.

He strode to the window and gazed at the moon, which rode resplendent and glorious.

"The moon is almost full, is it not, *Monsieur*?" he remarked, turning to me. I nodded, and I could have sworn that he shuddered.

"Your pardon, *Monsieur*. I will not annoy you further." He turned to go, but at the door turned and retraced his steps.

"*Monsieur*," he almost whispered, with a fierce intensity, "whatever you do, be sure you bar and bolt your door tonight!"

Then he was gone, leaving me to stare after him bewilderedly.

I dozed off to sleep, the distant shouts of the revelers in my ears, and though I was weary, or perhaps because of it, I slept lightly. While I never really awoke until morning, sounds and noises seemed to drift to me through my veil of slumber, and once it seemed that something was prying and shoving against the bolted door.

As is to be supposed, most of the guests were in a beastly humor the following day and remained in their rooms most of the morning or else straggled down late. Besides Dom Vincente there were really only three of the masculine members sober: de Montour; the Spaniard, de Seville (as he called himself); and myself. The Spaniard never touched wine, and though de Montour consumed incredible quantities of it, it never affected him in any way.

The ladies greeted us most graciously.

"S'truth, *Signor*," remarked that minx Marcita, giving me her hand with a gracious air that was like to make me snicker, "I am glad to see there are gentlemen among us who care more for our company than for the wine cup; for most of them are most surprisingly befuddled this morning."

Then with a most outrageous turning of her wondrous eyes, "Methinks someone was too drunk to be discreet last night—or not drunk enough. For unless my poor senses deceive me much, someone came fumbling at my door late in the night."

"Ha!" I exclaimed in quick anger, "some—!"

"No. Hush." She glanced about as if to see that we were alone, then: "Is it not strange that Signor de Montour, before he retired last night, instructed me to fasten my door firmly?"

"Strange," I murmured, but did not tell her that he had told me the same thing.

"And is it not strange, Pierre, that though Signor de Montour left the banquet hall even before you did, yet he has the appearance of one who has been up all night?"

I shrugged. A woman's fancies are often strange.

"Tonight," she said roguishly, "I will leave my door unbolted and see whom I catch."

"You will do no such thing."

She showed her little teeth in a contemptuous smile and displayed a small, wicked dagger.

"Listen, imp. De Montour gave me the same warning he did you. Whatever he knew, whoever prowled the halls last night, the object was more apt murder than amorous adventure. Keep you your doors bolted. The lady Ysabel shares your room, does she not?"

"Not she. And I send my woman to the slave quarters at night," she murmured, gazing mischievously at me from beneath drooping eyelids.

"One would think you a girl of no character from your talk," I told her, with the frankness of youth and of long friendship. "Walk with care, young lady, else I tell your brother to spank you."

And I walked away to pay my respects to Ysabel. The Portuguese girl was the very opposite of Marcita, being a shy, modest young thing, not so beautiful as the Italian, but exquisitely pretty in an appealing, almost childish air. I once had thoughts— Hi ho! To be young and foolish!

Your pardon, *Messieurs*. An old man's mind wanders. It was of de Montour that I meant to tell you—de Montour and Dom Vincente's mink-faced cousin.

A band of armed natives were thronged about the gates, kept at a distance by the Portuguese soldiers. Among them were some score of young men and women all naked, chained neck to neck. Slaves they were, captured by some warlike tribe and brought for sale. Dom Vincente looked them over personally.

Followed a long haggling and bartering, of which I quickly wearied and turned away, wondering that a man of Dom Vincente's rank could so demean himself as to stoop to trade.

But I strolled back when one of the natives of the village nearby came up and interrupted the sale with a long harangue to Dom Vincente.

While they talked de Montour came up, and presently Dom Vincente turned to us and said, "One of the woodcutters of the village was torn to pieces by a leopard or some such beast last night. A strong young man and unmarried."

"A leopard? Did they, see it?" suddenly asked de Montour, and when Dom Vincente said no, that it came and went in the night, de Montour lifted a trembling hand and drew it across his forehead, as if to brush away cold sweat.

"Look you, Pierre," quoth Dom Vincente, "I have here a slave who, wonder of wonders, desires to be your man. Though the devil only knows why."

He led up a slim young Jakri, a mere youth, whose main asset seemed a merry grin.

"He is yours," said Dom Vincente. "He is goodly trained and will make a fine servant. And look ye, a slave is of an advantage over a servant, for all he requires is food and a loincloth or so with a touch of the whip to keep him in his place."

It was not long before I learned why Gola wished to be "my man," choosing me among all the rest. It was because of my hair. Like many dandies of that day, I wore it long and curled, the strands falling to my shoulders. As it happened, I was the only man of the party who so wore my hair, and Gola would sit and gaze at it in silent admiration for hours at a time, or until, growing nervous under his unblinking scrutiny, I would boot him forth.

It was that night that a brooding animosity, hardly apparent, between Baron von Schiller and Jean Desmarie broke out into a flame.

As usual, a woman was the cause. Marcita carried on a most outrageous flirtation with both of them.

That was not wise. Desmarte was a wild young fool. Von Schiller was a lustful beast. But when, *Messieurs*, did woman ever use wisdom?

Their hate flamed to a murderous fury when the German sought to kiss Marcita.

Swords were clashing in an instant. But before Dom Vincente could thunder a command to halt, Luigi was between the combatants, and had beaten their swords down, hurling them back viciously.

"*Signori*," said he softly, but with a fierce intensity, "is it the part of high-bred *signorito* fight over my sister? Ha, by the toenails of Satan, for the toss of a coin I would call you both out! You, Marcita, go to your chamber, instantly, nor leave until I give you permission."

And she went, for, independent though she was, none cared to face the slim, effeminate-appearing youth when a tigerish snarl curled his lips, a murderous gleam lightened his dark eyes.

Apologies were made, but from the glances the two rivals threw at each other, we knew that the quarrel was not forgotten and would blaze forth again at the slightest pretext.

Late that night I woke suddenly with a strange, eerie feeling of horror. Why, I could not say. I rose, saw that the door was firmly bolted, and seeing Gola asleep on the floor, kicked him awake irritably.

And just as he got up, hastily, rubbing himself, the silence was broken by a wild scream, a scream that rang through the castle and brought a startled shout from the arquebusier pacing the palisade; a scream from the mouth of a girl, frenzied with terror.

Gola squawked and dived behind the divan. I jerked the door open and raced down the dark corridor. Dashing down a winding stair, I caromed into someone at the bottom and we tumbled headlong.

He gasped something and I recognized the voice of Jean Desmarte. I hauled him to his feet, and raced along, he following; the screams had ceased, but the whole castle was in an uproar, voices shouting, the clank of weapons, lights flashing up, Dom Vincente's voice shouting for the soldiers, the noise of armed men rushing through the rooms and falling over each other. With all the confusion, Desmarte, the Spaniard, and I reached Marcita's room just as Luigi darted inside and snatched his sister into his arms.

Others rushed in, carrying lights and weapons, shouting, demanding to know what was occurring.

The girl lay quietly in her brother's arms, her dark hair loose and rippling over her shoulders, her dainty night-garments torn to shreds and exposing her lovely body. Long scratches showed upon her arms, breasts and shoulders.

Presently, she opened her eyes, shuddered, then shrieked wildly and clung frantically to Luigi, begging him not to let something take her.

"The door!" she whimpered. "I left it unbarred. And *something* crept into my room through the darkness. I struck at it with my dagger and it hurled me to the floor, tearing, tearing at me. Then I fainted."

"Where is von Schiller?" asked the Spaniard, a fierce glint in his dark eyes. Every man glanced at his neighbor. All the guests were there except the German. I noted de Montour gazing at the terrified girl, his face more haggard than usual. And I thought it strange that he wore no weapon.

"Aye, von Schiller!" exclaimed Desmarte fiercely. And half of us followed Dom Vincente out into the corridor. We began a vengeful search through the castle, and in a small, dark hallway we found von Schiller. On his face he lay, in a crimson, ever-widening stain.

"This is the work of some native!" exclaimed Desmarte, face aghast.

"Nonsense," bellowed Dom Vincente. "No native from the outside could pass the soldiers. All slaves, von Schiller's among them, were barred and bolted in the slave quarters, except Gola, who sleeps in Pierre's room, and Ysabel's woman."

"But who else could have done this deed?" exclaimed Desmarte in a fury.

"You!" I said abruptly; "else why ran you so swiftly away from the room of Marcita?"

"Curse you, you lie!" he shouted, and his swift-drawn sword leaped for my breast; but quick as he was, the Spaniard was quicker. Desmarte's rapier clattered against the wall and Desmarte stood like a statue, the Spaniard's motionless point just touching his throat.

"Bind him," said the Spaniard without passion.

"Put down your blade, Don Florenzo," commanded Dom Vincente, striding forward and dominating the scene. "Signor Desmarte, you are one of my best friends, but I am the only law here and duty must be done. Give your word that you will not seek to escape."

"I give it," replied the Gascon calmly. "I acted hastily. I apologize. I was not intentionally running away, but the halls and corridors of this cursed castle confuse me."

Of us all, probably but one man believed him.

"*Messieurs*!" De Montour stepped forward. "This youth is not guilty. Turn the German over."

Two soldiers did as he asked. De Montour shuddered, pointing. The rest of us glanced once, then recoiled in horror.

"Could man have done that thing?"

"With a dagger—" began someone.

"No dagger makes wounds like that," said the Spaniard. "The German was torn to pieces by the talons of some frightful beast."

We glanced about us, half expecting some hideous monster to leap upon us from the shadows.

We searched that castle; every foot, every inch of it. And we found no trace of any beast.

Dawn was breaking when I returned to my room, to find that Gola had barred himself in; and it took me nearly a half-hour to convince him to let me in.

Having smacked him soundly and berated him for his

cowardice, I told him what had taken place, as he could understand French and could speak a weird mixture which he proudly called French.

His mouth gaped and only the whites of his eyes showed as the tale reached its climax.

"Ju ju!" he whispered fearsomely. "Fetish man!"

Suddenly an idea came to me. I had heard vague tales, little more than hints of legends, of the devilish leopard cult that existed on the West Coast. No white man had ever seen one of its votaries, but Dom Vincente had told us tales of beast-men, disguised in skins of leopards, who stole through the midnight jungle and slew and devoured. A ghastly thrill traveled up and down my spine, and in an instant I had Gola in a grasp which made him yell.

"Was that a leopard-man?" I hissed, shaking him viciously.

"Massa, massa!" he gasped. "Me good boy! Ju ju man get! More besser no tell!"

"You'll tell me!" I gritted, renewing my endeavors, until, his hands waving feeble protests, he promised to tell me what he knew.

"No leopard-man!" he whispered, and his eyes grew big with supernatural fear. "Moon, he full, woodcutter find, him heap clawed. Find 'nother woodcutter. Big Massa (Dom Vincente) say, 'leopard.' No leopard. But leopard-man, he come to kill. *Something kill leopard-man*! Heap claw! Hai, hai! Moon full again. Something come in, lonely hut; claw um woman, claw um pick'nin. Man find um claw up. Big Massa say 'leopard.' Full moon again, and woodcutter find, heap clawed. Now come in castle. No leopard. *But always footmarks of a man.*"

I gave a startled, incredulous exclamation.

It was true, Gola averred. Always the footprints of a man led away from the scene of the murder. Then why did the natives not tell the Big Massa that he might hunt down the fiend? Here Gola assumed a crafty expression and whispered in my ear, "*The footprints were of a man who wore shoes!*"

Even assuming that Gola was lying, I felt a thrill of unexplainable horror. Who, then, did the natives believe was doing these frightful murders?

And he answered: Dom Vincente!

By this time, *Messieurs*, my mind was in a whirl.

What was the meaning of all this? Who slew the German and sought to ravish Marcita? And as I reviewed the crime, it appeared to me that murder rather than rape was the object of the attack.

Why did de Montour warn us, and then appear to have knowledge of the crime, telling us that Desmarte was innocent and then proving it?

It was all beyond me.

The tale of the slaughter got among the natives, in spite of all we could do, and they appeared restless and nervous, and thrice that day Dom Vincente had a black lashed for insolence. A brooding atmosphere pervaded the castle.

I considered going to Dom Vincente with Gola's tale, but decided to wait awhile.

The women kept their chambers that day, the men were restless and moody. Dom Vincente announced that the sentries would be doubled and some would patrol the corridors of the castle itself. I found myself musing cynically that if Gola's suspicions were true, sentries would be of little good.

I am not, *Messieurs*, a man to brook such a situation with patience. And I was young then. So as we drank before retiring, I flung my goblet on the table and angrily announced that in spite of man, beast or devil, I slept that night with doors flung wide. And I tramped angrily to my chamber.

Again, as on the first night, de Montour came. And his face was as a man who has looked into the gaping gates of hell.

"I have come," he said, "to ask you—nay, *Monsieur*, to implore you to reconsider your rash determination."

I shook my head impatiently.

"You are resolved? Yes? Then I ask you do to this for me, that after I enter my chamber, you will bolt my doors from the outside."

I did as he asked, and then made my way back to my chamber, my mind in a maze of wonderment. I had sent Gola to the slave quarters, and I laid rapier and dagger close at hand. Nor did I go to bed, but crouched in a great chair, in the darkness. Then I had much ado to keep from sleeping. To keep myself awake, I fell to musing on the strange words of de Montour. He seemed to be laboring under great excitement; his eyes hinted of ghastly mysteries known to him alone. And yet his face was not that of a wicked man.

Suddenly the notion took me to go to his chamber and talk with him.

Walking those dark passages was a shuddersome task, but eventually I stood before de Montour's door. I called softly. Silence. I reached out a hand and felt splintered fragments of wood. Hastily I struck flint and steel which I carried, and the flaming tinder showed the great oaken door sagging on its mighty hinges; showed a door smashed and splintered from the inside. And the chamber of de Montour was unoccupied.

Some instinct prompted me to hurry back to my room, swiftly but silently, shoeless feet treading softly. And as I neared the door, I was aware of something in the darkness before me. Something which crept in from a side corridor and glided stealthily along.

In a wild panic of fear I leaped, striking wildly and aimlessly in the darkness. My clenched fist encountered a human head, and something went down with a crash. Again I struck a light; a man lay senseless on the floor, and he was de Montour.

I thrust a candle into a niche in the wall, and just then de Montour's eyes opened and he rose uncertainly.

"You!" I exclaimed, hardly knowing what I said. "You, of all men!"

He merely nodded.

"You killed von Schiller?"

"Yes."

I recoiled with a gasp of horror.

"Listen." He raised his hand. "Take your rapier and run me through. No man will touch you."

"No," I exclaimed. "I can not."

"Then, quick," he said hurriedly, "get into your chamber and bolt the door. Haste! It will return!"

"What will return?" I asked, with a thrill of horror. "If it will harm me, it will harm you. Come into the chamber with me."

"No, no!" he fairly shrieked, springing back from my outstretched arm. "Haste, haste! It left me for an instant, but it will return." Then in a low-pitched voice of indescribable horror: "It is returning. *It is here now!*"

And I felt a *something*, a formless, shapeless presence near. A thing of frightfulness.

De Montour was standing, legs braced, arms thrown back, fists clenched. The muscles bulged beneath his skin, his eyes widened and narrowed, the veins stood out upon his forehead as if in great physical effort. As I looked, to my horror, out of nothing, a shapeless, nameless *something* took vague form! Like a shadow it moved upon de Montour.

It was hovering about him! Good God, it was merging, becoming one with the man!

De Montour swayed; a great gasp escaped him. The dim thing vanished. De Montour wavered. Then he turned toward me, and may God grant that I never look on a face like that again!

It was a hideous, a bestial face. The eyes gleamed with a frightful ferocity; the snarling lips were drawn back from gleaming teeth, which to my startled gaze appeared more like bestial fangs than human teeth.

Silently the *thing* (I can not call it a human) slunk toward me. Gasping with horror I sprang back and through the door, just as the *thing* launched itself through the air, with a sinuous motion which even then made me think of a leaping wolf. I slammed the door, holding it against the frightful *thing* which hurled itself again and again against it.

Finally it desisted and I heard it slink stealthily off down the corridor. Faint and exhausted I sat down, waiting, listening. Through the open window wafted the breeze, bearing all the scents of Africa, the spicy and the foul. From the native village came the sound of a native drum. Other drums answered farther up the river and back in the bush. Then from somewhere in the jungle, horridly incongruous, sounded the long, high-pitched call of a timber wolf. My soul revolted.

Dawn brought a tale of terrified villagers, of a Negro woman torn by some fiend of the night, barely escaping. And to de Montour I went.

On the way I met Dom Vincente. He was perplexed and angry.

"Some hellish thing is at work in this castle," he said. "Last night, though I have said naught of it to anyone, something leaped upon the back of one of the arquebusiers, tore the leather jerkin from his shoulders and pursued him to the barbican. More, someone locked de Montour into his room last night, and he was forced to smash the door to get out."

He strode on, muttering to himself, and I proceeded down the stairs, more puzzled than ever.

De Montour sat upon a stool, gazing out the window. An indescribable air of weariness was about him.

His long hair was uncombed and tousled, his garments were tattered. With a shudder I saw faint crimson stains upon his hands, and noted that the nails were torn and broken.

He looked up as I came in, and waved me to a seat. His face was worn and haggard, but was that of a man.

After a moment's silence, he spoke.

"I will tell you my strange tale. Never before has it passed my lips, and why I tell you, knowing that you will not believe me, I can not say."

And then I listened to what was surely the wildest, the most fantastic, the weirdest tale ever heard by man.

"Years ago," said de Montour, "I was upon a military mission in northern France. Alone, I was forced to pass through the fiend-haunted woodlands of Villefère. In those frightful forests I

was beset by an inhuman, a ghastly *thing*—a werewolf. Beneath
a midnight moon we fought, and slew it. Now this is the truth:
that if a werewolf is slain in the half-form of a man, its ghost
will haunt its slayer through eternity. But if it is slain as a wolf,
hell gapes to receive it. The true werewolf is not (as many think)
a man who may take the form of a wolf, *but a wolf who takes
the form of a man!*

"Now listen, my friend, and I will tell you of the wisdom, the
hellish knowledge that is mine, gained through many a frightful
deed, imparted to me amid the ghastly shadows of midnight
forests where fiends and half-beasts roamed.

"In the beginning, the world was strange, misshapen. Grotesque
beasts wandered through its jungles. Driven from another world,
ancient demons and fiends came in great numbers and settled
upon this newer, younger world. Long the forces of good and
evil warred.

"A strange beast, known as man, wandered among the other
beasts, and since good or bad must have a concrete form ere
either accomplishes its desire, the spirits of good entered man.
The fiends entered other beasts, reptiles and birds; and long and
fiercely waged the age-old battle. But man conquered. The great
dragons and serpents were slain and with them the demons.
Finally, Solomon, wise beyond the ken of man, made great war
upon them, and by virtue of his wisdom, slew, seized and bound.
But there were some which were the fiercest, the boldest, and
though Solomon drove them out he could not conquer them.
Those had taken the form of wolves. As the ages passed, wolf
and demon became merged. No longer could the fiend leave the
body of the wolf at will. In many instances, the savagery of the
wolf overcame the subtlety of the demon and enslaved him, so
the wolf became again only a beast, a fierce, cunning beast, but
merely a beast. But of the werewolves, there are many, even yet.

"And during the time of the full moon, the wolf may take the
form, or the half-form of a man. When the moon hovers at her
zenith, however, the wolf-spirit again takes ascendency and the

werewolf becomes a true wolf once more. But if it is slain in
the form of a man, then the spirit is free to haunt its slayer
through the ages.

"Harken now. I had thought to have slain the *thing* after it
had changed to its true shape. But I slew it an instant too soon.
The moon, though it approached the zenith, had not yet reached
it, nor had the *thing* taken on fully the wolf-form."

"Of this I knew nothing and went my way. But when the
next time approached for the full moon, I began to be aware of
a strange, malicious influence. An atmosphere of horror hovered
in the air and I was aware of inexplicable, uncanny impulses.

"One night in a small village in the center of a great forest,
the influence came upon me with full power. It was night, and
the moon, nearly full, was rising over the forest. And between
the moon and me, I saw, floating in the upper air, ghostly and
barely discernible, *the outline of a wolf's head!*

"I remember little of what happened thereafter. I remember,
dimly, clambering into the silent street, remember struggling,
resisting briefly, vainly, and the rest is a crimson maze, until I
came to myself the next morning and found my garments and
hands caked and stained crimson; and heard the horrified chat-
tering of the villagers, telling of a pair of clandestine lovers,
slaughtered in a ghastly manner, scarcely outside the village, torn
to pieces as if by wild beasts, as if by wolves.

"From that village I fled aghast, but I fled not alone. In the
day I could not feel the drive of my fearful captor, but when
night fell and the moon rose, I ranged the silent forest, a
frightful *thing*, a slayer of humans, a fiend in a man's body.

"God, the battles I have fought! But always it overcame me
and drove me ravening after some new victim. But after the
moon had passed its fullness, the *thing's* power over me ceased
suddenly. Nor did it return until three nights before the moon
was full again.

"Since then I have roamed the world—fleeing, fleeing, seeking
to escape. Always the *thing* follows, taking possession of my

body when the moon is full. Gods, the frightful deeds I have done!

"I would have slain myself long ago, but I dare not. For the soul of a suicide is accurst, and my soul would be forever hunted through the flames of hell. And harken, most frightful of all, my slain body would for ever roam the earth, moved and inhabited by the soul of the werewolf! Can any thought be more ghastly?

"And I seem immune to the weapons of man. Swords have pierced me, daggers have hacked me. I am covered with scars. Yet never have they struck me down. In Germany they bound and led me to the block. There would I have willingly placed my head, but the *thing* came upon me, and breaking my bonds, I slew and fled. Up and down the world I have wandered, leaving horror and slaughter in my trail. Chains, cells can not hold me. The *thing* is fastened to me through all eternity.

"In desperation I accepted Dom Vincente's invitation, for look you, none knows of my frightful double life, since no one could recognize me in the clutch of the demon; and few, seeing me, live to tell of it.

"My hands are red, my soul doomed to everlasting flames, my mind is torn with remorse for my crimes. And yet I can do nothing to help myself. Surely, Pierre, no man ever knew the hell that I have known.

"Yes, I slew von Schiller, and I sought, to destroy the girl Marcita. Why I did not, I can not say, for I have slain both women and men.

"Now, if you will, take your sword and slay me, and with my last breath I will give you the good God's blessing. No?

"You know now my tale and you see before you a man, fiend-haunted for all eternity."

My mind was spinning with wonderment as I left the room of de Montour. What to do, I knew not. It seemed likely that he would yet murder us all, and yet I could not bring myself to tell Dom Vincente all. From the bottom of my soul I pitied de Montour.

So I kept my peace, and in the days that followed I made occasion to seek him out and converse with him. A real friendship sprang up between us.

About this time that black devil, Gola, began to wear an air of suppressed excitement, as if he knew something he wished desperately to tell, but would not or else dared not.

So the days passed in feasting, drinking and hunting, until one night de Montour came to my chamber and pointed silently at the moon which was just rising.

"Look ye," he said, "I have a plan. I will give it out that I am going into the jungle for hunting and will go forth, apparently for several days. But at night I will return to the castle, and you must lock me into the dungeon which is used as a storeroom."

This we did, and I managed to slip down twice a day and carry food and drink to my friend. He insisted on remaining in the dungeon even in the day, for though the fiend had never exerted its influence over him in the daytime, and he believed it powerless then, yet he would take no chances.

It was during this time that I began to notice that Dom Vincente's mink-faced cousin, Carlos, was forcing his attentions upon Ysabel, who was his second cousin, and who seemed to resent those attentions.

Myself, I would have challenged him for a duel for the toss of a coin, for I despised him, but it was really none of my affair. However, it seemed that Ysabel feared him.

My friend Luigi, by the way, had become enamored of the dainty Portuguese girl, and was making swift love to her daily.

And de Montour sat in his cell and reviewed his ghastly deeds until he battered the bars with his bare hands.

And Don Florenzo wandered about the castle grounds like a dour Mephistopheles.

And the other guests rode and quarreled and drank.

And Gola slithered about, eyeing me if always on the point of imparting momentous information. What wonder if my nerves became rasped to the shrieking point?

Each day the natives grew surlier and more and more sullen and intractable.

One night, not long before the full of the moon, I entered the dungeon where de Montour sat.

He looked up quickly.

"You dare much, coming to me in the night."

I shrugged my shoulders, seating myself.

A small barred window let in the night scents and sounds of Africa.

"Hark to the native drums," I said. "For the past week they have sounded almost incessantly."

De Montour assented.

"The natives are restless. Methinks 'tis deviltry they are planning. Have you noticed that Carlos is much among them?"

"No," I answered, "but 'tis like there will be a break between him and Luigi. Luigi is paying court to Ysabel."

So we talked, when suddenly de Montour became silent and moody, answering only in monosyllables.

The moon rose and peered in at the barred windows. De Montour's face was illuminated by its beams.

And then the hand of horror grasped me. On the wall behind de Montour appeared a shadow, a shadow clearly defined of a *wolf's head*!

At the same instant de Montour felt its influence. With a shriek he bounded from his stool.

He pointed fiercely, and as with trembling hands I slammed and bolted the door behind me, I felt him hurl his weight against it. As I fled up the stairway I heard a wild raving and battering at the iron-bound door. But with all the werewolf's might the great door held.

As I entered my room, Gola dashed in and gasped out the tale he had been keeping for days.

I listened, incredulously, and then dashed forth to find Dom Vincente.

I was told that Carlos had asked him to accompany him

to the village to arrange a sale of slaves.

My informer was Don Florenzo of Seville, and when I gave him a brief outline of Gola's tale; he accompanied me.

Together we dashed through the castle gate, flinging a word to the guards, and down the landing toward the village.

Dom Vincente, Dom Vincente, walk with care, keep sword loosened in its sheath! Fool, fool, to walk in the night with Carlos, the traitor!

They were nearing the village when we caught up with them. "Dom Vincente!" I exclaimed; "return instantly to the castle. Carlos is selling you into the hands of the natives! Gola has told me that he lusts for your wealth and for Ysabel! A terrified native babbled to him of booted footprints near the places where the woodcutters were murdered, and Carlos has made the blacks believe that the slayer was you! Tonight the natives were to rise and slay every man in the castle except Carlos! Do you not believe me, Dom Vincente?"

"Is this the truth, Carlos?" asked Dom Vincente, in amazement. Carlos laughed mockingly.

"The fool speaks truth," he said, "but it accomplishes you nothing. Ho!"

He shouted as he leaped for Dom Vincente. Steel flashed in the moonlight and the Spaniard's sword was through Carlos ere he could move.

And the shadows rose about us. Then it was back to back, sword and dagger, three men against a hundred. Spears flashed, and a fiendish yell went up from savage throats. I spitted three natives in as many thrusts and then went down from a stunning swing from a warclub, and an instant later Dom Vincente fell upon me, with a spear in one arm and another through the leg. Don Florenzo was standing above us, sword leaping like a live thing, when a charge of the arquebusiers swept the river bank clear and we were borne into the castle.

The black hordes came with a rush, spears flashing like a wave of steel, a thunderous roar of savagery going up to the skies.

Time and again they swept up the slopes, bounding the moat, until they were swarming over the palisades. And time and again the fire of the hundred-odd defenders hurled them back.

They had set fire to the plundered warehouses, and their light vied with the light of the moon. Just across the river there was a larger storehouse, and about this hordes of the natives gathered, tearing it apart for plunder.

"Would that they would drop a torch upon it," said Dom Vincente, "for naught is stored therein save some thousand pounds of gunpowder. I dared not store the treacherous stuff this side of the river. All the tribes of the river and coast have gathered for our slaughter and all my ships are upon the seas. We may hold out awhile, but eventually they will swarm the palisade and put us to the slaughter."

I hastened to the dungeon wherein de Montour sat. Outside the door I called to him and he bade me enter in voice which told me the fiend had left him for an instant.

"The blacks have risen," I told him.

"I guessed as much. How goes the battle?"

I gave him the details of the betrayal and the fight, and mentioned the powder-house across the river. He sprang to his feet.

"Now by my hag-ridden soul!" he exclaimed. "I will fling the dice once more with hell! Swift, let me out of the castle! I will essay to swim the river and set off yon powder!"

"It is insanity!" I exclaimed. "A thousand blacks lurk between the palisades and the river, and thrice that number beyond! The river itself swarms with crocodiles!"

"I will attempt it!" he answered, a great light in his face. "If I can reach it, some thousand natives will lighten the siege; if I am slain, then my soul is free and mayhap will gain some forgiveness for that I gave my life to atone for my crimes."

Then, "Haste," he exclaimed, "for the demon is returning! Already I feel his influence! Haste ye!"

For the castle gates we sped, and as de Montour ran he gasped as a man in a terrific battle.

At the gate he pitched headlong, then rose, to spring through it. Wild yells greeted him from the natives.

The arquebusiers shouted curses at him and at me. Peering down from the top of the palisades I saw him turn from side to side uncertainly. A score of natives were rushing recklessly forward, spears raised.

Then the eerie wolf-yell rose to the skies, and de Montour bounded forward. Aghast, the natives paused, and before a man of them could move he was among them. Wild shrieks, not of rage, but of terror.

In amazement the arquebusiers held their fire.

Straight through the group of blacks de Montour charged, and when they broke and fled, three of them fled not.

A dozen steps de Montour took in pursuit; then stopped stock-still. A moment he stood so while spears flew about him, then turned and ran swiftly in the direction of the river.

A few steps from the river another band of blacks barred his way. In the flaming light of the burning houses the scene was clearly illuminated. A thrown spear tore through de Montour's shoulder. Without pausing in his stride he tore it forth and drove it through a native, leaping over his body to get among the others.

They could not face the fiend-driven white man. With shrieks they fled, and de Montour, bounding upon the back of one, brought him down.

Then he rose, staggered and sprang to the river bank. An instant he paused there and then vanished in the shadows.

"Name of the devil!" gasped Dom Vincente at my shoulder. "What manner of man is that? Was that de Montour?"

I nodded. The wild yells of the natives rose above the crackle of the arquebus fire. They were massed thick about the great warehouse across the river.

"They plan a great rush," said Dom Vincente. "They will swarm clear over the palisade, methinks. Ha!"

A crash that seemed to rip the skies apart! A burst of flame that mounted to the stars! The castle rocked with the explosion.

Then silence, as the smoke, drifting away, showed only a great crater where the warehouse had stood.

I could tell of how Dom Vincente led a charge, crippled as he was, out of the castle gate and, down the slope, to fall upon the terrified blacks who had escaped the explosion. I could tell of the slaughter, of the victory and the pursuit of the fleeing natives.

I could tell, too, *Messieurs*, of how I became separated from the band and of how I wandered far into the jungle, unable to find my way back to the coast.

I could tell how I was captured by a wandering band of slave raiders, and of how I escaped. But such is not my intention. In itself it would make a long tale; and it is of de Montour that I am speaking.

I thought much of the things that had passed and wondered if indeed de Montour reached the storehouse to blow it to the skies or whether it was but the deed of chance.

That a man could swim that reptile-swarming river, fiend-driven though he was, seemed impossible. And if he blew up the storehouse, he must have gone up with it.

So one night I pushed my way wearily through the jungle and sighted the coast, and close to the shore a small, tumbledown hut of thatch. To it I went, thinking to sleep therein if insects and reptiles would allow.

I entered the doorway and then stopped short. Upon a make-shift stool sat a man. He looked up as I entered and the rays of the moon fell across his face.

I started back with a ghastly thrill of horror. *It was de Montour, and the moon was full!*

Then as I stood, unable to flee, he rose and came toward me. And his face, though haggard as of a man who has looked into hell, was the face of a sane man.

"Come in, my friend," he said, and there was a great peace in his voice. "Come in and fear me not. The fiend has left me forever."

"But tell me, how conquered you?" I exclaimed as I grasped his hand.

"I fought a frightful battle, as I ran to the river," he answered, "for the fiend had me in its grasp and drove me to fall upon the natives. But for the first, time my soul and mind gained ascendency for an instant, an instant just long enough to hold me to my purpose. And I believe the good saints came to my aid, for I was giving my life to save life.

"I leaped into the river and swam, and in an instant the crocodiles were swarming about me.

"Again in the clutch of the fiend I fought them, there in the river. Then suddenly the *thing* left me.

"I climbed from the river and fired the warehouse. The explosion hurled me hundreds of feet, and for days I wandered witless through the jungle."

"But the full moon came, and came again, and I felt not the influence of the fiend.

"I am free, free!" And a wondrous note of exultation, nay, *exaltation*, thrilled his words:

"My soul is free. Incredible as it seems, the demon lies drowned upon the bed of the river, or else inhabits the body of one of the savage reptiles that swim the ways of the Niger."

THE VALLEY OF THE WORM

I will tell you of Niord and the worm. You have heard the tale before in many guises wherein the hero was named Tyr, or Perseus, or Siegfried, or Beowulf, or St. George. But it was Niord who met the loathly demoniac thing that crawled hideously up from hell, and from which meeting sprang the cycle of hero-tales that revolves down the ages until the very substance of the truth is lost and passes into the limbo of all forgotten legends. I know whereof I speak, for I was Niord.

As I lie here awaiting death, which creeps slowly upon me like a blind slug, my dreams are filled with glittering visions and the pageantry of glory. It is not of the drab, disease-racked life of James Allison I dream, but all the gleaming figures of the mighty pageantry that have passed before, and shall come after; for I have faintly glimpsed, not merely the shapes that come after, as a man in a long parade glimpses, far ahead, the line of figures that precede him winding over a distant hill, etched shadow-like against the sky. I am one and all the pageantry of shapes and guises and masks which have been, are, and shall be the visible manifestations of that illusive, intangible, but vitally existent spirit now promenading under the brief and temporary name of James Allison.

Each man on earth, each woman, is part and all of a similar caravan of shapes and beings. But they cannot remember—their minds cannot bridge the brief, awful gulfs of blackness which lie between those unstable shapes, and which the spirit, soul or ego, in spanning, shakes off its fleshy masks. I remember. Why I can remember is the strangest tale of all; but as I lie here with death's black wings slowly unfolding over me, all the dim folds of my previous lives are shaken out before my eyes, and I see myself in many forms and guises—braggart, swaggering, fearful, loving, foolish, all that men have been or will be.

I have been man in many lands and many conditions; yet—and

here is another strange thing—my line of reincarnation runs straight down one unerring channel. I have never been any but a man of that restless race men once called Nordheimr and later Aryans, and today name by many names and designations. Their history is my history, from the first mewling wail of a hairless white ape cub in the wastes of the Arctic, to the death-cry of the last degenerate product of ultimate civilization, in some dim and unguessed future age.

My name has been Hialmar, Tyr, Bragi, Bran, Horsa, Eric and John. I strode red-handed through the deserted streets of Rome behind the yellow-maned Brennus; I wandered through the violated plantations with Alaric and his Goths when the flame of burning villas lit the land like day and an empire was gasping its last under our sandalled feet; I waded sword in hand through the foaming surf from Hengist's galley to lay the foundations of England in blood and pillage; when Leif the Lucky sighted the broad white beaches of an unguessed world, I stood beside him in the bows of the dragon-ship, my golden beard blowing in the wind; and when Godfrey of Bouillon led his Crusaders over the walls of Jerusalem, I was among them in steel cap and brigandine.

But it is of none of these things I would speak. I would take you back with me into an age beside which that of Brennus and Rome is as yesterday. I would take you back through, not merely centuries and millenniums, but epochs and dim ages unguessed by the wildest philosopher. Oh far, far and far will you fare into the nighted past before you win beyond the boundaries of my race, blue-eyed, yellow-haired, wanderers, slayers, lovers, mighty in rapine and wayfaring.

It is the adventure of Niord Worm's-bane of which I would speak—the rootstem of a whole cycle of herotales which has not yet reached its end, the grisly underlying reality that lurks behind time-distorted myths of dragons, fiends and monsters.

Yet it is not alone with the mouth of Niord that I will speak. I am James Allison no less than I was Niord, and as I unfold the tale, I will interpret some of his thoughts and dreams and deeds from the mouth of the modern I, so that the saga of Niord shall not be a meaningless chaos to you. His blood is your blood, who are sons of Aryan; but wide misty gulfs of aeons lie horrifically between, and the deeds and dreams of Niord seem as alien to your deeds and dreams as the primordial and lion-haunted forest seems alien to the white-walled city street.

It was a strange world in which Niord lived and loved and fought, so long ago that even my aeon-spanning memory cannot recognize landmarks. Since then the surface of the earth has changed, not once but a score of times; continents have risen and sunk, seas have changed their beds and rivers their courses, glaciers have waxed and waned, and the very stars and constellations have altered and shifted.

It was so long ago that the cradle-land of my race was still in Nordheim. But the epic drifts of my people had already begun, and blue-eyed, yellow-maned tribes flowed eastward and southward and westward, on century-long treks that carried them around the world and left their bones and their traces in strange lands and wild waste places. On one of these drifts I grew from infancy to manhood. My knowledge of that northern homeland was dim memories, like half-remembered dreams, of blinding white snow plains and ice fields, of great fires roaring in the circle of hide tents, of yellow manes flying in great winds, and a sun setting in a lurid wallow of crimson clouds, blazing on trampled snow where still dark forms lay in pools that were redder than the sunset.

That last memory stands out clearer than the others. It was the field of Jotunheim, I was told in later years, whereon had just been fought that terrible battle which was the Armageddon of the Æsir-folk, the subject of a cycle of hero-songs for long ages, and which still lives today in dim dreams of Ragnarok and Goetterdaemmerung. I looked on that battle as a mewling infant; so I must have lived about—but I will not name the age, for I would be called a madman, and historians and geologists alike would rise to refute me.

But my memories of Nordheim were few and dim, paled by memories of that long, long trek upon which I had spent my life. We had not kept to a straight course, but our trend had been for ever southward. Sometimes we had bided for a while in fertile upland valleys or rich river-traversed plains, but always we took up the trail again, and not always because of drouth or famine. Often we left countries teeming with game and wild grain to push into wastelands. On our trail we moved endlessly, driven only by our restless whim, yet blindly following a cosmic law, the workings of which we never guessed, any more than the wild geese guess in their flights around the world. So at last we came into the Country of the Worm.

I will take up the tale at the time when we came into jungle-clad hills reeking with rot and teeming with spawning life, where the tom-toms of a savage people pulsed incessantly through the hot breathless night. These people came forth to dispute our way short, strongly built men, black-haired, painted, ferocious, but indisputably white men. We knew their breed of old. They were Picts, and of all alien races the fiercest. We had met their kind before in thick forests, and in upland valleys beside mountain lakes. But many moons had passed since those meetings.

I believe this particular tribe represented the easternmost drift of the race. They were the most primitive and ferocious of any I ever met. Already they were exhibiting hints of characteristics I have noted among black savages in jungle countries, though they had dwelled in these environs only a few generations. The abysmal jungle was engulfing them, was obliterating their pristine characteristics and shaping them in its own horrific mould. They were drifting into head-hunting, and cannibalism was but a step which I believe they must have taken before they became extinct. These things are natural adjuncts to the jungle; the Picts did not learn them from the black people, for then there were no blacks among those hills. In later years they came up from the south, and the Picts first enslaved and then were absorbed by them. But with that my saga of Niord is not concerned.

We came into that brutish hill country, with its squalling abysms of savagery and black primitiveness. We were a whole tribe marching on foot, old men, wolfish with their long beards and gaunt limbs, giant warriors in their prime, naked children running along the line of march, women with tousled yellow locks carrying babies which never cried—unless it were to scream from pure rage. I do not remember our numbers, except that there were some 500 fighting-men—and by fighting-men I mean all males, from the child just strong enough to lift a bow, to the oldest of the old men. In that madly ferocious age all were fighters. Our women fought, when brought to bay, like tigresses, and I have seen a babe, not yet old enough to stammer articulate words, twist its head and sink its tiny teeth in the foot that stamped out its life.

Oh, we were fighters! Let me speak of Niord. I am proud of him, the more when I consider the paltry crippled body of James Allison, the unstable mask I now wear. Niord was tall, with great shoulders, lean hips and mighty limbs. His muscles were long and swelling, denoting endurance and speed as well as strength. He could run all day without tiring, and he possessed a coordination that made his movements a blur of blinding speed. If I told you his full strength, you would brand me a liar. But there is no man on earth today strong enough to bend the bow Niord handled with ease. The longest arrow-flight on record is that of a Turkish archer who sent a shaft 482 yards. There was not a stripling in my tribe who could not have bettered that flight.

As we entered the jungle country we heard the tom-toms booming across the mysterious valleys that slumbered between the brutish hills, and in a broad, open plateau we met our enemies. I do not believe these Picts knew us, even by legends, or they had never rushed so openly to the onset, though they outnumbered us. But there was no attempt at ambush. They swarmed out of the trees, dancing and singing their war-songs, yelling their barbarous threats. Our heads should hang in their idol-hut and our yellow-haired women should bear their sons. Ho! ho! ho! By

Ymir, it was Niord who laughed then, not James Allison. Just so we of the Æsir laughed to hear their threats—deep thunderous laughter from broad and mighty chests. Our trail was laid in blood and embers through many lands. We were the slayers and ravishers, striding sword in hand across the world, and that these folk threatened us woke our rugged humour.

We went to meet them, naked but for our wolfhides, swinging our bronze swords, and our singing was like rolling thunder in the hills. They sent their arrows among us, and we gave back their fire. They could not match us in archery. Our arrows hissed in blinding clouds among them, dropping them like autumn leaves, until they howled and frothed like mad dogs and changed to hand-grips. And we, mad with the fighting joy, dropped our bows and ran to meet them, as a lover runs to his love.

By Ymir, it was a battle to madden and make drunken with the slaughter and the fury. The Picts were as ferocious as we, but ours was the superior physique, the keener wit, the more highly developed fighting-brain. We won because we were a superior race, but it was no easy victory. Corpses littered the blood-soaked earth; but at last they broke, and we cut them down as they ran, to the very edge of the trees. I tell of that fight in a few bald words. I cannot paint the madness, the reek of sweat and blood, the panting, muscle-straining effort, the splintering of bones under mighty blows, the rending and hewing of quivering sentient flesh; above all the merciless abysmal savagery of the whole affair, in which there was neither rule nor order, each man fighting as he would or could. If I might do so, you would recoil in horror; even the modern I, cognizant of my close kinship with those times, stand aghast as I review that butchery. Mercy was yet unborn, save as some individual's whim, and rules of warfare were as yet undreamed of. It was an age in which each tribe and each human fought tooth and fang from birth to death, and neither gave nor expected mercy.

So we cut down the fleeing Picts, and our women came out on the field to brain the wounded enemies with stones, or cut their throats with copper knives. We did not torture. We were no more cruel than life demanded. The rule of life was ruthlessness, but there is more wanton cruelty today than ever we dreamed of. It was not wanton bloodthirstiness that made us butcher wounded and captive foes. It was because we knew our chances of survival increased with each enemy slain.

Yet there was occasionally a touch of individual mercy, and so it was in this fight. I had been occupied with a duel with an especially valiant enemy. His tousled thatch of black hair scarcely came above my chin, but he was a solid knot of steel-spring muscles, than which lightning scarcely moved faster. He had an iron sword and a hide-covered buckler. I had a knotty-headed bludgeon. That fight was one that glutted even my battle-lusting soul. I was bleeding from a score of flesh wounds before one of my terrible, lashing strokes smashed his shield like cardboard, and an instant later my bludgeon glanced from his unprotected head. Ymir! Even now I stop to laugh and marvel at the hardness of that Pict's skull. Men of that age were assuredly built on a rugged plan! That blow should have spattered his brains like water. It did lay his scalp open horribly, dashing him senseless to the earth, where I let him lie, supposing him to be dead, as I joined in the slaughter of the fleeing warriors.

When I returned reeking with sweat and blood, my club horridly clotted with blood and brains, I noticed that my antagonist was regaining consciousness, and that a naked tousle-headed girl was preparing to give him the finishing touch with a stone she could scarcely lift. A vagrant whim caused me to check the blow. I had enjoyed the fight, and I admired the adamantine quality of his skull.

We made camp a short distance away, burned our dead on a great pyre, and after looting the corpses of the enemy, we dragged them across the plateau and cast them down in a valley to make a feast for the hyenas, jackals and vultures which were already gathering. We kept close watch that night, but we were not attacked, though far away through the jungle we could make out the red gleam of fires, and could faintly hear, when the wind veered, the throb of tom-toms and demoniac screams and yells keenings for the slain or mere animal squallings of fury.

Nor did they attack us in the days that followed. We bandaged our captive's wounds and quickly learned his primitive tongue, which, however, was so different from ours that I cannot conceive of the two languages having ever had a common source.

His name was Grom, and he was a great hunter and fighter, he boasted. He talked freely and held no grudge, grinning broadly and showing tusk-like teeth, his beady eyes glittering from under the tangled black mane that fell over his low forehead. His limbs were almost ape-like in their thickness.

He was vastly interested in his captors, though he could never understand why he had been spared; to the end it remained an inexplicable mystery to him. The Picts obeyed the law of survival even more rigidly than did the Æsir. They were the more practical, as shown by their more settled habits. They never roamed as far or as blindly as we. Yet in every line we were the superior race.

Grom, impressed by our intelligence and fighting qualities, volunteered to go into the hills and make peace for us with his people. It was immaterial to us, but we let him go. Slavery had not yet been dreamed of.

So Grom went back to his people, and we forgot about him, except that I went a trifle more cautiously about my hunting, expecting him to be lying in wait to put an arrow through my back. Then one day we heard a rattle of tom-toms, and Grom appeared at the edge of the jungle, his face split in his gorilla grin, with the painted, skin-clad, feather-bedecked chiefs of the clans. Our ferocity had awed them, and our sparing of Grom further impressed them. They could not understand leniency; evidently we valued them too cheaply to bother about killing one when he was in our power.

So peace was made with much pow-wow, and sworn to with many strange oaths and rituals we swore only by Ymir, and an Æsir never broke that vow. But they swore by the elements, by the idol which sat in the fetish-hut where fires burned for ever and a withered crone slapped a leather-covered drum all night long, and by another being too terrible to be named.

Then we all sat around the fires and gnawed meat-bones, and drank a fiery concoction they brewed from wild grain, and the wonder is that the feast did not end in a general massacre; for that liquor had devils in it and made maggots writhe in our brains. But no harm came of our vast drunkenness, and thereafter we dwelled at peace with our barbarous neighbours. They taught us many things, and learned many more from us. But they taught us iron-workings, into which they had been forced by the lack of copper in those hills, and we quickly excelled them.

We went freely among their villages—mud-walled clusters of huts in hilltop clearings, overshadowed by giant trees—and we allowed them to come at will among our camps—straggling lines of hide tents on the plateau where the battle had been fought. Our young men cared not for their squat beady-eyed women, and our rangy clean-limbed girls with their tousled yellow heads were not drawn to the hairy-breasted savages. Familiarity over a period of years would have reduced the repulsion on either side, until the two races would have flowed together to form one hybrid people, but long before that time the Æsir rose and departed, vanishing into the mysterious hazes of the haunted south. But before that exodus there came to pass the horror of the Worm.

I hunted with Grom and he led me into brooding, uninhabited valleys and up into silence-haunted hills where no men had set foot before us. But there was one valley, off in the mazes of the south-west, into which he would not go. Stumps of shattered columns, relics of a forgotten civilization, stood among the trees on the valley floor. Grom showed them to me, as we stood on the cliffs that flanked the mysterious vale, but he would not go down into it, and he dissuaded me when I would have gone alone. He would not speak plainly of the danger that lurked there, but it was greater than that of serpent or tiger, or the trumpeting elephants which occasionally wandered up in devastating droves from the south.

Of all beasts, Grom told me in the gutturals of his tongue, the Picts feared only Satha, the great snake, and they shunned the jungle where he lived. But there was another thing they feared, and it was connected in some manner with the Valley of Broken Stones, as the Picts called the crumbling pillars. Long ago, when his ancestors had first come into the country, they had dared that grim vale, and a whole clan of them had perished, suddenly, horribly and unexplainably. At least Grom did not explain. The horror had come up out of the earth, somehow, and it was not good to talk of it, since it was believed that It might be summoned by speaking of It—whatever It was.

But Grom was ready to hunt with me anywhere else; for he was the greatest hunter among the Picts, and many and fearful were our adventures. Once I killed, with the iron sword I had forged with my own hands, that most terrible of all beasts—old sabre-tooth, which men today call a tiger because he was more like a tiger than anything else. In reality he was almost as much like a bear in build, save for his unmistakably feline head. Sabre-tooth was massive-limbed, with a low-hung, great, heavy body, and he vanished from the earth because he was too terrible a fighter, even for that grim age. As his muscles and ferocity grew, his brain dwindled until at last even the instinct of self-preservation vanished. Nature, who maintains her balance in such things, destroyed him because, had his super-fighting powers been allied with an intelligent brain, he would have destroyed all other forms of life on earth. He was a freak on the road of evolution organic development gone mad and run to fangs and talons, to slaughter and destruction.

I killed sabre-tooth in a battle that would make a saga in itself, and for months afterwards I lay semi-delirious with ghastly wounds that made the toughest warriors shake their heads. The Picts said that never before had a man killed a sabre-tooth single-handed. Yet I recovered, to the wonder of all.

While I lay at the doors of death there was a secession from the tribe. It was a peaceful secession, such as continually occurred and contributed greatly to the peopling of the world by yellow-haired tribes. Forty-five of the young men took themselves mates simultaneously and wandered off to found a clan of their own. There was no revolt; it was a racial custom which bore fruit in all the later ages, when tribes sprung from the same roots met, after centuries of separation, and cut one another's throats with joyous abandon. The tendency of the Aryan and the pre-Aryan was always towards disunity, clans splitting off the main stem, and scattering.

So these young men, led by one Bragi, my brother-in-arms, took their girls and venturing to the south-west, took up their abode in the Valley of Broken Stones. The Picts expostulated, hinting vaguely of a monstrous doom that haunted the vale, but the Æsir laughed. We had left our own demons and weirds in the icy wastes of the far blue north, and the devils of other races did not much impress us.

When my full strength was returned, and the grisly wounds were only scars, I girt on my weapons and strode over the plateau to visit Bragi's clan. Grom did not accompany me. He had not been in the Æsir camp for several days. But I knew the way. I remembered well the valley, from the cliffs of which I had looked down and seen the lake at the upper end, the trees thickening into forest at the lower extremity. The sides of the valley were high sheer cliffs, and a steep broad ridge at either end cut it off from the surrounding country. It was towards the lower or southwestern end that the valley floor was dotted thickly with ruined columns, some towering high among the trees, some fallen into heaps of lichen-clad stones. What race reared them none knew. But Grom had hinted fearsomely of a hairy, apish monstrosity dancing loathsomely under the moon to a demoniac piping that induced horror and madness.

I crossed the plateau whereon our camp was pitched, descended the slope, traversed a shallow vegetation-choked valley, climbed another slope, and plunged into the hills. A half-day's leisurely travel brought me to the ridge on the other side of which lay the valley of the pillars. For many miles I had seen no sign of human life. The settlements of the Picts all lay many miles to the east. I topped the ridge and looked down into the dreaming valley with its still blue lake, its brooding cliffs and its broken columns jutting among the trees. I looked for smoke. I saw none, but I saw vultures wheeling in the sky over a cluster of tents on the lake shore.

I came down the ridge warily and approached the silent camp. In it I halted, frozen with horror. I was not easily moved. I had seen death in many forms, and had fled from or taken part in red massacres that spilled blood like water and heaped the earth with corpses. But here I was confronted with an organic devastation that staggered and appalled me. Of Bragi's embryonic clan, not one remained alive, and not one corpse was whole. Some of the hide tents still stood erect. Others were mashed down and flattened out, as if crushed by some monstrous weight, so that at first I wondered if a drove of elephants had stampeded across the camp. But no elephants ever wrought such destruction as I saw strewn on the bloody ground. The camp was a shambles, littered with bits of flesh and fragments of bodies—hands, feet, heads, pieces of human debris. Weapons lay about, some of them stained with a greenish slime like that which spurts from a crushed caterpillar.

No human foe could have committed this ghastly atrocity. I looked at the lake, wondering if nameless amphibian monsters had crawled from the calm waters whose deep blue told of unfathomed depths. Then I saw a print left by the destroyer. It was a track such as a titanic worm might leave, yards broad, winding back down the valley. The grass lay flat where it ran, and bushes and small trees had been crushed down into the earth, all horribly smeared with blood and greenish slime.

With berserk fury in my soul I drew my sword and started to follow it, when a call attracted me. I wheeled, to see a stocky form approaching me from the ridge. It was Grom the Pict, and when I think of the courage it must have taken for him to have overcome all the instincts planted in him by traditional teachings and personal experience, I realize the full depths of his friendship for me.

Squatting on the lake shore, spear in his hands, his black eyes ever roving fearfully down the brooding tree-waving reaches of the valley, Grom told me of the horror that had come upon Bragi's clan under the moon. But first he told me of it, as his sires had told the tale to him.

Long ago the Picts had drifted down from the north-west on a long, long trek, finally reaching these jungle-covered hills, where, because they were weary, and because the game and fruit were plentiful and there were no hostile tribes, they halted and built their mud-walled villages.

Some of them, a whole clan of that numerous tribe, took up their abode in the Valley of the Broken Stones. They found the columns and a great ruined temple back in the trees, and in that temple there was no shrine or altar, but the mouth of a shaft that vanished deep into the black earth, and in which there were no steps such as a human being would make and use. They built their village in the valley, and in the night, under the moon, horror came upon them and left only broken walls and bits of slime-smeared flesh.

In those days the Picts feared nothing. The warriors of the other clans gathered and sang their war-songs and danced their war-dances, and followed a broad track of blood and slime to the shaft-mouth in the temple. They howled defiance and hurled down boulders which were never heard to strike bottom. Then began a thin demoniac piping, and up from the well pranced a hideous anthropomorphic figure dancing to the weird strains of a pipe it held in its monstrous hands. The horror of its aspect froze the fierce Picts with amazement, and close behind it a vast white bulk heaved up from the subterranean darkness. Out of the shaft came a slavering mad nightmare which arrows pierced but could not check, which swords carved but could not slay. It fell slobbering upon the warriors, crushing them to crimson pulp, tearing them to bits as an octopus might tear small fishes, sucking their blood from their mangled limbs and devouring them even as they screamed and struggled. The survivors fled, pursued to the very ridge, up which, apparently, the monster could not propel its quaking mountainous bulk.

After that they did not dare the silent valley. But the dead came to their shamans and old men in dreams and told them strange and terrible secrets. They spoke of an ancient, ancient race of semi-human beings which once inhabited that valley and reared those columns for their own weird inexplicable purposes. The white monster in the pits was their god, summoned up from the nighted abysses of mid-earth uncounted fathoms below the black mould by sorcery unknown to the sons of men. The hairy anthropomorphic being was its servant, created to serve the god, a formless elemental spirit drawn up from below and cased in flesh, organic but beyond the understanding of humanity. The Old Ones had long vanished into the limbo from whence they crawled in the black dawn of the universe, but their bestial god and his inhuman slave lived on. Yet both were organic after a fashion, and could be wounded, though no human weapon had been found potent enough to slay them.

Bragi and his clan had dwelled for weeks in the valley before the horror struck. Only the night before, Grom, hunting above the cliffs, and by that token daring greatly, had been paralyzed by a high-pitched demon piping, and then by a mad clamour of human screaming. Stretched face down in the dirt, hiding his head in a tangle of grass, he had not dared to move, even when the shrieks died away in the slobbering, repulsive sounds of a hideous feast. When dawn broke he had crept shuddering to the cliffs to look down into the valley, and the sight of the devastation, even when seen from afar, had driven him in yammering flight far into the hills. But it had occurred to him, finally, that he should warn the rest of the tribe, and returning, on his way to the camp on the plateau, he had seen me entering the valley.

So spoke Grom, while I sat and brooded darkly, my chin on my mighty fist. I cannot frame in modern words the clan feeling that in those days was a living vital part of every man and woman. In a world where talon and fang were lifted on every hand, and the hands of all men raised against an individual, except those of his own clan, tribal instinct was more than the phrase it is today. It was as much a part of a man as was his heart or his right hand. This was necessary, for only thus banded together in unbreakable groups could mankind have survived in the terrible environments of the primitive world. So now the personal grief I felt for Bragi and the clean-limbed young men and laughing white-skinned girls was drowned in a deeper sea of grief and fury that was cosmic in its depth and intensity. I sat grimly, while the Pict squatted anxiously beside me, his gaze roving from me to the menacing deeps of the valley where the accursed columns loomed like broken teeth of cackling hags among the waving leafy reaches.

I, Niord, was not one to use my brain over-much. I lived in a physical world, and there were the old men of the tribe to do my thinking. But I was one of a race destined to become dominant mentally as well as physically, and I was no mere muscular animal. So as I sat there, there came dimly and then clearly a thought to me that brought a short fierce laugh from my lips.

Rising, I bade Grom aid me, and we built a pyre on the lake shore of dried wood, the ridge-poles of the tents, and the broken shafts of spears. Then we collected the grisly fragments that had been parts of Bragi's band, and we laid them on the pile, and struck flint and steel to it.

The thick sad smoke crawled serpent-like into the sky, and, turning to Grom, I made him guide me to the jungle where lurked that scaly horror, Satha, the great serpent. Grom gaped at me; not the greatest hunters among the Picts sought out the mighty crawling one. But my will was like a wind that swept him along my course, and at last he led the way. We left the valley by the upper end, crossing the ridge, skirting the tall cliffs, and plunged into the fastnesses of the south, which was peopled only by the grim denizens of the jungle. Deep into the jungle we went, until we came to a low-lying expanse, dank and dark beneath the great creeper-festooned trees, where our feet sank deep into the spongy silt, carpeted by rotting vegetation, and slimy moisture oozed up beneath their pressure. This, Grom told me, was the realm haunted by Satha, the great serpent.

Let me speak of Satha. There is nothing like him on earth today, nor has there been for countless ages. Like the meat-eating dinosaur, like old sabre-tooth, he was too terrible to exist. Even then he was a survival of a grimmer age when life and its forms were cruder and more hideous. There were not many of his kind then, though they may have existed in great numbers in the reeking ooze of the vast jungle-tangled swamps still further south. He was larger than any python of modern ages, and his fangs dripped with poison a thousand times more deadly than that of a king cobra.

He was never worshipped by the pure-blood Picts, though the blacks that came later deified him, and that adoration persisted in the hybrid race that sprang from the negroes and their white conquerors. But to other peoples he was the nadir of evil horror, and tales of him became twisted into demonology; so in later ages Satha became the veritable devil of the white races, and the Stygians first worshipped, and then, when they became Egyptians, abhorred him under the name of Set, the Old Serpent, while to the Semites he became Leviathan and Satan. He was terrible enough to be a god, for he was a crawling death. I had seen a bull elephant fall dead in his tracks from Satha's bite. I had seen him, had glimpsed him writhing his horrific way through the dense jungle, had seen him take his prey, but I had never hunted him. He was too grim, even for the slayer of old sabre-tooth.

But now I hunted him, plunging further and further into the hot, breathless reek of his jungle, even when friendship for me could not drive Grom further. He urged me to paint my body and sing my death-song before I advanced further, but I pushed on unheeding.

In a natural runway that wound between the shouldering trees, I set a trap. I found a large tree, soft and spongy of fibre, but thick-boled and heavy, and I hacked through its base close to the ground with my great sword, directing its fall so that when it toppled, its top crashed into the branches of a smaller tree, leaving it leaning across the runway, one end resting on the earth, the other caught in the small tree. Then I cut away the branches on the underside, and cutting a slim, tough sapling I trimmed it and stuck it upright like a prop-pole under the leaning tree. Then, cutting away the tree which supported it, I left the great trunk poised precariously on the prop-pole, to which I fastened a long vine, as thick as my wrist.

Then I went alone through that primordial twilight jungle until an overpowering fetid odour assailed my nostrils, and from the rank vegetation in front of me Satha reared up his hideous head, swaying lethally from side to side, while his forked tongue jetted in and out, and his great yellow terrible eyes burned icily on me with all the evil wisdom of the black elder world that was when man was not. I backed away, feeling no fear, only an icy sensation along my spine, and Satha came sinuously after me, his shining 80-foot barrel rippling over the rotting vegetation in mesmeric silence. His wedge-shaped head was bigger than the head of the hugest stallion, his trunk was thicker than a man's body, and his scales shimmered with a thousand changing scintillations. I was to Satha as a mouse is to a king cobra, but I was fanged as no mouse ever was. Quick as I was, I knew I could not avoid the lightning stroke of that great triangular head; so I dared not let him come too close. Subtly I fled down the runway, and behind me the rush of the great supple body was like the sweep of wind through the grass.

He was not far behind me when I raced beneath the dead-fall, and as the great shining length glided under the trap, I gripped the vine with both hands and jerked desperately. With a crash the great trunk fell across Satha's scaly back, some 6 feet back of his wedge-shaped head.

I had hoped to break his spine but I do not think it did, for the great body coiled and knotted, the mighty tail lashed and thrashed, mowing down the bushes as if with a giant flail. At the instant of the fall, the huge head had whipped about and struck the tree with a terrific impact, the mighty fangs shearing through bark and wood like scimitars. Now, as if aware he fought an inanimate foe, Satha turned on me, standing out of his reach. The scaly neck writhed and arched, the mighty jaws gaped, disclosing fangs a foot in length, from which dripped venom that might have burned through solid stone.

I believe, what of his stupendous strength, that Satha would have writhed from under the trunk, but for a broken branch that had been driven deep into his side, holding him like a barb. The sound of his hissing filled the jungle and his eyes glared at me with such concentrated evil that I shook despite myself. Oh, he knew it was I who had trapped him! Now I came as close as I dared, and with a sudden powerful cast of my spear transfixed his neck just below the gaping jaws, nailing him to the tree-trunk. Then I dared greatly, for he was far from dead, and I knew he would in an instant tear the spear from the wood and be free to strike. But in that instant I ran in, and swinging my sword with all my great power, I hewed off his terrible head.

The heavings and contortions of Satha's prisoned form in life were naught to the convulsions of his headless length in death. I retreated, dragging the gigantic head after me with a crooked pole, and at a safe distance from the lashing, flying tail, I set to work. I worked with naked death then, and no man ever toiled more gingerly than did I. For I cut out the poison sacs at the base of the great fangs, and in the terrible venom I soaked the heads of eleven arrows, being careful that only the bronze points were in the liquid, which else had corroded away the wood of the tough shafts. While I was doing this, Grom, driven by comradeship and curiosity, came stealing nervously through the jungle, and his mouth gaped as he looked on the head of Satha.

For hours I steeped the arrowheads in the poison, until they were caked with a horrible green scum, and showed tiny flecks of corrosion where the venom had eaten into the solid bronze. I wrapped them carefully in broad, thick, rubber-like leaves, and then, though night had fallen and the hunting beasts were roaring on every hand, I went back through the jungled hills, Grom with me, until at dawn we came again to the high cliffs that loomed above the Valley of Broken Stones.

At the mouth of the valley I broke my spear, and I took all the unpoisoned shafts from my quiver, and snapped them. I painted my face and limbs as the Æsir painted themselves only when they went forth to certain doom, and I sang my death-song to the sun as it rose over the cliffs, my yellow mane blowing in the morning wind.

Then I went down into the valley, bow in hand.

Grom could not drive himself to follow me. He lay on his belly in the dust and howled like a dying dog.

I passed the lake and the silent camp where the pyre-ashes still smouldered, and came under the thickening trees beyond. About me the columns loomed, mere shapeless heads from the ravages of staggering aeons. The trees grew more dense, and under their vast leafy branches the very light was dusky and evil. As in twilight shadow I saw the ruined temple, cyclopean walls staggering up from masses of decaying masonry and fallen blocks of stone. About 600 yards in front of it a great column reared up in an open glade, 80 or 90 feet in height. It was so worn and pitted by weather and time that any child of my tribe could have climbed it, and I marked it and changed my plan.

I came to the ruins and saw huge crumbling walls upholding a domed roof from which many stones had fallen, so that it seemed like the lichen-grown ribs of some mythical monster's skeleton arching above me. Titanic columns flanked the open doorway through which ten elephants could have stalked abreast.

Once there might have been inscriptions and hieroglyphics on the pillars and walls, but they were long worn away. Around the great room, on the inner side, ran columns in better state of preservation. On each of these columns was a flat pedestal, and some dim instinctive memory vaguely resurrected a shadowy scene wherein black drums roared madly, and on these pedestals monstrous beings squatted loathsomely in inexplicable rituals rooted in the black dawn of the universe.

There was no altar only the mouth of a great well-like shaft in the stone floor, with strange obscene carvings all about the rim. I tore great pieces of stone from the rotting floor and cast them down the shaft which slanted down into utter darkness. I heard them bound along the side, but I did not hear them strike bottom. I cast down stone after stone, each with a searing curse, and at last I heard a sound that was not the dwindling rumble of the falling stones. Up from the well floated a weird demon-piping that was a symphony of madness. Far down in the darkness I glimpsed the faint fearful glimmering of a vast white bulk.

I retreated slowly as the piping grew louder, falling back through the broad doorway. I heard a scratching, scrambling noise, and up from the shaft and out of the doorway between the colossal columns came a prancing incredible figure. It went erect like a man, but it was covered with fur, that was shaggiest where its face should have been. If it had ears, nose and a mouth I did not discover them. Only a pair of staring red eyes leered from the furry mask. Its misshapen hands held a strange set of pipes, on which it blew weirdly as it pranced towards me with many a grotesque caper and leap.

Behind it I heard a repulsive obscene noise as of a quaking unstable mass heaving up out of a well. Then I nocked an arrow, drew the cord and sent the shaft singing through the furry breast of the dancing monstrosity. It went down as though struck by a thunderbolt, but to my horror the piping continued, though the pipes had fallen from the malformed hands. Then I turned and ran fleetly to the column, up which I swarmed before I looked back. When I reached the pinnacle I looked, and because of the shock and surprise of what I saw, I almost fell from my dizzy perch.

Out of the temple the monstrous dweller in the darkness had come, and I, who had expected a horror yet cast in some terrestrial mould, looked on the spawn of nightmare. From what subterranean hell it crawled in the long ago I know not, nor what black age it represented. But it was not a beast, as humanity knows beasts. I call it a worm for lack of a better term. There is no earthly language that has a name for it. I can only say that it looked somewhat more like a worm than it did an octopus, a serpent or a dinosaur.

It was white and pulpy, and drew its quaking bulk along the ground, worm-fashion. But it had wide flat tentacles, and fleshy feelers, and other adjuncts the use of which I am unable to explain. And it had a long proboscis which it curled and uncurled like an elephant's trunk. Its forty eyes, set in a horrific circle, were composed of thousands of facets of as many scintillant colours which changed and altered in never-ending transmutation. But through all interplay of hue and glint, they retained their evil intelligence intelligence there was behind those flickering facets, not human nor yet bestial, but a night-born demoniac intelligence such as men in dreams vaguely sense throbbing titanically in the black gulfs outside our material universe. In size the monster was mountainous; its bulk would have dwarfed a mastodon.

But even as I shook with the cosmic horror of the thing, I drew a feathered shaft to my ear and arched it singing on its way. Grass and bushes were crushed flat as the monster came towards me like a moving mountain and shaft after shaft I sent with terrific force and deadly precision. I could not miss so huge a target. The arrows sank to the feathers or clear out of sight in the unstable bulk, each bearing enough poison to have stricken dead a bull elephant. Yet on it came, swiftly, appallingly, apparently heedless of both the shafts and the venom in which they were steeped. And all the time the hideous music played a maddening accompaniment, whining thinly from the pipes that lay untouched on the ground.

My confidence faded; even the poison of Satha was futile against this uncanny being. I drove my last shaft almost straight downward into the quaking white mountain, so close was the monster under my perch. Then suddenly its colour altered. A wave of ghastly blue surged over it, and the vast bulk heaved in earthquake-like convulsions. With a terrible plunge it struck the lower part of the column, which crashed to falling shards of stone. But even with the impact, I leaped far out and fell through the empty air full upon the monster's back.

The spongy skin yielded and gave beneath my feet, and I drove my sword hilt deep, dragging it through the pulpy flesh, ripping a horrible yard-long wound, from which oozed a green slime. Then a flip of a cable-like-tentacle flicked me from the titan's back and spun me 300 feet through the air to crash among a cluster of giant trees.

The impact must have splintered half the bones in my frame, for when I sought to grasp my sword again and crawl anew to the combat, I could not move hand or foot, could only writhe helplessly with my broken back. But I could see the monster and I knew that I had won, even in defeat. The mountainous bulk was heaving and billowing, the tentacles were lashing madly, the antennae writhing and knotting, and the nauseous whiteness had changed to a pale and grisly green. It turned ponderously and lurched back towards the temple, rolling like a crippled ship in a heavy swell. Trees crashed and splintered as it lumbered against them.

I wept with pure fury because I could not catch up my sword and rush in to die glutting my berserk madness in mighty strokes. But the worm-god was death-stricken and needed not my futile sword. The demon pipes on the ground kept up their infernal tune, and it was like the fiend's death-dirge. Then as the monster veered and floundered, I saw it catch up the corpse of its hairy slave. For an instant the apish form dangled in mid-air, gripped round by the trunk-like proboscis, then was dashed against the temple wall with a force that reduced the hairy body to a mere shapeless pulp. At that the pipes screamed out horribly, and fell silent for ever.

The titan staggered on the brink of the shaft; then another change came over it—a frightful transfiguration the nature of which I cannot yet describe. Even now when I try to think of it clearly, I am only chaotically conscious of a blasphemous, unnatural transmutation of form and substance, shocking and indescribable. Then the strangely altered bulk tumbled into the shaft to roll down into the ultimate darkness from whence it came, and I knew that it was dead. And as it vanished into the well, with a rending, grinding groan the ruined walls quivered from dome to base. They bent inward and buckled with deafening reverberation, the columns splintered, and with a cataclysmic crash the dome itself came thundering down. For an instant the air seemed veiled with flying debris and stone-dust, through which the treetops lashed madly as in a storm or an earthquake convulsion. Then all was clear again and I stared, shaking the blood from my eyes. Where the temple had stood there lay only a colossal pile of shattered masonry and broken stones, and every column in the valley had fallen, to lie in crumbling shards.

In the silence that followed I heard Grom wailing a dirge over me. I bade him lay my sword in my hand, and he did so, and bent close to hear what I had to say, for I was passing swiftly.

"Let my tribe remember," I said, speaking slowly. "Let the tale be told from village to village, from camp to camp, from tribe to tribe, so that men may know that not man nor beast nor devil may prey in safety on the golden-haired people of Asgard. Let them build me a cairn where I lie and lay me therein with my bow and sword at hand, to guard this valley for ever; so if the ghost of the god I slew comes up from below, my ghost will ever be ready to give it battle."

And while Grom howled and beat his hairy breast, death came to me in the Valley of the Worm.

THE GARDEN OF FEAR

Once I was Hunwulf, the Wanderer. I cannot explain my knowledge of this fact by any occult or esoteric means, nor shall I try. A man remembers his past life; I remember my past *lives*. Just as a normal individual recalls the shapes that were him in childhood, boyhood and youth, so I recall the shapes that have been James Allison in forgotten ages. Why this memory is mine I cannot say, any more than I can explain the myriad other phenomena of nature which daily confront me and every other mortal. But as I lie waiting for death to free me from my long disease, I see with a clear, sure sight the grand panorama of lives that trail out behind me. I see the men who have been me, and I see the beasts that have been me.

For my memory does not end at the coming of Man. How could it, when the beast so shades into Man that there is no clearly divided line to mark the boundaries of bestiality? At this instant I see a dim twilight vista, among the gigantic trees of a primordial forest that never knew the tread of a leather-shod foot. I see a vast, shaggy, shambling bulk that lumbers clumsily yet swiftly, sometimes upright, sometimes on all fours. He delves under rotten logs for grubs and insects, and his small ears twitch continually. He lifts his head and bares yellow fangs. He is primordial, bestial, anthropoid; yet I recognize his kinship with the entity now called James Allison. Kinship? Say rather oneness. I am he; he is I. My flesh is soft and white and hairless; his is dark and tough and shaggy. Yet we were one, and already in his feeble, shadowed brain are beginning to stir and tingle the man-thoughts and the man dreams, crude, chaotic, fleeting, yet the basis for all the high and lofty visions men have dreamed in all the following ages.

Nor does my knowledge cease there. It goes back, back, down immemorial vistas I dare not follow, to abysses too dark and awful for the human mind to plumb. Yet even there I am aware of my identity, my individuality. I tell you the individual is never lost, neither in the black pit from which we once crawled, blind, squalling and noisome, or in that eventual Nirvana in which we shall one day sink—which I have glimpsed afar off, shining as a blue twilight lake among the mountains of the stars.

But enough. I would tell you of Hunwulf. Oh, it was long, long ago! How long ago I dare not say. Why should I seek for paltry human comparisons to describe a realm indescribably, incomprehensibly distant? Since that age the earth had altered her contours not once but a dozen times, and whole cycles I of mankind have completed their destinies.

I was Hunwulf, a son of the golden-haired Æsir, who, from the icy plains of shadowy Asgard, sent I blue-eyed tribes around the world in century-long drifts to leave their trails in strange places. On one of those southward drifts I was born, for I never saw the homeland of my people, where the bulk of the Nordheimer still dwelt in their horse-hide tents among the snows.

I grew to manhood on that long wandering, to the fierce, sinewy, untamed manhood of the Æsir, who knew no gods but Ymir of the frost-rimmed beard, and whose axes are stained with the blood of many nations. My thews were like woven steel cords. My yellow hair fell in a lion-like mane to my mighty shoulders. My loins were girt with leopard skin. With either hand I could wield my heavy flint-headed axe. Year by year my tribe drifted southward, sometimes swinging in long arcs to east or west, sometimes lingering for months or years in fertile valleys or plains where the grass-eaters swarmed, but always forging slowly and inevitably southward. Sometimes our way led through vast and breathless solitudes that had never known a human cry; sometimes strange tribes disputed our course, and our trail passed over bloodstained ashes of butchered villages. And amidst this wandering, hunting and slaughtering, I came to full manhood and the love of Gudrun.

What shall I say of Gudrun? How describe color to the blind? I can say that her skin was whiter than milk, that her hair was living gold with the flame of the sun caught in it, that the supple beauty of her body would shame the dream that shaped the Grecian goddesses. But I cannot make you realize the fire and wonder that was Gudrun. You have no basis for comparison; you know womanhood only by the women of your epoch, who, beside her are like candles beside the glow of the full moon. Not for a millennium of millenniums have women like Gudrun walked the earth. Cleopatra, Thais, Helen of Troy, they were but pallid shadows of her beauty, frail mimicries of the blossom that blooms to full glory only in the primordial.

For Gudrun I forsook my tribe and my people, and went into the wilderness, an exile and an outcast, with blood on my hands. She was of my race, but not of my tribe: a waif whom we found as a child wandering in a dark forest, lost from some wandering tribe of our blood. She grew up in the tribe, and when she came to the full ripeness of her glorious young womanhood, she was given to Heimdul the Strong, the mightiest hunter of the tribe.

But the dream of Gudrun was madness in my soul, a flame that burned eternally, and for her I slew Heimdul, crushing his skull with my flint-headed axe ere he could bear her to his horse-hide tent. And then follows our long flight from the vengeance of the tribe. Willingly she went with me, for she loved me with the love of the Æsir women, which is a devouring flame that destroys weakness. Oh, it was a savage age, when life was grim and bloodstained, and the weak died quickly. There was nothing mild or gentle about us, our passions were those of the tempest, the surge and impact of battle, the challenge of the lion. Our loves were as terrible as our hates.

And so I carried Gudrun from the tribe, and the killers were hot on our trail. For a night and a day they pressed us hard, until we swam a rising river, a roaring, foaming torrent that even the men of the Æsir dared not attempt. But in the madness of our love and recklessness we buffetted our way across, beaten and torn by the frenzy of the flood, and reached the farther bank alive.

Then for many days we traversed upland forests haunted by tigers and leopards, until we came to a great barrier of mountains, blue ramparts climbing awesomely to the sky. Slope piled upon slope.

In those mountains we were assailed by freezing winds and hunger, and by giant condors which swept down upon us with a thunder of gigantic wings. In grim battles in the passes I shot away all my arrows and splintered my flintheaded spear, but at last we crossed the bleak backbone of the range and descending the southern slopes, came upon a village of mud huts among the cliffs inhabited by a peaceful, brown-skinned people who spoke a strange tongue and had strange customs. But they greeted us with the sign of peace, and brought us into their village, where they set meat and barley-bread and fermented milk before us, and squatted in a ring about us while we ate, and a woman slapped softly on a bowl-shaped tom-tom to do us honor.

We had reached their village at dusk, and night fell while we feasted. On all sides rose the cliffs and peaks shouldering massively against the stars. The little cluster of mud huts and the tiny fires were drowned and lost in the immensity of the night. Gudrun felt the loneliness, the crowding desolation of that darkness, and she pressed close to me, her shoulder against my breast. But my axe was close at my hand, and I had never known the sensation of fear.

The little brown people squatted before us, men and women, and tried to talk to us with motions of their slender hands. Dwelling always in one place, in comparative security, they lacked both the strength and the uncompromising ferocity of the nomadic Æsir. Their hands fluttered with friendly gestures in the firelight.

I made them understand that we had come from the north, had crossed the backbone of the great mountain range, and that on the morrow it was our intention to descend into the green tablelands which we had glimpsed southward of the peaks. When they understood my meaning they set up a great cry shaking their heads violently, and beating madly on the drum. They were all so eager to impart something to me, and all waving their hands at once, that they bewildered rather than enlightened me. Eventually they did make me understand that they did not wish me to descend the mountains. Some menace lay to the south of the village, but whether of man or beast, I could not learn.

It was while they were all gesticulating and my whole attention was centered on their gestures, that the blow fell. The first intimation was a sudden thunder of wings in my ears; a dark shape rushed out of the night, and a great pinion dealt me a buffet over the head as I turned. I was knocked sprawling, and in that instant I heard Gudrun scream as she was torn from my side. Bounding up, quivering with a furious eagerness to rend and slay, I saw the dark shape vanish again into the darkness, a white, screaming, writhing figure trailing from its talons.

Roaring my grief and fury I caught up my axe and charged into the dark—then halted short, wild, desperate, knowing not which way to turn.

The little brown people had scattered, screaming, knocking sparks from their fires as they rushed over them in their haste to gain their huts, but now they crept out fearfully, whimpering like wounded dogs. They gathered around me and plucked at me with timid hands and chattered in their tongue while I cursed in sick impotency, knowing they wished to tell me something which I could not understand.

At last I suffered them to lead me back to the fire, and there the oldest man of the tribe brought forth a strip of cured hide, a clay pot of pigments, and a stick. On the hide he painted a crude picture of a winged thing carrying a white woman—oh, it was very crude, but I made out his meaning. Then all pointed southward and cried out loudly in their own tongue; and I knew that the menace they had warned me against was the thing that had carried off Gudrun. Until then I supposed that it had been one of the great mountain condors which had carried her away, but the picture the old man drew, in black paint, resembled a winging man more than anything else.

Then, slowly and laboriously, he began to trace something I finally recognized as a map—oh, yes, even in those dim days we had our primitive maps, though no modern man would be able to comprehend them so greatly different was our symbolism.

It took a long time; it was midnight before the old man had finished and I understood his tracings. But at last the matter was made clear. If I followed the course traced on the map, down the long narrow valley where stood the village, across a plateau, down a series of rugged slopes and along another valley, I would come to the place where lurked the being which had stolen my woman. At that spot the old man drew what looked like a mis-shapen hut, with many strange markings all about it in red pigments. Pointing to these, and again to me, he shook his head, with those loud cries that seemed to indicate peril among these people.

Then they tried to persuade me not to go, but afire with eagerness I took the piece of hide and pouch of food they thrust into my hands (they were indeed a strange people for that age), grasped my axe and set off in the moonless darkness. But my eyes were keener than a modern mind can comprehend, and my sense of direction was as a wolfs. Once the map was fixed in my mind, I could have thrown it away and come unerring to the place I sought but I folded it and thrust it into my girdle.

I traveled at my best speed through the starlight, taking no heed of any beasts that might be seeking their prey—cave bear or saber-toothed tiger. At times I heard gravel slide under stealthy padded paws; I glimpsed fierce yellow eyes burning in the darkness, and caught sight of shadowy, skulking forms. But I plunged on recklessly, in too desperate a mood to give the path to any beast however fearsome.

I traversed the valley, climbed a ridge and came out on a broad plateau, gashed with ravines and strewn with boulders. I crossed this and in the darkness before dawn commenced my climb down the treacherous slopes. They seemed endless, falling away in a long steep incline until their feet were lost in darkness.

But I went down recklessly, not pausing to unsling the rawhide rope I carried about my shoulders, trusting to my luck and skill to bring me down without a broken neck.

And just as dawn was touching the peaks with a white glow, I dropped into a broad valley, walled by stupendous cliffs. At that point it was wide from east to west, but the cliffs converged toward the lower end, giving the valley the appearance of a great fan, narrowing swiftly toward the south.

The floor was level, traversed by a winding stream. Trees grew thinly; there was no underbrush, but a carpet of tall grass, which at that time of year were somewhat dry. Along the stream where the green lush grew, wandered mammoths, hairy mountains of flesh and muscle.

I gave them a wide berth, giants too mighty for me to cope with, confident in their power, and afraid of only one thing on earth. They bent forward their great ears and lifted their trunks menacingly when I approached too near, but they did not attack me. I ran swiftly among the trees, and the sun was not yet above the eastern ramparts which its rising edged with golden flame, when I came to the point where the cliffs converged. My night-long climb had not affected my iron muscles. I felt no weariness; my fury burned unabated. What lay beyond the cliffs I could not know; I ventured no conjecture. I had room in my brain only for red wrath and killing-lust.

The cliffs did not form a solid wall. That is, the extremities of the converging palisades did not meet, leaving a notch or gap a few hundred feet wide, and emerged into a second valley, or rather into a continuance of the same valley which broadened out again beyond the pass.

The cliffs slanted away swiftly to east and west, to form a giant rampart that marched clear around the valley in the shape of a vast oval. It formed a blue rim all around the valley without a break except for a glimpse of the clear sky that seemed to mark another notch at the southern end. The inner valley was shaped much like a great bottle, with two necks.

The neck by which I entered was crowded with trees, which grew densely for several hundred yards, when they gave way abruptly to a field of crimson flowers. And a few hundred yards beyond the edges of the trees, I saw a strange structure.

I must speak of what I saw not alone as Hunwulf, but as James Allison as well. For Hunwulf only vaguely comprehended the things he saw, and, as Hunwulf, he could not describe them at all. I, as Hunwulf, knew nothing of architecture. The only man-built dwelling I had ever seen had been the horse-hide tents of my people, and the thatched mud huts of the barley people— and other people equally primitive.

So as Hunwulf I could only say that I looked upon a great hut the construction of which was beyond my comprehension. But I, James Allison, know that it was a tower, some seventy feet in height, of a curious green stone, highly polished, and of a substance that created the illusion of semi-translucency. It was cylindrical, and, as near as I could see, without doors or windows. The main body of the building was perhaps sixty feet in height, and from its center rose a smaller tower that completed its full stature. This tower, being much inferior in girth to the main body of the structure, and thus surrounded by a sort of gallery, with a crenellated parapet, and was furnished with both doors, curiously arched, and windows, thickly barred as I could see, even from where I stood.

That was all. No evidence of human occupancy. No sign of life in all the valley. But it was evident that this castle was what the old man of the mountain village had been trying to draw, and I was certain that in it I would find Gudrun–if she still lived.

Beyond the tower I saw the glimmer of a blue lake into which the stream, following the curve of the western wall, eventually flowed. Lurking amid the trees I glared at the tower and at the flowers surrounding it on all sides, growing thick along the walls and extending for hundreds of yards in all directions. There were trees at the other end of the valley, near the lake; but no trees grew among the flowers.

They were not like any plants I had ever seen. They grew close together, almost touching each other. They were some four feet in height, with only one blossom on each stalk, a blossom larger than a man's head, with broad, fleshy petals drawn close together. These petals were a livid crimson, the hue of an open wound. The stalks were thick as a man's wrist, colorless, almost transparent. The poisonously green leaves were shaped like spearheads, drooping on long snaky stems. Their whole aspect was repellent, and I wondered what their denseness concealed.

For all my wild-born instincts were roused in me. I felt lurking peril, just as I had often sensed the ambushed lion before my external senses recognized him. I scanned the dense blossoms closely, wondering if some great serpent lay coiled among them. My nostrils expanded as I quested for a scent, but the wind was blowing away from me. But there was something decidedly unnatural about that vast garden. Though the north wind swept over it, not a blossom stirred, not a leaf rustled; they hung motionless, sullen, like birds of prey with drooping heads, and I had a strange feeling that they were watching me like living things.

It was like a landscape in a dream: on either hand the blue cliffs lifting against the cloud-fleeced sky; in the distance the dreaming lake; and that fantastic green tower rising in the midst of that livid crimson field.

And there was something else: in spite of the wind that was blowing away from me, I caught a scent, a charnel-house reek of death and decay and corruption that rose from the blossoms.

Then suddenly I crouched closer in my covert. There was life and movement on the castle. A figure emerged from the tower, and coming to the parapet, leaned upon it and looked out across the valley. It was a man, but such a man as I had never dreamed of, even in nightmares.

He was tall, powerful, black with the hue of polished ebony; but the feature which made a human nightmare of him was the batlike wings which folded on his shoulders. I knew they were wings: the fact was obvious and indisputable.

I, James Allison, have pondered much on that phenomenon which I witnessed through the eyes of Hunwulf. Was that winged man merely a freak, an isolated example of distorted nature, dwelling in solitude and immemorial desolation? Or was he a survival of a forgotten race, which had risen, reigned and vanished before the coming of man as we know him? The little brown people of the hills might have told me, but we had no speech in common. Yet I am inclined to the latter theory. Winged men are not uncommon in mythology; they are met with in the folk-lore of many nations and many races. As far back as man may go in myth, chronicle and legend, he finds tales of harpies and winged gods, angels and demons. Legends are distorted shadows of pre-existent realities, I believe that once a race of winged black men ruled a pre-Adamite world, and that I, Hunwulf, met the last survivor of that race in the valley of the red blossoms.

These thoughts I think as James Allison, with my modern knowledge which is as imponderable as my modern ignorance.

I, Hunwulf, indulged in no such speculations. Modern skepticism was not a part of my nature, nor did I seek to rationalize what seemed not to coincide with a natural universe. I acknowledged no gods but Ymir and his daughters, but I did not doubt the existence—as demons—of other deities, worshipped by other races. Supernatural beings of all sorts fitted into my conception of life and the universe. I no more doubted the existence of dragons, ghosts, fiends and devils than I doubted the existence of lions and buffaloes and elephants. I accepted this freak of nature as a supernatural demon and did not worry about its origin or source. Nor was I thrown into a panic of superstitious fear. I was a son of Asgard, who feared neither man nor devil, and I had more faith in the crushing power of my flint axe than in the spells of priests or the incantations of sorcerers.

But I did not immediately rush into the open and charge the tower. The wariness of the wild was mine, and I saw no way to climb the castle. The winged man needed no doors on the side, because he evidently entered at the top, and the slick surface of the walls seemed to defy the most skillful climber. Presently a way of getting upon the tower occurred to me, but I hesitated, waiting to see if any other winged people appeared, though I had an unexplainable feeling that he was the only one of his kind in the valley–possibly in the world. While I crouched among the trees and watched, I saw him lift his elbows from the parapet and stretch lithely, like a great cat. Then he strode across the circular gallery and entered the tower. A muffled cry rang out on the air which caused me to stiffen, though even so I realized that it was not the cry of a woman. Presently the black master of the castle emerged, dragging a smaller figure with him–a figure which writhed and struggled and cried out piteously. I saw that it was a small brown man, much like those of the mountain village. Captured, I did not doubt, as Gudrun had been captured.

He was like a child in the hands of his huge foe. The black man spread broad wings and rose over the parapet, carrying his captive as a condor might carry a sparrow. He soared out over the field of blossoms, while I crouched in my leafy retreat, glaring in amazement.

The winged man, hovering in mid-air, voiced a strange weird cry; and it was answered in horrible fashion. A shudder of awful life passed over the crimson field beneath him. The great red blossoms trembled, opened, spreading their fleshy petals like the mouths of serpents. Their stalks seemed to elongate, stretching upward eagerly. Their broad leaves lifted and vibrated with a curious lethal whirring, like the singing of a rattlesnake. A faint but flesh-crawling hissing sounded over all the valley. The blossoms gasped, straining upward. And with a fiendish laugh, the winged man dropped his writhing captive.

With a scream of a lost soul the brown man hurtled downward, crashing among the flowers. And with a rustling hiss, they were on him. Their thick flexible stalks arched like the necks of serpents, their petals closed on his flesh. A hundred blossoms clung to him like the tentacles of an octopus, smothering and crushing him down. His shrieks of agony came muffled; he was completely hidden by the hissing, threshing flowers. Those beyond reach swayed and writhed furiously as if seeking to tear up their roots in their eagerness to join their brothers. All over the field the great red blossoms leaned and strained toward the spot where the grisly battle went on. The shrieks sank lower and lower and lower, and ceased. A dread silence reigned over the valley. The black man flapped his way leisurely back to the tower, and vanished within it.

Then presently the blossoms detached themselves one by one from their victim who lay very white and still. Aye, his whiteness was more than that of death; he was like a wax image, a staring effigy from which every drop of blood had been sucked. And a startling transmutation was evident in the flowers directly about him. Their stalks no longer colorless; they were swollen and dark red, like transparent bamboos filled to the bursting with fresh blood.

Drawn by an insatiable curiosity, I stole from the trees and glided to the very edge of the red field. The blossoms hissed and bent toward me, spreading their petals like the hood of a roused cobra. Selecting one farthest from its brothers, I severed the stalk with a stroke of my axe, and the thing tumbled to the ground, writhing like a beheaded serpent.

When its struggles ceased I bent over it in wonder. The stalk was not hollow as I had supposed--that is, hollow like a dry bamboo. It was traversed by a network of thread-like veins, some empty and some exuding a colorless sap. The stems which held the leaves to the stalk were remarkably tenacious and pliant, and the leaves themselves were edged with curved spines, like sharp hooks.

Once those spines were sunk in the flesh, the victim would be forced to tear up the whole plant by the roots if he escaped.

The petals were each as broad as my hand, and as thick as a prickly pear, and on the inner side covered with innumerable tiny mouths, not larger than the head of a pin. In the center, where the pistil should be, there was a barbed spike, of a substance like thorn, and narrow channels between the four serrated edges.

From my investigations of this horrible travesty of vegetation, I looked up suddenly, just in time to see the winged man appear again on the parapet. He did not seem particularly surprised to see me. He shouted in his unknown tongue and made a mocking gesture, while I stood statue-like, gripping my axe. Presently he turned and entered the tower as he had done before; and as before, he emerged with a captive. My fury and hate were almost submerged by the flood of joy that Gudrun was alive.

In spite of her supple strength, which was that of a she-panther, the black man handled Gudrun as easily as he had handled the brown man. Lifting her struggling white body high above his head, he displayed her to me and yelled tauntingly. Her golden hair streamed over her white shoulders as she fought vainly, crying to me in the terrible extremity of her fright and horror. Not lightly was a woman of the Æsir reduced to cringing terror. I measured the depths of her captor's diabolism by her frenzied cries.

But I stood motionless. If it would have saved her, I would have plunged into that crimson morass of hell, to be hooked and pierced and sucked white by those fiendish flowers. But that would help her none. My death would merely leave her without a defender. So I stood silent while she writhed and whimpered, and the black man's laughter sent red waves of madness surging across my brain. Once he made as if to cast her down among the flowers, and my iron control almost snapped and sent me plunging into that red sea of hell. But it was only a gesture. Presently he dragged her back to the tower and tossed her inside. Then he turned back to the parapet, rested his elbows upon it, and fell to watching me. Apparently he was playing with us as a cat plays with a mouse before he destroys it.

But while he watched, I turned my back and strode into the forest. I, Hunwulf, was not a thinker, as modern men understand the term. I lived in an age where emotions were translated by the smash of a flint axe rather than by emanations of the intellect. Yet I was not the senseless animal the black man evidently supposed me to be. I had a human brain, whetted by the eternal struggle for existence and supremacy.

I knew I could not cross that red strip that banded the castle, alive. Before I could take a half dozen steps a score of barbed spikes would be thrust into my flesh, their avid mouths sucking the flood from my veins to feed their demoniac lust. Even my tigerish strength would not avail to hew a path through them.

The winged man did not follow. Looking back, I saw him still lounging in the same position. When I, as James Allison, dream again the dreams of Hunwulf, that, image is etched in my mind, that gargoyle figure with elbows propped on the parapet, like a medieval devil brooding on the battlements of hell.

I passed through the straits of the valley and came into the vale beyond where the trees thinned and the mammoths lumbered along the stream. Beyond the herd I stopped and drawing a pair of flints into my pouch, stooped and struck a spark in the dry grass. Running swiftly from chosen place to place, I set a dozen fires, in a great semi-circle. The north wind caught them, whipped them into eager life, drove them before it. In a few moments a rampart of flame was sweeping down the valley.

The mammoths ceased their feeding, lifted their great ears and bellowed alarm. In all the world they feared only fire. They began to retreat southward, the cows herding the calves before them, bulls trumpeting like the blast of Judgement Day. Roaring like a storm the fire rushed on, and the mammoths broke and stampeded, a crushing hurricane of flesh, a thundering earthquake of hurtling bone and muscle. Trees splintered and went down before them, the ground shook under their headlong tread. Behind them came the racing fire and on the heels of the fire came I, so closely that the smouldering earth burnt the moose-hide sandals off my feet.

Through the narrow neck they thundered, levelling the dense thickets like a giant scythe. Trees were torn up by the roots; it was as if a tornado had ripped through the pass.

With a deafening thunder of pounding feet and trumpeting, they stormed across the sea of red blossoms. Those devilish plants might have even pulled down and destroyed a single mammoth; but under the impact of the whole herd, they were no more than common flowers. The maddened titans crashed through and over them, battering them to shreds, hammering, stamping them into the earth which grew soggy with their juice.

I trembled for an instant, fearing the brutes would not turn aside for the castle, and dubious of even it being able to withstand that battering ram concussion. Evidently the winged man shared my fears, for he shot up from the tower and raced off through the sky toward the lake. But one of the bulls butted head-on into the wall, was shunted off the smooth curving surface, caromed into the one next to him, and the herd split and roared by the tower on either hand, so closely their hairy sides rasped against it. They thundered on through the red field toward the distant lake.

The fire, reaching the edge of the trees, was checked; the smashed sappy fragments of the red flowers would not burn. Trees, fallen or standing, smoked and burst into flame, and burning branches showered around me as I ran through the trees and out into the gigantic swath the charging herd had cut through the livid field.

As I ran I shouted to Gudrun and she answered me. Her voice was muffled and accompanied by a hammering on something. The winged man had locked her in a tower.

As I came under the castle wall, treading on remnants of red petals and snaky stalks, I unwound my rawhide rope, swung it, and sent its loop shooting upward to catch on one of the merlons of the crenellated parapet. Then I went up it, hand over hand, gripping the rope between my toes, bruising my knuckles and elbows against the sheer wall as I swung about.

I was within five feet of the parapet when I was galvanized by the beat of wings about my head. The black man shot out of the air and landed on the gallery. I got a good look at him as he leaned over the parapet. His features were straight and regular; there was no suggestion of the negroid about him. His eyes were slanted slits, and his teeth gleamed in a savage grin of hate and triumph. Long, long he had ruled the valley of the red blossoms, levelling tribute of human lives from the miserable tribes of the hills, for writhing victims to feed the carnivorous half-bestial flowers which were his subjects and protectors. And now I was in his power, my fierceness, and craft gone for naught. A stroke of the crooked dagger in his hand and I would go hurtling to my death. Somewhere Gudrun, seeing my peril, was screaming like a wild thing, and then a door crashed with a splintering of wood.

The black man, intent upon his gloating, laid the keen edge of his dagger on the rawhide strand–then a strong white arm locked about his neck from behind, and he was jerked violently backward. Over his shoulder I saw the beautiful face of Gudrun, her hair standing on end, her eyes dilated with terror and fury.

With a roar he turned in her grasp, tore loose her clinging arms and hurled her against the tower with such force that she lay half stunned. Then he turned again to me, but in that instant I had swarmed up and over the parapet, and leaped upon the gallery, unslinging my axe.

For an instant he hesitated, his wings half-lifted, his hand poising on his dagger, as if uncertain whether to fight or take to the air. He was a giant in stature, with muscles standing out in corded ridges all over him, but he hesitated, as uncertain as a man when confronted by a wild beast.

I did not hesitate. With a deep-throated roar I sprang, swinging my axe with all my giant strength. With a strangled cry he threw up his arms; but down between them the axe plunged and blasted his head to red ruin.

I wheeled toward Gudrun; and struggling to her knees, she threw her white arms about me in a desperate clasp of love and terror, staring awedly to where lay the winged lord of the valley, the crimson pulp that had been his head drowned in a puddle of blood and brains.

I had often wished that it were possible to draw these various lives of mine together in one body, combining the experiences of Hunwulf with the knowledge of James Allison. Could that be so, Hunwulf would have gone through the ebony door which Gudrun in her desperate strength had shattered, into that weird chamber he glimpsed through the ruined panels, with fantastic furnishing, and shelves heaped with rolls of parchment. He would have unrolled those scrolls and pored over their characters until he deciphered them, and read, perhaps, the chronicles of that weird race whose last survivor he had just slain. Surely the tale was stranger than an opium dream, and marvelous as the story of lost Atlantis.

But Hunwulf had no such curiosity. To him the tower, the ebony furnished chamber and the rolls of parchment were mean-ingless, inexplicable emanations of sorcery, whose significance lay only in their diabolism. Though the solution of mystery lay under his fingers, he was a far removed from it as James Allison, millenniums yet unborn.

To me, Hunwulf, the castle was but a monstrous trap, concerning which I had but one emotion, and that a desire to escape from it as quickly as possible.

With Gudrun clinging to me I slid to the ground, then with a dextrous flip I freed my rope and wound it; and after that we went hand and hand along the path made by the mammoths, now vanishing in the distance, toward the blue lake at the southern end of the valley and the notch in the cliffs beyond it.

RATTLE OF BONES

"Landlord, ho!" The shout broke the lowering silence and reverberated through the black forest with sinister echoing. "This place hath a forbidding aspect, meseemeth."

Two men stood in front of the forest tavern. The building was low, long and rambling, built of heavy logs. Its small windows were heavily barred and the door was closed. Above the door its sinister sign showed faintly—a cleft skull.

This door swung slowly open and a bearded face peered out. The owner of the face stepped back and motioned his guests to enter—with a grudging gesture it seemed. A candle gleamed on a table; a flame smoldered in the fireplace.

"Your names?"

"Solomon Kane," said the taller man briefly.

"Gaston l'Armon," the other spoke curtly. "But what is that to you?"

"Strangers are few in the Black Forest," grunted the host, "bandits many. Sit at yonder table and I will bring food."

The two men sat down, with the bearing of men who have traveled far. One was a tall gaunt man, clad in a featherless hat and somber black garments, which set off the dark pallor of his forbidding face. The other was of a different type entirely, bedecked with lace and plumes, although his finery was somewhat stained from travel. He was handsome in a bold way, and his restless eyes shifted from side to side, never still an instant.

The host brought wine and food to the rough-hewn table and then stood back in the shadows, like a somber image. His features, now receding into vagueness, now luridly etched in the firelight as it leaped and flickered, were masked in a beard which seemed almost animal-like in thickness. A great nose curved above this beard and two small red eyes stared unblinkingly at his guests.

"Who are you?" suddenly asked the younger man.

"I am the host of the Cleft Skull Tavern," sullenly replied the other. His tone seemed to challenge his questioner to ask further.

"Do you have many guests?" l'Armon pursued.

"Few come twice," the host grunted.

Kane started and glanced up straight into those small red eyes, as if he sought for some hidden meaning in the host's words. The flaming eyes seemed to dilate, then dropped sullenly before the Englishman's cold stare.

"I'm for bed," said Kane abruptly, bringing his meal to a close. "I must take up my journey by daylight."

"And I," added the Frenchman. "Host, show us to our chambers."

Black shadows wavered on the walls as the two followed their silent host down a long, dark hall. The stocky, broad body of their guide seemed to grow and expand in the light of the small candle which he carried, throwing a long, grim shadow behind him.

At a certain door he halted, indicating that they were to sleep there. They entered; the host lit a candle with the one he carried, then lurched back the way he had come.

In the chamber the two men glanced at each other. The only furnishings of the room were a couple of bunks, a chair or two and a heavy table.

"Let us see if there be any way to make fast the door," said Kane. "I like not the looks of mine host."

"There are racks on door and jamb for a bar," said Gaston, "but no bar."

"We might break up the table and use its pieces for a bar," mused Kane.

"*Mon Dieu*," said l'Armon, "you are timorous, *m'sieu*."

Kane scowled. "I like not being murdered in my sleep," he answered gruffly.

"My faith!" the Frenchman laughed. "We are chance met—until I overtook you on the forest road an hour before sunset, we had never seen each other."

"I have seen you somewhere before," answered Kane, "though I can not now recall where. As for the other, I assume every man is an honest fellow until he shows me he is a rogue; moreover, I am a light sleeper and slumber with a pistol at hand."

The Frenchman laughed again.

"I was wondering how *m'sieu* could bring himself to sleep in the room with a stranger! Ha! Ha! All right, *m'sieu* Englishman, let us go forth and take a bar from one of the other rooms."

Taking the candle with them, they went into the corridor. Utter silence reigned and the small candle twinkled redly and evilly in the thick darkness.

"Mine host hath neither guests nor servants," muttered Solomon Kane. "A strange tavern! What is the name, now? These German words come not easily to me—the Cleft Skull? A bloody name, i'faith."

They tried the rooms next to theirs, but no bar rewarded their search. At last they came to the last room at the end of the corridor. They entered. It was furnished like the rest, except that the door was provided with a small barred opening, and fastened from the outside with a heavy bolt, which was secured at one end to the door-jamb. They raised the bolt and looked in.

"There should be an outer window, but there is not," muttered Kane. "Look!"

The floor was stained darkly. The walls and the one bunk were hacked in places, great splinters having been torn away.

"Men have died in here," said Kane, somberly. "Is yonder not a bar fixed in the wall?"

"Aye, but 'tis made fast," said the Frenchman, tugging at it. "The—"

A section of the wall swung back and Gaston gave a quick exclamation. A small, secret room was revealed, and the two men bent over the grisly thing that lay upon its floor.

"The skeleton of a man!" said Gaston. "And behold, how his bony leg is shackled to the floor! He was imprisoned here and died."

"Nay," said Kane, "the skull is cleft—methinks mine host had a grim reason for the name of his hellish tavern. This man, like us, was no doubt a wanderer who fell into the fiend's hands."

"Likely," said Gaston without interest; he was engaged in idly working the great iron ring from the skeleton's leg bones. Failing in this, he drew his sword and with an exhibition of remarkable strength cut the chain which joined the ring on the leg to a ring set deep in the log floor.

"Why should he shackle a skeleton to the floor?" mused the Frenchman. "*Monbleu*! 'Tis a waste of good chain. Now, *m'sieu*," he ironically addressed the white heap of bones, "I have freed you and you may go where you like!"

"Have done!" Kane's voice was deep. "No good will come of mocking the dead."

"The dead should defend themselves," laughed l'Armon. "Somehow, I will slay the man who kills me, though my corpse climb up forty fathoms of ocean to do it."

Kane turned toward the outer door, closing the door of the secret room behind him. He liked not this talk which smacked of demonry and witchcraft; and he was in haste to face the host with the charge of his guilt.

As he turned, with his back to the Frenchman, he felt the touch of cold steel against his neck and knew that a pistol muzzle was pressed close beneath the base of his brain.

"Move not, *m'sieu*!" The voice was low and silky. "Move not, or I will scatter your few brains over the room."

The Puritan, raging inwardly, stood with his hands in air while l'Armon slipped his pistols and sword from their sheaths.

"Now you can turn," said Gaston, stepping back.

Kane bent a grim eye on the dapper fellow, who stood bareheaded now, hat in one hand, the other hand leveling his long pistol.

"Gaston the Butcher!" said the Englishman somberly. "Fool that I was to trust a Frenchman! You range far, murderer! I remember you now, with that cursed great hat off—I saw you in Calais some years agone."

"Aye—and now you will see me never again. What was that?"

"Rats exploring yon skeleton," said Kane, watching the bandit like a hawk, waiting for a single slight wavering of that black gun muzzle. "The sound was of the rattle of bones."

"Like enough," returned the other. "Now, *M'sieu* Kane, I know you carry considerable money on your person. I had thought to wait until you slept and then slay you, but the opportunity presented itself and I took it. You trick easily."

"I had little thought that I should fear a man with whom I had broken bread," said Kane, a deep timbre of slow fury sounding in his voice.

The bandit laughed cynically. His eyes narrowed as he began to back slowly toward the outer door. Kane's sinews tensed involuntarily; he gathered himself like a giant wolf about to launch himself in a death leap, but Gaston's hand was like a rock and the pistol never trembled.

"We will have no death plunges after the shot," said Gaston. "Stand still, *m'sieu*; I have seen men killed by dying men, and I wish to have distance enough between us to preclude that possibility. My faith—I will shoot, you will roar and charge, but you will die before you reach me with your bare hands. And mine host will have another skeleton in his secret niche. That is, if I do not kill him myself. The fool knows me not nor I him, moreover—"

The Frenchman was in the doorway now, sighting along the barrel. The candle, which had been stuck in a niche on the wall, shed a weird and flickering light which did not extend past the doorway. And with the suddenness of death, from the darkness behind Gaston's back, a broad, vague form rose up and a gleaming blade swept down. The Frenchman went to his knees like a butchered ox, his brains spilling from his cleft skull. Above him towered the figure of the host, a wild and terrible spectacle, still holding the hanger with which he had slain the bandit.

"Ho! ho!" he roared. "Back!"

Kane had leaped forward as Gaston fell, but the host thrust into his very face a long pistol which he held in his left hand.

"Back!" he repeated in a tigerish roar, and Kane retreated from the menacing weapon and the insanity in the red eyes.

The Englishman stood silent, his flesh crawling as he sensed a deeper and more hideous threat than the Frenchman had offered. There was something inhuman about this man, who now swayed to and fro like some great forest beast while his mirthless laughter boomed out again.

"Gaston the Butcher!" he shouted, kicking the corpse at his feet. "Ho! ho! My fine brigand will hunt no more! I had heard of this fool who roamed the Black Forest—he wished gold and he found death! Now your gold shall be mine; and more than gold—vengeance!"

"I am no foe of yours," Kane spoke calmly.

"All men are my foes! Look—the marks on my wrists! See—the marks on my ankles! And deep in my back—the kiss of the knout! And deep in my brain, the wounds of the years of the cold, silent cells where I lay as punishment for a crime I never committed!" The voice broke in a hideous, grotesque sob.

Kane made no answer. This man was not the first he had seen whose brain had shattered amid the horrors of the terrible Continental prisons.

"But I escaped!" the scream rose triumphantly. "And here I make war on all men... What was that?"

Did Kane see a flash of fear in those hideous eyes?

"My sorcerer is rattling his bones!" whispered the host, then laughed wildly. "Dying, he swore his very bones would weave a net of death for me. I shackled his corpse to the floor, and now, deep in the night, I hear his bare skeleton clash and rattle as he seeks to be free, and I laugh, I laugh! Ho! ho! How he yearns to rise and stalk like old King Death along these dark corridors when I sleep, to slay me in my bed!"

Suddenly the insane eyes flared hideously: "You were in that secret room, you and this dead fool! Did he talk to you?"

Kane shuddered in spite of himself. Was it insanity or did he actually hear the faint rattle of bones, as if the skeleton had moved slightly? Kane shrugged his shoulders; rats will even tug at dusty bones.

The host was laughing again. He sidled around Kane, keeping the Englishman always covered, and with his free hand opened the door. All was darkness within, so that Kane could not even see the glimmer of the bones on the floor.

"All men are my foes!" mumbled the host, in the incoherent manner of the insane. "Why should I spare any man? Who lifted a hand to my aid when I lay for years in the vile dungeons of Karlsruhe—and for a deed never proven? Something happened to my brain, then. I became as a wolf—a brother to these of the Black Forest to which I fled when I escaped.

"They have feasted, my brothers, on all who lay in my tavern— all except this one who now clashes his bones, this magician from Russia. Lest he come stalking back through the black shadows when night is over the world, and slay me—for who may slay the dead?—I stripped his bones and shackled him. His sorcery was not powerful enough to save him from me, but all men know that a dead magician is more evil than a living one. Move not, Englishman! Your bones I shall leave in this secret room beside this one, to—"

The maniac was standing partly in the doorway of the secret room, now, his weapon still menacing Kane. Suddenly he seemed to topple backward, and vanished in the darkness; and at the same instant a vagrant gust of wind swept down the outer corridor and slammed the door shut behind him. The candle on the wall flickered and went out. Kane's groping hands, sweeping over the floor, found a pistol, and he straightened, facing the door where the maniac had vanished. He stood in the utter darkness, his blood freezing, while a hideous muffled screaming came from the secret room, intermingled with the dry, grisly rattle of fleshless bones. Then silence fell.

Kane found flint and steel and lighted the candle. Then, holding it in one hand and the pistol in the other, he opened the secret door.

"Great God!" he muttered as cold sweat formed on his body. "This thing is beyond all reason, yet with mine own eyes I see it! Two vows have here been kept, for Gaston the Butcher swore that even in death he would avenge his slaying, and his was the hand which set yon fleshless monster free. And he—"

The host of the Cleft Skull lay lifeless on the floor of the secret room, his bestial face set in lines of terrible fear; and deep in his broken neck were sunk the bare fingerbones of the sorcerer's skeleton.

THE HAUNTER OF THE RING

As I entered John Kirowan's study I was too much engrossed in my own thoughts to notice, at first, the haggard appearance of his visitor, a big, handsome young fellow well known to me.

"Hello, Kirowan," I greeted. "Hello, Gordon. Haven't seen you for quite a while. How's Evelyn?" And before he could answer, still on the crest of the enthusiasm which had brought me there, I exclaimed: "Look here, you fellows, I've got something that will make you stare! I got it from that robber Ahmed Mektub, and I paid high for it, but it's worth it. Look!" From under my coat I drew the jewel-hilted Afghan dagger which had fascinated me as a collector of rare weapons.

Kirowan, familiar with my passion, showed only polite interest, but the effect on Gordon was shocking.

With a strangled cry he sprang up and backward, knocking the chair clattering to the floor. Fists clenched and countenance livid he faced me, crying: "Keep back! Get away from me, or—"

I was frozen in my tracks.

"What in the—" I began bewilderedly, when Gordon, with another amazing change of attitude, dropped into a chair and sank his head in his hands. I saw his heavy shoulders quiver. I stared helplessly from him to Kirowan, who seemed equally dumbfounded.

"Is he drunk?" I asked.

Kirowan shook his head, and filling a brandy glass, offered it to the man. Gordon looked up with haggard eyes, seized the drink and gulped it down like a man half famished. Then he straightened up and looked at us shamefacedly.

"I'm sorry I went off my handle, O'Donnel" he said. "It was the unexpected shock of you drawing that knife."

"Well," I retorted, with some disgust, "I suppose you thought I was going to stab you with it!"

"Yes, I did!" Then, at the utterly blank expression on my face, he added: "Oh, I didn't actually *think* that; at least, I didn't reach that conclusion by any process of reasoning. It was just the blind primitive instinct of a hunted man, against whom anyone's hand may be turned."

His strange words and the despairing way he said them sent a queer shiver of nameless apprehension down my spine.

"What are you talking about?" I demanded uneasily. "Hunted? For what? You never committed a crime in your life."

"Not in this life, perhaps," he muttered.

"What do you mean?"

"What if retribution for a black crime committed in a previous life were hounding me?" he muttered.

"That's nonsense," I snorted.

"Oh, is it?" he exclaimed, stung. "Did you ever hear of my great-grandfather, Sir Richard Gordon of Argyle?"

"Sure; but what's that got to do with—"

"You've seen his portrait: doesn't it resemble me?"

"Well, yes," I admitted, "except that your expression is frank and wholesome whereas his is crafty and cruel."

"He murdered his wife," answered Gordon. "Suppose the theory of reincarnation were true? Why shouldn't a man suffer in one life for a crime committed in another?"

"You mean you think you are the reincarnation of your great-grandfather? Of all the fantastic—well, since he killed his wife, I suppose you'll be expecting Evelyn to murder you!" This last was delivered in searing sarcasm, as I thought of the sweet, gentle girl Gordon had married. His answer stunned me.

"My wife," he said slowly, "has tried to kill me three times in the past week."

There was no reply to that. I glanced helplessly at John Kirowan. He sat in his customary position, chin resting on his strong, slim hands; his white face was immobile, but his dark eyes gleamed with interest. In the silence I heard a clock ticking like a death-watch.

"Tell us the full story, Gordon," suggested Kirowan, and his calm, even voice was like a knife that cut a strangling, relieving the unreal tension.

"You know we've been married less than a year," Gordon began, plunging into the tale as though he were bursting for utterance; his words stumbled and tripped over one another. "All couples have spats, of course, but we've never had any real quarrels. Evelyn is the best-natured girl in the world.

"The first thing out of the ordinary occurred about a week ago. We had driven up in the mountains, left the car, and were wandering around picking wild flowers. At last we came to a steep slope, some thirty feet in height, and Evelyn called my attention to the flowers which grew thickly at the foot. I was looking over the edge and wondering if I could climb down without tearing my clothes to ribbons, when I felt a violent shove from behind that toppled me over.

"If it had been a sheer cliff, I'd have broken my neck. As it was, I went tumbling down, rolling and sliding, and brought up at the bottom scratched and bruised, with my garments in rags. I looked up and saw Evelyn staring down, apparently frightened half out of her wits.

"'Oh Jim!' she cried. 'Are you hurt? How came you to fall?'

"It was on the tip of my tongue to tell her that there was such a thing as carrying a joke too far, but these words checked me. I decided that she must have stumbled against me unintentionally, and actually didn't know it was she who precipitated me down the slope.

"So I laughed it off, and went home. She made a great fuss over me, insisted on swabbing my scratches with iodine, and lectured me for my carelessness! I hadn't the heart to tell her it was her fault.

"But four days later, the next thing happened. I was walking along our driveway, when I saw her coming up it in the automobile. I stepped out on the grass to let her by, as there isn't any curb along the driveway. She was smiling as she approached me, and slowed down the car, as if to speak to me. Then, just before she reached me, a most horrible change came over her expression. Without warning the car leaped at me like a living thing as she drove her foot down on the accelerator. Only a frantic leap backward saved me from being ground under the wheels. The car shot across the lawn and crashed into a tree. I ran to it and found Evelyn dazed and hysterical, but unhurt. She babbled of losing control of the machine.

"I carried her into the house and sent for Doctor Donnelly. He found nothing seriously wrong with her, and attributed her dazed condition to fright and shock. Within half an hour she regained her normal senses, but she's refused to touch the wheel since. Strange to say, she seemed less frightened on her own account than on mine. She seemed vaguely to know that she'd nearly run me down, and grew hysterical again when she spoke of it. Yet she seemed to take it for granted that I knew the machine had got out of her control. But I distinctly saw her wrench the wheel around, and I know she deliberately tried to hit me—why, God alone knows."

"Still I refused to let my mind follow the channel it was getting into. Evelyn had never given any evidence of any psychological weakness or 'nerves'; she's always been a level-headed girl, wholesome and natural. But I began to think she was subject to crazy impulses. Most of us have felt the impulse to leap from tall buildings. And sometimes a person feels a blind, childish and utterly reasonless urge to harm someone. We pick up a pistol, and the thought suddenly enters our mind how easy it would be to send our friend, who sits smiling and unaware, into eternity with a touch of the trigger. Of course we don't do it, but the impulse is there. So I thought perhaps some lack of mental discipline made Evelyn susceptible to these unguided impulses, and unable to control them."

"Nonsense," I broke in. "I've known her since she was a baby. If she has any such trait, she's developed it since she married you."

It was an unfortunate remark. Gordon caught it up with a despairing gleam in his eyes. "That's just it—since she married me! It's a curse—a black, ghastly curse, crawling like a serpent out of the past! I tell you, I was Richard Gordon and she—she was Lady Elizabeth, his murdered wife!" His voice sank to a blood-freezing whisper.

I shuddered; it is an awful thing to look upon the ruin of a keen clean brain, and such I was certain that I surveyed in James Gordon. Why or how, or by what grisly chance it had come about I could not say, but I was certain the man was mad.

"You spoke of three attempts." It was John Kirowan's voice again, calm and stable amid the gathering webs of horror and unreality.

"Look here!" Gordon lifted, his arm, drew back the sleeve and displayed a bandage, the cryptic significance of which was intolerable.

"I came into the bathroom this morning looking for my razor," he said. "I found Evelyn just on the point of using my best shaving implement for some feminine purpose—to cut out a pattern, or something. Like many women she can't seem to realize the difference between a razor and a butcher-knife or a pair of shears.

"I was a bit irritated, and I said: 'Evelyn, how many times have I told you not to use my razors for such things? Bring it here; I'll give you my pocket-knife.'

"'I'm sorry, Jim,' she said. 'I didn't know it would hurt the razor. Here it is.'

"She was advancing, holding the open razor toward me. I reached for it—then something warned me. It was the same look in her eyes, just as I had seen it the day she nearly ran over me. That was all that saved my life, for I instinctively threw up my hand just as she slashed at my throat with all her power. The blade gashed my arm as you see, before I caught her wrist. For an instant she fought me like a wild thing; her slender body was taut as steel beneath my hands. Then she went limp and the look in her eyes was replaced by a strange dazed expression. The razor slipped out of her fingers.

"I let go of her and she stood swaying as if about to faint. I went to the lavatory—my wound was bleeding in a beastly fashion—and the next thing I heard her cry out, and she was hovering over me.

"'Jim!' she cried. 'How did you cut yourself so terribly?'"

Gordon shook his head and sighed heavily. "I guess I was a bit out of my head. My self-control snapped.

"'Don't keep up this pretense, Evelyn,' I said. 'God knows what's got into you, but you know as well as I that you've tried to kill me three times in the past week.'

"She recoiled as if I'd struck her, catching at her breast and staring at me as if at a ghost. She didn't say a word—and just what I said I don't remember. But when I finished I left her standing there white and still as a marble statue. I got my arm bandaged at a drug store, and then came over here, not knowing what else to do.

"Kirowan—O'Donnel—it's damnable! Either my wife is subject to fits of insanity—" He choked on the word. "No, I can't believe it. Ordinarily her eyes are too clear and level—too utterly sane. But every time she has an opportunity to harm me, she seems to become a temporary maniac."

He beat his fists together in his impotence and agony.

"But it isn't insanity! I used to work in a psychopathic ward, and I've seen every form of mental unbalance. My wife is *not* insane!"

"Then what—" I began, but he turned haggard eyes on me.

"Only one alternative remains," he answered. "It is the old curse—from the days when I walked the earth with a heart as black as hell's darkest pits, and did evil in the sight of man and of God. *She* knows, in fleeting snatches of memory. People have *seen* before—have glimpsed forbidden things in momentary liftings of the veil, which bars life from life. She was Elizabeth Douglas, the ill-fated bride of Richard Gordon, whom he murdered in jealous frenzy, and the vengeance is hers. I shall die by her hands, as it was meant to be. And she—" he bowed his head in his hands.

"Just a moment." It was Kirowan again. "You have mentioned a strange look in your wife's eyes. What sort of a look? Was it of maniacal frenzy?"

Gordon shook his head. "It was an utter blankness. All the life and intelligence simply vanished, leaving her eyes dark wells of emptiness."

Kirowan nodded, and asked a seemingly irrelevant question. "Have you any enemies?"

"Not that I know of."

"You forget Joseph Roelocke," I said. "I can't imagine that elegant sophisticate going to the trouble of doing you actual harm, but I have an idea that if he could discomfort you without any physical effort on his part, he'd do it with a right good will."

Kirowan turned on me an eye that had suddenly become piercing.

"And who is this Joseph Roelocke?"

"A young exquisite who came into Evelyn's life and nearly rushed her off her feet for a while. But in the end she came back to her first love—Gordon here. Roelocke took it pretty hard. For all his suaveness there's a streak of violence and passion in the man that might have cropped out but for his infernal indolence and blasé indifference."

"Oh, there's nothing to be said against Roelocke," interrupted Gordon impatiently. "He must know that Evelyn never really loved him. He merely fascinated her temporarily with his romantic Latin air."

"Not exactly Latin, Jim," I protested. "Roelocke does look foreign, but it isn't Latin. It's almost Oriental."

"Well, what has Roelocke to do with this matter?" Gordon snarled with the irascibility of frayed nerves. "He's been as friendly as a man could be since Evelyn and I were married. In fact, only a week ago he sent her a ring which he said was a peace-offering and a belated wedding gift; said that after all, her jilting him was a greater misfortune for her than it was for him—the conceited jackass!"

"A ring?" Kirowan had suddenly come to life; it was as if something hard and steely had been sounded in him. "What sort of a ring?"

"Oh, a fantastic thing—copper, made like a scaly snake coiled three times, with its tail in its mouth and yellow jewels for eyes. I gather he picked it up somewhere in Hungary."

"He has traveled a great deal in Hungary?"

Gordon looked surprized at this questioning but answered: "Why, apparently the man's traveled everywhere. I put him down as the pampered son of a millionaire. He never did any work, so far as I know."

"He's a great student," I put in. "I've been up to his apartment several times, and I never saw such a collection of books—"

Gordon leaped to his feet with an oath, "Are we all crazy?" he cried. "I came up here hoping to get some help—and you fellows fall to talking of Joseph Roelocke. I'll go to Doctor Donnelly—"

"Wait!" Kirowan stretched out a detaining hand. "If you don't mind, we'll go over to your house. I'd like to talk to your wife."

Gordon dumbly acquiesced. Harried and haunted by grisly forebodings, he knew not which way to turn, and welcomed anything that promised aid.

We drove over in his car, and scarcely a word was spoken on the way. Gordon was sunk in moody ruminations, and Kirowan had withdrawn himself into some strange aloof domain of thought beyond my ken. He sat like a statue, his dark vital eyes staring into space, not blankly, but as one who looks with understanding into some far realm.

Though I counted the man as my best friend, I knew but little of his past. He had come into my life as abruptly and unannounced as Joseph Roelocke had come into the life of Evelyn Ash. I had met him at the Wanderer's Club, which is composed of the drift of the world, travelers, eccentrics, and all manner of men whose paths lie outside the beaten tracks of life. I had been attracted to him, and intrigued by his strange powers and deep knowledge. I vaguely knew that he was the black sheep younger son of a titled Irish family, and that he had walked many strange ways. Gordon's mention of Hungary struck a chord in my memory; one phase of his life Kirowan had once let drop fragmentarily. I only knew that he had once suffered a bitter grief and a savage wrong, and that it had been in Hungary. But the nature of the episode I did not know.

At Gordon's house Evelyn met us calmly, showing inner agitation only by the over-restraint of her manner. I saw the beseeching look she stole at her husband. She was a slender, soft-spoken girl, whose dark eyes were always vibrant and alight with emotion. That child try to murder her adored husband? The idea was monstrous. Again I was convinced that James Gordon himself was deranged.

Following Kirowan's lead, we made a pretense of small talk, as if we had casually dropped in, but I felt that Evelyn was not deceived. Our conversation rang false and hollow, and presently Kirowan said: "Mrs. Gordon, that is a remarkable ring you are wearing. Do you mind if I look at it?"

"I'll have to give you my hand," she laughed. "I've been trying to get it off today, and it won't come off."

She held out her slim white hand for Kirowan's inspection, and his face was immobile as he looked at the metal snake that coiled about her slim finger. He did not touch it. I myself was aware of an unaccountable repulsion. There was something almost obscene about that dull copperish reptile wound about the girl's white finger.

"It's evil-looking, isn't it?" She involuntarily shivered. "At first I liked it, but now I can hardly bear to look at it. If I can get it off I intend to return it to Joseph—Mr. Roelocke."

Kirowan was about to make some reply, when the doorbell rang. Gordon jumped as if shot, and Evelyn rose quickly.

"I'll answer it, Jim—I know who it is."

She returned an instant later with two more mutual friends, those inseparable cronies, Doctor Donnelly, whose burly body, jovial manner and booming voice were combined with as keen a brain as any in the profession, and Bill Bain, elderly, lean, wiry, acidly witty. Both were old friends of the Ash family. Doctor Donnelly had ushered Evelyn into the world, and Bain was always Uncle Bill to her.

"Howdy, Jim! Howdy, Mr. Kirowan!" roared Donnelly. "Hey, O'Donnel, have you got any firearms with you? Last time your nearly blew my head off showing me an old flintlock pistol that wasn't supposed to be loaded!"

"Doctor Donnelly!"

We all turned. Evelyn was standing beside a wide table, holding it as if for support. Her face was white. Our badinage ceased instantly. A sudden tension was in the air.

"Doctor Donnelly," she repeated, holding her voice steady by an effort, "I sent for you and Uncle Bill—for the same reason for which I know Jim has brought Mr. Kirowan and Michael. There is a matter Jim and I can no longer deal with alone. There is something between us—something black and ghastly and terrible."

"What are you talking about, girl?" All the levity was gone from Donnelly's great voice.

"My husband—" She choked, then went blindly on: "My husband has accused me of trying to murder him."

The silence that fell was broken by Bain's sudden and energetic rise. His eyes blazed and his fists quivered.

"You young pup!" he shouted at Gordon. "I'll knock the living daylights—"

"Sit down, Bill!" Donnelly's huge hand crushed his smaller companion back into his chair. "No use goin' off half cocked. Go ahead, honey."

"We need help. We can not carry this thing alone." A shadow crossed her comely face. "This morning Jim's arm was badly cut. He said I did it. I don't know. I was handing him the razor. Then

I must have fainted. At least, everything faded away. When I came to myself he was washing his arm in the lavatory—and—and he accused me of trying to kill him."

"Why, the young fool!" barked the belligerent Bain. "Hasn't he sense enough to know that if you did cut him, it was an accident?"

"Shut up, won't you?" snorted Donnelly. "Honey, did you say you fainted? That isn't like you."

"I've been having fainting spells," she answered. "The first time was when we were in the mountains and Jim fell down a cliff. We were standing on the edge—then everything went black, and when my sight cleared, he was rolling down the slope." She shuddered at the recollection.

"Then when I lost control of the car and it crashed into the tree. You remember—Jim called you over."

Doctor Donnelly nodded his head ponderously.

"I don't remember you ever having fainting spells before."

"But Jim says I pushed him over the cliff!" she cried hysterically. "He says I tried to run him down in the car! He says I purposely slashed him with the razor!"

Doctor Donnelly turned perplexedly, toward the wretched Gordon.

"How about it, son?"

"God help me," Gordon burst out in agony; "it's true!"

"Why, you lying hound!" It was Bain who gave tongue, leaping again to his feet. "If you want a divorce, why don't you get it in a decent way, instead of resorting to these despicable tactics—"

"Damn you!" roared Gordon, lunging up, and losing control of himself completely. "If you say that I'll tear your jugular out!"

Evelyn screamed; Donnelly grabbed Bain ponderously and banged him back into his chair with no overly gentle touch, and Kirowan laid a hand lightly on Gordon's shoulder. The man seemed to crumple into himself. He sank back into his chair and held out his hands gropingly toward his wife.

"Evelyn," he said, his voice thick with laboring emotion, "you know I love you. I feel like a dog. But God help me, it's true. If we go on this way, I'll be a dead man, and you—"

"Don't say it!" she screamed. "I know you wouldn't lie to me, Jim. If you say I tried to kill you, I know I did. But I swear, Jim, I didn't do it consciously. Oh, I must be going mad! That's why my dreams have been so wild and terrifying lately—"

"Of what have you dreamed, Mrs. Gordon?" asked Kirowan gently.

She pressed her hands to her temples and stared dully at him, as if only half comprehending.

"A black thing," she muttered. "A horrible faceless black thing that mows and mumbles and paws over me with apish hands. I dream of it every night. And in the daytime I try to kill the only man I ever loved. I'm going mad! Maybe I'm already crazy and don't know it."

"Calm yourself, honey." To Doctor Donnelly, with all his science, it was only another case of feminine hysteria. His matter-of-fact voice seemed to soothe her, and she sighed and drew a weary hand through her damp locks.

"We'll talk this all over, and everything's goin' to be okay," he said, drawing a thick cigar from his vest pocket. "Gimme a match, honey."

She began mechanically to feel about the table, and just as mechanically Gordon said: "There are matches in the drawer, Evelyn."

She opened the drawer and began groping in it, when suddenly, as if struck by recollection and intuition, Gordon sprang up, white-faced, and shouted: "No, no! Don't open that drawer-don't—"

Even as he voiced that urgent cry, she stiffened, as if at the feel of something in the drawer. Her change of expression held us all frozen, even Kirowan. The vital intelligence vanished from her eyes like a blown-out flame, and into them came the look Gordon had described as blank. The term was descriptive. Her beautiful eyes were dark wells of emptiness, as if the soul had been withdrawn from behind them.

Her hand came out of the drawer holding a pistol, and she fired point-blank. Gordon reeled with a groan and went down, blood starting from his head. For a flashing instant she looked down stupidly at the smoking gun in her hand, like one suddenly waking from a nightmare. Then her wild scream of agony smote our ears.

"Oh God, I've killed him! Jim! *Jim!* "

She reached him before any of us, throwing herself on her knees and cradling his bloody head in her arms, while she sobbed in an unbearable passion of horror and anguish. The emptiness was gone from her eyes; they were alive and dilated with grief and terror.

I was making toward my prostrate friend with Donnelly and Bain, but Kirowan caught my arm. His face was no longer immobile; his eyes glittered with a controlled savagery.

"Leave him to them!" he snarled. "We are hunters, not healers! Lead me to the house of Joseph Roelocke!"

I did not question him. We drove there in Gordon's car.

I had the wheel, and something about the grim face of my companion caused me to hurl the machine recklessly through the traffic. I had the sensation of being part of a tragic drama which was hurtling with headlong speed toward a terrible climax.

I wrenched the car to a grinding halt at the curb before the building where Roelocke lived in a bizarre apartment high above the city. The very elevator that shot us skyward seemed imbued with something of Kirowan's driving urge for haste. I pointed out Roelocke's door, and he cast it open without knocking and shouldered his way in. I was close at his heels.

Roelocke, in a dressing-gown of Chinese silk worked with dragons, was lounging on a divan, puffing quickly at a cigarette. He sat up, overturning a wine-glass which stood with a half-filled bottle at his elbow.

Before Kirowan could speak, I burst out with our news. "James Gordon has been shot!"

He sprang to his feet. "Shot? When? When did she kill him?"

"*She?*" I glared in bewilderment. "How did you know—"

With a steely hand Kirowan thrust me aside, and as the men faced each other, I saw recognition flare up in Roelocke's face. They made a strong contrast: Kirowan, tall, pale with some white-hot passion; Roelocke, slim, darkly handsome, with the saracenic arch of his slim brows above his black eyes. I realized that whatever else occurred, it lay between those two men. They were not strangers; I could sense like a tangible thing the hate that lay between them.

"John Kirowan!" softly whispered Roelocke.

"You remember me, Yosef Vrolok!" Only an iron control kept Kirowan's voice steady. The other merely stared at him without speaking.

"Years ago," said Kirowan more deliberately, "when we delved in the dark mysteries together in Budapest, I saw whither you were drifting. I drew back; I would not descend to the foul depths of forbidden occultism and diabolism to which you sank. And because I would not, you despised me, and you robbed me of the only woman I ever loved; you turned her against me by means of your vile arts, and then you degraded and debauched her, sank her into your own foul slime. I had killed you with my hands then, Yosef Vrolok—vampire by nature as well as by name that you are—but your arts protected you from physical vengeance. But you have trapped yourself at last!"

Kirowan's voice rose in fierce exultation. All his cultured restraint had been swept away from him, leaving a primitive, elemental man, raging and gloating over a hated foe.

"You sought the destruction of James Gordon and his wife, because she unwittingly escaped your snare; you—"

Roelocke shrugged his shoulders and laughed. "You are mad. I have not seen the Gordons for weeks. Why blame me for their family troubles?"

Kirowan snarled. "Liar as always. What did you say just now when O'Donnel told you Gordon had been shot? 'When did *she* kill him?' You were expecting to hear that the girl had killed her husband. Your psychic powers had told you that a climax was close at hand. You were nervously awaiting news of the success of your devilish scheme.

"But I did not need a slip of your tongue to recognize your handiwork. I knew as soon as I saw the ring on Evelyn Gordon's finger; the ring she could not remove; the ancient and accursed ring of Thoth-amon, handed down by foul cults of sorcerers since the days of forgotten Stygia, I knew that ring was yours, and I knew by what ghastly rites you came to possess it. And I knew its power. Once she put it on her finger, in her innocence and ignorance, she was in your power. By your black magic you summoned the black elemental spirit, *the haunter of the ring*, out of the gulfs of Night and the ages. Here in your accursed chamber you performed unspeakable rituals to drive Evelyn Gordon's soul from her body, and to cause that body to be possessed by that godless sprite from *outside* the human universe.

"She was too clean and wholesome, her love for her husband too strong, for the fiend to gain complete and permanent possession of her body; only for brief instants could it drive her own spirit into the void and animate her form. But that was enough for your purpose. But you have brought ruin upon yourself by your vengeance!"

Kirowan's voice rose to a feline screech.

"What was the price demanded by the fiend you drew from the Pits? Ha, you blench! Yosef Vrolok is not the only man to have learned forbidden secrets! After I left Hungary, a broken man, I took up again the study of the black arts, to trap you, you cringing serpent! I explored the ruins of Zimbabwe, the lost mountains of inner Mongolia, and the forgotten jungle islands of the southern seas. I learned what sickened my soul so that I forswore occultism for ever—but I learned of the black spirit that deals death by the hand of a beloved one, and is controlled by a master of magic.

"But, Yosef Vrolok, you are not an adept! You have not the power to control the fiend you have invoked. And you have sold your soul!"

The Hungarian tore at his collar as if it were a strangling noose. His face had changed, as if a mask had dropped away; he looked much older.

"You lie!" he panted. "I did not promise him my soul—"

"I do not lie!" Kirowan's shriek was shocking in its wild exultation. "I know the price a man must pay for calling forth the nameless shape that roams the gulfs of Darkness. Look! There in the corner behind you! A nameless, sightless thing is laughing— is mocking you! It has fulfilled its bargain, and it has come for you, Yosef Vrolok!"

"No! No!" shrieked Vrolok, tearing his limp collar away from his sweating throat. His composure had crumpled, and his demoralization was sickening to see. "I tell you it was not *my* soul—I promised it a soul, but not *my* soul—he must take the soul of the girl, or of James Gordon."

"Fool!" roared Kirowan. "Do you think *he* could take the souls of innocence? That he would not know they were beyond his reach? The girl and the youth he could kill; their souls were not his to take or yours to give. But *your* black soul is not beyond his reach, and he will have his wage. Look! He is materializing behind you! He is growing out of thin air!"

Was it the hypnosis inspired by Kirowan's burning words that caused me to shudder and grow cold, to feel an icy chill that was not of earth pervade the room? Was it a trick of light and shadow that seemed to produce the effect of a black anthropomorphic shadow on the wall behind the Hungarian? *No*, by heaven! It grew, it swelled-Vrolok had not turned. He stared at Kirowan with eyes starting from his head, hair standing stiffly on his scalp, sweat dripping from his livid face.

Kirowan's cry started shudders down my spine.

"Look behind you, fool! *I see him!* He has come! He is here! His grisly mouth gapes in awful laughter! His mis-shapen paws reach for you!"

And then at last Vrolok wheeled, with an awful shriek, throwing his arms above his head in a gesture of wild despair. And for one brain-shattering instant he was *blotted out* by a great black shadow—Kirowan grasped my arm and we fled from that accursed chamber, blind with horror.

The same paper which bore a brief item telling of James Gordon having suffered a slight scalp-wound by the accidental discharge of a pistol in his home, headlined the sudden death of Joseph Roelocke, wealthy and eccentric clubman, in his sumptuous apartments—apparently from heart-failure.

I read it at breakfast, while I drank cup after cup of black coffee, from a hand that was not too steady, even after the lapse of a night. Across the table from me Kirowan likewise seemed to lack appetite. He brooded, as if he roamed again through bygone years.

"Gordon's fantastic theory of reincarnation was wild enough," I said at last. "But the actual facts were still more incredible. Tell me, Kirowan, was that last scene the result of hypnosis? Was it the power of your words that made me seem to see a black horror grow out of the air and rip Yosef Vrolok's soul from his living body?"

He shook his head. "No human hypnotism would strike that black-hearted devil dead on the floor. No; there are beings outside the ken of common humanity, foul shapes of transcosmic evil. Such a one it was with which Vrolok dealt."

"But how could it claim his soul?" I persisted. "If indeed such an awful bargain had been struck, it had not fulfilled its part, for James Gordon was not dead, but merely knocked senseless."

"Vrolok did not know it," answered Kirowan. "He thought that Gordon was dead, and I convinced him that he himself had been trapped, and was doomed. In his demoralization he fell easy prey to the thing he called forth. *It*, of course, was always watching for a moment of weakness on his part. The powers of Darkness never deal fairly with human beings; he who traffics with them is always cheated in the end."

"It's a mad nightmare," I muttered. "But it seems to me, then, that you as much as anything else brought about Vrolok's death."

"It is gratifying to think so," Kirowan answered. "Evelyn Gordon is safe now; and it is a small repayment for what he did to another girl, years ago, and in a far country."

GRAVEYARD RATS

Chapter One

THE HEAD FROM THE GRAVE

S aul Wilkinson awoke suddenly, and lay in the darkness with beads of cold sweat on his hands and face. He shuddered at the memory of the dream from which he had awakened.

But horrible dreams were nothing uncommon. Grisly nightmares had haunted his sleep since early childhood. It was another fear that clutched his heart with icy fingers—fear of the sound that had roused him. It had been a furtive step—hands fumbling in the dark.

And now a small scurrying sounded in the room—a rat running back and forth across the floor.

He groped under his pillow with trembling fingers. The house was still, but imagination peopled its darkness with shapes of horror. But it was not all imagination. A faint stir of air told him the door that gave on the broad hallway was open. He knew he had closed that door before he went to bed. And he knew it was not one of his brothers who had come so subtly to his room.

In that fear-tense, hate-haunted household, no man came by night to his brother's room without first making himself known.

This was especially the case since an old feud had claimed the eldest brother four days since—John Wilkinson, shot down in the streets of the little hill-country town by Joel Middleton, who had escaped into the post oak grown hills, swearing still greater vengeance against the Wilkinsons.

All this flashed through Saul's mind as he drew the revolver from under his pillow.

As he slid out of bed, the creak of the springs brought his heart into his throat, and he crouched there for a moment, holding his breath and straining his eyes into the darkness.

Richard was sleeping upstairs, and so was Harrison, the city detective Peter had brought out to hunt down Joel Middleton. Peter's room was on the ground floor, but in another wing. A yell for help might awaken all three, but it would also bring a hail of lead at him, if Joel Middleton were crouching over there in the blackness.

Saul knew this was his fight, and must be fought out alone, in the darkness he had always feared and hated. And all the time sounded that light, scampering patter of tiny feet, racing up and down, up and down...

Crouching against the wall, cursing the pounding of his heart, Saul fought to steady his quivering nerves. He was backed against the wall which formed the partition between his room and the hall.

The windows were faint gray squares in the blackness, and he could dimly make out objects of furniture in all except one side of the room. Joel Middleton must be over there, crouching by the old fireplace, which was invisible in the darkness.

But why was he waiting? And why was that accursed rat racing up and down before the fireplace, as if in a frenzy of fear and greed? Just so Saul had seen rats race up and down the floor of the meat-house, frantic to get at flesh suspended out of reach.

Noiselessly, Saul moved along the wall toward the door. If a man was in the room, he would presently be lined between himself and a window. But as he glided along the wall like a night-shirted ghost, no ominous bulk grew out of the darkness. He reached the door and closed it soundlessly, wincing at his nearness to the unrelieved blackness of the hall outside.

But nothing happened. The only sounds were the wild beating of his heart, the loud ticking of the old clock on the mantelpiece—the maddening patter of the unseen rat. Saul clenched his teeth against the shrieking of his tortured nerves. Even in his growing terror he found time to wonder frantically why that rat ran up and down before the fireplace.

The tension became unbearable. The open door proved that Middleton, or someone—or *something*—had come into that room. Why would Middleton come save to kill? But why in God's name had he not struck already? What was he waiting for?

Saul's nerve snapped suddenly. The darkness was strangling him and those pattering rat-feet were red-hot hammers on his crumbling brain. He must have light, even though that light brought hot lead ripping through him.

In stumbling haste he groped to the mantelpiece, fumbling for the lamp. And he cried out—a choked, horrible croak that could not have carried beyond his room. For his hand, groping in the dark on the mantel, had touched the hair on a human scalp!

A furious squeal sounded in the darkness at his feet and a sharp pain pierced his ankle as the rat attacked him, as if he were an intruder seeking to rob it of some coveted object.

But Saul was hardly aware of the rodent as he kicked it away and reeled back, his brain a whirling turmoil. Matches and candles were on the table, and to it he lurched, his hands sweeping the dark and finding what he wanted.

He lighted a candle and turned, gun lifted in a shaking hand. There was no living man in the room except himself. But his distended eyes focused themselves on the mantelpiece—and the object on it.

He stood frozen, his brain at first refusing to register what his eyes revealed. Then he croaked inhumanly and the gun crashed on the hearth as it slipped through his numb fingers.

John Wilkinson was dead, with a bullet through his heart. It had been three days since Saul had seen his body nailed into the crude coffin and lowered into the grave in the old Wilkinson family graveyard. For three days the hard clay soil had baked in the hot sun above the coffined form of John Wilkinson.

Yet from the mantel John Wilkinson's face leered at him— white and cold and dead.

It was no nightmare, no dream of madness. There, on the mantelpiece rested John Wilkinson's severed head.

And before the fireplace, up and down, up and down, scampered a creature with red eyes, that squeaked and squealed—a great gray rat, maddened by its failure to reach the flesh its ghoulish hunger craved.

Saul Wilkinson began to laugh—horrible, soul-shaking shrieks that mingled with the squealing of the gray ghoul. Saul's body rocked to and fro, and the laughter turned to insane weeping, that gave way in turn to hideous screams that echoed through the old house and brought the sleepers out of their sleep.

They were the screams of a madman. The horror of what he had seen had blasted Saul Wilkinson's reason like a blown-out candle flame.

Chapter Two

MADMAN'S HATE

It was those screams which roused Steve Harrison, sleeping in an upstairs chamber. Before he was fully awake he was on his way down the unlighted stairs, pistol in one hand and flashlight in the other.

Down in the hallway he saw light streaming from under a closed door, and made for it. But another was before him. Just as Harrison reached the landing, he saw a figure rushing across the hall, and flashed his beam on it.

It was Peter Wilkinson, tall and gaunt, with a poker in his hand. He yelled something incoherent, threw open the door and rushed in.

Harrison heard him exclaim: "Saul! What's the matter? What are you looking at—" Then a terrible cry: *"My God!"*

The poker clanged on the floor, and then the screams of the maniac rose to a crescendo of fury.

It was at this instant that Harrison reached the door and took in the scene with one startled glance. He saw two men in nightshirts grappling in the candlelight, while from the mantel a cold, dead, white face looked blindly down on them, and a gray rat ran in mad circles about their feet.

Into that scene of horror and madness Harrison propelled his powerful, thick-set body. Peter Wilkinson was in sore straits. He had dropped his poker and now, with blood streaming from a wound in his head, he was vainly striving to tear Saul's lean fingers from his throat.

The glare in Saul's eyes told Harrison the man was mad. Crooking one massive arm about the maniac's neck, he tore him loose from his victim with an exertion of sheer strength that not even the abnormal energy of insanity could resist.

The madman's stringy muscles were like steel wires under the detective's hands, and Saul twisted about in his grasp, his teeth snapping, beastlike, for Harrison's bull-throat. The detective shoved the clawing, frothing fury away from him and smashed a fist to the madman's jaw. Saul crashed to the floor and lay still, eyes glazed and limbs quivering.

Peter reeled back against a table, purple-faced and gagging.

"Get cords, quick!" snapped Harrison, heaving the limp figure off the floor and letting it slump into a great arm-chair. "Tear that sheet in strips. We've got to tie him up before he comes to. Hell's fire!"

The rat had made a ravening attack on the senseless man's bare feet. Harrison kicked it away, but it squeaked furiously and came charging back with ghoulish persistence. Harrison crushed it under his foot, cutting short its maddened squeal.

Peter, gasping convulsively, thrust into the detective's hands the strips he had torn from the sheet, and Harrison bound the limp limbs with professional efficiency. In the midst of his task he looked up to see Richard, the youngest brother, standing in the doorway, his face like chalk.

"Richard!" choked Peter. "Look! My God! John's head!"

"I see!" Richard licked his lips. "But why are you tying up Saul?"

"He's crazy," snapped Harrison. "Get me some whiskey, will you?"

As Richard reached for a bottle on a curtained shelf, booted feet hit the porch outside, and a voice yelled: "Hey, there! Dick! What's wrong?"

"That's our neighbor, Jim Allison," muttered Peter.

He stepped to the door opposite the one that opened into the hall and turned the key in the ancient lock. That door opened upon a side porch. A tousle-headed man with his pants pulled on over his nightshirt came blundering in.

"What's the matter?" he demanded. "I heard somebody hollerin', and run over quick as I could. What you doin' to Saul—good God Almighty!"

He had seen the head on the mantel, and his face went ashen.

"Go get the marshal, Jim!" croaked Peter. "This is Joel Middleton's work!"

Allison hurried out, stumbling as he peered back over his shoulder in morbid fascination.

Harrison had managed to spill some liquor between Saul's livid lips. He handed the bottle to Peter and stepped to the mantel. He touched the grisly object, shivering slightly as he did so. His eyes narrowed suddenly.

"You think Middleton dug up your brother's grave and cut off his head?" he asked.

"Who else?" Peter stared blankly at him.

"Saul's mad. Madmen do strange things. Maybe Saul did this."

"No! No!" exclaimed Peter, shuddering. "Saul hasn't left the house all day. John's grave was undisturbed this morning, when I stopped by the old graveyard on my way to the farm. Saul was sane when he went to bed. It was seeing John's head that drove him mad. Joel Middleton has been here, to take this horrible revenge!" He sprang up suddenly, shrilling, "My God, he may still be hiding in the house somewhere!"

"We'll search it," snapped Harrison. "Richard, you stay here with Saul. You might come with me, Peter."

In the hall outside the detective directed a beam of light on the heavy front door. The key was turned in the massive lock.

He turned and strode down the hall, asking: "Which door is farthest from any sleeping chamber?"

"The back kitchen door!" Peter answered, and led the way. A few moments later they were standing before it. It stood partly open, framing a crack of starlit sky.

"He must have come and gone this way," muttered Harrison. "You're sure this door was locked?"

"I locked all outer doors myself," asserted Peter. "Look at those scratches on the outer side! And there's the key lying on the floor inside."

"Old-fashioned lock," grunted Harrison. "A man could work the key out with a wire from the outer side and force the lock easily. And this is the logical lock to force, because the noise of breaking it wouldn't likely be heard by anybody in the house."

He stepped out onto the deep back porch. The broad back yard was without trees or brushes, separated by a barbed-wire fence from a pasture lot, which ran to a wood-lot thickly grown with post oaks, part of the woods which hemmed in the village of Lost Knob on all sides.

Peter stared toward that woodland, a low, black rampart in the faint starlight, and he shivered.

"He's out there, somewhere!" he whispered. "I never suspected he'd dare strike at us in our own house. I brought you here to hunt him down. I never thought we'd need you to protect us!"

Without replying, Harrison stepped down into the yard. Peter cringed back from the starlight, and remained crouching at the edge of the porch.

Harrison crossed the narrow pasture and paused at the ancient rail fence which separated it from the woods. They were black as only post oak thickets can be.

No rustle of leaves, no scrape of branches betrayed a lurking presence. If Joel Middleton had been there, he must have already sought refuge in the rugged hills that surrounded Lost Knob.

Harrison turned back toward the house. He had arrived at Lost Knob late the preceding evening. It was now somewhat past midnight. But the grisly news was spreading, even in the dead of night.

The Wilkinson house stood at the western edge of the town, and the Allison house was the only one within a hundred yards of it. But Harrison saw lights springing up in distant windows.

Peter stood on the porch, head out-thrust on his long, buzzard-like neck.

"Find anything?" he called anxiously.

"Tracks wouldn't show on this hard-baked ground," grunted the detective. "Just what did you see when you ran into Saul's room?"

"Saul standing before the mantelboard, screaming with his mouth wide open," answered Peter. "When I saw—what he saw, I must have cried out and dropped the poker. Then Saul leaped on me like a wild beast."

"Was his door locked?"

"Closed, but not locked. The lock got broken accidentally a few days ago."

"One more question: has Middleton ever been in this house before?"

"Not to my knowledge," replied Peter grimly. "Our families have hated each other for twenty-five years. Joel's the last of his name."

Harrison re-entered the house. Allison had returned with the marshal, McVey, a tall, taciturn man who plainly resented the detective's presence. Men were gathering on the side porch and in the yard. They talked in low mutters, except for Jim Allison, who was vociferous in his indignation.

"This finishes Joel Middleton!" he proclaimed loudly. "Some folks sided with him when he killed John. I wonder what they think now? Diggin' up a dead man and cuttin' his head off! That's Injun work! I reckon folks won't wait for no jury to tell 'em what to do with Joel Middleton!"

"Better catch him before you start lynchin' him," grunted McVey. "Peter, I'm takin' Saul to the county seat."

Peter nodded mutely. Saul was recovering consciousness, but the mad glaze of his eyes was unaltered. Harrison spoke:

"Suppose we go to the Wilkinson graveyard and see what we can find? We might be able to track Middleton from there."

"They brought you in here to do the job they didn't think I was good enough to do," snarled McVey. "All right. Go ahead and do it—alone. I'm takin' Saul to the county seat."

With the aid of his deputies he lifted the bound maniac and strode out. Neither Peter nor Richard offered to accompany him. A tall, gangling man stepped from among his fellows and awkwardly addressed Harrison:

"What the marshal does is his own business, but all of us here are ready to help all we can, if you want to git a posse together and comb the country."

"Thanks, no." Harrison was unintentionally abrupt. "You can help me by all clearing out, right now. I'll work this thing out alone, in my own way, as the marshal suggested."

The men moved off at once, silent and resentful, and Jim Allison followed them, after a moment's hesitation. When all had gone, Harrison closed the door and turned to Peter.

"Will you take me to the graveyard?"

Peter shuddered. "Isn't it a terrible risk? Middleton has shown he'll stop at nothing."

"Why should he?" Richard laughed savagely. His mouth was bitter, his eyes alive with harsh mockery, and lines of suffering were carven deep in his face.

"We never stopped hounding him," said he. "John cheated him out of his last bit of land—that's why Middleton killed him. For which you were devoutly thankful!"

"You're talking wild!" exclaimed Peter.

Richard laughed bitterly. "You old hypocrite! We're all beasts of prey, we Wilkinsons—like this thing!" He kicked the dead rat viciously. "We all hated each other. You're glad Saul's crazy! You're glad John's dead. Only me left now, and I have a heart disease. Oh, stare if you like! I'm no fool. I've seen you poring over Aaron's lines in *Titus Andronicus*:

"Oft have I digg'd up dead men from their graves, and set them upright at their dear friends' doors!"

"You're mad yourself!" Peter sprang up, livid.

"Oh, am I?" Richard had lashed himself almost into a frenzy. "What proof have we that you didn't cut off John's head? You knew Saul was a neurotic, that a shock like that might drive him mad! And you visited the graveyard yesterday!"

Peter's contorted face was a mask of fury. Then, with an effort of iron control, he relaxed and said quietly: "You are over-wrought, Richard."

"Saul and John hated you," snarled Richard. "I know why. It was because you wouldn't agree to leasing our farm on Wild River to that oil company. But for your stubbornness we might all be wealthy."

"You know why I wouldn't lease," snapped Peter. "Drilling there would ruin the agricultural value of the land—certain profit, not a risky gamble like oil."

"So you say," sneered Richard. "But suppose that's just a smoke screen? Suppose you dream of being the sole, surviving heir, and becoming an oil millionaire all by yourself, with no brothers to share—"

Harrison broke in: "Are we going the chew the rag all night?"

"No!" Peter turned his back on his brother. "I'll take you to the graveyard. I'd rather face Joel Middleton in the night than listen to the ravings of this lunatic any longer."

"I'm not going," snarled Richard. "Out there in the black night there's too many chances for you to remove the remaining heir. I'll go and stay the rest of the night with Jim Allison."

He opened the door and vanished in the darkness.

Peter picked up the head and wrapped it in a cloth, shivering lightly as he did so.

"Did you notice how well preserved the face is?" he muttered. "One would think that after three days—Come on. I'll take it and put it back in the grave where it belongs."

"I'll kick this dead rat outdoors," Harrison began, turning—and then stopped short. "The damned thing's gone!"

Peter Wilkinson paled as his eyes swept the empty floor.

"It was there!" he whispered. "It was dead. You smashed it! It couldn't come to life and run away."

"We'll, what about it?" Harrison did not mean to waste time on this minor mystery.

Peter's eyes gleamed wearily in the candlelight.

"It was a graveyard rat!" he whispered. "I never saw one in an inhabited house, in town, before! The Indians used to tell strange tales about them! They said they were not beasts at all, but evil, cannibal demons, into which entered the spirits of wicked, dead men at whose corpses they gnawed!"

"Hell's fire!" Harrison snorted, blowing out the candle. But his flesh crawled. After all, a dead rat could not crawl away by itself.

Chapter Three

THE FEATHERED SHADOW

Clouds had rolled across the stars. The air was hot and stifling. The narrow, rutty road that wound westward into the hills was atrocious. But Peter Wilkinson piloted his ancient Model T Ford skillfully, and the village was quickly lost to sight behind them. They passed no more houses. On each side the dense post oak thickets crowded close to the barbed-wire fences.

Peter broke the silence suddenly:

"How did that rat come into our house? They overrun the woods along the creeks, and swarm in every country graveyard in the hills. But I never saw one in the village before. It must have followed Joel Middleton when he brought the head—"

A lurch and a monotonous bumping brought a curse from Harrison. The car came to a stop with a grind of brakes.

"Flat," muttered Peter. "Won't take me long to change tires. You watch the woods. Joel Middleton might be hiding anywhere."

That seemed good advice. While Peter wrestled with rusty metal and stubborn rubber, Harrison stood between him and the nearest clump of trees, with his hand on his revolver. The night wind blew fitfully through the leaves, and once he thought he caught the gleam of tiny eyes among the stems.

"That's got it," announced Peter at last, turning to let down the jack. "We've wasted enough time."

"Listen!" Harrison started, tensed. Off to the west had sounded a sudden scream of pain or fear. Then there came the impact of racing feet on the hard ground, the crackling of brush, as if someone fled blindly through the bushes within a few hundred yards of the road. In an instant Harrison was over the fence and running toward the sounds.

"Help! Help!" it was the voice of dire terror. "Almighty God! Help!"

"This way!" yelled Harrison, bursting into an open flat. The unseen fugitive evidently altered his course in response, for the heavy footfalls grew louder, and then there rang out a terrible shriek, and a figure staggered from the bushes on the opposite side of the glade and fell headlong.

The dim starlight showed a vague writhing shape, with a darker figure on its back. Harrison caught the glint of steel, heard the sound of a blow. He threw up his gun and fired at a venture. At the crack of the shot, the darker figure rolled free, leaped up and vanished in the bushes. Harrison ran on, a queer chill crawling along his spine because of what he had seen in the flash of the shot.

He crouched at the edge of the bushes and peered into them. The shadowy figure had come and gone, leaving no trace except the man who lay groaning in the glade.

Harrison bent over him, snapping on his flashlight. He was an old man, a wild, unkempt figure with matted white hair and beard. That beard was stained with red now, and blood oozed from a deep stab in his back.

"Who did this?" demanded Harrison, seeing that it was useless to try to stanch the flow of blood. The old man was dying. "Joel Middleton?"

"It couldn't have been!" Peter had followed the detective. "That's old Joash Sullivan, a friend of Joel's. He's half crazy, but I've suspected that he's been keeping in touch with Joel and giving his tips—"

"Joel Middleton," muttered the old man. "I'd been to find him, to tell the news about John's head—"

"Where's Joel hiding?" demanded the detective.

Sullivan choked on a flow of blood, spat and shook his head.

"You'll never learn from me!" He directed his eyes on Peter with the eerie glare of the dying. "Are you taking your brother's head back to his grave, Peter Wilkinson? Be careful you don't find your own grave before this night's done! Evil on all your name! The devil owns your souls and the graveyard rats'll eat your flesh! The ghost of the dead walks the night!"

"What do you mean?" demanded Harrison. "Who stabbed you?"

"A dead man!" Sullivan was going fast. "As I come back from meetin' Joel Middleton I met him. Wolf Hunter, the Tonkawa chief your grandpap murdered so long ago, Peter Wilkinson! He chased me and knifed me. I saw him plain, in the starlight—naked in his loin-clout and feathers and paint, just as I saw him when I was a child, before your grandpap killed him!

"Wolf Hunter took your brother's head from the grave!" Sullivan's voice was a ghastly whisper. "He's come back from Hell to fulfill the curse he laid onto your grandpa, when your grandpap shot him in the back, to get the land his tribe claimed. Beware! His ghost walks the night! The graveyard rats are his servants. The graveyard rats—"

Blood burst from his white-bearded lips and he sank back, dead.

Harrison rose somberly.

"Let him lie. We'll pick up his body as we go back to town. We're going on to the graveyard."

"Dare we?" Peter's face was white. "A human I do not fear, not even Joel Middleton, but a ghost—"

"Don't be a fool!" snorted Harrison. "Didn't you say the old man was half crazy?"

"But what if Joel Middleton is hiding somewhere near—"

"I'll take care of him!" Harrison had an invincible confidence in his own fighting ability. What he did not tell Peter, as they returned to the car, was that he had had a glimpse of the slayer in the flash of his shot. The memory of that glimpse still had the short hair prickling at the base of his skull.

That figure had been naked but for a loin-cloth and moccasins and a headdress of feathers.

"Who was Wolf Hunter?" he demanded as they drove on.

"A Tonkawa chief," muttered Peter. "He befriended my grand-father and was later murdered by him, just as Joash said. They say his bones lie in the old graveyard to this day."

Peter lapsed into silence, seemingly a prey of morbid broodings.

Some four miles from town the road wound past a dim clearing. That was the Wilkinson graveyard. A rusty barbed-wire fence surrounded a cluster of graves whose white headstones leaned at crazy angles. Weeds grew thick, straggling over the low mounds.

The post oaks crowded close on all sides, and the road wound through them, past the sagging gate. Across the tops of the trees, nearly half a mile to the west, there was visible a shapeless bulk which Harrison knew was the roof of a house.

"The old Wilkinson farmhouse," Peter answered in reply to his question. "I was born there, and so were my brothers. Nobody's lived in it since we moved to town, ten years ago."

Peter's nerves were taut. He glanced fearfully at the black woods around him, and his hands trembled as he lighted a lantern he took from the car. He winced as he picked up the round cloth-wrapped object that lay on the back seat; perhaps he was visualizing the cold, white, stony face that cloth concealed.

As he climbed over the low gate and led the way between the weed-grown mounds he muttered: "We're fools. If Joel

Middleton's laying out there in the woods he could pick us both off easy as shooting rabbits."

Harrison did not reply, and a moment later Peter halted and shone the light on a mound which was bare of weeds. The surface was tumbled and disturbed, and Peter exclaimed: "Look! I expected to find an open grave. Why do you suppose he took the trouble of filling it again?"

"We'll see," grunted Harrison. "Are you game to open that grave?"

"I've seen my brother's head," answered Peter grimly. "I think I'm man enough to look on his headless body without fainting. There are tools in the tool-shed in the corner of the fence. I'll get them."

Returning presently with pick and shovel, he set the lighted lantern on the ground, and the cloth-wrapped head near it. Peter was pale, and sweat stood on his brow in thick drops. The lantern cast their shadows, grotesquely distorted, across the weed-grown graves. The air was oppressive. There was an occasional dull flicker of lightning along the dusky horizons.

"What's that?" Harrison paused, pick lifted. All about them sounded rustlings and scurryings among the weeds. Beyond the circle of lantern light clusters of tiny red beads glittered at him.

"Rats!" Peter hurled a stone and the beads vanished, though the rustlings grew louder. "They swarm in this graveyard. I believe they'd devour a living man, if they caught him helpless. Begone, you servants of Satan!"

Harrison took the shovel and began scooping out mounds of loose dirt.

"Ought not to be hard work," he grunted. "If he dug it out today or early tonight, it'll be loose all the way down—"

He stopped short, with his shovel jammed hard against the dirt, and a prickling in the short hairs at the nape of his neck. In the tense silence he heard the graveyard rats running through the grass.

"What's the matter?" A new pallor greyed Peter's face.

"I've hit solid ground," said Harrison slowly. "In three days, this clayey soil bakes hard as a brick. But if Middleton or anybody else had opened this grave and refilled it today, the soil would be loose all the way down. It's not. Below the first few inches it's packed and baked hard! The top has been scratched, but the grave has never been opened since it was first filled, three days ago!"

Peter staggered with an inhuman cry.

"Then it's true!" he screamed. "Wolf Hunter *has* come back! He reached up from Hell and took John's head without opening the grave! He sent his familiar devil into our house in the form of a rat! A ghost-rat that could not be killed! Hands off, curse you!"

For Harrison caught at him, growling: "Pull yourself together, Peter!"

But Peter struck his arm aside and tore free. He turned and ran—not toward the car parked outside the graveyard, but toward the opposite fence. He scrambled across the rusty wires with a ripping of cloth and vanished in the woods, heedless of Harrison's shouts.

"Hell!" Harrison pulled up, and swore fervently. Where but in the black-hill country could such things happen? Angrily he picked up the tools and tore into the close-packed clay, baked by a blazing sun into almost iron hardness.

Sweat rolled from him in streams, and he grunted and swore, but persevered with all the power of his massive muscles. He meant to prove or disprove a suspicion growing in his mind—a suspicion that the body of John Wilkinson had never been placed in that grave.

The lightning flashed oftener and closer, and a low mutter of thunder began in the west. An occasional gust of wind made the lantern flicker, and as the mound beside the grave grew higher, and the man digging there sank lower and lower in the earth, the rustling in the grass grew louder and the red beads began to glint in the weeds. Harrison heard the eerie gnashings of tiny teeth all about him, and swore at the memory of grisly legends, whispered by the Negroes of his boyhood region about the graveyard rats.

The grave was not deep. No Wilkinson would waste much labor on the dead. At last the rude coffin lay uncovered before him. With the point of the pick he pried up one corner of the lid, and held the lantern close. A startled oath escaped his lips. The coffin was not empty. It held a huddled, headless figure.

Harrison climbed out of the grave, his mind racing, fitting together pieces of the puzzle. The stray bits snapped into place, forming a pattern, dim and yet incomplete, but taking shape. He looked for the cloth-wrapped head, and got a frightful shock.

The head was gone!

For an instant Harrison felt cold sweat clammy on his hands. Then he heard a clamorous squeaking, the gnashing of tiny fangs.

He caught up the lantern and shone the light about. In its reflection he saw a white blotch on the grass near a straggling clump of bushes that had invaded the clearing. It was the cloth in which the head had been wrapped. Beyond that a black, squirming mound heaved and tumbled with nauseous life.

With an oath of horror he leaped forward, striking and kicking. The graveyard rats abandoned the head with rasping squeaks, scattering before him like darting black shadows. And Harrison shuddered. It was no face that stared up at him in the lantern light, but a white, grinning skull, to which clung only shreds of gnawed flesh.

While the detective burrowed into John Wilkinson's grave, the graveyard rats had torn the flesh from John Wilkinson's head.

Harrison stooped and picked up the hideous thing, now triply hideous. He wrapped it in the cloth, and as he straightened, something like fright took hold of him.

He was ringed in on all sides by a solid circle of gleaming red sparks that shone from the grass. Held back by their fear, the graveyard rats surrounded him, squealing their hate.

Demons, the Negroes called them, and in that moment Harrison was ready to agree.

They gave back before him as he turned toward the grave, and he did not see the dark figure that slunk from the bushes behind him. The thunder boomed out, drowning even the squeaking of the rats, but he heard the swift footfall behind him an instant before the blow was struck.

He whirled, drawing his gun, dropping the head, but just as he whirled, something like a louder clap of thunder exploded in his head, with a shower of sparks before his eyes.

As he reeled backward he fired blindly, and cried out as the flash showed him a horrific, half-naked, painted, feathered figure, crouching with a tomahawk uplifted—the open grave was behind Harrison as he fell.

Down into the grave he toppled, and his head struck the edge of the coffin with a sickening impact. His powerful body went limp; and like darting shadows, from every side raced the graveyard rats, hurling themselves into the grave in a frenzy of hunger and blood-lust.

Chapter Four

RATS IN HELL

It seemed to Harrison's stunned brain that he lay in blackness on the darkened floors of Hell, a blackness lit by darts of flame from the eternal fires. The triumphant shrieking of demons was in his ears as they stabbed him with red-hot skewers.

He saw them, now—dancing monstrosities with pointed noses, twitching ears, red eyes and gleaming teeth—a sharp pain knifed through his flesh.

And suddenly the mists cleared. He lay, not on the floor of Hell, but on a coffin in the bottom of a grave; the fires were lightning flashes from the black sky; and the demons were rats that swarmed over him, slashing with razor-sharp teeth.

Harrison yelled and heaved convulsively, and at his movement the rats gave back in alarm. But they did not leave the grave; they massed solidly along the walls, their eyes glittering redly.

Harrison knew he could have been senseless only a few seconds. Otherwise, these gray ghouls would have already stripped the living flesh from his bones—as they had ripped the dead flesh from the head of the man on whose coffin he lay.

Already his body was stinging in a score of places, and his clothing was damp with his own blood.

Cursing, he started to rise—and a chill of panic shot through him! Falling, his left arm had been jammed into the partly-open coffin, and the weight of his body on the lid clamped his hand fast. Harrison fought down a mad wave of terror.

He would not withdraw his hand unless he could lift his body from the coffin lid—and the imprisonment of his hand held him prostrate there.

Trapped!

In a murdered man's grave, his hand locked in the coffin of a headless corpse, with a thousand gray ghoul-rats ready to tear the flesh from his living frame!

As if sensing his helplessness, the rats swarmed upon him. Harrison fought for his life, like a man in a nightmare. He kicked, he yelled, he cursed, he smote them with the heavy six-shooter he still clutched in his hand.

Their fangs tore at him, ripping cloth and flesh, their acrid scent nauseated him; they almost covered him with their squirming, writhing bodies. He beat them back, smashed and crushed them with blows of his six-shooter barrel.

The living cannibals fell on their dead brothers. In desperation he twisted half-over and jammed the muzzle of his gun against the coffin lid.

At the flash of fire and the deafening report, the rats scurried in all directions.

Again and again, he pulled the trigger until the gun was empty. The heavy slugs crashed through the lid, splitting off a great sliver from the edge. Harrison drew his bruised hand from the aperture.

Gagging and shaking, he clambered out of the grave and rose groggily to his feet. Blood was clotted in his hair from the gash the ghostly hatchet had made in his scalp, and blood trickled from a score of tooth-wounds in his flesh. Lightning played constantly, but the lantern was still shining. But it was not on the ground.

It seemed to be suspended in mid-air—and then he was aware that it was held in the hand of a man—a tall man in a black slicker, whose eyes burned dangerously under his broad hat-brim. In his other hand a black pistol muzzle menaced the detective's midriff.

"You must be that damn' low-country law Pete Wilkinson brung up here to run me down!" growled this man.

"Then you're Joel Middleton!" grunted Harrison.

"Sure I am!" snarled the outlaw. "Where's Pete, the old devil?"

"He got scared and ran off."

"Crazy, like Saul, maybe," sneered Middleton. "Well, you tell him I been savin' a slug for his ugly mug a long time. And one for Dick, too."

"Why did you come here?" demanded Harrison.

"I heard shootin'. I got here just as you was climbin' out of the grave. What's the matter with you? Who was it that broke your head?"

"I don't know his name," answered Harrison, caressing his aching head.

"Well, it don't make no difference to me. But I want to tell you that I didn't cut John's head off. I killed him because he needed it." The outlaw swore and spat. "But I didn't do that other!"

"I know you didn't," Harrison answered.

"Eh?" The outlaw was obviously startled.

"Do you know which rooms the Wilkinsons sleep in, in their house in town?"

"Naw," snorted Middleton. "Never was in their house in my life."

"I thought not. Whoever put John's head on Saul's mantel knew. The back kitchen door was the only one where the lock could have been forced without waking somebody up. The lock on Saul's door was broken. You couldn't have known those things. It looked like an inside job from the start. The lock was forced to make it look like an outside job.

"Richard spilled some stuff that cinched my belief that it was Peter. I decided to bring him out to the graveyard and see if his nerve would stand up under an accusation across his brother's open coffin. But I hit hard-packed soil and knew the grave hadn't been opened. It gave me a turn and I blurted out what I'd found. But it's simple, after all.

"Peter wanted to get rid of his brothers. When you killed John, that suggested a way to dispose of Saul. John's body stood in its coffin in the Wilkinsons' parlor until it was placed in the grave the next day. No death watch was kept. It was easy for Peter to go into the parlor while his brothers slept, pry up the coffin lid and cut off John's head. He put it on ice somewhere to preserve it. When I touched it I found it was nearly frozen.

"No one knew what had happened, because the coffin was not opened again. John was an atheist, and there was the briefest sort of ceremony. The coffin was not opened for his friends to take a last look, as is the usual custom. Then tonight the head was placed in Saul's room. It drove him raving mad.

"I don't know why Peter waited until tonight, or why he called me into the case. He must be partly insane himself. I don't think he meant to kill me when we drove out here tonight. But when he discovered I knew the grave hadn't been opened tonight, he saw the game was up. I ought to have been smart enough to keep my mouth shut, but I was so sure that Peter had opened the grave to get the head, that when I found it *hadn't* been opened, I spoke involuntarily, without stopping to think of the other alternative. Peter pretended a panic and ran off. Later he sent back his partner to kill me."

"Who's he?" demanded Middleton.

"How should I know? Some fellow who looks like an Indian!"

"That old yarn about a Tonkawa ghost has went to your brain!" scoffed Middleton.

"I didn't say it was a ghost," said Harrison, nettled. "It was real enough to kill your friend Joash Sullivan!"

"What?" yelled Middleton. "Joash killed? Who done it?"

"The Tonkawa ghost, whoever he is. The body is lying about a mile back, beside the road, amongst the thickets, if you don't believe me."

Middleton ripped out a terrible oath.

"By God, I'll kill somebody for that! Stay where you are! I ain't goin' to shoot no unarmed man, but if you try to run me down I'll kill you sure as Hell. So keep off my trail. I'm goin', and don't you try to follow me!"

The next instant Middleton had dashed the lantern to the ground where it went out with a clatter of breaking glass.

Harrison blinked in the sudden darkness that followed, and the next lightning flash showed him standing alone in the ancient graveyard.

The outlaw was gone.

Chapter Five

THE RATS EAT

Cursing, Harrison groped on the ground, lit by the lightning flashes. He found the broken lantern, and he found something else.

Rain drops splashed against his face as he started toward the gate. One instant he stumbled in velvet blackness, the next the tombstones shone white in the dazzling glare. Harrison's head ached frightfully. Only chance and a tough skull had saved his life. The would-be killer must have thought the blow was fatal and fled, taking John Wilkinson's head for what grisly purpose there was no knowing. But the head was gone.

Harrison winced at the thought of the rain filling the open grave, but he had neither the strength nor the inclination to shovel the dirt back in it. To remain in that dark graveyard might well be death. The slayer might return.

Harrison looked back as he climbed the fence. The rain had disturbed the rats; the weeds were alive with scampering, flame-eyed shadows. With a shudder, Harrison made his way to the flivver. He climbed in, found his flashlight and reloaded his revolver.

The rain grew in volume. Soon the rutty road to Lost Knob would be a welter of mud. In his condition he did not feel able to the task of driving back through the storm over that abominable road. But it could not be long until dawn. The old farmhouse would afford him a refuge until daylight.

The rain came down in sheets, soaking him, dimming the already uncertain lights as he drove along the road, splashing noisily through the mud-puddles. Wind ripped through the post oaks. Once he grunted and batted his eyes. He could have sworn that a flash of lightning had fleetingly revealed a painted, naked, feathered figure gliding among the trees!

The road wound up a thickly wooded eminence, rising close to the bank of a muddy creek. On the summit the old house squatted. Weeds and low bushes straggled from the surrounding woods up to the sagging porch. He parked the car as close to the house as he could get it, and climbed out, struggling with the wind and rain.

He expected to have to blow the lock off the door with his gun, but it opened under his fingers. He stumbled into a musty-smelling room, weirdly lit by the flickering of the lightning through the cracks of the shutters.

His flashlight revealed a rude bunk built against a side wall, a heavy hand-hewn table, a heap of rags in a corner. From this pile of rags black furtive shadows darted in all directions.

Rats! Rats again!

Could he never escape them?

He closed the door and lit the lantern, placing it on the table. The broken chimney caused the flame to dance and flicker, but not enough wind found its way into the room to blow it out. Three doors, leading into the interior of the house, were closed. The floor and walls were pitted with holes gnawed by the rats.

Tiny red eyes glared at him from the apertures.

Harrison sat down on the bunk, flashlight and pistol on his lap. He expected to fight for his life before day broke. Peter Wilkinson was out there in the storm somewhere, with a heart full of murder, and either allied to him or working separately—in either case an enemy to the detective—was that mysterious painted figure.

And that figure was Death, whether living masquerader or Indian ghost. In any event, the shutters would protect him from a shot from the dark, and to get at him his enemies would have to come into the lighted room where he would have an even chance—which was all the big detective had ever asked.

To get his mind off the ghoulish red eyes glaring at him from the floor, Harrison brought out the object he had found lying near the broken lantern, where the slayer must have dropped it.

It was a smooth oval of flint, made fast to a handle with rawhide thongs—the Indian tomahawk of an elder generation. And Harrison's eyes narrowed suddenly; there was blood on the flint, and some of it was his own. But on the other point of the oval there was more blood, dark and crusted, with strands of hair lighter than his, clinging to the clotted point.

Joash Sullivan's blood? No. The old man had been knifed. But someone else had died that night. The darkness had hidden another grim deed....

Black shadows were stealing across the floor. The rats were coming back—ghoulish shapes, creeping from their holes, converging on the heap of rags in the far corner—a tattered carpet, Harrison now saw, rolled in a long compact heap. Why should the rats leap upon that rag? Why should they race up and down along it, squealing and biting at the fabric?

There was something hideously suggestive about its contour—a shape that grew more definite and ghastly as he looked.

The rats scattered, squeaking, as Harrison sprang across the room. He tore away the carpet—and looked down on the corpse of Peter Wilkinson.

The back of the head had been crushed. The white face was twisted in a leer of awful terror.

For an instant Harrison's brain reeled with the ghastly possibilities his discovery summoned up. Then he took a firm grasp on himself, fought off the whispering potency of the dark, howling night, the thrashing wet black woods and the abysmal aura of the ancient hills, and recognized the only sane solution of the riddle.

Somberly he looked down on the dead man. Peter Wilkinson's fright had been genuine, after all. In his blind panic he had reverted to the habits of his boyhood and fled toward his old home—and met death instead of security.

Harrison started convulsively as a weird sound smote his ears above the roar of the storm—the wailing horror of an Indian war-whoop. The killer was upon him!

Harrison sprang to a shuttered window, peered through a crack, waiting for a flash of lightning. When it came he fired through the window at a feathered head he saw peering around a tree close to the car.

In the darkness that followed the flash he crouched, waiting—there came another white glare—he grunted explosively but did not fire. The head was still there, and he got a better look at it. The lightning shone weirdly white upon it.

It was John Wilkinson's fleshless skull, clad in a feathered headdress and bound in place—and it was the bait of a trap.

Harrison wheeled and sprang toward the lantern on the table. That grisly ruse had been to draw his attention to the front of the house while the killer slunk upon him through the rear of the building! The rats squealed and scattered. Even as Harrison whirled an inner door began to open. He smashed a heavy slug through the panels, heard a groan and the sound of a falling body, and then, just as he reached a hand to extinguish the lantern, the world crashed over his head.

A blinding burst of lightning, a deafening clap of thunder, and the ancient house staggered from gables to foundations! Blue fire crackled from the ceiling and ran down the walls and over the floor. One livid tongue just flicked the detective's shin in passing.

It was like the impact of a sledgehammer. There was in instant of blindness and numb agony, and Harrison found himself sprawling, half-stunned on the floor. The lantern lay extinguished beside the overturned table, but the room was filled with a lurid light.

He realized that a bolt of lightning had struck the house, and that the upper story was ablaze. He hauled himself to his feet, looking for his gun. It lay halfway across the room, and as he started toward it, the bullet-split door swung open. Harrison stopped dead in his tracks.

Through the door limped a man naked but for a loin-cloth and moccasins on his feet. A revolver in his hand menaced the detective. Blood oozing from a wound in his thigh mingled with the paint with which he had smeared himself.

"So it was you who wanted to be the oil millionaire, Richard!" said Harrison.

The other laughed savagely. "Aye, and I will be! And no cursed brothers to share with—brothers I always hated, damn them! Don't move! You nearly got me when you shot through the door. I'm taking no chances with you! Before I send you to Hell, I'll tell you everything.

"As soon as you and Peter started for the graveyard, I realized my mistake in merely scratching the top of the grave—knew you'd hit hard clay and know the grave hadn't been opened. I knew then I'd have to kill you, as well as Peter. I took the rat you mashed when neither of you were looking, so its disappearance would play on Peter's superstitions.

"I rode to the graveyard through the woods, on a fast horse. The Indian disguise was one I thought up long ago. What with that rotten road, and the flat that delayed you, I got to the grave-yard before you and Peter did. On the way, though, I dismounted and stopped to kill that old fool Joash Sullivan. I was afraid he might see and recognize me.

"I was watching when you dug into the grave. When Peter got panicky and ran through the woods I chased him, killed him, and brought his body here to the old house. Then I went back after you. I intended bringing your body here, or rather your bones, after the rats finished you, as I thought they would. Then I heard Joel Middleton coming and had to run for it—I don't care to meet that gun-fighting devil anywhere!

"I was going to burn this house with both your bodies in it. People would think, when they found the bones in the ashes, that Middleton killed you both and burnt the house! And now you play right into my hands by coming here! Lightning has struck the house and it's burning! Oh, the gods fight for me tonight!"

A light of unholy madness played in Richard's eyes, but the pistol muzzle was steady, as Harrison stood clenching his great fists helplessly.

"You'll lie here with that fool Peter!" raved Richard. "With a bullet through your head, until your bones are burnt to such a crisp that nobody can tell how you died! Joel Middleton will be shot down by some posse without a chance to talk. Saul will rave out his days in a madhouse! And I, who will be safely sleeping in my house in town before sun-up, will live out my allotted years in wealth and honor, never suspected—never—"

He was sighting along the black barrel, eyes blazing, teeth bared like the fangs of a wolf between painted lips—his finger was curling on the trigger.

Harrison crouched tensely, desperately, poising the hurl himself with bare hands at the killer and try to pit his naked strength against hot lead spitting from that black muzzle—then—

The door crashed inward behind him and the lurid glare framed a tall figure in a dripping slicker.

An incoherent yell rang to the roof and the gun in the outlaw's hand roared. Again, and again, and yet again it crashed, filling the room with smoke and thunder, and the painted figure jerked to the impact of the tearing lead.

Through the smoke Harrison saw Richard Wilkinson toppling—but he too was firing as he fell. Flames burst through the ceiling, and by their brighter glare Harrison saw a painted figure writhing on the floor, a taller figure wavering in the doorway. Richard was screaming in agony.

Middleton threw his empty gun at Harrison's feet.

"Heard the shootin' and come," he croaked. "Reckon that settles the feud for good!" He toppled, and Harrison caught him in his arms, a lifeless weight.

Richard's screams rose to an unbearable pitch. The rats were swarming from their holes. Blood streaming across the floor had dripped into their holes, maddening them. Now they burst forth in a ravening horde that heeded not cries, or movement, or the devouring flames, but only their own fiendish hunger.

In a gray-black wave they swept over the dead man and the dying man. Peter's white face vanished under that wave. Richard's screaming grew thick and muffled. He writhed, half covered by grey, tearing figures who sucked at his gushing blood, tore at his flesh.

Harrison retreated through the door, carrying the dead outlaw. Joel Middleton, outlaw and killer, yet deserved a better fate than was befalling his slayer.

To save that ghoul, Harrison would not have lifted a finger, had it been in his power.

It was not. The graveyard rats had claimed their own. Out in the yard, Harrison let his burden fall limply. Above the roar of the flames still rose those awful, smothered cries.

Through the blazing doorway he had a glimpse of a horror, a gory figure rearing upright, swaying, enveloped by a hundred clinging, tearing shapes. He glimpsed a face that was not a face at all, but a blind, bloody skull-mask. Then the awful scene was blotted out as the flaming roof fell with a thundering, ear-rending crash.

Sparks showered against the sky, the flames rose as the walls fell in, and Harrison staggered away, dragging the dead man, as a storm-wrapped dawn came haggardly over the oak-clad ridges.

SKULL-FACE

Chapter One

THE FACE IN THE MIST

"We are no other than a moving row
Of Magic Shadow-shapes that come and go."

—*Omar Khayyam*

The horror first took concrete form amid that most unconcrete of all things—a hashish dream. I was off on a timeless, space-less journey through the strange lands that belong to this state of being, a million miles away from earth and all things earthly; yet I became cognizant that something was reaching across the unknown voids—something that tore ruthlessly at the separating curtains of my illusions and intruded itself into my visions.

I did not exactly return to ordinary waking life, yet I was conscious of a seeing and a recognizing that was unpleasant and seemed out of keeping with the dream I was at that time enjoying. To one who has never known the delights of hashish, my explanation must seem chaotic, and impossible. Still, I was aware of a rending of mists and then the Face intruded itself into my sight. I thought at first it was merely a skull; then I saw that it was a hideous yellow instead of white, and was endowed with some horrid form of life. Eyes glimmered deep in the sockets and the jaws moved as if in speech. The body, except for the high, thin shoulders, was vague and indistinct, but the hands, which floated in the mists before and below the skull, were horribly vivid and filled me crawling fears. They were like the hands of a mummy, long, lean and yellow, with knobby joints and cruel curving talons.

Then, to complete the vague horror which was swiftly taking possession of me, a voice spoke—imagine a man so long dead that his vocal organ had grown rusty and unaccustomed to speech. This was the thought which made my flesh crawl as I listened.

"A strong brute and one who might be useful somehow. See that he is given all the hashish he requires."

Then the face began to recede, even as I sensed that I was the subject of conversation, and the mists billowed and began to close again. Yet for a single instant a scene stood out with startling clarity. I gasped—or sought to. For over the high, strange shoulder of the apparition another face stood out clearly for an instant, as if the owner peered at me. Red lips, half parted, long dark eyelashes. shading vivid eyes, a shimmery cloud of hair. Over the shoulder of Horror, breath-taking beauty for an instant looked at me.

Chapter Two

THE HASHISH SLAVE

"Up from Earth's center through the Seventh Gate
I rose, and on the Throne of Saturn sate."

—*Omar Khayyam*

My dream of the skull-face was borne over that usually uncrossable gap that lies between hashish enchantment and humdrum reality. I sat cross-legged on a mat in Yun Shatu's Temple of Dreams and gathered the fading forces of my decaying brain to the task of remembering events and faces.

This last dream was so entirely different from any I had ever had before, that my waning interest was roused to the point of inquiring as to its origin. When I first began to experiment with hashish, I sought to find a physical or psychic basis for the wild flights of illusion pertaining thereto, but of late I had been content to enjoy without seeking cause and effect.

Whence this unaccountable sensation of familiarity in regard to that vision? I took my throbbing head between my hands and laboriously sought a clue. A living dead man and a girl of rare beauty who had looked over his shoulder. Then I remembered.

Back in the fog of days and nights which veils a hashish addict's memory, my money had given out. It seemed years or possibly centuries, but my stagnant reason told me that it had probably been only a few days. At any rate, I had presented myself at Yun Shatu's sordid dive as usual and had been thrown out by the great Negro, Hassim, when it was learned I had no more money.

My universe crashing to pieces about me, and my nerves humming like taut piano wires for the vital need that was mine, I crouched in the gutter and gibbered bestially, till Hassim swaggered out and stilled my yammerings with a blow that felled me, half stunned.

Then as I presently rose, staggeringly and with no thought save of the river; which flowed with cool murmur so near me— as I rose, a light hand was laid like the touch of a rose on my arm. I turned with a frightened start, and stood spellbound before the vision of loveliness which met my gaze. Dark eyes, limpid with pity surveyed me and the little hand on my ragged sleeve drew me toward the door of the Dream Temple. I shrank back, but a low voice, soft and musical, urged me, and filled with a trust that was strange. I shambled along with my beautiful guide.

At the door Hassim met us, cruel hands lifted and a dark scowl on his ape-like brow, but as I cowered there, expecting a blow, he halted before the girl's upraised hand and her word of command which had taken on an imperious note.

I did not understand what she said, but I saw dimly, as in a fog, that she gave the black man money, and she led me to a couch where she had me recline and arranged the cushions as if I were king of Egypt instead of a ragged, dirty renegade who lived only for hashish. Her slim hand was cool on my brow for a moment, and then she was gone and Yussef Ali came bearing the stuff for which my very soul shrieked—and soon I was wandering again through those strange and exotic countries that only a hashish slave knows.

Now as I sat on the mat and pondered the dream of the skull-face I wondered more. Since the unknown girl had led me back into the dive, I had come and gone as before, when I had plenty of money to pay Yun Shatu. Someone certainly was paying him for me, and while my subconscious mind had told me it was the girl, my rusty brain had failed to grasp the fact entirely, or to wonder why. What need of wondering? So someone paid and the vivid-hued dreams continued, what cared I? But now I wondered. For the girl who had protected me from Hassim and had brought the hashish for me was the same girl I had seen in the skull-face dream.

Through the soddenness of my degradation the lure of her struck like a knife piercing my heart and strangely revived the memories of the days when I was a man like other men—not yet a sullen, cringing slave of dreams. Far and dim they were, shimmery islands in the mist of years—and what a dark sea lay between!

I looked at my ragged sleeve and the dirty, claw-like hand protruding from it; I gazed through the hanging smoke which fogged the sordid room, at the low bunks along the wall whereon lay the blankly staring dreamers—slaves, like me, of hashish or of opium. I gazed at the slippered Chinamen gliding softly to and fro bearing pipes or roasting balls of concentrated purgatory over tiny flickering fires. I gazed at Hassim standing, arms folded, beside the door like a great statue of black basalt.

And I shuddered and hid my face in my hands because with the faint dawning of returning manhood, I knew that this last and most cruel dream was futile—I had crossed an ocean over which I could never return, had cut myself off from the world of normal men or women. Naught remained now but to drown this dream as I had drowned all my others—swiftly and with hope that I should soon attain that Ultimate Ocean which lies beyond all dreams.

So these fleeting moments of lucidity, of lodging, that tear aside the veils of all dope slaves—unexplainable, without hope of attainment.

So I went back to my empty dreams, to my fantasmagoria of illusions; but sometimes, like a sword cleaving a mist, through the high lands and the low lands and seas of my visions floated, like half-forgotten music, the sheen of dark eyes and shimmery hair.

You ask how I, Stephen Costigan, American and a man of some attainments and culture, came to lie in a filthy dive of London's Limehouse? The answer is simple—no jaded debauchee, I, seeking new sensations in the mysteries of the Orient. I answer—Argonne! Heavens, what deeps and heights of horror lurk in that one word alone! Shell-shocked—shell-torn. Endless days and nights without end and roaring red hell over No Man's Land where I lay shot and bayoneted to shreds of gory flesh. My body recovered, how I know not; my mind never did.

And the leaping fires and shifting shadows in my tortured brain drove me down and down, along the stairs of degradation, uncaring until at last I found surcease in Yun Shatu's Temple of Dreams, where I slew my red dreams in other dreams—the dreams of hashish whereby a man may descend to the lower pits of the reddest hells or soar into those unnamable heights where the stars are diamond pinpoints beneath his feet.

Not the visions of the sot, the beasts, were mine. I attained the unattainable, stood face to face with the unknown and in cosmic calmness knew the unguessable. And was content after a fashion, until the sight of burnished hair and scarlet lips swept away my dream-built universe and left me shuddering among its ruins.

Chapter Three

THE MASTER OF DOOM

"And He that toss'd you down into the Field,
He knows about it all—He knows! He knows!"

—Omar Khayyam

A hand shook me roughly as I emerged languidly from my latest debauch.

"The master wishes you! Up! Swine!"

Hassim it was who spoke.

"To hell with the Master!" I answered, for I hated Hassim—and feared him.

"Up with you or you get no more hashish," was the brutal response, and I rose in trembling haste.

I followed the huge black man and he led the way to the rear of the building, stepping in and out among the wretched dreamers on the floor.

"Muster all hands on deck!" droned a sailor in a bunk. "All hands!"

Hassim flung open the door at the rear and motioned me to enter. I had never before passed through that door and had supposed it led into Yun Shatu's private quarters. But it was furnished only with a cot, a bronze idol of some sort before which incense burned, and a heavy table.

Hassim gave me a sinister glance and seized the table as if to spin it about. It turned as if it stood on a revolving platform and a section of the floor turned with it, revealing a hidden doorway in the floor. Steps led downward in the darkness.

Hassim lighted a candle and with a brusk gesture invited me to descend. I did so, with the sluggish obedience of the dope addict, and he followed, closing the door above us by means of an iron lever fastened to the underside of the floor. In the semi-darkness we went down the rickety steps, some nine or ten I should say, and then came upon a narrow corridor.

Here Hassim again took the lead, holding the candle high in front of him. I could scarcely see the sides of this cave-like passage-way but knew that it was not wide. The flickering light showed it to be bare of any sort of furnishings save for a number of strange-looking chests which lined the walls—receptacles containing opium and other dope, I thought.

A continuous scurrying and the occasional glint of small red eyes haunted the shadows, betraying the presence of vast numbers of the great rats which infest the Thames waterfront of that section.

Then more steps loomed out of the dark in front of us as the corridor came to an abrupt end. Hassim led the way up and at the top knocked four times against what seemed the underside of a floor. A hidden door opened and a flood of soft, illusive light streamed through.

Hassim hustled me up roughly and I stood blinking in such a setting as I had never seen in my wildest flights of vision. I stood in a jungle of palm-trees through which wriggled a million vivid-hued dragons! Then, as my startled eyes became accustomed to the light, I saw that I had not been suddenly transferred to some other planet, as I had at first thought. The palm-trees were there, and the dragons, but the trees were artificial and stood in great pots and the dragons writhed across heavy tapestries which hid the walls.

The room itself was a monstrous affair—inhumanly large, it seemed to me. A thick smoke, yellowish and tropical in sugges-tion, seemed to hang over all, veiling the ceiling and baffling upward glances. This smoke, I saw, emanated from an altar in front of the wall to my left. I started. Through the saffron billowing fog two eyes, hideously large and vivid, glittered at me. The vague outlines of some bestial idol took indistinct shape. I flung an uneasy glance about, marking the Oriental divans and couches and the bizarre furnishings, and then my eyes halted and rested on a lacquer screen just in front of me.

I could not pierce it and no sound came from beyond it, yet I felt eyes searing into my consciousness through it, eyes that burned through my very soul. A strange aura of evil flowed from that strange screen with its weird carvings and unholy decorations.

Hassim salaamed profoundly before it and then, without speaking, stepped back and folded his arms, statue-like.

A voice suddenly broke the heavy and oppressive silence.

"You who are a swine, would you like to be a man again?"

I started. The tone was inhuman, cold—more, there was a suggestion of long disuse of the vocal organs—the voice I had heard in my dream!

"Yes," I replied, trance-like, "I would like to be a man again."

Silence ensued for a space; then the voice came again with a sinister whispering undertone at the back of its sound like bats flying through a cavern.

"I shall make you a man again because I am a friend to all broken men. Not for a price shall I do it, nor for gratitude. And I give you a sign to seal my promise and my vow. Thrust your hand through the screen."

At these strange and almost unintelligible words I stood perplexed, and then, as the unseen one repeated the last command, I stepped forward and thrust my hand through a slit which opened silently in the screen. I felt my wrist seized in an iron grip and something seven times colder than ice touched the inside of my hand. Then my wrist was released, and drawing forth my hand I saw a strange symbol traced in blue close to the base of my thumb—a thing that resembled a scorpion.

The voice spoke again in a sibilant language I did not understand, and Hassim stepped forward deferentially. He reached about the screen and then turned to me, holding a goblet of some amber-colored liquid which he proffered me with an ironical bow. I took it hesitatingly.

"Drink and fear not," said the unseen one. "It is only an Egyptian wine with life-giving qualities."

So I raised the goblet and emptied it; the taste was not unpleasant, and even as I handed the beaker to Hassim again, I seemed to feel new life and vigor whip along my jaded veins.

"Remain at Yun Shatu's house," said the voice. "You will be given food and a bed until you are strong enough to work for yourself. You will use no hashish nor will you require any. Go!"

As in a daze, I followed Hassim back through the hidden door, down the steps, along the dark corridor and up through the other door that led us into the Temple of Dreams.

An we stepped from the rear chamber into the main room of the dreamers, I turned to the Negro wonderingly.

"Master? Master of what? Of Life?"

Hassim laughed, fiercely and sardonically.

"Master of Doom!"

Chapter Four

THE SPIDER AND THE FLY

"There was the Door to which I found no Key;
There was the Veil through which I might not
see."

—Omar Khayyam

I sat on Yun Shatu's cushions and pondered with a clearness of mind new and strange to me. As for that, all my sensations were new and strange. I felt as if I had wakened from a monstrously long sleep, and though my thoughts were sluggish, I felt as though the cobwebs which had clogged them for so long had been partly brushed away.

I drew my hand across my brow, noting how it trembled. I was weak and shaky and felt the stirrings of hunger—not for dope but for food. What had been in the draft I had quaffed in the chamber of mystery? And why had the "Master" chosen me, out of all the other wretches of Yun Shatu's, for regeneration?

And who was this Master? Somehow the word sounded vaguely familiar—I sought laboriously to remember. Yes—I had heard it, lying half-waking in the bunks or on the floor—whispered sibilantly by Yun Shatu or by Hassim or by Yussef Ali, the Moor, muttered in their low-voiced conversation and mingled always with words I could not understand. Was not Yun Shatu, then, Master of the Temple of Dreams?

I had thought and the other addicts thought that the withered Chinaman held undisputed sway over this drab kingdom and that Hassim and Yussef Ali were his servants. And the four China boys who roasted opium with Yun Shatu and Yar Khan the Afghan and Santiago the Haitian and Ganra Singh the renegade Sikh—all in the pay of Yun Shatu, we supposed—bound to the opium lord by bonds of gold or fear.

For Yun Shatu was a power in London's Chinatown and I had heard that his tentacles reached across the seas into high places of mighty and mysterious tongues. Was that Yun Shatu behind the lacquer screen? No; I knew the Chinaman's voice and besides I had seen him puttering about in the front of the Temple just as I went through the back door.

Another thought came to me. Often, lying half torpid, in the late hours of night or in the early grayness of dawn, I had seen men and women steal into the Temple, whose dress and bearing were strangely out of place and incongruous. Tall, erect men, often in evening dress, with their hats drawn low about their brows, and fine ladies, veiled, in silks and furs. Never two of them came together, but always they came separately and, hiding their features, hurried to the rear door, where they entered and presently came forth again, hours later sometimes.

Knowing that the lust for dope finds resting-place in high

positions sometimes, I had never wondered overmuch, supposing that these were wealthy men and women of society who had fallen victims to the craving, and that somewhere in the back of the building there was a private chamber for such. Yet now I wondered—sometimes these persons had remained only a few moments—was it always opium for which they came, or did they, too, traverse that strange corridor and converse with the One behind the screen?

My mind dallied with the idea of a great specialist to whom came all classes of people to find surcease from the dope habit. Yet it was strange that such a one should select a dope-joint from which to work—strange, too, that the owner of that house should apparently look on him with so much reverence.

I gave it up as my head began to hurt with the unwonted effort of thinking, and shouted for food. Yussef Ali brought it to me on a tray, with a promptness which was surprising. More, he salaamed as he departed, leaving me to ruminate on the strange shift of my status in the Temple of Dreams.

I ate, wondering what the One of the screen wanted with me. Not for an instant did I suppose that his actions had been prompted by the reasons he pretended: the life of the underworld had taught me that none of its denizens leaned toward philanthropy. And underworld the chamber of mystery had been, in spite of its elaborate and bizarre nature. And where could it be located? How far had I walked along the corridor? I shrugged my shoulders, wondering if it were not all a hashish-induced dream; then my eye fell upon my hand—and the scorpion traced thereon.

"Muster all hands!" droned the sailor in the bunk. "All hands!"

To tell in detail of the next few days would be boresome to any who have not tasted the dire slavery of dope. I waited for the craving to strike me again—waited with sure sardonic hopelessness. All day, all night—another day—then the miracle was forced upon my doubting brain. Contrary to all theories and supposed facts of science and common sense the craving had left me as suddenly and completely as a bad dream!

At first I could not credit my senses but believed myself to be still in the grip of a dope nightmare. But it was true. From the time I quaffed the goblet in the room of mystery, I felt not the slightest desire for the stuff which had been life itself to me. This, I felt vaguely, was somehow unholy and certainly opposed to all rules of nature. If the dread being behind the screen had discovered the secret of breaking hashish's terrible power, what other monstrous secrets had he discovered and what unthinkable dominance was his? The suggestion of evil crawled serpent-like through my mind.

I remained at Yun Shatu's house, lounging in a bunk or on cushions spread upon the floor, eating and drinking at will, but now that I was becoming a normal man again, the atmosphere became most revolting to me and the sight of the wretches writhing in their dreams reminded me unpleasantly of what I myself had been, and it repelled, nauseated me.

So one day, when no one was watching me, I rose and went out on the street and walked along the waterfront. The air, burdened though it was with smoke and foul scents, filled my lungs with strange freshness and aroused new vigor in what had once been a powerful frame. I took new interest in the sounds of men living and working, and the sight of a vessel being unloaded at one of the wharfs actually thrilled me. The force of longshoremen was short, and presently I found myself heaving and lifting and carrying, and though the sweat coursed down my brow and my limbs trembled at the effort, I exulted in the thought that at last I was able to labor for myself again, no matter how low or drab the work might be. As I returned to the door of Yun Shatu's that evening—hideously weary but with the renewed feeling of manhood that comes of honest toil—Hassim met me at the door.

"You been where?" he demanded roughly.

"I've been working on the docks," I answered shortly.

"You don't need to work on docks," he snarled. "The Master got work for you."

He led the way, and again I traversed the dark stairs and the corridor under the earth. This time my faculties were alert and I decided that the passageway could not be over thirty or forty feet in length. Again I stood before the lacquer screen and again I heard the inhuman voice of living death.

"I can give you work," said the voice. "Are you willing to work for me?"

I quickly assented. After all, in spite of the fear which the voice inspired, I was deeply indebted to the owner.

"Good. Take these."

As I started toward the screen a sharp command halted me and Hassim stepped forward and, reaching behind, took what was offered. This was a bundle of pictures and papers, apparently.

"Study these," said the One behind the screen, "and learn all you can about the man portrayed thereby. Yun Shatu will give you money; buy yourself such clothes as seamen wear and take a room at the front of the Temple. At the end of two days, Hassim will bring you to me again. Go!"

The last impression I had, as the hidden door closed above me, was that the eyes of the idol, blinking through the everlasting smoke, leered mockingly at me.

The front of the Temple of Dreams consisted of rooms for rent, masking the true purpose of the building under the guise of a waterfront boarding-house. The police had made several visits to Yun Shatu but had never got any incriminating evidence against him.

So in one of these rooms I took up my abode and set to work studying the material given me.

The pictures were all of one man, a large man, not unlike me in build, and general facial outline, except that he wore a heavy beard and was inclined to blondness whereas I am dark. The name, as written on the accompanying papers, was Major Fairlan Morley, special commissioner to Natal and the Transvaal. This office and title were new to me and I wondered at the connection between an African commissioner and an opium house on the Thames waterfront.

The papers consisted of extensive data evidently copied from authentic sources and all dealing with Major Morley, and a number of private documents considerably illuminating on the major's private life.

An exhaustive description was given of the man's personal appearance and habits, some of which seemed very trivial to me. I wondered what the purpose could be, and how the One behind the screen had come in possession of papers of such intimate nature.

I could find no clue in answer to this question but bent all my energies to the task set out for me. I owed a deep debt of gratitude to the unknown man who required this of me and I was determined to repay him to the best of my ability. Nothing, at this time, suggested a snare to me.

Chapter Five

THE MAN ON THE COUCH

*"What dam of lances sent thee forth
to jest at dawn with Death?"*

—Kipling

At the expiration of two days, Hassim beckoned me as I stood in the opium room. I advanced with a springy, resilient tread, secure in the confidence that I had culled the Morley papers of all their worth. I was a new man; my mental swiftness and physical readiness surprised me—sometimes it seemed unnatural.

Hassim eyed me through narrowed lids and motioned me to follow, as usual. As we crossed the room, my gaze fell upon a man who lay on a couch close to the wall, smoking opium. There was nothing at all suspicious about his ragged, unkempt clothes, his dirty, bearded face or the blank stare, but my eyes, sharpened to an abnormal point, seemed to sense a certain incongruity in the clean-cut limbs which not even the slouchy garments could efface.

Hassim spoke impatiently and I turned away. We entered the rear room, and as he shut the door and turned to the table, it moved of itself and a figure bulked up through the hidden doorway. The Sikh, Ganra Singh, a lean sinister-eyed giant, emerged and proceeded to the door opening into the opium room, where he halted until we should have descended and closed the secret doorway.

Again I stood amid the billowing yellow smoke and listened to the hidden, voice.

"Do you think you know enough about Major Morley to impersonate him successfully?"

Startled, I answered, "No doubt I could, unless I met someone who was intimate with him."

"I will take care of that. Follow me closely. Tomorrow you sail on the first boat for Calais. There you will meet an agent of mine who will accost you the instant you step upon the wharfs, and give you further instructions. You will sail second class and avoid all conversation with strangers or anyone. Take the papers with you. The agent will aid you in making up and your masquerade will start in Calais. That is all. Go!"

I departed, my wonder growing. All this rigmarole evidently had a meaning, but one which I could not fathom. Back in the opium room Hassim bade me be seated on some cushions to await his return. To my question he snarled that he was going forth as he had been ordered, to buy me a ticket on the Channel boat. He departed and I sat down, leaning my back against the wall. As I ruminated, it seemed suddenly that eyes were fixed on me so intensely as to disturb my sub-mind. I glanced up quickly but no one seemed to be looking at me. The smoke drifted through the hot atmosphere as usual; Yussef Ali and the Chinese glided back and forth tending to the wants of the sleepers.

Suddenly the door to the rear room opened and a strange and hideous figure came haltingly out. Not all of those who found entrance to Yun Shatu's back room were aristocrats and society members. This was one of the exceptions, and one whom I remembered as having often entered and emerged therefrom—a tall, gaunt figure, shapeless and ragged wrappings and nondescript garments, face entirely hidden. Better that the face be hidden, I thought, for without doubt the wrapping concealed a grisly sight. The man was a leper, who had somehow managed to escape the attention of the public guardians and who was occasionally seen haunting the lower and more mysterious regions of East End—a mystery even to the lowest denizens of Limehouse.

Suddenly my supersensitive mind was aware of a swift tension in the air. The leper hobbled out the door, closed it behind him. My eyes instinctively sought the couch whereon lay the man who had aroused my suspicions earlier in the day. I could have sworn that cold steely eyes gleamed menacingly before they flickered shut. I crossed to the couch in one stride and bent over the prostrate man. Something about his face seemed unnatural—a healthy bronze seemed to underlie the pallor of complexion.

"Yun Shatu!" I shouted. "A spy is in the house!"

Things happened then with bewildering speed. The man on the couch with one tigerish movement leaped erect and a revolver gleamed in his hand. One sinewy arm flung me aside as I sought to grapple with him and a sharp decisive voice sounded over the babble which broke forth:

"You there! Halt! Halt!"

The pistol in the stranger's hand was leveled at the leper, who was making for the door in long strides!

All about was confusion; Yun Shatu was shrieking volubly in Chinese and the four China boys and Yussef Ali were rushing in from all sides, knives glittering in their hands.

All this I saw with unnatural clearness even as I marked the stranger's face. As the flying leper gave no evidence of halting, I saw the eyes harden to steely points of determination, sighting along the pistol barrel—the features set with the grim purpose of the slayer. The leper was almost to the outer door, but death would strike him down ere he could reach it.

And then, just as the finger of the stranger tightened on the trigger, I hurled myself forward and my right fist crashed against his chin. He went, down as though struck by a trip-hammer, the revolver exploding harmlessly in the air.

In that instant, with the blinding flare of light that sometimes comes to one, I knew that the leper was none other than the Man Behind the Screen!

I bent over the fallen man, who though not entirely senseless had been rendered temporarily helpless by that terrific blow. He was struggling dazedly to rise but I shoved him roughly down again and seizing the false beard he wore, tore it away. A lean bronzed face was revealed, the strong lines of which not even the artificial dirt and grease-paint could alter.

Yussef Ali leaned above him now, dagger in hand, eyes slits of murder. The brown sinewy hand went up—I caught the wrist.

"Not so fast, you black devil! What are you about to do?"

"This is John Gordon," he hissed, "the Master's greatest foe! He must die, curse you!"

John Gordon! The name was familiar somehow, and yet I did not seem to connect it with the London police nor account for the man's presence in Yun Shatu's dope-joint.

The false leper had vanished. Yun Shatu stood gazing at me as immobile as an idol, hands in his wide sleeves, and Yussef Ali stood back, muttering murderously and thumbing his dagger edge, as I led Gordon out of the opium room and through the innocent-appearing bar which lay between that room and the street.

Out in the street I said to him: "I have no idea as to who you are or what you are doing here, but you see what an unhealthful place it is for you. Hereafter be advised by me and stay away."

His only answer was a searching glance, and then he turned and walked swiftly though somewhat unsteadily up the street.

Chapter Six

THE DREAM GIRL

*"I have reached these lands but newly
From an ultimate dim Thule."*

—Poe

Outside my room sounded a light footstep. The door-knob turned cautiously and slowly; the door opened. I sprang erect with a gasp. Red lips, half parted, dark eyes like limpid seas of wonder, a mass of shimmering hair—framed in my drab doorway stood the girl of my dreams!

She entered, and half turning with a sinuous motion, closed the door. I sprang forward, my hands outstretched, then halted as she put a finger to her lips.

"You must not talk loudly," she almost whispered; "*He* did not say I could not come; yet—"

Her voice was soft and musical, with just a touch of foreign accent which I found delightful. As for the girl herself, every intonation, every movement proclaimed the Orient. She was a fragrant breath from the East. From her night-black hair, piled high above her alabaster forehead, to her little feet, encased in high-heeled pointed slippers, she portrayed the highest ideal of Asiatic loveliness—an effect which was heightened rather than lessened by the English blouse and skirt which she wore.

"You are beautiful!" I said dazedly. "Who are you?"

"I am Zuleika," she answered with a shy smile. "I—I am glad you like me. I am glad you no longer dream hashish dreams."

Strange that so small a thing should set my heart to leaping wildly!

"I owe it all to you, Zuleika," I said huskily. "Had not I dreamed of you every hour since you first lifted me from the gutter, I had lacked the power of even hoping to be freed from my curse."

She blushed prettily and intertwined her white fingers as if in nervousness.

"You leave England tomorrow?" she said suddenly.

"Yes. Hassim has not returned with my ticket—" I hesitated suddenly, remembering the command of silence.

"Yes, I know, I know!" she whispered swiftly, her eyes widening. "And John Gordon has been here! He saw you!"

"Yes!"

She came close to me with a quick lithe movement.

"You are to impersonate some man! Listen, while you are doing this, you must not ever let Gordon see you! He would know you, no matter what your disguise! He is a terrible man!"

"I don't understand," I said, completely bewildered. "How did the Master break me of my hashish craving? Who is this Gordon and why did he come here? Why does the Master go disguised as a leper—and who is he? Above all, why am I to impersonate a man I never saw or heard of?"

"I cannot—I dare not tell you!" she whispered, her face paling. "I—"

Somewhere in the house sounded the faint tones of a Chinese gong. The girl started like a frightened gazelle.

"I must go! *He* summons me!"

She opened the door, darted through, halted a moment to electrify me with her passionate exclamation: "Oh, be careful, be very careful, sahib!" Then she was gone.

Chapter Seven

THE MAN OF THE SKULL

"What the hammer? what the chain?
In what furnace was thy brain?
What the anvil? what dread grasp
Dare its deadly terrors clasp?"

—Blake

A while after my beautiful and mysterious visitor had left, I sat in meditation. I believed that I had at last stumbled on to an explanation of a part of the enigma, at any rate. This was the conclusion I had reached: Yun Shatu, the opium lord, was simply the agent or servant of some organization or individual whose work was on a far larger scale than merely supplying dope addicts in the Temple of Dreams. This man or these men needed co-workers among all classes of people; in other words, I was being let in with a group of opium smugglers on a gigantic scale. Gordon no doubt had been investigating the case, and his presence alone showed that it was no ordinary one, for I knew that he held a high position with the English government, though just what, I did not know.

Opium or not, I determined to carry out my obligation to the Master. My moral sense had been blunted by the dark ways I had traveled, and the thought of despicable crime did not enter my head. I was indeed hardened.

More, the mere debt of gratitude was now increased a thousandfold, by the thought of the girl.

To the Master I owed it that I was still able to stand up on my feet and look into her clear eyes as a man should. So if he wished my services as a smuggler of dope, he should have them. No doubt I was to impersonate some man so high in governmental esteem that the usual actions of the customs officers would be deemed unnecessary; was I to bring some rare dream-producer into England somehow?

These thoughts were in my mind as I went downstairs, but ever back of them hovered other and more alluring suppositions—what was the reason for the girl, here in this vile dive—a rose in a garbage-heap—and who was she?

As I entered the outer bar, Hassim came in, his brows set in a dark scowl of anger, and, I believed, fear. He carried a newspaper in his hand, folded.

"I told you to wait in opium room," he snarled.

"You were gone so long that I went up to my room. Have you the ticket?"

He merely grunted and pushed on past me into the opium room; and standing at the door I saw him cross the floor and disappear into the rear room. I stood there, my bewilderment increasing. For as Hassim had brushed past me, I had noted an item on the face of the paper, against which his black thumb was tightly pressed as if to mark that special column of news.

And with the unnatural celerity of action and judgment which seemed to be mine those days, I had in that fleeting instant read the following:

AFRICAN SPECIAL COMMISSIONER
FOUND MURDERED!

The body of Major Fairlan Morley was yesterday discovered in a rotting ship's hold at Bordeaux...

No more I saw of the details, but that alone was enough to make me think!

The affair seemed to be taking, on an ugly aspect. Yet—

Another day passed. To my inquiries, Hassim snarled that the plans had been changed and I was not to go to France. Then, late in the evening, he came to bid me once more to the room of mystery.

I stood before the lacquer screen, the yellow smoke acrid in my nostrils, the woven dragons writhing along the tapestries, the palm-trees rearing thick and oppressive.

"A change has come in our plans," said the voice. "You will not sail as was decided before. But I have other work that you may do. Mayhap this will be more to your type of usefulness for I admit you have somewhat disappointed me in regard to subtlety. You interfered the other day in such manner as will no doubt cause me great inconvenience in the future."

I said nothing, but a feeling of resentment began to stir in me.

"Even after the assurance of one of my most trusted servants," the toneless voice continued, with no mark of any emotion save a slightly rising note, "you insisted on releasing my most deadly enemy. Be more circumspect in the future."

"I saved your life!" I said angrily.

"And for that reason alone I overlook your mistake—this time!"

A slow fury suddenly surged up inside of me.

"This time! Make the best of it this time, for I assure you there will be no next time. I owe you a greater debt than I can ever hope to pay, but that does not make me your slave. I have saved your life—the debt is as near paid as a man can pay it. Go your way and I go mine!"

A low, hideous laugh answered me, like a reptilian hiss.

"You fool! You will pay with your whole life's toil! You say you are not my slave? I say you are—just as black Hassim there beside you is my slave—just as the girl Zuleika is my slave, who has bewitched you with her wonderful beauty."

These words sent a wave of hot blood to my brain and I was conscious of a flood of fury which completely engulfed my reason for a second. Just as all my moods and senses seemed sharpened and exaggerated those days, so now this burst of rage transcended every moment of anger I had ever had in my life before.

"Hell's fiends!" I shrieked. "You devil—who are you and what is your hold on me? I'll see you or die!"

Hassim sprang at me, but I hurled him backward and with one stride reached the screen and flung it aside with an incredible effort of strength. Then I shrank back, hands outflung, shrieking. A tall, gaunt figure stood before me, a figure arrayed grotesquely in a silk brocaded gown which fell stiffly to the floor.

From the sleeves of this gown protruded hands which filled me with crawling horror—long, predatory hands, with thin bony fingers and curved talons—withered skin of a parchment brownish-yellow, like the hands of a man long dead.

The hands—but, oh God, the face! A skull to which no vestige of flesh seemed to remain but on which taut brownish-yellow skin grew fast, etching out every detail of that terrible death's-head. The forehead was high and in a way magnificent, but the head was curiously narrow through the temples, and from under penthouse brows great eyes glimmered like pools of yellow fire. The nose was high-bridged and very thin; the mouth was a mere colorless gash between thin, cruel lips. A long, bony neck supported this frightful vision and completed the effect of a reptilian demon from some medieval hell.

I was face to face with the skull-faced man of my dreams!

Chapter Eight

BLACK WISDOM

The terrible spectacle drove for the instant all thoughts of rebellion from my mind. My very blood froze in my veins and I stood motionless. I heard Hassim laugh grimly behind me. The eyes in the cadaverous face blazed fiendishly at me and I blanched from the concentrated satanic fury I saw in them.

Then the horror laughed sibilantly, wickedly.

"I do you a great honor, Mr. Costigan; among a very few, even of my own servants, you may say that you saw my face and lived. I think you will be more useful to me living than dead."

I was silent, completely unnerved. It was difficult to believe that this man lived, for his appearance certainly belied the thought. He seemed horribly like a mummy. Yet his lips moved when he spoke and his eyes flamed with hideous life.

"You will do as I say," he said abruptly, and his voice, had taken on a note of command. "You doubtless know, or know of, Sir Haldred Frenton?"

"Yes."

Every man of culture in Europe and America was familiar with the travel books of Sir Haldred Frenton, author and soldier of fortune.

"You will go to Sir Haldred's estate tonight—"

"Yes?"

"*And kill him!*"

I staggered, literally. This order was incredible—unspeakable! I had sunk low, low enough to smuggle opium, but to deliberately murder a man I had never seen, a man noted for his kindly deeds!

That was too monstrous, I thought, even to contemplate.

"You do not refuse?"

The tone was as loathing and as mocking as the hiss of a serpent.

"Refuse?" I screamed, finding my voice at last. "Refuse? You incarnate devil! Of course I refuse! You—"

Something in the cold assurance of his manner halted me— froze me into apprehensive silence.

"You fool!" he said calmly. "I broke the hashish chains—do you know how? Four minutes from now you will know and curse the day you were born! Have you not thought it strange, the swiftness of brain, the resilience of body—the brain that should be rusty and slow, the body that should be weak and sluggish from years of abuse? That blow that felled John Gordon— have you not wondered at its might? The ease with which you mastered Major Morley's records—have you not wondered at that?

You fool, you are bound to me by chains of steel and blood and fire! I have kept you alive and sane—I alone. Each day the life-saving elixir has been given you in your wine. You could not live and keep your reason without it. And I and only I know its secret!"

He glanced at a queer timepiece which stood on a table at his elbow.

"This time I had Yun Shatu leave the elixir out—I anticipated rebellion. The time is near—ha, it strikes!"

Something else he said, but I did not hear. I did not see, nor did I feel in the human sense of the word. I was writhing at his feet, screaming and gibbering in the flames of such hells as men have never dreamed of.

Aye, I knew now! He had simply given me a dope so much stronger that it drowned the hashish. My unnatural ability was explainable now—I had simply been acting under the stimulus of something which combined all the hells in its make-up, which stimulated, something like heroin, but whose effect was unnoticed by the victim. What it was, I had no idea, nor did I believe anyone knew save that hellish being who stood watching me with grim amusement. But it had held my brain together, instilling into my system a need for it, and now my frightful craving tore my soul asunder.

Never, in my moments of worst shell-shock or my moments of hashish craving, have I ever experienced anything like that, I burned with the heat of a thousand hells and froze with an iciness that was colder than any ice, a hundred times, I swept down to the deepest pits of torture and up to the highest crags of torment—a million yelling devils hemmed me in, shrieking and stabbing. Bone by bone, vein by vein, cell by cell I felt my body disintegrate and fly in bloody atoms all over the universe—and each separate cell was an entire system of quivering, screaming nerves. And they gathered from far voids and reunited with a greater torment.

Through the fiery bloody mists I heard my own voice screaming, a monotonous yammering.

Then, with distended eyes I saw a golden goblet, held by a clawlike hand, swim into view—a goblet filled with a clear amber liquid.

With a bestial screech I seized it with both hands, being dimly aware that the metal stem gave beneath my fingers and brought the brim to my lips. I drank in frenzied haste, the liquid slopping down onto my breast.

Chapter Nine

KATHULOS OF EGYPT

"Night shall be thrice night over you.
And Heaven an iron cope."

—Chesterton

The Skull-faced One stood watching me critically as I sat panting on a couch, completely exhausted. He held in his hand the goblet and surveyed the golden stem, which was crushed out of all shape. This my maniac fingers had done in the instant of drinking.

"Superhuman strength, even for a man in your condition," he said with sort of creaky pedantry. "I doubt if even Hassim here could equal it. Are you ready for your instructions now?"

I nodded, wordless. Already the hellish strength of the elixir was flowing through my veins, renewing my burnt-out force. I wondered how long a man could live as I lived being constantly burned out and artificially rebuilt.

"You will be given a disguise and will go alone to the Frenton estate. No one suspects any design against Sir Haldred and your entrance into the estate and the house itself should be a matter of comparative ease. You will not don the disguise—which will be of unique nature—until you are ready to enter the estate. You will then proceed to Sir Haldred's room and kill him, breaking his neck with your bare hands—this is essential—"

The voice droned on, giving its ghastly orders in a frightfully casual and matter-of-fact way. The cold sweat beaded my brow.

"You will then leave the estate, taking care to leave the imprint of your hand somewhere plainly visible, and the automobile, which will be waiting for you at some safe place near by, will bring you back here, you having first removed the disguise. I have, in case of later complications, any amount of men who will swear that you spent the entire night in the Temple of Dreams and never left it. But there must be no detection! Go warily and perform your task surely, for you know the alternative."

I did not return to the opium house but was taken through winding corridors, hung with heavy tapestries, to a small room containing only an Oriental couch. Hassim gave me to understand that I was to remain there until after nightfall and then left me. The door was closed but I made no effort to discover if it was locked. The Skull-faced Master held me with stronger shackles than locks and bolts.

Seated upon the couch in the bizarre setting of a chamber which might have been a room in an Indian zenana, I faced fact squarely and fought out my battle. There was still in me some trace of manhood left—more than the fiend had reckoned, and added to this were black despair and desperation. I chose and determined on my only course.

Suddenly the door opened softly. Some intuition told me whom to expect, nor was I disappointed. Zuleika stood, a glorious vision before me—a vision which mocked me, made blacker my despair and yet thrilled me with wild yearning and reasonless joy.

She bore a tray of food which she set beside me, and then she seated herself on the couch, her large eyes fixed upon my face. A flower in a serpent den she was, and the beauty of her look, took hold of my heart.

"Stephen!" she whispered and I thrilled as she spoke my name for the first time.

Her luminous eyes suddenly shone with tears and she laid her little hand on my arm. I seized it in both my rough hands.

"They have set you a task which you fear and hate!" she faltered.

"Aye!" I almost laughed. "But I'll fool them yet! Zuleika, tell me—what is the meaning of all this?"

She glanced fearfully around her.

"I do not know all." She hesitated. "Your plight is all my fault but I—I hoped—Stephen, I have watched you every time you came to Yun Shatu's for months. You did not see me but I saw you, and I saw in you, not the broken sot your rags proclaimed, but a wounded soul, a soul bruised terribly on the ramparts of life. And from my heart I pitied you. Then when Hassim abused you that day"—again tears started to her eyes—"I could not bear it and I knew how you suffered for want of hashish. So I paid Yun Shatu, and going to the Master I—I—oh, you will hate me for this!" she sobbed.

"No—no—never—"

"I told him that you were a man who might be of use to him and begged him to have Yun Shatu supply you with what you needed. He had already noticed you, for his is the eye of the slaver and all the world is his slave market! So he bade Yun Shatu do as I asked: and now—better if you had remained as you were, my friend."

"No! No!" I exclaimed. "I have known a few days of regeneration, even if it was false! I have stood before you as a man, and that is worth all else!"

And all that I felt for her must have looked forth from my eyes, for she dropped hers and flushed. Ask me not how love comes to a man: but I knew that I loved Zuleika—had loved this mysterious Oriental girl since first I saw her—and somehow I felt that she, in a measure, returned my affection. This realization made blacker and more barren the road I had chosen, yet—for pure love must ever strengthen a man—it nerved me to do what I must do.

"Zuleika," I said, speaking hurriedly, "time flies and there are things I must learn: tell me—who are you and why do you remain in this den of Hades?"

"I am Zuleika—that is all I know. I am Circassian by blood and birth. When I was very little I was captured in a Turkish raid and raised in a Stamboul harem. While I was yet too young to marry, my master gave me as a present to—to *Him*."

"And who is he—this skull-faced man?"

"He is Kathulos of Egypt—that is all I know. My Master."

"An Egyptian? Then what is he doing in London—why all this mystery?"

She intertwined her fingers nervously.

"Stephen, please speak lower; always there is someone listening everywhere. I do not know who the Master is or why he is here or why he does these things; I swear by Allah! If I knew I would tell you. Sometimes distinguished-looking men come here to the room where the Master receives them—not the room where you saw him—and he makes me dance before them and afterward flirt with them a little. And always I must repeat exactly what they say to me. That is what I must always do—in Turkey, in the Barbary States, in Egypt, in France and in England. The Master taught me French and English and educated me in many ways himself. He is the greatest sorcerer in all the world and knows all ancient magic and everything."

"Zuleika," I said, "my race is soon run, but let me get you out of this—come with me and I swear I'll get you away from this fiend!"

She shuddered and hid her face.

"No, no, I cannot!"

"Zuleika," I asked gently, "what hold has he over you, child—dope also?"

"No, no!" she whimpered. "I do not know—I do not know—but I cannot—I never can escape him!"

I sat, baffled for a few moments; then I asked, "Zuleika, where are we right now?"

"This building is a deserted storehouse back of the Temple of Silence."

"I thought so. What is in the chests in the tunnel?"

"I do not know."

Then suddenly she began weeping softly. "You too, a slave, like me—you who are so strong and kind—oh, Stephen, I cannot bear it!"

I smiled. "Lean closer, Zuleika, and I will tell you how I am going to fool this Kathulos."

She glanced apprehensively at the door.

"You must speak low. I will lie in your arms and while you pretend to caress me, whisper your words to me."

She glided into my embrace, and there on the dragon-worked couch in that house of horror I first knew the glory of Zuleika's slender form nestling in my arms—of Zuleika's soft cheek pressing my breast. The fragrance of her was in my nostrils, her hair in my eyes, and my senses reeled. Then with my lips hidden by her silky hair I whispered, swiftly:

"I am going to warn Sir Haldred Frenton—then to find John Gordon and tell him of this den. I will lead the police here and you must watch closely and be ready to hide from *Him*—until we can break through and kill or capture him. Then you will be free."

"But you!" she gasped, paling. "You must have the elixir, and only he—"

"I have a way of outdoing him, child," I answered.

She went pitifully white and her woman's intuition sprang to the right conclusion.

"You are going to kill yourself!"

And much as it hurt me to see her emotion, I yet felt a torturing thrill that she should feel so on my account. Her arms tightened about my neck.

"Don't, Stephen!" she begged. "It is better to live, even—"

"No, not at that price. Better to go out clean while I have the manhood left."

She stared at me wildly for an instant; then, pressing her red lips suddenly to mine, she sprang up and fled from the room. Strange, strange are the ways of love. Two stranded ships on the shores of life, we had drifted inevitably together, and though no word of love had passed between us, we knew each other's heart. Through grime and rags, and through accouterments of the slave, we knew each other's heart and from the first loved as naturally and as purely as it was intended from the beginning of Time.

The beginning of life now and the end for me, for as soon as I had completed my task, ere I felt again the torments of my curse, love and life and beauty and torture should be blotted out together in the stark finality of a pistol ball scattering my rotting brain. Better a clean death than—

The door opened again and Yussef Ali entered.

"The hour arrives for departure," he said briefly. "Rise and follow."

I had no idea, of course, as to the time. No window opened from the room I occupied—I had seen no outer window whatever. The rooms were lighted by tapers in censers swinging from the ceiling. As I rose the slim young Moor slanted a sinister glance in my direction.

"This lies between you and me," he said sibilantly. "Servants of the same Master we—but this concerns ourselves alone. Keep your distance from Zuleika—the Master has promised her to me in the days of the empire."

My eyes narrowed to slits as I looked into the frowning, handsome face of the Oriental, and such hate surged up in me as I have seldom known. My fingers involuntarily opened and closed, and the Moor, marking the action, stepped back, hand in his girdle.

"Not now—there is work for us both—later perhaps"; then in a sudden cold gust of hatred, "Swine! Ape-man! When the Master is finished with you, I shall quench my dagger in your heart!"

I laughed grimly.

"Make it soon, desert-snake, or I'll crush your spine between my hands."

Chapter Ten

THE DARK HOUSE

"Against all man-made shackles and
a man-made Hell—
Alone—at last—unaided—I rebel!"

—Mundy

I followed Yussef Ali along the winding hallways, down the steps—Kathulos was not in the idol-room—and along the tunnel. Then through the rooms of the Temple of Dreams and out into the street, where the street lamps gleamed drearily through the fogs and a slight drizzle. Across the street stood an automobile, curtains closely drawn.

"That is yours," said Hassim, who had joined us. "Saunter across natural-like. Don't act suspicious. The place may be watched. The driver knows what to do."

Then he and Yussef Ali drifted back into the bar and I took a single step toward the curb.

"Stephen!"

A voice that made my heart leap spoke my name! A white hand beckoned from the shadows of the doorway. I stepped quickly there.

"Zuleika!"

"Shh!"

She clutched my arm, slipped something into my hand; I made out vaguely a small flask of gold.

"Hide this quick!" came her urgent whisper.

"Don't come back, go away and hide. This is full of elixir—I will try to get you some more before that is all gone. You must find a way of communicating with me."

"Yes, but how did you get this?" I asked amazedly.

"I stole it from the Master! Now please, I must go before he misses me."

And she sprang back into the doorway and vanished. I stood undecided. I was sure that she had risked nothing less than her life in doing this and I was torn by the fear of what Kathulos might do to her, were the theft discovered. But to return to the house of mystery would certainly invite suspicion, and I might carry out my plan and strike back before the Skull-faced One learned of his slave's duplicity.

So I crossed the street to the waiting automobile. The driver was a Negro whom I had never seen before, a lanky man of medium height. I stared hard at him, wondering how much he had seen. He gave no evidence of having seen anything, and I decided that even if he had noticed me step back into the shadows he could not have seen what passed there nor have been able to recognize the girl.

He merely nodded as I climbed in the back seat, and a moment later we were speeding away down the deserted and fog-haunted streets. A bundle beside me I concluded to be the disguise mentioned by the Egyptian.

To recapture the sensations I experienced as I rode through the rainy, misty night would be impossible. I felt as if I were already dead and the bare and dreary streets about me were the roads of death over which my ghost had been doomed to roam forever. A torturing joy was in my heart, and bleak despair—the despair of a doomed man. Not that death itself was so repellent—a dope victim dies too many deaths to shrink from the last—but it was hard to go out just as love had entered my barren life. And I was still young.

A sardonic smile crossed my lips—they were young, too, the men who died beside me in No Man's Land. I drew back my sleeve and clenched my fists, tensing my muscles. There was no surplus weight on my frame, and much of the firm flesh had wasted away, but the cords of the great biceps still stood out like knots of iron, seeming to indicate massive strength. But I knew my might was false, that in reality I was a broken husk of a man, animated by the artificial fire of the elixir, without which a frail girl might topple me over.

The automobile came to a halt among some trees. We were on the outskirts of an exclusive suburb and the hour was past midnight. Through the trees I saw a large house looming darkly against the distant flares of night-time London.

"This is where I wait," said the Negro. "No one can see the automobile from the road or from the house."

Holding a match so its light could not be detected outside the car, I examined the "disguise" and was hard put to restrain an insane laugh. The disguise was the complete hide of a gorilla! Gathering the bundle under my arm I trudged toward the wall which surrounded the Frenton estate. A few steps and the trees where the Negro hid with the car merged into one dark mass. I did not believe he could see me, but for safety's sake, I made, not for the high iron gate at the front but for the wall at the side where there was no gate.

No light showed in the house. Sir Haldred was a bachelor and I was sure that the servants were all in bed long ago. I negotiated the wall with ease and stole across the dark lawn to a side door, still carrying the grisly "disguise" under my arm. The door was locked, as I anticipated, and I did not wish to arouse anyone until I was safely in the house, where the sound of voices would not carry to one who might have followed me. I took hold of the knob with both hands, and exerting slowly the inhuman strength that was mine, began to twist. The shaft turned in my hands and the lock within shattered suddenly, with a noise that was like the crash of a cannon in the stillness. An instant more and I was inside and had closed the door behind me.

I took a single stride in the darkness in the direction I believed the stair to be, then halted as a beam of light flashed into my face. At the side of the beam I caught the glimmer of a pistol muzzle. Beyond, a lean shadowy, face floated.

"Stand where you are and put up your hands!"

I lifted my hands, allowing the bundle to slip to the floor. I had heard that voice only once but I recognized it—knew instantly that the man who held that light was John Gordon.

"How many are with you?"

His voice was sharp, commanding.

"I am alone," I answered. "Take me into a room where a light cannot be seen from the outside and, I'll tell you some things you want to know."

He was silent; then, bidding me take up the bundle I had dropped, he stepped to one side and motioned me to precede him into the next room. There he directed me to a stairway and at the top landing opened a door and switched on lights.

I found myself in a room whose curtains were closely drawn. During this journey Gordon's alertness had not relaxed, and now he stood still covering me with his revolver. Clad in conventional garments, he stood revealed a tall, leanly but powerfully built man, taller than I but not so heavy—with steel-gray eyes and clean-cut features. Something about the man attracted me, even as I noted a bruise on his jawbone where my fist had struck in our last meeting.

"I cannot believe," he said crisply, "that this apparent clumsiness and lack of subtlety is real. Doubtless you have your own reasons for wishing me to be in a secluded room at this time, but Sir Haldred is efficiently protected even now. Stand still."

Muzzle pressed against my chest, he ran his hand over my garments for concealed weapons, seeming slightly surprised when he found none.

"Still," he murmured as if to himself, "a man who can burst an iron lock with his bare hands has scant need of weapons."

"You are wasting valuable time," I said impatiently. "I was sent here tonight to kill Sir Haldred Frenton—"

"By whom?" the question was shot at me.

"By the man who sometimes goes disguised as a leper."

He nodded, a gleam in his scintillant eyes.

"My suspicions were correct, then."

"Doubtless. Listen to me closely—do you desire the death or arrest of that man?"

Gordon laughed grimly.

"To one who wears the mark of the scorpion on his hand, my answer would be superfluous."

"Then follow my directions and your wish shall be granted."

His eyes narrowed suspiciously.

"So that was the meaning of this open entry and non-resistance," he said slowly. "Does the dope which dilates your eyeballs so warp your mind that you think to lead me into ambush?"

I pressed my hands against my temples. Time was racing and every moment was precious—how could I convince this man of my honesty?

"Listen; my name is Stephen Costigan of America. I was a frequenter of Yun Shatu's dive and a hashish addict—as you have guessed, but just now a slave of stronger dope. By virtue of this slavery, the man you know as a false leper, whom Yun Shatu and his friends call 'Master', gained dominance over me and sent me here to murder Sir Haldred—why, God only knows. But I have gained a space of respite by coming into possession of some of this dope which I must have in order to live, and I fear and hate this Master. Listen to me and I swear, by all things holy and unholy, that before the sun rises the false leper shall be in your power!"

I could tell that Gordon was impressed in spite of himself.

"Speak fast!" he rapped.

Still I could sense his disbelief and a wave of futility swept over me.

"If you will not act with me," I said, "let me go and somehow I'll find a way to get to the Master and kill him. My time is short—my hours are numbered and my vengeance is yet to be realized."

"Let me hear your plan, and talk fast," Gordon answered.

"It is simple enough. I will return to the Master's lair and tell him I have accomplished that which he sent me to do. You must follow closely with your men and while I engage the Master in conversation surround the house. Then, at the signal, break in and kill or seize him."

Gordon frowned. "Where is this house?"

"The warehouse back of Yun Shatu's has been converted into a veritable Oriental palace."

"The warehouse!" he exclaimed. "How can that be? I had thought of that first, but I have carefully examined it from without. The widows are closely barred and spiders have built webs across them. The doors are nailed fast on the outside and the seals that mark the warehouse as deserted were never broken."

"They tunneled up from beneath," I answered. "The Temple of Dreams is directly connected with the warehouse. A tunnel connects the building, with one door in the rear room of Yun Shatu's and the other in the idol-room of the warehouse."

"I have been in Yun Shatu's back room and found no such door."

"The table rests upon it. You noted the heavy table in the center of the room? Had you turned it around, the secret door would have opened in the floor. Now this is my plan: I will go in through the Temple of Dreams and meet the Master in the idol-room. You will have men secretly stationed in front of the warehouse and others upon the other street, in front of the Temple of Dreams.

"Yun Shatu's building, as you know, faces the waterfront, while the warehouse, fronting the opposite direction, faces a narrow street running parallel with the river. At the signal let the men in this street break open the front of the warehouse and rush in, while simultaneously those in front of Yun Shatu's make an invasion through the Temple of Dreams. Let these make for the rear room, shooting without mercy any who may seek to deter them, and there open the secret door as I have said.

"There being, to the best of my knowledge, no other exit from the Master's lair, he and his servants will necessarily seek to make their escape through the tunnel. Thus we will have them on both sides."

"This may be a snare," he muttered, "or an attempt to draw me away from Sir Haldred, but—"

I held my breath.

"I am a gambler by nature," he said slowly. "I am going to follow what you Americans call a hunch—but God help you if you are lying to me!"

I sprang erect.

"Thank God! Now aid me with this suit, for I must be wearing it when I return to the automobile waiting for me."

His eyes narrowed as I shook out the horrible masquerade and prepared to don it.

"This shows, as always, the touch of the master hand. You were doubtless instructed to leave marks of your hands, encased in those hideous gauntlets?"

"Yes—though I have no idea why."

"I think I have—the Master is famed for leaving no real clues to mark his crimes—a great ape escaped from a neighboring zoo earlier in the evening and it seems too obvious for mere chance, in the light of this disguise. The ape would have gotten the blame of Sir Haldred's death."

The thing was easily gotten into and the illusion of reality it created was so perfect as to draw a shudder from me as I viewed myself in a mirror.

"It is now two o'clock," said Gordon. "Allowing for the time it will take you to get back to Limehouse and the time it will take me to get my men stationed, I promise you that at half-past four the house will be closely surrounded. Give me a start—wait here until I have left this house, so I will arrive at least as soon as you."

"Good!" I impulsively grasped his hand. "There will doubtless be a girl there who is in no way implicated with the Master's evil doings, but only a victim of circumstances such as I have been. Deal gently with her."

"It shall be done. What signal shall I look for?"

"I have no way of signaling for you and I doubt if any sound in the house could be heard on the street. Let your men make their raid on the stroke of five."

I turned to go.

"A man is waiting for you with a car, I take it? Is he likely to suspect anything?"

"I have a way of finding out, and if he does," I replied grimly, "I will return alone to the Temple of Dreams."

Chapter Eleven

FOUR THIRTY-FOUR

*"Doubting, dreaming dreams no
mortal ever dared to dream before."*

The door closed softly behind me, the great dark house looming up more starkly than ever. Stooping, I crossed the wet lawn at a run, a grotesque and unholy figure, I doubt not, since any man had at a glance sworn me to be not a man but a giant ape.

So craftily had the Master devised!

I clambered the wall, dropped to the earth beyond and made my way through the darkness and the drizzle to the group of trees which masked the automobile.

The Negro driver leaned out of the front seat.

I was breathing hard and sought in various ways to simulate the actions of a man who has just murdered in cold blood and fled the scene of his crime.

"You heard nothing, no sound, no scream?" I hissed, gripping his arm.

"No noise except a slight crash when you first went in," he answered. "You did a good job—nobody passing along the road could have suspected anything."

"Have you remained in the car all the time?" I asked. And

when he replied that he had, I seized his ankle ánd ran my hand over the soles of his shoe; it was perfectly dry, as was the cuff of his trouser leg. Satisfied, I climbed into the back seat. Had he taken a step on the earth, shoe and garment would have showed it by the telltale dampness.

I ordered him to refrain from starting the engine until I had removed the apeskin, and then we sped through the night and I fell victim to doubts and uncertainties. Why should Gordon put any trust in the word of a stranger and a former ally of the Master's? Would he not put my tale down as the ravings of a dope-crazed addict, or a lie to ensnare or befool him?

Still, if he had not believed me, why had he let me go?

I could but trust. At any rate, what Gordon did or did not do would scarcely affect my fortunes ultimately, even though Zuleika had furnished me with that which would merely extend the number of my days. My thoughts centered on her, and more than my hope of vengeance on Kathulos was the hope that Gordon might be able to save her from the clutches of the fiend. At any rate, I thought grimly if Gordon failed me, I still had my hands and if I might lay them upon the bony frame of the Skull-faced One—

Abruptly I found myself thinking of Yussef Ali and his strange words, the import of which just occurred to me:

"*The Master, has promised her to me in the days of the empire!*"

The days of the empire—what could that mean?

The automobile at last drew up in front of the building which hid the Temple of Silence—now dark and still. The ride had seemed interminable and as I dismounted I glanced at the time-piece on the dashboard of the car. My heart leaped—it was four thirty-four, and unless my eyes tricked me, I saw a movement in the shadows across the street, out of the flare of the street lamp. At this time of night it could mean only one of two things—some menial of the Master watching for my return or else Gordon had kept his word. The Negro drove away and I opened the door, crossed the deserted bar and entered the opium room. The bunks and the floor were littered with the dreamers, for such places as these knew nothing of day or night as normal people know, but all lay deep in that well-known sottish slumber.

The lamps glimmered through the smoke and a silence hung mistily over all.

Chapter Twelve

THE STROKE OF FIVE

*"He saw gigantic tracks of death,
And many a shape of doom."*

—Chesterton

Two of the China boys squatted among the smudge fires, staring at me unwinkingly as I threaded my way among the recumbent bodies and made my way to the rear door. For the first time I traversed the corridor alone and found time to wonder again as to the contents of the strange chests which lined the walls.

Four raps on the under side of the floor, and a moment later I stood in the idol-room. I gasped in amazement—the fact that across a table from me sat Kathulos in all his horror was not the cause of my exclamation. Except for the table, the chair on which the Skull-face sat and the altar—now bare of incense—the room was perfectly bare! Drab, unlovely, the unused warehouse met my gaze instead of the costly tapestries I had become accustomed to. The palms, the idol, the lacquered screens—all were gone.

"Ah, Mr. Costigan, you are wondering, no doubt."

The dead voice of the Master broke in on my thoughts. His serpent eyes glittered balefully. The long yellow fingers-twined sinuously upon the table.

"You thought me to be a trusting fool, no doubt!" he rapped suddenly. "Did you think I would not have you followed? You fool, Yussef Ali was at your heels every moment!"

An instant I stood speechless, frozen by the crash of these words against my brain; then as their import sank home, I launched myself forward with a roar. At the same instant, before my clutching fingers could close on the mocking horror on the other side of the table, men rushed from every side. I whirled, and with the clarity of hate, from the swirl of savage faces I singled out Yussef Ali, and crashed my right fist against his temple with every ounce of my strength. Even as he dropped, Hassim struck me to my knees and a Chinaman flung a man-net over my shoulders. I heaved erect, bursting the stout cords as if they were strings, and then a blackjack in the hands of Ganra Singh stretched me stunned and bleeding on the floor.

Lean sinewy hands seized and bound me with cords that cut cruelly into my flesh. Emerging from the mists of semi-unconsciousness, I found myself lying on the altar with the masked Kathulos towering over me like a gaunt ivory tower. About in a semicircle stood Ganra Singh, Yar Khan, Yun Shatu and several others whom I knew as frequenters of the Temple of Dreams. Beyond them—and the sight cut me to the heart—I saw Zuleika crouching in a doorway, her face white and her hands pressed against her cheeks, in an attitude of abject terror.

"I did not fully trust you," said Kathulos sibilantly, "so I sent Yussuf Ali to follow you. He reached the group of trees before you and, following you into the estate, heard your very interesting conversation with John Gordon—for he scaled the house-wall like a cat and clung to the window-ledge! Your driver delayed purposely so as to give Yussuf Ali plenty of time to get back—I have decided to change my abode anyway. My furnishings are already on their way to another house—and as soon as we have disposed of the traitor—you—we shall depart also, leaving a little surprise for your friend Gordon when he arrives at five-thirty."

My heart gave a sudden leap of hope. Yussef Ali had misunderstood, and Kathulos lingered here in false security while the London detective force had already silently surrounded the house. Over my shoulder I saw Zuleika vanish from the door.

I eyed Kathulos, absolutely unaware of what he was saying. It was not long until five—if he dallied longer—then I froze as the Egyptian spoke a word and Li Kung, a gaunt, cadaverous Chinaman, stepped from the silent semicircle and drew from his sleeve a long thin dagger. My eyes sought the time-piece that still rested on the table and my heart sank. It was still ten minutes until five. My death did not matter so much since it simply hastened the inevitable, but in my mind's eye I could see Kathulos and his murderers escaping while the police awaited the stroke of five.

The Skull-face halted in some harangue, and stood in a listening attitude. I believe his uncanny intuition warned him of danger. He spoke a quick staccato command to Li Kung and the Chinaman sprang forward, dagger lifted above my breast.

The air was suddenly supercharged with dynamic tension. The keen dagger-point hovered high above me—loud and clear sounded the skirl of a police whistle and on the heels of the sound there came a terrific crash from the front of the warehouse!

Kathulos leaped into frenzied activity. Hissing orders like a cat spitting, he sprang for the hidden door and the rest followed him. Things happened with the speed of a nightmare. Li Kung had followed the rest, but Kathulos flung a command over his shoulder and the Chinaman turned back and came rushing toward the altar where I lay, dagger high, desperation in his countenance.

A scream broke through the clamor and as I twisted desperately about to avoid the descending dagger, I caught a glimpse of Kathulos dragging Zuleika away. Then with a frenzied wrench I toppled from the altar just as Li Kung's dagger, grazing my breast, sank inches deep into the dark-stained surface and quivered there.

I had fallen on the side next to the wall and what was taking place in the room I could not see, but it seemed as if far away I could hear men screaming faintly and hideously. Then Li Kung wrenched his blade free and sprang, tigerishly, around the end of the altar. Simultaneously a revolver cracked from the doorway—the Chinaman spun clear around, the dagger flying from his hand—he slumped to the floor.

Gordon, came running from the doorway where a few moments earlier Zuleika had stood, his pistol still smoking in his hand. At his heels were three rangy, clean-cut men in plainclothes. He cut my bonds and dragged me upright.

"Quick! Where have they gone?"

The room was empty of life save for myself, Gordon and his men, though two dead men lay on the floor.

I found the secret door and after a few seconds' search located the lever which opened it. Revolvers drawn, the men groped about me and peered nervously into the dark stairway. Not a sound came up from the total darkness.

"This is uncanny!" muttered Gordon. "I suppose the Master and his servants went this way when they left the building—as they are certainly not here now!—and Leary and his men should have stopped them either in the tunnel itself or in the rear room of Yun Shatu's. At any rate, in either event they should have communicated with us by this time."

"Look out, sir!" one of the men exclaimed suddenly, and Gordon, with an ejaculation, struck out with his pistol barrel and crushed the life from a huge snake which had crawled silently up the steps from the blackness beneath.

"Let us see into this matter," said he, straightening.

But before he could step onto the first stair, I halted him; for flesh crawling, I began dimly to understand something of what had happened—I began to understand the silence in the tunnel, the absence of detectives, the screams I had heard some minutes previously while I lay on the altar. Examining the lever which opened the door, I found another smaller lever—I began to believe I knew what those mysterious chests in the tunnel contained.

"Gordon," I said hoarsely, "have you an electric torch?"

One of the men produced a large one.

"Direct the light into the tunnel, but as you value your life, do not put a foot upon the steps."

The beam of light struck through the shadows, lighting the tunnel, etching out boldly a scene that will haunt my brain all the rest of my life. On the floor of the tunnel, between the chests which now gaped open, lay two men who were members of London's finest secret service. Limbs twisted and faces horribly distorted they lay, and above and about them writhed, in long glittering scaly shimmerings, scores of hideous reptiles.

The clock struck five.

Chapter Thirteen

THE BLIND BEGGAR WHO RODE

*"He seemed a beggar such as lags
Looking for crusts and ale."*

—Chesterton

The cold gray dawn was stealing over the river as we stood in the deserted bar of the Temple of Dreams. Gordon was questioning the two men who had remained on guard outside the building while their unfortunate companions went in to explore the tunnel.

"As soon as we heard the whistle, sir, Leary and Murken rushed the bar and broke into the opium room, while we waited here at the bar door according to orders. Right away several ragged elopers came tumbling out and we grabbed them. But no one else came out and we heard nothing from Leary and Murken; so we just waited until you came, sir."

"You saw nothing of a giant Negro, or of the Chinaman Yun Shatu?"

"No, sir. After a while the patrolmen arrived and we threw a cordon around the house, but no one was seen."

Gordon shrugged his shoulders; a few cursory questions had satisfied him that the captives were harmless addicts and he had them released.

"You are sure no one else came out?"

"Yes, sir—no, wait a moment. A wretched old blind beggar did come out, all rags and dirt and with a ragged girl leading him. We stopped him but didn't hold him—a wretch like that couldn't be harmful.".

"No?" Gordon jerked out. "Which way did he go?"

"The girl led him down the street to the next block and then an automobile stopped and they got in and drove off, sir."

Gordon glared at him.

"The stupidity of the London detective has rightfully become an international jest," he said acidly. "No doubt it never occurred to you as being strange that a Limehouse beggar should ride about in his own automobile."

Then impatiently waving aside the man, who sought to speak further, he turned to me.

"Mr. Costigan, if you will come to my apartment we may be able to clear up some new things."

Chapter Fourteen

THE BLACK EMPIRE

"Oh the new spears dipped in life-blood
as the woman shrieked in vain!
Oh the days before the English!
When will those days come again?"

—Mundy

Gordon struck a match and absently allowed it to flicker and go out in his hand. His Turkish cigarette hung unlighted between his fingers.

"This is the most logical conclusion to be reached," he was saying. "The weak link in our chain was lack of men. But curse it, one cannot round up an army at two o'clock in the morning, even with the aid of Scotland Yard. I went on to Limehouse, leaving orders for a number of patrolmen to follow me as quickly as they could be got together, and to throw a cordon about the house.

"They arrived too late to prevent the Master's servants slipping out of the side doors and windows, as they could easily do, with only Finnegan and Hansen on guard at the front of the building. However, they arrived in time to prevent the Master himself from slipping out in that way—no doubt he lingered to effect his disguise and was caught in that manner. He owes his escape to his craft and boldness and to the carelessness of Finnegan and Hansen. The girl who accompanied him—"

"She was Zuleika, I am sure."

I answered listlessly, wondering anew what shackles bound her inexorably to the Egyptian sorcerer.

"You owe your life to her," Gordon rapped out, lighting another match. "We were standing in the shadows in front of the warehouse, waiting for the hour to strike, and of course ignorant as to what was going on in the house, when a girl appeared at one of the barred windows and begged us for God's sake to do something; that a man was being murdered. So we broke in at once. However, she was not to be seen anywhere when we entered."

"She probably returned to the room," I muttered, "and was forced to accompany the Master. God grant he knows nothing of her trickery."

"I do not know," said Gordon, dropping the charred match stem, "whether she guessed at our true identity or whether she just made the appeal in desperation.

"However, the main point is this: evidence points to the fact that, on hearing the whistle, Leary and Murken invaded Yun

Shatu's from the front at the same instant my three men and I made our attack on the warehouse front. As it took us some seconds to batter down the door, it is logical to suppose that they found the secret door and entered the tunnel before we effected an entrance into the warehouse.

"The Master, knowing our plans before hand, and being aware that an invasion would be made through the tunnel and having long ago made preparations for such an exigency—"

An involuntary shudder shook me.

"—the Master worked the lever that opened the chests—the screams you heard as you lay upon the altar were the death shrieks of Leary and Murken. Then, leaving the Chinaman behind to finish you, the Master and the rest descended into the tunnel—incredible as it seems—and threading their way unharmed among the serpents, entered Yun Shatu's house and escaped therefrom as I have said."

"That seems impossible. Why should not the snakes turn on them?"

Gordon finally ignited his cigarette and puffed a few seconds before replying.

"The reptiles might still have been giving their full and hideous attention to the dying men, or else—I have on previous occasions been confronted with indisputable proof of the Master's dominance over beasts and reptiles of even the lowest and most dangerous orders. How he and his slaves passed unhurt among those scaly fiends must remain, at present, one of the many unsolved mysteries pertaining to that strange man."

I stirred restlessly in my chair. This brought up a point which I had come to Gordon's neat but bizarre apartments to clear up.

"You have not yet told me," I said abruptly, "who this man is and what is his mission."

"As to who he is, I can only say that he is known as you name him—the Master. I have never seen him unmasked, nor do I know his real name nor his nationality."

"I can enlighten you to an extent there," I broke in. "I have seen him unmasked and have heard the name his slaves call him."

Gordon's eyes blazed and he leaned forward.

"His name," I continued, "is Kathulos and he claims to be an Egyptian."

"Kathulos!" Gordon repeated. "You say he claims to be an Egyptian—have you any reason for doubting his claim to that nationality?"

"He may be of Egypt," I answered slowly, "but he is different, somehow, from any human I ever saw or hope to see. Great age might account for some of his peculiarities, but there are certain lineal differences that my anthropological studies tell me have been present since birth—features which would be abnormal to any other man but which are perfectly normal in Kathulos. That sounds paradoxical, I admit, but to appreciate fully the horrid inhumanness of the man, you would have to see him yourself."

Gordon sat all attention while I swiftly sketched the appearance of the Egyptian as I remembered him—and that appearance was indelibly etched on my brain forever.

As I finished he nodded.

"As I have said, I never saw Kathulos except when disguised as a beggar, a leper or some such thing—when he was fairly swathed in rags. Still, I too have been impressed with a strange *difference* about him—something that is not present at all in other men."

Gordon tapped his knee with his fingers—a habit of his when deeply engrossed by a problem.

"You have asked as to the mission of this man," he began slowly. "I will tell you all I know."

"My position with the British Government is a unique and peculiar one. I hold what might be called a roving commission—an office created solely for the purpose of suiting my special needs. As a secret service official during the first World War, I convinced the powers of a need of such an office and of my ability to fill it.

"Somewhat over seventeen months ago I was sent to South Africa to investigate the unrest which has been growing among the natives of the interior ever since the World War and which has of late assumed alarming proportions. There I first got on the track of this man Kathulos. I found in roundabout ways, that Africa was a seething cauldron of rebellion from Morocco to Cape Town. The old, old vow had been made again—the Negroes and the Mohammedans, banded together, should drive the white men into the sea.

"This pact has been made before but always, hitherto, broken. Now, however, I sensed a giant intellect and a monstrous genius behind the veil, a genius powerful enough to accomplish this union and hold it together. Working entirely on hints and vague whispered clues, I followed the trail up through Central Africa and into Egypt. There, at last, I came upon definite evidence that such a man existed. The whispers hinted of a living dead man—a *skull-faced* man. I learned that this man was the high priest of the mysterious Scorpion society of northern Africa. He was spoken of variously as Skull-face, the Master, and the Scorpion.

"Following a trail of bribed officials and filched state secrets, I at last trailed him to Alexandria, where I had my first sight of him in a dive in the native quarter—disguised as a leper. I heard him distinctly addressed as 'mighty Scorpion' by the natives, but he escaped me.

"All trace vanished then; the trail ran out entirely until rumors of strange happenings in London reached me and I came back to England to investigate an apparent leak in the war office.

"As I thought, the Scorpion had preceded me. This man, whose education and craft transcend anything I ever met with, is simply the leader and instigator of a world-wide movement such as mankind has never seen before. He plots, in a word, the overthrow of the white races!

"His ultimate aim is a black empire, with himself as emperor of the world! And to that end he has banded together in one monstrous conspiracy the black, the brown and the yellow."

"I understand now what Yussef Ali meant when he said 'the days of the empire,'" I muttered.

"Exactly," Gordon rapped with suppressed excitement. "Kathulos' power is unlimited and unguessed. Like an octopus his tentacles stretch to the high places of civilization and to the far corners of the world. And his main weapon is—dope! He has flooded Europe and no doubt America with opium and hashish, and in spite of all effort it has been impossible to discover the break in the barriers through which the hellish stuff is coming. With this he ensnares and enslaves men and women.

"You have told me of the aristocratic men and women you saw coming to Yun Shatu's dive. Without doubt they were dope addicts—for, as I said, the habit lurks in high places—holders of governmental positions, no doubt, coming to trade for the stuff they craved and giving in return state secrets, inside information and promise of protection for the Master's crimes.

"Oh, he does not work haphazardly! Before ever the black flood breaks, he will be prepared; if he has his way, the governments of the white races will be honeycombs of corruption—the strongest men of the white races will be dead. The white men's secrets of war will be his. When it comes, I look for a simultaneous uprising against white supremacy, of all the colored races—races who, in the last war, learned the white men's ways of battle, and who, led by such a man as Kathulos and armed with the white man's finest weapons, will be almost invincible.

"A steady stream of rifles and ammunition has been pouring into East Africa and it was not until I discovered the source that it was stopped. I found that a staid and reliable Scotch firm was smuggling these arms among the natives and I found more: the manager of this firm was an opium slave. That was enough. I saw Kathulos' hand in the matter. The manager was arrested and committed suicide in his cell—that is only one of the many situations with which I am called upon to deal.

"Again the case of Major Fairlan Morley. He, like myself, held a very flexible commission and had been sent to the Transvaal to work upon the same case. He sent to London a number of secret papers for safe-keeping. They arrived some weeks ago and were put in a bank vault. The letter accompanying them gave explicit instructions that they were to be delivered to no one but the Major himself, when he called for them in person, or in event of his death, to myself.

"As soon as I learned that he had sailed from Africa I sent trusted men to Bordeaux, where he intended to make his first landing in Europe. They did not succeed in saving the Major's life, but they certified his death, for they found his body in a deserted ship whose hulk was stranded on the beach. Efforts were made to keep the affair a secret but somehow it leaked into the papers with the result—"

"I began to understand why I was to impersonate the unfortunate major," I interrupted.

"Exactly. A false beard furnished you, and your black hair dyed blond, you would have presented yourself at the bank, received the papers from the banker, who knew Major Morley just intimately enough to be deceived by your appearance, and the papers would have then fallen into the hands of the Master.

"I can only guess at the contents of those papers, for events have been taking place too swiftly for me to call for and obtain them. But they must deal with subjects closely connected with the activities of Kathulos. How he learned of them and of the provisions of the letter accompanying them, I have no idea, but as I said, London is honeycombed with his spies.

"In my search for clues, I often frequented Limehouse disguised as you first saw me. I went often to the Temple of Dreams and even managed once to enter the back room, for I suspected some sort of rendezvous in the rear of the building. The absence of any exit baffled me and I had no time to search for secret doors before I was ejected by the giant black man Hassim, who had no suspicion of my true identity. I noticed that very often the leper entered or left Yun Shatu's, and finally it was borne on me that this supposed leper was the Scorpion himself.

"That night you discovered me on the couch in the opium room, I had come there with no especial plan in mind. Seeing Kathulos leaving, I determined to rise and follow him, but you spoiled that."

He fingered his chin and laughed grimly.

"I was an amateur boxing champion in Oxford," said he, "but Tom Cribb himself could not have withstood that blow—or have dealt it."

"I regret it as I regret few things."

"No need to apologize. You saved my life immediately afterward—I was stunned, but not too much to know that that brown devil Yussef Ali was burning to cut out my heart."

"How did you come to be at Sir Haldred Frenton's estate? And how is it that you did not raid Yun Shatu's dive?"

"I did not have the place raided because I knew somehow Kathulos would be warned and our efforts would come to naught. I was at Sir Haldred's that night because I have contrived to spend at least part of each night with him since he returned from the Congo. I anticipated an attempt upon his life when I learned from his own lips that he was preparing, from the studies he made on this trip, a treatise on the secret native societies of West Africa. He hinted that the disclosures he intended to make therein might prove sensational, to say the least. Since it is to Kathulos' advantage to destroy such men as might be able to arouse the Western world to its danger, I knew that Sir Haldred was a marked man. Indeed, two distinct attempts were made upon his life on his journey to the coast from the African interior. So I put two trusted men on guard and they are at their post even now.

"Roaming about the darkened house, I heard the noise of your entry, and, warning my men, I strode down to intercept you. At the time of our conversation, Sir Haldred was sitting in his unlighted study, a Scotland Yard man with drawn pistol on each side of him. Their vigilance no doubt accounts for Yussef Ali's failure to attempt what you were sent to do.

"Something in your manner convinced me in spite of yourself," he meditated. "I will admit I had some bad moments of doubt as I waited in the darkness that precedes dawn, outside the warehouse."

Gordon rose suddenly and going to a strong-box which stood in a corner of the room, drew thence a thick envelope.

"Although Kathulos has checkmated me at almost every move," he said, "I have not been entirely idle. Noting the frequenters of Yun Shatu's, I have compiled a partial list of the Egyptian's right-hand men, and their records. What you have told me has enabled me to complete that list. As we know, his henchmen are scattered all over the world, and there are possibly hundreds of them here, in London. However, this is a list of those I believe to be in his closest council, now with him in England. He told you himself that few even of his followers ever saw him unmasked."

We bent together over the list, which contained the following names: "Yun Shatu, Hongkong Chinese, suspected opium smuggler—keeper of Temple of Dreams—resident of Limehouse seven years. Hassim—ex-Senegalese chief—wanted in French Congo for murder. Santiago, Negro—fled from Haiti under suspicion of voodoo worship atrocities. Yar Khan, Afridi, record unknown. Yussef Ali, Moor, slave-dealer in Morocco—suspected of being a German spy in the World War—an instigator of the Fellaheen Rebellion on the upper Nile. Ganra Singh, Lahore, India, Sikh—smuggler of arms into Afghanistan—took an active part in the Lahore and Delhi riots—suspected of murder on two occasions—a dangerous man. Stephen Costigan, American—resident of England since the war—hashish addict—man of remarkable strength. Li Kung, northern China, opium smuggler."

Lines were drawn significantly through three names—mine, Li Kung's and Yussef Ali's. Nothing was written next to mine, but following Li Kung's name was scrawled briefly in Gordon's rambling character: "Shot by John Gordon during the raid on Yun Shatu's." And following the name of Yussef Ali: "Killed by Stephen

Costigan during the Yun Shatu raid."

I laughed mirthlessly. Black empire or not, Yussef Ali would never hold Zuleika in his arms, for he had never risen from where I felled him.

"I know not," said Gordon somberly as he folded the list and replaced it in the envelope, "what power Kathulos has that draws together black men and yellow men to serve him—that unites world-old foes. Hindoo, Moslem, and pagan are among his followers. And back in the mists of the East where mysterious and gigantic forces are at work, this uniting is culminating on a monstrous scale."

He glanced at his watch.

"It is nearly ten. Make yourself at home here, Mr. Costigan, while I visit Scotland Yard and see if any clue has been found as to Kathulos' new quarters. I believe that the webs are closing on him, and with your aid I promise you we will have the gang located within a week at most."

Chapter Fifteen

THE MARK OF THE TULWAR

*"The fed world curls by his drowsy mate
In a tight-trod earth; but the lean wolves wait."*

—Mundy

I sat alone in John Gordon's apartments and laughed mirthlessly. In spite of the elixir's stimulus, the strain of the previous night, with its loss of sleep and its heartrending action, was telling on me. My mind was a chaotic whirl wherein the faces of Gordon, Kathulos and Zuleika shifted with numbing swiftness. All the mass of information Gordon had given to me seemed jumbled and incoherent.

Through this state of being, one fact stood out boldly, I must find the latest hiding-place of the Egyptian and get Zuleika out of his hands—if indeed she still lived.

A week, Gordon had said—I laughed again—a week and I would be beyond aiding anyone. I had found the proper amount of elixir to use—knew the minimum amount my system required—and knew that I could make the flask last me four days at most. Four days! Four days in which to comb the rat-holes of Limehouse and Chinatown—four days in which to ferret out, somewhere in the mazes of East End, the lair of Kathulos.

I burned with impatience to begin, but nature rebelled, and staggering to a couch, I fell upon it and was asleep instantly.

Then someone was shaking me.

"Wake up, Mr. Costigan!"

I sat up, blinking. Gordon stood over me, his face haggard.

"There's devil's work done, Costigan! The Scorpion has struck again!"

I sprang up, still half asleep and only partly realizing what he was saying. He helped me into my coat, thrust my hat at me, and then his firm grip on my arm was propelling me out of his door and down the stairs. The street lights were blazing; I had slept an incredible time.

"A logical victim!" I was aware that my companion was saying. "He should have notified me the instant of his arrival!"

"I don't understand—" I began dazedly.

We were at the curb now and Gordon hailed a taxi, giving the address of a small and unassuming hotel in a staid and prim section of the city.

"The Baron Rokoff," he rapped as we whirled along at reckless speed, "a Russian free-lance, connected with the war office. He returned from Mongolia yesterday and apparently went into hiding. Undoubtedly he had learned something vital in regard to the slow waking of the East. He had not yet communicated with us, and I had no idea that he was in England until just now."

"And you learned—"

"The baron was found in his room, his dead body mutilated in a frightful manner!"

The respectable and conventional hotel which the doomed baron had chosen for his hiding place was in a state of wild uproar, being suppressed by the police. The management had attempted to keep the matter quiet, but somehow the guests had learned of the atrocity and many were leaving in haste—or preparing to, as the police were planning to hold all for investigation.

The baron's room, which was on the top floor, was in a state to defy description. Not even in the great war have I seen a more complete shambles. Nothing had been touched; all remained just as the chamber-maid had found it a half hour since. Tables and chairs lay shattered on the floor, and the furniture, floor and walls were spattered with blood. The baron, a tall, muscular man in life, lay in the middle of the room, a fearful spectacle. His skull had been cleft to the brows, a deep gash under his left armpit had shorn through his ribs, and his left arm hung by a shred of flesh. The cold bearded face was set in a look of indescribable horror.

"Some heavy, curved weapon must have been used," said Gordon, "something like a saber, wielded with terrific force. See where a chance blow sank inches deep into the window-sill. And again, the thick back of this heavy chair has been split like a shingle. A saber, surely."

"A tulwar," I muttered, somberly. "Do you not recognize the handiwork of the Central Asian butcher? Yar Khan has been here."

"The Afghan! He came across the roofs, of course, and descended to the window-ledge by means of a knotted rope made fast to something on the edge of the roof. About one-thirty the maid, passing through the corridor, heard a terrific commotion in the baron's room—smashing of chairs and a sudden short shriek which died abruptly into a ghastly gurgle and then ceased—to the sound of heavy blows, curiously muffled, such as a sword might make when driven deep into human flesh. Then all noises stopped suddenly.

"She called the manager and they tried the door and, finding it locked, and receiving no answer to their shouts, opened it with the desk key. Only the corpse was there, but the window was open. This is strangely unlike Kathulos' usual procedure. It lacks subtlety. Often his victims appear to have died from natural causes. I scarcely understand."

"I see little difference in the outcome," I answered. "There is nothing that can be done to apprehend the murderer as it is."

"True," Gordon scowled. "We know who did it but there is no proof—not even a fingerprint. Even if we knew where the Afghan is hiding and arrested him, we could prove nothing—there would be a score of men to swear alibis for him. The baron returned only yesterday. Kathulos probably did not know of his arrival until tonight. He knew that, tomorrow, Rokoff would make known his presence to me and impart what he learned in northern Asia. The Egyptian knew he must strike quickly, and lacking time to prepare a safer and more elaborate form of murder, he sent the Afridi with his tulwar. There is nothing we can do, at least not until we discover the Scorpion's hiding-place. What the baron had learned in Mongolia, we shall never know, but that it dealt with the plans and aspirations of Kathulos, we may be sure."

We went down the stairs again and out on the street accompanied by one of the Scotland Yard men, Hansen. Gordon suggested that we walk back to his apartment, and I greeted the opportunity to let the cool night air blow some of the cobwebs out of my mazed brain.

As we walked along the deserted streets, Gordon suddenly cursed savagely.

"This is a veritable labyrinth we are following, leading nowhere! Here, in the very heart of civilization's metropolis, the direct enemy of that civilization commits crimes of the most outrageous nature and goes free! We are children, wandering in the night, struggling with an unseen evil—dealing with an incarnate devil, of whose true identity we know nothing and whose true ambitions we can only guess.

"Never have we managed to arrest one of the Egyptian's direct henchmen, and the few dupes and tools of his we have apprehended have died mysteriously before they could tell us anything. Again I repeat: what strange power has Kathulos that dominates these men of different creeds and races? The men in London with him are, of course, mostly renegades, slaves of dope, but his tentacles stretch all over the East. Some dominance is his: the power that sent the Chinaman, Li Kung, back to kill you, in the face of certain death; that sent Yar Khan and Moslem over the roofs of London to do murder; that holds Zuleika the Circassian in unseen bonds of slavery.

"Of course we know," he continued after a brooding silence, "that the East has secret societies which are behind and above all considerations of creeds. There are cults in Africa and the Orient whose origin dates back to Ophir and the fall of Atlantis. This man must be a power in some or possibly all of these societies. An Egyptian by his own word, he controls the lives and destinies of orthodox Moslems, Hindoos, Shintos and devil-worshippers. It's unnatural.

"Have you ever"—he turned to me abruptly—"heard the ocean mentioned in connection with Kathulos?"

"Never."

"There is a widespread superstition in northern Africa, based on a very ancient legend, that the great leader of the colored races would come out of the sea! And I once heard a Berber speak of the Scorpion as 'The Son of the Ocean'."

"That is a term of respect among that tribe, is it not?"

"Yes; still I wonder sometimes."

Chapter Sixteen

THE MUMMY WHO LAUGHED

"Laughing as littered skulls that lie
After lost battles turn to the sky
An everlasting laugh."

—Chesterton

"A shop open this late!" Gordon remarked suddenly.

A fog had descended on London and along the quiet street we were traversing the lights glimmered with the peculiar reddish haze characteristic of such atmospheric conditions. Our footfalls echoed drearily. Even in the heart of a great city there are always sections which seem overlooked and forgotten. Such a street was this. Not even a policeman was in sight.

The shop which had attracted Gordon's attention was just in front of us, on the same side of the street. There was no sign over the door, merely some sort of emblem something like a dragon. Light flowed from the open doorway and the small show windows on each side. As it was neither a café nor the entrance to a hotel, we found ourselves idly speculating over its reason for being open. Ordinarily, I suppose neither of us would have given the matter a thought, but our nerves were so keyed up that we found ourselves instinctively suspicious of anything out of the ordinary. Then something occurred which was distinctly out of the ordinary.

A tall, very thin man, considerably stooped, suddenly loomed up out of the fog in front of us, and beyond the shop. I had only a glance of him—an impression of incredible gauntness, of worn, wrinkled garments, a high silk, hat drawn close over the brows, a face hidden by a muffler; then he turned aside and entered the shop. A cold wind whispered down the street, twisting the fog into wispy ghosts, but the coldness that came upon me transcended the wind's.

"Gordon!" I exclaimed in a fierce, low voice. "My senses are no longer reliable or else Kathulos himself has just gone into that house!"

Gordon's eyes blazed. We were now close to the shop, and lengthening his strides into a run, he hurled himself into the door, the detective and I close upon his heels.

A weird assortment of merchandise met our eyes. Antique weapons covered the walls, and the floor was piled high with curious things. Maori idols shouldered Chinese josses, and suits of mediaeval armor bulked darkly against stacks of rare Oriental rugs and Latin-made shawls. The place was an antique shop. Of the figure who had aroused our interest we saw nothing.

An old man clad bizarrely in red fez, brocaded jacket and Turkish slippers came from the back of the shop; he was a Levantine of some sort.

"You wish something, sirs?"

"You keep open rather late," Gordon said abruptly, his eyes traveling swiftly over the shop for some secret hiding-place that might conceal the object of our search.

"Yes, sir. My customers number many eccentric professors and students who keep very irregular hours. Often the night boats unload special pieces for me and very often I have customers later than this. I remain open all night, sir."

"We are merely looking around," Gordon returned, and in an aside to Hansen: "Go to the back and stop anyone who tries to leave that way."

Hansen nodded and strolled casually to the rear of the shop. The back door was clearly visible to our view, through a vista of antique furniture and tarnished hangings strung up for exhibition. We had followed the Scorpion—if he it was—so closely that I did not believe he would have had time to traverse the full length of the shop and make his exit without our having seen him as we came in. For our eyes had been on the rear door ever since we had entered.

Gordon and I browsed around casually among the curios, handling and discussing some of them, but I have no idea as to their nature. The Levantine had seated himself crosslegged on a Moorish mat close to the center of the shop and apparently took only a polite interest in our explorations.

After a time Gordon whispered to me, "There is no advantage in keeping up this pretense. We have looked everywhere the Scorpion might be hiding, in the ordinary manner. I will make known my identity and authority and we will search the entire building openly."

Even as he spoke, a truck drew up outside the door and two burly Negroes entered. The Levantine seemed to have expected them, for he merely waved them toward the back of the shop and they responded with a grunt of understanding.

Gordon and I watched them closely as they made their way to a large mummy-case which stood upright against the wall not far from the back. They lowered this to a level position and then started for the door, carrying it carefully between them.

"Halt!" Gordon stepped forward, raising his hand authoritatively.

"I represent Scotland Yard," he said swiftly, "and have sanction for anything I choose to do. Set that mummy down; nothing leaves this shop until we have thoroughly searched it."

The Negroes obeyed without a word, and my friend turned to the Levantine, who, apparently not perturbed or even interested, sat smoking a Turkish water-pipe.

"Who was that tall man who entered just before we did, and where did he go?"

"No one entered before you, sir. Or, if anyone did, I was at the back of the shop and did not see him. You are certainly at liberty to search my shop, sir."

And search it we did, with the combined craft of a secret service expert and a denizen of the underworld—while Hansen stood stolidly at his post, the two Negroes standing over the carved mummy-case watched us impassively. And the Levantine sat like a sphinx on his mat, puffing a fog of smoke into the air. The whole thing had a distinct effect of unreality.

At last, baffled, we returned to the mummy-case, which was certainly long enough to conceal even a man of Kathulos' height. The thing did not appear to be sealed as is the usual custom, and Gordon opened it without difficulty. A formless shape, swathed in moldering wrappings, met our eyes. Gordon parted some of the wrappings and revealed an inch or so of withered, brownish, leathery arm. He shuddered involuntarily as he touched it, as a man will do at the touch of a reptile or some inhumanly cold thing. Taking a small metal idol from a stand near by, he rapped on the shrunken breast and the arm. Each gave out a solid thumping, like some sort of wood.

Gordon shrugged his shoulders. "Dead for two thousand years, anyway, and I don't suppose I should risk destroying a valuable mummy simply to prove that which we know to be true."

He closed the case again.

"The mummy may have crumbled some, even from this much exposure, but perhaps it did not."

This last was addressed to the Levantine, who replied merely by a courteous gesture of his hand, and the Negroes once more lifted the case and carried it to the truck, where they loaded it on, and a moment later mummy, truck and Negroes had vanished in the fog.

Gordon still nosed about the shop, but I stood stock-still in the center of the floor. To my chaotic and dope-ridden brain I attributed it, but the sensation had been mine, that through the wrappings of the mummy's face, great eyes had burned into mine, eyes like pools of yellow fire, that seared my soul and froze me where I stood. And as the case had been carried through the door, I knew that the lifeless thing in it, dead, God only knows how many centuries, was *laughing*, hideously and silently.

Chapter Seventeen

THE DEAD MAN FROM THE SEA

Gordon puffed savagely at his Turkish cigarette, staring abstract-edly and unseeingly at Hansen, who was sitting opposite him.

"I suppose we must chalk up another failure against ourselves. That Levantine, Kamonos, is evidently a creature of the Egyptian's, and the walls and floors of his shop are probably honeycombed with secret panels and doors which would baffle a magician."

Hansen made some answer but I said nothing. Since our return to Gordon's apartment, I had been conscious of a feeling of intense languor and sluggishness which not even my condition could account for. I knew that my system was full of the elixir—but my mind seemed strangely slow and hard of comprehension in direct contrast with the average state of my mentality when stimulated by the hellish dope.

This condition was slowly leaving me, like mist floating from the surface of a lake, and I felt as if I were waking gradually from a long and unnaturally sound sleep.

Gordon was saying, "I would give a good deal to know if Kamonos is really one of Kathulos' slaves or if the Scorpion managed to make his escape through some natural exit as we entered."

"Kamonos is his servant, true enough," I found myself saying slowly, as if searching for the proper words. "As we left, I saw his gaze light upon the scorpion which is traced on my hand. His eyes narrowed, and as we were leaving he contrived to brush close against me—and to whisper in a quick low voice: 'Soho, Forty-eight.'"

Gordon came erect like a loosened steel bow.

"Indeed!" he rapped. "Why did you not tell me at the time?"

"I don't know."

My friend eyed me sharply.

"I noticed you seemed like a man intoxicated all the way from the shop," said he. "I attributed it to some aftermath of hashish. But no. Kathulos is undoubtedly a masterful disciple of Mesmer—his power over venomous reptiles shows that, and I am beginning to believe it is the real source of his power over humans.

"Somehow, the Master caught you off your guard in that shop and partly asserted his dominance over your mind. From what hidden nook he sent his thought waves to shatter your brain, I do not know, but Kathulos was somewhere in that shop, I am sure."

"He was. He was in the mummy-case."

"The mummy-case!" Gordon exclaimed rather impatiently. "That is impossible! The mummy quite filled it and not even such a thin being as the Master could have found room there."

I shrugged my shoulders, unable to argue the point but somehow sure of the truth of my statement.

"Kamonos," Gordon continued, "doubtless is not a member of the inner circle and does not know of your change of allegiance. Seeing the mark of the scorpion, he undoubtedly supposed you to be a spy of the Master's. The whole thing may be a plot to ensnare us, but I feel that the man was sincere—Soho, Forty-eight can be nothing less than the Scorpion's new rendezvous."

I, too, felt that Gordon was right, though a suspicion lurked in my mind.

"I secured the papers of Major Morley yesterday," he continued, "and while you slept, I went over them. Mostly they but corroborated what I already knew—touched on the unrest of the natives and repeated the theory that one vast genius was behind all: But there was one matter which interested me greatly and which I think will interest you also."

From his strongbox he took a manuscript written in the close, neat characters of the unfortunate major, and, in a monotonous droning which betrayed little of his intense excitement, he read the following nightmarish narrative:

"This matter I consider worth jotting down—as to whether it has any bearing oh the case at hand, further developments will show: At Alexandria, where I spent some weeks seeking further clues as to the identity of the man known as the Scorpion, I made the acquaintance, through my friend Ahmed Shah, of the noted Egyptologist, Professor Ezra Schuyler of New York. He verified the statement made by various laymen, concerning the legend of the 'ocean-man.' This myth, handed down from generation to generation, stretches back into the very mists of antiquity and is, briefly, that some day a man shall come up out of the sea and shall lead the people of Egypt to victory over all others.

"This legend has spread over the continent so that now all black races consider that it deals with the coming of a universal emperor. Professor Schuyler gave it as his opinion that the myth was somehow connected with the lost Atlantis, which, he maintains, was located between the African and South American continents and to whose inhabitants the ancestors of the Egyptians were tributary. The reasons for his connection are too lengthy and vague to note here, but following the line of his theory he told me a strange and fantastic tale.

"He said that a close friend of his, Von Lorfmon of Germany, a sort of free-lance scientist, now dead, was sailing off the coast of Senegal some years ago, for the purpose of investigating and classifying the rare specimens of sealife found there. He was using for his purpose a small trading vessel, manned by a crew of Moors, Greeks and Negroes.

"Some days out of sight of land, something floating was sighted, and this object, being grappled and brought aboard, proved to be a *mummy-case of a most curious kind*. Professor Schuyler explained to me the features whereby it differed from the ordinary Egyptian style, but from his rather technical account I merely got the impression that it was a strangely shaped affair carved with characters neither cuneiform nor hieroglyphic. The case was heavily lacquered, being watertight and air-tight, and Von Lorfmon had considerable difficulty in opening it.

"However, he managed to do so without damaging the case, and a most unusual mummy was revealed. Schuyler said that he never saw either the mummy or the case, but that from descriptions given him by the Greek skipper who was present at the opening of the case, the mummy differed as much from the ordinary man as the case differed from the conventional type.

"Examination proved that the subject had not undergone the usual procedure of mummification. All parts were intact just as in life, but the whole form was shrunk and hardened to a wood-like consistency. Cloth wrappings swathed the thing and they crumbled to dust and vanished the instant air was let in upon them.

"Von Lorfmon was impressed by the effect upon the crew. The Greeks showed no interest beyond that which would ordinarily be shown by any man, but the Moors, and even more the Negroes, seemed to be rendered temporarily insane! As the case was hoisted on board, they all fell prostrate on the deck and raised a sort of worshipful chant, and it was necessary to use force in order to exclude them from the cabin wherein the mummy was exposed.

"A number of fights broke out between them and the Greek element of the crew, and the skipper and Von Lorfmon thought best to put back to the nearest port in all haste. The skipper attributed it to the natural aversion of seamen toward having a corpse on board, but Von Lorfmon seemed to sense a deeper meaning."

"They made port in Lagos, and that very night Von Lorfmon was murdered in his stateroom and the mummy and its case vanished. All the Moor and Negro sailors deserted ship the same night. Schuyler said—and here the matter took on a most sinister and mysterious aspect—that immediately afterward this widespread unrest among the natives began to smolder and take tangible form; he connected it in some manner with the old legend.

"An aura of mystery, also, hung over Von Lorfmon's death. He had taken the mummy into his stateroom, and anticipating an attack from the fanatical crew, had carefully barred and bolted door and portholes. The skipper, a reliable man, swore that it was virtually impossible to effect an entrance from without. And what signs were presented pointed to the fact that the locks had been worked from *within*. The scientist was killed by a dagger which formed part of his collection and which was left in his breast.

"As I have said, immediately afterward the African cauldron began to seethe. Schuyler said that in his opinion the natives considered the ancient prophecy fulfilled. The mummy was *the man from the sea*.

"Schuyler gave as his opinion that the thing was the work of Atlanteans and that the man in the mummy-case was a native of lost Atlantis.

"How the case came to float up through the fathoms of water which cover the forgotten land, he does not venture to offer a theory. He is sure that somewhere in the ghost-ridden mazes of the African jungles the mummy has been enthroned as a god, and, inspired by the dead thing, the black warriors are gathering for a wholesale massacre. He believes, also, that some crafty Moslem is the direct moving power of the threatened rebellion."

Gordon ceased speaking and looked up at me.

"Mummies seem to weave a weird dance through the warp of the tale," he said. "The German scientist took several pictures of the mummy with his camera, and it was after seeing these— which strangely enough were not stolen along with the thing—that Major Morley began to think himself on the brink of some monstrous discovery. His diary reflects his state of mind and becomes incoherent—his condition seems to have bordered on insanity. What did he learn to unbalance him so? Do you suppose that the mesmeric spells of Kathulos were used in some way against him?"

"These pictures—" I began.

"They fell into Schuyler's hands and he gave one to Morley. I found it among the manuscripts."

He handed the thing to me, watching me narrowly.

I stared, then rose unsteadily and poured myself a tumbler of wine.

"Not a dead idol in a voodoo hut," I said shakily, "but a monster animated by fearsome life, roaming the world for victims. Morley had seen the Master—that is why his brain crumbled. Gordon, as I hope to live again, that face is the face of Kathulos!"

Gordon stared wordlessly at me.

"The Master hand, Gordon!" I laughed. A certain grim enjoyment penetrated the mists of my horror, at the sight of the steel-nerved Englishman struck speechless, doubtless for the first time in his life.

He moistened his lips and said in a scarcely recognizable voice, "Then, in God's name, Costigan, nothing is stable or certain, and mankind hovers at the brink of untold abysses of nameless horror. If that dead monster found by Von Lorfmon is in truth the Scorpion, brought to life in some hideous fashion, what can mortal effort accomplish against him?"

"The mummy at Kamonos'—" I began, but he interrupted.

"Aye, the man whose flesh, hardened by a thousand years of nonexistence—that must have been Kathulos himself! He would have just had time to strip, wrap himself in the linens and step into the case before we entered. You remember that the case, leaning upright against the wall, stood partly concealed by a large Burmese idol, which obstructed our view and doubtless gave him time to accomplish his purpose. My God, Costigan, with what horror of the prehistoric world are we dealing?"

"I have heard of Hindoo fakirs who could induce a condition closely resembling death," I began. "Is it not possible that Kathulos, a shrewd and crafty Oriental, could have placed himself in this state and his followers have placed the case in the ocean where it was sure to be found? And might not he have been in this shape tonight at Kamonos'?"

Gordon shook his head.

"No. I have seen these fakirs. None of them ever feigned death to the extent of becoming shriveled and hard—in a word, dried up. Morley, narrating in another place the description of the mummy-case as jotted down by Von Lorfmon and passed on to Schuyler, mentions the fact that large portions of seaweed adhered to it—seaweed of a kind found only at great depths, on the bottom of the ocean. The wood, too, was of a kind which Von Lorfmon failed to recognize or classify, in spite of the fact that he was one of the greatest living authorities on flora. And his notes again and again emphasize the enormous *age* of the thing. He admitted that there was no way of telling how old the mummy was, but his hints intimate that he believed it to be not thousands of years old, but millions of years!

"No. We must face the facts. Since you are positive that the picture of the mummy is the picture of Kathulos—and there is little room for fraud—one of two things is practically certain. The Scorpion was never dead but ages ago was placed in that mummy-case and his life preserved in some manner, or else—he was dead and has been brought to life! Either of these theories, viewed in the cold light of reason, is absolutely untenable. Are we all insane?"

"Had you ever walked the road to hashish land," I said somberly, "you could believe anything to be true. Had you ever gazed into the terrible reptilian eyes of Kathulos the sorcerer, you would not doubt that he was both dead and alive."

Gordon gazed out the window, his fine face haggard in the gray light.

"At any rate," said he, "there are two places which I intend exploring thoroughly before the sun rises again—Kamonos' antique shop and Soho, Forty-eight."

Chapter Eighteen

THE GRIP OF THE SCORPION

*"While from a proud tower in the town
Death looks gigantically down."*

—Poe

Hansen snored on the bed as I paced the room. Another day had passed over London and again the street lamps glimmered through the fog. Their lights affected me strangely. They seemed to beat, solid waves of energy, against my brain. They twisted the fog into strange sinister shapes. Footlights of the stage that is the streets of London, how many grisly scenes had they lighted?

Gordon I had not seen since dawn. Following the clue of "Soho Forty-eight" he had gone forth to arrange a raid upon the place and he thought it best that I should remain under cover. He anticipated an attempt upon my life, and again he feared that if I went searching among the dives I formerly frequented it would arouse suspicion.

Hansen snored on. I seated myself and began to study the Turkish shoes which clothed my feet. Zuleika had worn Turkish slippers—how she floated through my waking dreams, gilding prosaic things with her witchery! Her face smiled at me from the fog; her phantom footfalls re-echoed through the misty chambers of my skull.

They beat an endless tattoo, luring and haunting till it seemed that these echoes found echoes, soft and stealthy, in the hallway outside the room where I stood. A sudden rap at the door, and I started.

Hansen slept on as I crossed the room and flung the door swiftly open. A swirling wisp of fog had invaded the corridor, and through it, like a silver veil, I saw her—Zuleika stood before me with her shimmering hair and her red lips parted and her great dark eyes.

Like a speechless fool I stood and she glanced quickly down the hallway and then stepped inside and closed the door.

"Gordon!" she whispered in a thrilling undertone. "Your friend! The Scorpion has him!"

Hansen had awakened and now sat gaping stupidly at the strange scene which met his eyes.

Zuleika did not heed him.

"And, oh, Stephen!" she cried, and tears shone in her eyes, "I have tried so hard to secure some more elixir, but I could not."

"Never mind that." I finally found my speech. "Tell me about Gordon."

"He went back to Kamonos' alone, and Hassim and Ganra Singh took him captive and brought him to the Master's house. Tonight assemble a great host of the people of the Scorpion for the sacrifice."

"Sacrifice!" A grisly thrill of horror coursed down my spine. Was there no limit to the ghastliness of this business?

"Quick, Zuleika, where is this house of the Master's?"

"Soho, Forty-eight. You must summon the police and send many men to surrounded it, but you must not go yourself—"

Hansen sprang up, quivering for action, but I turned to him. My brain was clear now, or seemed to be, and racing unnaturally.

"Wait!" I turned back to Zuleika. "When is this sacrifice to take place?"

"At the rising of the moon."

"That is only a few hours before dawn. Time to save him, but if we raid the house they'll kill him before we can reach them. And God only knows how many diabolical things guard all approaches."

"I do not know," Zuleika whimpered. "I must go now, or the Master will kill me."

Something gave way in my brain at that; something like a flood of wild and terrible exultation swept over me.

"The Master will kill no one!" I shouted, flinging my arms on high. "Before ever the east turns red for dawn, the Master dies! By all things holy and unholy I swear it!"

Hansen stared wildly at me, and Zuleika shrank back as I turned on her. To my dope-inspired brain had come a sudden burst of light, true and unerring.

I knew Kathulos was a mesmerist—that he understood fully the secret of dominating another's mind and soul. And I knew that at last I had hit upon the reason of his power over the girl. Mesmerism! As a snake fascinates and draws to him a bird, so the Master held Zuleika to him with unseen shackles. So absolute was his rule over her that it held even when she was out of his sight, working over great distances.

There was but one thing which would break that hold: the magnetic power of some other person whose control was stronger with her than Kathulos'. I laid my hands on her slim little shoulders and made her face me.

"Zuleika," I said commandingly, "here you are safe; you shall not return to Kathulos. There is no need of it. Now you are free."

But I knew I had failed before I ever started. Her eyes held a look of amazed, unreasoning fear and she twisted timidly in my grasp.

"Stephen, please let me go!" she begged. "I must—I must!"

I drew her over to the bed and asked Hansen for his handcuffs. He handed them to me wonderingly, and I fastened one cuff to the bedpost and the other to her slim wrist. The girl whimpered but made no resistance, her limpid eyes seeking mine in mute appeal.

It cut me to the quick to enforce my will upon her in this apparently brutal manner, but I steeled myself.

"Zuleika," I said tenderly, "you are now my prisoner. The Scorpion cannot blame you for not returning to him when you are unable to do so—and before dawn you shall be free of his rule entirely."

I turned to Hansen and spoke in a tone which admitted of no argument.

"Remain here, just without the door, until I return. On no account allow any strangers to enter—that is, anyone whom you do not personally know. And I charge you, on your honor as a man, do not release this girl, no matter what she may say. If neither I nor Gordon have returned by ten o'clock tomorrow, take her to this address—that family once were friends of mine and will take care of a homeless girl. I am going to Scotland Yard."

"Stephen," Zuleika wailed, "you are going to the Master's lair? You will be killed. Send the police, do not go!"

I bent, drew her into my arms, felt her lips against mine, then tore myself away.

The fog plucked at me with ghostly fingers, cold as the hands of dead men, as I raced down the street. I had no plan, but one was forming in my mind, beginning to seethe in the stimulated cauldron that was my brain. I halted at the sight of a policeman pacing his beat, and beckoning him to me, scribbled a terse note on a piece of paper torn from a notebook, and handed it to him.

"Get this to Scotland Yard; it's a matter of life and death and it has to do with the business of John Gordon."

At that name, a gloved hand came up in swill assent, but his assurance of haste died out behind me as I renewed my flight. The note stated briefly that Gordon was a prisoner at Soho Forty-eight and advised an immediate raid in force—advised, nay, in Gordon's name, commanded it.

My reason for my actions was simple; I knew that the first noise of the raid sealed John Gordon's doom. Somehow I first must reach him and protect or free him before the police arrived.

The time seemed endless, but at last the grim gaunt outlines of the house that was Soho Forty-eight rose up before me, a giant ghost in the fog. The hour grew late; few people dared the mists and the dampness as I came to a halt in the street before this forbidding building. No lights showed from the windows, either upstairs or down. It seemed deserted. But the lair of the scorpion often seems deserted until the silent death strikes suddenly.

Here I halted and a wild thought struck me. One way or another, the drama would be over by dawn. Tonight was the climax of my career, the ultimate top of life. Tonight I was the strongest link in the strange chain of events. Tomorrow it would not matter whether I lived or died. I drew the flask of elixir from my pocket and gazed at it. Enough for two more days if properly eked out. Two more days of life! Or—I needed stimulation as I never needed it before; the task in front of me was one no mere human could hope to accomplish.

If I drank the entire remainder of the elixir, I had no idea as to the duration of its effect, but it would last the night through. And my legs were shaky; my mind had curious periods of utter vacuity; weakness of brain and body assailed me. I raised the flask and with one draft drained it.

For an instant I thought it was death. Never had I taken such an amount.

Sky and world reeled, and I felt as if I would fly into a million vibrating fragments, like the bursting of a globe of brittle steel. Like fire, like hell-fire, the elixir raced along my veins and I was a giant! Monster! A superman!

Turning, I strode to the menacing, shadowy doorway. I had no plan; I felt the need of none. As a drunken man walks blithely into danger, I strode to the lair of the Scorpion, magnificently aware of my superiority, imperially confident of my stimulation and sure as the unchanging stars that the way would open before me.

Oh, there never was a superman like that who knocked commandingly on the door of Soho Forty-eight that night in the rain and the fog!

I knocked four times, the old signal that we slaves had used to be admitted into the idol room at Yun Shatu's. An aperture opened in the center of the door, and slanted eyes looked warily out. They slightly widened as the owner recognized me, then narrowed wickedly.

"You fool!" I said angrily. "Don't you see the mark?"

I held my hand to the aperture.

"Don't you recognize me? Let me in, curse you!"

I think the very boldness of the trick made for its success. Surely by now all the Scorpion's slaves knew of Stephen Costigan's rebellion, knew that he was marked for death. And the very fact that I came there, inviting doom, confused the doorman.

The door opened, and I entered. The man who had admitted me was a tall, lank Chinaman I had known as a servant at Kathulos'. He closed the door behind me, and I saw we stood in a sort of vestibule, lighted by a dim lamp whose glow could not be seen from the street for the reason that the windows were heavily curtained. The Chinaman glowered at me, undecided. I looked at him, tensed. Then suspicion flared in his eyes and his hand flew, to his sleeve. But at the instant I was on him and his lean neck broke like a rotten bough between my hands.

I eased his corpse to the thickly carpeted floor, and listened. No sound broke the silence. Stepping as stealthily as a wolf, fingers spread like talons, I stole into the next room. This was furnished in Oriental style, with couches and rugs and gold-worked drapery, but was empty of human life. I crossed it and went into the next one. Light flowed softly from the censers which were swung from the ceiling, and the Eastern rugs dead-ened the sound of my footfalls; I seemed to be moving through a castle of enchantment.

Every moment I expected a rush of silent assassins from the doorways or from behind the curtains or screen with their writhing dragons. Utter silence reigned. Room after room I explored, and at last halted at the foot of the stairs. The inevitable censer shed an uncertain light, but most of the stairs were veiled in shadows. What horrors awaited me above?

But fear and the elixir are strangers and I mounted that stair of lurking terror as boldly as I had entered that house of terror.

The upper rooms I found to be much like those below, and with them they had this fact in common: they were empty of human life. I sought an attic but there seemed no door letting into one. Returning to the first floor, I made a search for an entrance into the basement, but again my efforts were fruitless. The amazing truth was borne in upon me: except for myself and that dead man who lay sprawled so grotesquely in the outer vestibule, there were no men in that house, dead or living.

I could not understand it. Had the house been bare of furniture I should have reached the natural conclusion that Kathulos had fled—but no signs of flight met my eye. This was unnatural, uncanny. I stood in the great shadowy library and pondered. No. I had made no mistake in the house.

Even if the broken corpse in the vestibule were not there to furnish mute testimony, everything in the room pointed toward the presence of the Master. There were the artificial palms, the lacquered screen, the tapestries, even the idol, though now no incense smoke rose before it. About the walls were ranged long shelves of books, bound in strange and costly fashion—books in every language in the world, I found from a swift examination, and on every subject—outré and bizarre, most of them.

Remembering the secret passage in the Temple of Dreams, I investigated the heavy mahogany table which stood in the center of the room. But nothing resulted. A sudden blaze of fury surged up in me, primitive and unreasoning. I snatched a statuette from the table and dashed it against the shelf-covered wall. The noise of its breaking would surely bring the gang from their hiding-place. But the result was much more startling than that!

The statuette struck the edge of a shelf and instantly the whole section of shelves with their load of books swung silently outward, revealing a narrow doorway! As in the other secret door, a row of steps led downward. At another time I would have shuddered at the thought of descending, with the horrors of the other tunnel fresh in my mind, but inflamed as I was by the elixir, I strode forward without an instant's hesitancy.

Since there was no one in the house, they must be somewhere in the tunnel or in whatever lair to which the tunnel led. I stepped through the doorway, leaving the door open. The police might find it that way and follow me, though somehow I felt as if mine would be a lone hand from the start to grim finish.

I went down a considerable distance and then the stair debouched into a level corridor some twenty feet wide—a remarkable thing. In spite of the width, the ceiling was rather low and from it hung small, curiously shaped, lamps which flung a dim light. I stalked hurriedly along the corridor like old Death seeking victims, and as I went I noted the work of the thing. The floor was of great broad flags and the walls seemed to be of huge blocks of evenly set stone. This passage was clearly no work of modern days; the slaves of Kathulos never tunneled there. Some secret way of mediaeval times, I thought— and after all, who knows what catacombs lie below London, whose secrets are greater and darker than those of Babylon and Rome?

On and on I went, and now I knew that I must be far below the earth. The air was dank and heavy, and cold moisture dripped from the stones of walls and ceiling. From time to time I saw smaller passages leading away in the darkness, but I determined to keep to the larger main one.

A ferocious impatience gripped me. I seemed to have been walking for hours, and still only dank damp walls and bare flags and guttering lamps met my eyes. I kept a close watch for sinister-appearing chests or the like—saw no such things.

Then as I was about to burst into savage curses, another stair loomed up in the shadows in front of me.

Chapter Nineteen

DARK FURY

"The ringed wolf glared the circle round
Through baleful, blue-lit eye,
Not unforgetful of his debt.
Quoth he, 'I'll do some damage yet
Or ere my turn to die.'"

—Mundy

Like a lean wolf, I glided up the stairs. Some twenty feet up there
was a sort of landing from which other corridors diverged, much
like the lower one by which I had come. The thought came to
me that the earth below London must be honeycombed with
such secret passages, one above the other. Some feet above this
landing the steps halted at a door, and here I hesitated, uncertain
as to whether I should chance knocking or not. Even as I meditated, the door began to open. I shrank back against the wall,
flattening myself out as much as possible. The door swung wide
and a Moor came through. Only a glimpse I had of the room
beyond, out of the corner of my eye, but my unnaturally alert
senses registered the fact that the room was empty.

And on the instant, before he could turn, I smote the Moor
a single deathly blow behind the angle of the jawbone, and he
toppled headlong down the stairs, to lie in a crumpled heap on
the landing, his limbs tossed grotesquely about.

My left hand caught the door as it started to slam shut, and
in an instant I was through and standing in the room beyond.
As I had thought, there was no occupant of this room. I crossed
it swiftly and entered the next. These rooms were furnished in
a manner before which the furnishings of the Soho house paled
into insignificance.

Barbaric, terrible, unholy—these words alone convey some slight idea of the ghastly sights which met my eyes. Skulls, bones and complete skeletons formed much of the decorations, if such they were. Mummies leered from their cases and mounted reptiles ranged the walls. Between these sinister relics hung African shields of hide and bamboo, crossed with assagais and war daggers. Here and there reared obscene idols, black and horrible.

And in between and scattered about among these evidences of savagery and barbarism were vases, screens, rugs and hangings of the highest Oriental workmanship; a strange and incongruous effect.

I had passed through two of these rooms without seeing a human being, when I came to stairs leading upward. Up these I went, several flights, until I came to a door in a ceiling. I wondered if I were still under the earth. Surely the first stairs had led into a house of some sort. I raised the door cautiously. Starlight met my eyes, and I drew myself warily up and out. There I halted. A broad flat roof stretched away on all sides, and beyond its rim on all sides glimmered the lights of London. Just what building I was on, I had no idea, but that it was a tall one, I could tell, for I seemed to be above most of the lights I saw. Then I saw that I was not alone.

Over against the shadows of the ledge that ran around the roof's edge, a great menacing form bulked in starlight. A pair of eyes glinted at me with a light not wholly sane; the star-light glanced silver from a curving length of steel. Yar Khan, the Afghan killer, fronted me in the silent shadows.

A fierce wild exultation surged over me. Now I could begin to pay the debt I owed Kathulos and all his hellish band! The dope fired my veins and sent waves of inhuman power and dark fury through me. A spring, and I was on my feet in a silent, deathly rush.

Yar Khan was a giant, taller and bulkier than I. He held a tulwar, and from the instant I saw him, I knew that he was full of the dope to the use of which he was addicted—heroin.

As I came in, he swung his heavy weapon high in air, but before he could strike I seized his sword wrist in an iron grip, and with my free hand drove smashing blows into his midriff.

Of that hideous battle, fought in silence above the sleeping city with only the stars to see, I remember little. I remember tumbling back and forth, locked in a death embrace. I remember the stiff beard rasping my flesh as his dope-fired eyes gazed wildly into mine. I remember the taste of hot blood in my mouth, the tang of fearful exultation in my soul, the onrushing and upsurging of inhuman strength and fury.

God, what a sight for a human eye, had anyone looked upon that grim roof where two human leopards, dope maniacs, tore each other to pieces!

I remember his arm breaking like rotten wood in my grip, and the tulwar falling from his useless hand. Handicapped as he was by a broken arm, the end was inevitable, and with one wild uproaring flood of might, I rushed him to the edge of the roof and bent him backward far out over the ledge. An instant, we struggled there; then I tore loose his hold and hurled him over, and one single shriek came up as he hurtled into the darkness below.

I stood upright, arms hurled up toward the stars, a terrible statue of primordial triumph. And down my breast trickled streams of blood from the long wounds left by the Afghan's frantic nails, on neck and face.

Then I turned with the craft of the maniac. Had no one heard the sound of that battle? My eyes were on the door through which I had come, but a noise made me turn; and for the first time I noticed a small affair like a tower jutting up from the roof. There was no window there, but there was a door, and even as I looked that door opened and a huge black form framed itself in the light that streamed from within. Hassim!

He stepped out on the roof and closed the door, his shoulders hunched and neck outthrust as he glanced this way and that. I struck him senseless to the roof with one hate-driven smash. I crouched over him, waiting some sign of returning consciousness. Then, away in the sky, close to the horizon, I saw a faint red tint. The rising of the moon!

Where in God's name was Gordon? Even as I stood undecided, a strange noise reached me. It was curiously like the droning of many bees.

Striding in the direction from which it seemed to come, I crossed the roof and leaned over the ledge. A sight nightmarish and incredible met my eyes.

Some twenty feet below the level of the roof on which I stood, there was another roof, of the same size and clearly a part of the same building. On one side it was bounded by the wall; on the other three sides a parapet several feet high took the place of a ledge.

A great throng of people stood, sat and squatted, close-packed on the roof—and without exception they were *Negroes*! There were hundreds of them, and it was their low-voiced conversation which I had heard. But what held my gaze was that upon which their eyes were fixed.

About the center of the roof rose a sort of teocalli some ten feet high, almost exactly like those found in Mexico and on which the priests of the Aztecs sacrificed human victims. This, allowing for its infinitely smaller scale, was an exact type of those sacrificial pyramids. On the flat top of it was a curiously carved altar, and beside it stood a lank, dusky form whom even the ghastly mask he wore could not disguise to my gaze—Santiago, the Haiti voodoo fetish man. On the altar lay John Gordon, stripped to the waist and bound hand and foot, but conscious.

I reeled back from the roof edge, rent in twain by indecision. Even the stimulus of the elixir was not equal to this. Then a sound brought me about to see Hassim struggling dizzily to his knees. I reached him with two long strides, and ruthlessly smashed him down again. Then I noticed a queer sort of contrivance dangling from his girdle. I bent and examined it. It was a mask similar to that worn by Santiago. Then my mind leaped,

swift and sudden, to a wild desperate plan, which to my dope-
ridden brain seemed not at all wild or desperate.

I stepped softly to the tower and, opening the door, peered
inward. I saw no one who might need to be silenced, but I saw
a long silken robe hanging upon a peg in the wall. The luck of
the dope fiend! I snatched it and closed the door again. Hassim
showed no signs of consciousness, but I gave him another smash
on the chin to make sure and, seizing his mask, hurried to the
ledge.

A low guttural chant floated up to me, jangling, barbaric, with
an undertone of maniacal blood-lust. The Negroes, men and
women, were swaying back and forth to the wild rhythm of their
death chant. On the teocalli, Santiago stood like a statue of black
basalt, facing the east, dagger held high—a wild and terrible sight,
naked as he was save for a wide silken girdle and that inhuman
mask on his face. The moon thrust a red rim above the eastern
horizon and a faint breeze stirred the great black plumes which
nodded above the voodoo man's mask. The chant of the worshippers dropped to a low, sinister whisper.

I hurriedly slipped on the death mask, gathered the robe close
about me and prepared for the descent. I was prepared to drop
the full distance, being sure in the superb confidence of my
insanity that I would land unhurt, but as I climbed over the ledge
I found a steel ladder leading down. Evidently Hassim, one of
the voodoo priests, intended descending this way. So down I
went, and in haste, for I knew that the instant the moon's lower
rim cleared the city's skyline, that motionless dagger would
descend into Gordon's breast.

Gathering the robe close about me so as to conceal my white
skin, I stepped down upon the roof, and strode forward through
rows of black worshippers who shrank aside to let me through.
To the foot of the teocalli I stalked and up the stairs that ran
about it, until I stood beside the death altar and marked the dark
red stains upon it. Gordon lay on his back, his eyes open, his
face drawn and haggard, but his gaze dauntless and unflinching.

Santiago's eyes blazed at me through the slits of his mask, but I read no suspicion in his gaze until I reached forward and took the dagger from his hand. He was too much astonished to resist, and the black throng fell suddenly silent. That he saw my hand was not that of a Negro it is certain, but he was simply struck speechless with astonishment. Moving swiftly I cut Gordon's bonds and hauled him erect. Then Santiago, with a shriek, leaped upon me—shrieked again and, arms flung high, pitched headlong from the teocalli, with his own dagger burred to the hilt in his breast.

Then the black worshippers were on us with a screech and a roar—leaping on the steps of the teocalli like black leopards in the moonlight, knives flashing, eyes gleaming whitely.

I tore mask and robe from me and answered Gordon's exclamation with a wild laugh. I had hoped that by virtue of my disguise I might get us both safely away, but now I was content to die there at his side.

He tore a great metal ornament from the altar, and as the attackers came he wielded this. A moment, we held them at bay, and then they flowed over us like a black wave. This to me was Valhalla! Knives stung me, and blackjacks smashed against me, but I laughed and drove my iron fists in straight, steam-hammer smashes that shattered flesh and bone. I saw Gordon's crude weapon rise and fall, and each time a man went down. Skulls shattered and blood splashed and the dark fury swept over me. Nightmare faces swirled about me, and I was on my knees; up again, and the faces crumpled before my blows. Through far mists, I seemed to hear a hideous familiar voice raised in imperious command. Gordon was swept away from me, but from the sounds I knew that the work of death still went on. The stars reeled through fogs of blood, but hell's exaltation was on me, and I reveled in the dark tides of fury, until a darker deeper tide swept over me and I knew no more.

Chapter Twenty

ANCIENT HORROR

"Here now in his triumph where all things falter
Stretched out on the spoils that his own hand spread,
As a God self-slain on his own strange altar,
Death lies dead."

—Swinburne

Slowly, I drifted back into life—slowly, slowly. A mist held me, and in the mist I saw a Skull—

I lay in a steel cage like a captive wolf, and the bars were too strong, I saw, even for my strength. The cage seemed to be set in a sort of niche in the wall, and I was looking into a large room. This room was under the earth; for the floor was of stone flags and the walls and ceiling were composed of gigantic blocks of the same material. Shelves ranged the walls, covered with weird appliances, apparently of a scientific nature, and more were on the great table that stood in the center of the room. Beside this sat Kathulos.

The Sorcerer was clad in a snaky yellow robe, and those hideous hands and that terrible head were more pronouncedly reptilian than ever. He turned his great yellow eyes toward me, like pools of livid fire, and his parchment-thin lips moved in what probably, passed for a smile.

I staggered erect and gripped the bars, cursing.

"Gordon, curse you, where is Gordon?"

Kathulos took a test-tube from the table, eyed it closely and emptied it into another.

"Ah, my friend awakes," he murmured in his voice—the voice of a living dead man.

He thrust his hands into his long sleeves and turned fully to me.

"I think in you," he said distinctly, "I have created a Frankenstein monster. I made of you a superhuman creature to serve my wishes and you broke from me. You are the bane of my might, worse than Gordon, even. You have killed valuable servants and interfered with my plans. However, your evil comes to an end tonight. Your friend Gordon broke away but he is being hunted through the tunnels and cannot escape.

"You," he continued with the sincere interest of the scientist, "are a most interesting subject. Your brain must be formed differently from any other man that ever lived. I will make a close study of it and add it to my laboratory. How a man with apparent need of the elixir in his system, has managed to go on for two days still stimulated by the last draft, is more than I can understand."

My heart leaped. With all his wisdom, little Zuleika had tricked him, and he evidently did not know that she had filched a flask of the life-giving stuff from him.

"The last draft you had from me," he went on, "was sufficient only for some eight hours. I repeat, it has me puzzled. Can you offer any suggestion?"

I snarled wordlessly. He sighed.

"As always the barbarian. Truly the proverb speaks: 'Jest with the wounded tiger and warm the adder in your bosom before you seek to lift the savage from his savagery!'"

He meditated awhile in silence. I watched him uneasily. There was about him a vague and curious indifference—his long fingers emerging from the sleeves drummed on the chair arms, and some hidden exultation strummed at the back of his voice, lending it unaccustomed vibrancy.

"And you might have been king of the new regime," he said suddenly. "Aye, the new—new and inhumanly old!"

He bent his head as if listening. From far off seemed to come a hum of guttural voices. His lips writhed in a smile.

"My black children," he murmured. "They tear my enemy Gordon to pieces in the tunnels. They, Mr. Costigan, are my real henchmen, and it was for their edification tonight that I laid John Gordon on the sacrificial stone. I would have preferred to have made some experiments with him, based on certain scientific theories, but my children must be humored. Later, under my tutelage, they will outgrow their childish superstitions and throw aside their foolish customs, but now they must be led gently by the hand.

"How do you like these under-the-earth corridors, Mr. Costigan?" he switched suddenly. "You thought of them—what? No doubt that the white savages of your Middle Ages built them? Faugh? These tunnels are older than your world! They were brought into being by mighty kings, too many eons ago for your mind to grasp, when an imperial city towered where now this crude village of London stands. All trace of that metropolis has crumbled to dust and vanished but these corridors were built by more than human skill—ha! ha! Of all the teeming thousands who move daily above them, none knows of their existence save my servants—and not all of them. Zuleika, for instance, does not know of them, for of late I have begun to doubt her loyalty and shall doubtless soon make of her an example."

At that I hurled myself blindly against the side of the cage, a red wave of hate and fury tossing me in its grip. I seized the bars and strained until the veins stood out on my forehead and the muscles bulged and crackled in my arms and shoulders. And the bars bent before my onslaught—a little but no more, and finally the power flowed from my limbs and I sank down trembling and weakened.

"The bars hold," he announced with something almost like relief in his tone. "Frankly, I prefer to be on the opposite side of them. You are a human ape if there was ever one."

He laughed suddenly and wildly.

"But why do you seek to oppose me?" he shrieked unexpectedly. "Why defy me, who am Kathulos, the Sorcerer, great even in the days of the old empire? Today, invincible! A magician, a scientist, among ignorant savages! Ha, ha!"

I shuddered, and sudden blinding light broke in on me. Kathulos himself was an addict, and was fired by the stuff of his choice! What hellish concoction was strong enough, terrible enough to thrill the Master and inflame him, I do not know, nor do I wish to know. Of all the uncanny knowledge that was his, I, knowing the man as I did, count this the most weird and grisly.

"You, you paltry fool!" he was ranting, his face lit supernaturally. "Know you who I am? Kathulos of Egypt! Bah! They knew me in the old days! I reigned in the dim misty sea lands ages and ages before the sea rose and engulfed the land. I died, not as men die; the magic draft of life everlasting was ours! I drank deep and slept. Long I slept in my lacquered case! My flesh withered and grew hard: my blood dried in my veins. I became as one dead. But still within me burned the spirit of life, sleeping but anticipating the awakening. The great cities crumbled to dust. The sea drank the land. The tall shrines and the lofty spires sank beneath the green waves. All this I knew as I slept, as a man knows in dreams. Kathulos of Egypt? Faugh! *Kathulos of Atlantis*!"

I uttered a sudden involuntary cry. This was too grisly for sanity.

"Aye, the magician, the Sorcerer.

"And down the long years of savagery, through which the barbaric races struggled to rise without their masters, the legend came of the day of empire, when one of the Old Race would rise up from the sea. Aye, and lead to victory the black people who are our slaves in the old days.

"These brown and yellow people, what care I for them? The blacks were the slaves of my race, and I am their god today. They will obey me. The yellow and the brown people are fools—I make them my tools and the day will come when my black warriors will turn on them and slay at my word. And you, you white barbarians, whose ape-ancestors forever defied my race and me, your doom is at hand! And when I mount my universal throne, the only whites shall be white slaves!

"The day came as prophesied, when my case, breaking free from the halls where it lay—where it had lain when Atlantis was still sovran of the world—where since her empery it had sunk into the green fathoms—when my case, I say, was smitten by the deep sea tides and moved and stirred, and thrust aside the clinging seaweed that masks temples and minarets, and came floating up past the lofty sapphire and golden spires, up through the green waters, to float upon the lazy waves of the sea.

"Then came a white fool carrying out the destiny of which he was not aware. The men on his ship, true believers, knew that the time had come. And I—the air entered my nostrils and I awoke from the long, long sleep.

"I stirred and I moved and lived. And rising in the night, I slew the fool that had lifted me from the ocean, and my servants made obeisance to me and took me into Africa, where I abode awhile and learned new languages and new ways of a new world, and became strong.

"The wisdom of your dreary world—ha ha! I who delved deeper in the mysteries of the old than any man dared go! All that men know today, I know, and the knowledge beside that which I have brought down the centuries is as a grain of sand beside a mountain! You should know something of that knowledge! By it I lifted you from one hell to plunge you into a greater! You fool, here at my hand is that which would lift you from this! Aye, would strike from you the chains whereby I have bound you!"

He snatched up a golden vial and shook it before my gaze. I eyed it as men dying in the desert must eye the distant mirages. Kathulos fingered it meditatively. His unnatural excitement seemed to have passed suddenly, and when he spoke again it was in the passionless, measured tones of the scientist.

"That would indeed be an experiment worth while—to free you of the elixir habit and see if your dope-riddled body would sustain life. Nine times out of ten the victim, with the need and stimulus removed, would die—but you are such a giant of a brute—"

He sighed and set the vial down.

"The dreamer opposes the man of destiny. My time is not my own or I should choose to spend my life in my laboratories, carrying out my experiments. But now, as in the days of the old empire when kings sought my counsel, I must work and labor for the good of the race at large. Aye, I must toil and sow the seed of glory against the full coming of the imperial days when the seas give up all their living dead."

I shuddered. Kathulos laughed wildly again. His fingers began to drum his chair arms and his face gleamed with the unnatural light once more. The red visions had begun to seethe in his skull again.

"Under the green seas they lie, the ancient masters, in their lacquered cases, dead as men reckon death, but only sleeping. Sleeping through the long ages as hours, awaiting the day of awakening! The old masters, the wise men, who foresaw the day when the sea would gulp the land, and who made ready. Made ready that they might rise again in the barbaric days to come. As did I. Sleeping they lie, ancient kings and grim wizards, who died as men die, before Atlantis sank. Who, sleeping, sank with her but who shall rise again!

"Mine the glory! I rose first. And I sought out the site of old cities, on shores that did not sink. Vanished, long vanished. The barbarian tide swept over them thousands of years ago as the green waters swept over their elder sister of the deeps. On some, the deserts stretch bare. Over some, as here, young barbarian cities rise."

He halted suddenly. His eyes sought one of the dark openings that marked a corridor. I think his strange intuition warned him of some impending danger but I do not believe that he had any inkling of how dramatically our scene would be interrupted.

As he looked, swift footsteps sounded and a man appeared suddenly in the doorway—a man disheveled, tattered and bloody. *John Gordon*! Kathulos sprang erect with a cry, and

Gordon, gasping as from superhuman exertion, brought down the revolver he held in his hand and fired point-blank. Kathulos staggered, clapping his hand to his breast, and then, groping wildly, reeled to the wall and fell against it. A doorway opened and he reeled through, but as Gordon leaped fiercely across the chamber, a blank stone surface met his gaze, which yielded not to his savage hammerings.

He whirled and ran drunkenly to the table where lay a bunch of keys the Master had dropped there.

"The vial!" I shrieked. "Take the vial!" And he thrust it into his pocket.

Back along the corridor through which he had come sounded a faint clamor, growing swiftly like a wolf-pack in full cry. A few precious seconds spent with fumbling for the right key, then the cage door swung open and I sprang out. A sight for the gods we were, the two of us! Slashed, bruised and cut, our garments hanging in tatters—my wounds had ceased to bleed, but now as I moved they began again, and from the stiffness of my hands I knew that my knuckles were shattered. As for Gordon, he was fairly drenched in blood from crown to foot.

We made off down a passage in the opposite direction from the menacing noise, which I knew to be the black servants of the Master in full pursuit of us. Neither of us was in good shape for running, but we did our best. Where we were going I had no idea. My superhuman strength had deserted me, and I was going on will power alone. We switched off into another corridor, and we had not gone twenty steps when, looking back, I saw the first of the black devils rounding the corner.

A desperate effort increased our lead a trifle, but they had seen us, were in full view now, and a yell of fury broke from them, to be succeeded by a more sinister silence as they bent all efforts to overhauling us.

There, a short distance in front of us, we saw a stair loom suddenly in the gloom. If we might reach that—but we saw something else.

Against the ceiling, between us and the stairs, hung a huge thing like an iron grill, with great spikes along the bottom—a portcullis.

And even as we looked, without halting in our panting strides, it began to move.

"They're lowering the portcullis!" Gordon croaked, his blood-streaked face a mask of exhaustion and will.

Now the blacks were only ten feet behind us—now the huge grate, gaining momentum, with a creak of rusty, unused mechanism, rushed downward. A final spurt, a gasping straining nightmare of pure nerve-strength, hurled us under and through, and the grate crashed behind us!

A moment we lay gasping, not heeding the frenzied horde who raved and screamed on the other side of the grate. So close had that final leap been, that the great spikes in their descent had torn shreds from our clothing.

The blacks were thrusting at us with daggers through the bars, but we were out of reach and it seemed to me that I was content to lie there and die of exhaustion. But Gordon weaved unsteadily erect and hauled me with him.

"Got to get out," he croaked; "got to warn—Scotland Yard—honeycombs in heart of London—high explosives—arms —ammunition."

We blundered up the steps, and in front of us I seemed to hear a sound of metal grating against metal. The stairs ended abruptly, on a landing that terminated in a blank wall. Gordon hammered against this and the inevitable secret doorway opened. Light streamed in, through the bars of a sort of grille. Men in the uniform of London police were sawing at these with hacksaws, and even as they greeted us, an opening was made through which we crawled.

"You're hurt, sir!" One of the men took Gordon's arm.

My companion shook him off.

"There's no time to lose! Out of here, as quick as we can go!"

I saw that we were in a basement of some sort. We hastened

up the steps and out into the early dawn which was turning the east scarlet. Over the tops of smaller houses I saw in the distance a great gaunt building on the roof of which, I felt instinctively, that wild drama had been enacted the night before.

"That building was leased some months ago by a mysterious Chinaman," said Gordon, following my gaze. "Office building originally—the neighborhood deteriorated and the building stood vacant for some time. The new tenant added several stories to it but left it apparently empty. Had my eye on it for some time."

This was told in Gordon's jerky swift manner as we started hurriedly along the sidewalk. I listened mechanically, like a man in a trance. My vitality was ebbing fast, and I knew that I was going to crumple at any moment.

"The people living in the vicinity had been reporting strange sights and noises. The man who owned the basement we just left heard queer sounds emanating from the wall of the basement, and called the police. About that time I was racing back and forth among those cursed corridors like a hunted rat, and I heard the police banging on the wall.

"I found the secret door and opened it, but found it barred by a grating. It was while I was telling the astounded policemen to procure a hacksaw that the pursuing Negroes, whom I had eluded for the moment, came in sight, and I was forced to shut the door and run for it again. By pure luck I found you and by pure luck managed to find the way back to the door.

"Now we must get to Scotland Yard. If we strike swiftly, we may capture the entire band of devils. Whether I killed Kathulos or not I do not know, or if he can be killed by mortal weapons. But to the best of my knowledge all of them are now in those subterranean corridors and—"

At that moment the world shook! A brain-shattering roar seemed to break the sky with its incredible detonation; houses tottered and crashed to ruins; a mighty pillar of smoke and flame burst from the earth, and on its wings great masses of débris soared skyward. A black fog of smoke and dust and falling timbers enveloped the world, a prolonged thunder seemed to rumble up from the center of the earth as of walls and ceilings falling, and amid the uproar and the screaming I sank down and knew no more.

Chapter Twenty-one

THE BREAKING OF THE CHAIN

"And like a soul belated,
In heaven and hell unmated,
By cloud and mist abated,
Comes out of darkness morn."

—Swinburne

There is little need to linger on the scenes of horror of that terrible London morning. The world is familiar with and knows most of the details attendant to the great explosion which wiped out a tenth of that great city with a resultant loss of lives and property. For such a happening some reason must needs be given; the tale of the deserted building got out, and many wild stories were circulated.

Finally, to still the rumors, the report was unofficially given out that this building had been the rendezvous and secret stronghold of a gang of international anarchists, who had stored its basement full of high explosives and who had supposedly ignited these accidentally. In a way there was a good deal to this tale, as you know, but the threat that had lurked there far transcended that one.

All this was told to me, for when I sank unconscious, Gordon, attributing my condition to exhaustion and a need of the hashish to the use of which he thought I was addicted, lifted me, and with the aid of the stunned policeman, got me to his rooms before returning to the scene of the explosion. At his rooms he found Hansen, and Zuleika handcuffed to the bed as I had left her. He released her and left her to tend to me, for all London was in a terrible turmoil, and he was needed elsewhere.

When I came to myself at last, I looked up into her starry eyes and lay quiet, smiling up at her. She sank down upon my bosom, nestling my head in her arms and covering my face with her kisses.

"Stephen!" she sobbed over and over, as her tears splashed hot on my face.

I was scarcely strong enough to put my arms about her, but I managed it. And we lay there for a space, in silence except for the girl's hard, racking sobs.

"Zuleika, I love you," I murmured.

"And I love you, Stephen," she sobbed. "Oh, it is so hard to part now—but I'm going with you, Stephen; I can't live without you!"

"My dear child," said John Gordon, entering the room suddenly, "Costigan's not going to die. We will let him have enough hashish to tide him along, and when he is stronger we will take him off the habit slowly."

"You don't understand, sahib; it is not hashish Stephen must have. It is something which only the Master knew, and now that he is dead or is fled, Stephen cannot get it and must die."

Gordon shot a quick, uncertain glance at me. His fine face was drawn and haggard, his clothes sooty and torn from his work among the débris of the explosion.

"She's right, Gordon," I said languidly. "I'm dying. Kathulos killed the hashish-craving with a concoction he called the elixir. I've been keeping myself alive on some of the stuff that Zuleika stole from him and gave me, but I drank it all last night."

I was aware of no craving of any kind, no physical or mental discomfort, even. All my mechanism was slowing down fast; I had passed the stage where the need of the elixir would tear and rend me. I felt only a great lassitude and a desire to sleep. And I knew that the moment I closed my eyes, I would die.

"A strange dope, that elixir," I said with growing languor. "It burns and freezes, and then at last the craving kills easily and without torment."

"Costigan, curse it," said Gordon desperately, "you can't go like this! That vial I took from the Egyptian's table—what is in it?"

"The Master swore it would free me of my curse and probably kill me also," I muttered. "I'd forgotten about it. Let me have it; it can no more than kill me, and I'm dying now."

"Yes, quick, let me have it!" exclaimed Zuleika fiercely, springing to Gordon's side, her hands passionately, outstretched. She returned with the vial which he had taken from his pocket, and knelt beside me, holding it to my lips, while she murmured to me gently and soothingly in her own language.

I drank, draining the vial, but feeling little interest in the whole matter. My outlook was purely impersonal, at such a low ebb was my life, and I cannot even remember how the stuff tasted. I only remember feeling a curious sluggish fire burn faintly along my veins, and the last thing I saw was Zuleika crouching over me, her great eyes fixed with a burning intensity on me. Her tense little hand rested inside her blouse, and remembering her vow to take her own life if I died, I tried to lift a hand and disarm her, tried to tell Gordon to take away the dagger she had hidden in her garments. But speech and action failed me and I drifted away into a curious sea of unconsciousness.

Of that period I remember nothing. No sensation fired my sleeping brain to such an extent as to bridge the gulf over which I drifted. They say I lay like a dead man for hours, scarcely breathing, while Zuleika hovered over me, never leaving my side an instant, and fighting like a tigress when anyone tried to coax her away to rest. Her chain was broken.

As I had carried the vision of her into that dim land of nothingness, so her dear eyes were the first thing which greeted my returning consciousness. I was aware of a greater weakness than I thought possible for a man to feel, as if I had been an invalid for months, but the life in me, faint though it was, was sound and normal, caused by no artificial stimulation. I smiled up at my girl, and murmured weakly:

"Throw away your dagger, little Zuleika: I'm going to live."

She screamed and fell on her knees beside me, weeping and laughing at the same time. Women are strange beings, of mixed and powerful emotions, truly.

Gordon entered and grasped the hand which I could not lift from the bed.

"You're a case for an ordinary human physician now, Costigan," he said. "Even a layman like myself can tell that. For the first time, since I've known you, the look in your eyes is entirely sane. You look like a man who has had a complete nervous breakdown, and needs about a year of rest and quiet. Great heavens, man, you've been through enough, outside your dope experience, to last you a lifetime."

"Tell me first," said I, "was Kathulos killed in the explosion?"

"I don't know," answered Gordon somberly. "Apparently the entire system of subterranean passages was destroyed. I know my last bullet—the last bullet that was in the revolver which I wrested from one of my attackers—found its mark in the Master's body, but whether he died from the wound, or whether a bullet can hurt him, I do not know. And whether in his death agonies he ignited the tons and tons of high explosives which were stored in the corridors, or whether the Negroes did it unintentionally, we shall never know.

"My God, Costigan, did you ever see such a honeycomb? And we know not how many miles in either direction the passages reached. Even now Scotland Yard men are combing the subways and basements of the town for secret openings. All known openings, such as the one through which we came and the one in Soho, Forty-eight, were blocked by falling walls. The office building was simply blown to atoms."

"What about the men who raided Soho, Forty-eight?"

"The door in the library wall had been closed. They found the Chinaman you killed, but searched the house without avail.

Lucky for them, too, else they had doubtless been in the tunnels when the explosion came, and perished with the hundreds of Negroes who must have died there."

"Every Negro in London must have been there."

"I daresay. Most of them are voodoo worshippers at heart, and the power the Master wielded was incredible."

My tale draws to a close. The months that followed passed uneventfully, except for the growing happiness which to me was paradise, but which would bore you were I to relate it. But one day Gordon and I again discussed the mysterious happenings that had had their being under the grim hand of the Master.

"Since that day," said Gordon, "the world has been quiet. Africa has subsided and the East seems to have returned to her ancient sleep. There can be but one answer—living or dead, Kathulos was destroyed that morning when his world crashed all about him."

"Gordon," said I, "what is the answer to that greatest of all mysteries?"

My friend shrugged his shoulders.

"I have come to believe that mankind eternally hovers on the brinks of secret oceans of which it knows nothing. Races have lived and vanished before our race rose out of the slime of the primitive, and it is likely still others will live upon the earth after ours has vanished. Scientists have long upheld the theory that the Atlanteans possessed a higher civilization than our own and on very different lines. Certainly Kathulos himself was proof that our boasted culture and knowledge were nothing beside that of whatever fearful civilization produced him."

"I have him to thank for two things," I said slowly: "the regaining of my lost manhood—and Zuleika. Kathulos, then, is dead, as far as any mortal thing can die. But what of those others—those 'ancient masters' who still sleep in the sea?"

Gordon shuddered.

"As I said, perhaps mankind loiters on the brink of unthinkable chasms of horror. But a fleet of gunboats is even now patrolling the oceans unobtrusively, with orders to destroy instantly any strange case that may be found."

"At night I dream of them, sometimes," I muttered, "sleeping in their lacquered cases, which drip with strange seaweed, far down among the green surges—where unholy spires and strange towers rise in the dark ocean."

"We have been face to face with an ancient horror," said Gordon somberly, "with a fear too dark and mysterious for the human brain to cope with. Fortune has been with us; she may not again favor the sons of men. It is best that we be ever on our guard. The universe was not made for humanity alone; life takes strange phases and it is the first instinct of nature for the different species to destroy each other. No doubt we seemed as horrible to the Master as he did to us. We have scarcely tapped the chest of secrets which nature has stored, and I shudder to think of what that chest may hold for the human race."

"That's true," said I, inwardly rejoicing at the vigor which was beginning to course through my wasted veins, "but men will meet obstacles as they come, as men have always risen to meet them. Now, I am beginning to know the full worth of life and love, and not all the devils from all the abysses can hold me."

Gordon smiled.

"You have it coming to you, old comrade. The best thing is to forget all about that dark interlude, for in that course lies light and happiness."

THE THING ON THE ROOF

They lumber through the night
With their elephantine tread;
I shudder in affright
As I cower in my bed.
They lift colossal wings
On the high gable roofs
Which tremble to the trample
Of their mastodonic hoofs.

—Justin Geoffrey: Out of the Old Land

Let me begin by saying that I was surprised when Tussmann called on me. We had never been close friends; the man's mercenary instincts repelled me; and since our bitter controversy of three years before, when he attempted to discredit my *Evidences of Nahua Culture in Yucatan*, which was the result of years of careful research, our relations had been anything but cordial. However, I received him and found his manner hasty and abrupt, but rather abstracted, as if his dislike for me had been thrust aside in some driving passion that had hold of him.

His errand was quickly stated. He wished my aid in obtaining a volume in the first edition of Von Junzt's *Nameless Cults*—the edition known as the Black Book, not from its color, but because of its dark contents. He might almost as well have asked me for the original Greek translation of the *Necronomicon*. Though since my return from Yucatan I had devoted practically all my time to my avocation of book collecting, I had not stumbled onto any hint that the book in the Dusseldorf edition was still in existence.

A word as to this rare work. Its extreme ambiguity in spots, coupled with its incredible subject matter, has caused it long to be regarded as the ravings of a maniac and the author was damned with the brand of insanity. But the fact remains that much of his assertions are unanswerable, and that he spent the full forty-five years of his life prying into strange places and discovering secret and abysmal things. Not a great many volumes were printed in the first edition and many of these were burned by their frightened owners when Von Junzt was found strangled in a mysterious manner, in his barred and bolted chamber one night in 1840, six months after he had returned from a mysterious journey to Mongolia.

Five years later a London printer, one Bridewall, pirated the work, and issued a cheap translation for sensational effect, full of grotesque woodcuts, and riddled with misspellings, faulty translations and the usual errors of a cheap and unscholarly printing. This still further discredited the original work, and publishers and public forgot about the book until 1909 when the Golden Goblin Press of New York brought out an edition.

Their production was so carefully expurgated that fully a fourth of the original matter was cut out; the book was handsomely bound and decorated with the exquisite and weirdly imaginative illustrations of Diego Vasquez. The edition was intended for popular consumption but the artistic instinct of the publishers defeated that end, since the cost of issuing the book was so great that they were forced to cite it at a prohibitive price.

I was explaining all this to Tussmann when he interrupted brusquely to say that he was not utterly ignorant in such matters. One of the Golden Goblin books ornamented his library, he said, and it was in it that he found a certain line which aroused his interest. If I could procure him a copy of the original 1839 edition, he would make it worth my while; knowing, he added, that it would be useless to offer me money, he would, instead, in return for my trouble on his behalf, make a full retraction of his former accusations in regard to my Yucatan researches, and offer a complete apology in *The Scientific News*.

I will admit that I was astounded at this, and realized that if the matter meant so much to Tussmann that he was willing to

make such concessions, it must indeed be of the utmost importance. I answered that I considered that I had sufficiently refuted
his charges in the eyes of the world and had no desire to put
him in a humiliating position, but that I would make the utmost
efforts to procure him what he wanted.

He thanked me abruptly and took his leave, saying rather vaguely
that he hoped to find a complete exposition of something in the
Black Book which had evidently been slighted in the later edition.

I set to work, writing letters to friends, colleagues and book
dealers all over the world, and soon discovered that I had assumed
a task of no small magnitude. Three months elapsed before my
efforts were crowned with success, but at last, through the aid
of Professor James Clement of Richmond, Virginia, I was able to
obtain what I wished.

I notified Tussmann and he came to London by the next train.
His eyes burned avidly as he gazed at the thick, dusty volume
with its heavy leather covers and rusty iron hasps, and his fingers
quivered with eagerness as he thumbed the time-yellowed pages.

And when he cried out fiercely and smashed his clenched
fist down on the table I knew that he had found what he hunted.

"Listen!" he commanded, and he read to me a passage that
spoke of an old, old temple in a Honduras jungle where a strange
god was worshipped by an ancient tribe which became extinct
before the coming of the Spaniards. And Tussmann read aloud
of the mummy that had been, in life, the last high priest of that
vanished people, and which now lay in a chamber hewn in the
solid rock of the cliff against which the temple was built. About
that mummy's withered neck was a copper chain, and on that
chain a great red jewel carved in the form of a toad. This jewel
was a key, Von Junzt went on to say, to the treasure of the temple
which lay hidden in a subterranean crypt far below the temple's
altar.

Tussmann's eyes blazed.

"I have seen that temple! I have stood before the altar. I have
seen the sealed-up entrance of the chamber in which, the natives

say, lies the mummy of the priest. It is a very curious temple, no more like the ruins of the prehistoric Indians than it is like the buildings of the modern Latin-Americans. The Indians in the vicinity disclaim any former connection with the place; they say that the people who built that temple were a different race from themselves, and were there when their own ancestors came into the country. I believe it to be a remnant of some long-vanished civilization which began to decay thousands of years before the Spaniards came.

"I would have liked to have broken into the sealed-up chamber, but I had neither the time nor the tools for the task. I was hurrying to the coast, having been wounded by an accidental gunshot in the foot, and I stumbled onto the place purely by chance.

"I have been planning to have another look at it, but circumstances have prevented—now I intend to let nothing stand in my way! By chance I came upon a passage in the Golden Goblin edition of this book, describing the temple. But that was all; the mummy was only briefly mentioned. Interested, I obtained one of Bridewall's translations but ran up against a blank wall of baffling blunders. By some irritating mischance the translator had even mistaken the location of the Temple of the Toad, as Von Junzt calls it, and has it in Guatemala instead of Honduras. The general description is faulty, the jewel is mentioned and the fact that it is a 'key'. But a key to what, Bridewall's book does not state. I now felt that I was on the track of a real discovery, unless Von Junzt was, as many maintain, a madman. But that the man was actually in Honduras at one time is well attested, and no one could so vividly describe the temple—as he does in the Black Book—unless he had seen it himself. How he learned of the jewel is more than I can say. The Indians who told me of the mummy said nothing of any jewel. I can only believe that Von Junzt found his way into the sealed crypt somehow—the man had uncanny ways of learning hidden things.

"To the best of my knowledge only one other white man has seen the Temple of the Toad besides Von Junzt and myself—the Spanish traveler Juan Gonzales, who made a partial exploration of that country in 1793. He mentioned, briefly, a curious fane that differed from most Indian ruins, and spoke skeptically of a legend current among the natives that there was 'something unusual' hidden under the temple. I feel certain that he was referring to the Temple of the Toad.

"Tomorrow I sail for Central America. Keep the book; I have no more use for it. This time I am going fully prepared and I intend to find what is hidden in that temple, if I have to demolish it. It can be nothing less than a great store of gold! The Spaniards missed it, somehow; when they arrived in Central America, the Temple of the Toad was deserted; they were searching for living Indians from whom torture could wring gold; not for mummies of lost peoples. But I mean to have that treasure."

So saying Tussmann took his departure. I sat down and opened the book at the place where he had left off reading, and I sat until midnight, wrapt in Von Junzt's curious, wild and at times utterly vague expoundings. And I found pertaining to the Temple of the Toad certain things which disquieted me so much that the next morning I attempted to get in touch with Tussmann, only to find that he had already sailed.

Several months passed and then I received a letter from Tussmann, asking me to come and spend a few days with him at his estate in Sussex; he also requested me to bring the Black Book with me.

I arrived at Tussmann's rather isolated estate just after nightfall. He lived in almost feudal state, his great ivy-grown house and broad lawns surrounded by high stone walls. As I went up the hedge-bordered way from the gate to the house, I noted that the place had not been well kept in its master's absence. Weeds grew rank among the trees, almost choking out the grass. Among some unkempt bushes over against the outer wall, I heard what appeared to be a horse or an ox blundering and lumbering about. I distinctly heard the clink of its hoof on a stone.

A servant who eyed me suspiciously admitted me and I found Tussmann pacing to and fro in his study like a caged lion. His giant frame was leaner, harder than when I had last seen him; his face was bronzed by a tropic sun. There were more and harsher lines in his strong face and his eyes burned more intensely than ever. A smoldering, baffled anger seemed to underlie his manner.

"Well, Tussmann," I greeted him, "what success? Did you find the gold?"

"I found not an ounce of gold," he growled. "The whole thing was a hoax—well, not all of it. I broke into the sealed chamber and found the mummy—"

"And the jewel?" I exclaimed.

He drew something from his pocket and handed it to me.

I gazed curiously at the thing I held. It was a great jewel, clear and transparent as crystal, but of a sinister crimson, carved, as Von Junzt had declared, in the shape of a toad. I shuddered involuntarily; the image was peculiarly repulsive. I turned my attention to the heavy and curiously wrought copper chain which supported it.

"What are these characters carved on the chain?" I asked curiously.

"I can not say," Tussmann replied. "I had thought perhaps you might know. I find a faint resemblance between them and certain partly defaced hieroglyphics on a monolith known as the Black Stone in the mountains of Hungary. I have been unable to decipher them."

"Tell me of your trip," I urged, and over our whiskey-and-sodas he began, as if with a strange reluctance.

"I found the temple again with no great difficulty, though it lies in a lonely and little-frequented region. The temple is built against a sheer stone cliff in a deserted valley unknown to maps and explorers. I would not endeavor to make an estimate of its

antiquity, but it is built of a sort of unusually hard basalt, such
as I have never seen anywhere else, and its extreme weathering
suggests incredible age.

"Most of the columns which form its facade are in ruins,
thrusting up shattered stumps from worn bases, like the scattered
and broken teeth of some grinning hag. The outer walls are
crumbling, but the inner walls and the columns which support
such of the roof as remains intact, seem good for another thousand years, as well as the walls of the inner chamber.

"The main chamber is a large circular affair with a floor
composed of great squares of stone. In the center stands the
altar, merely a huge, round, curiously carved block of the same
material. Directly behind the altar, in the solid stone cliff which
forms the rear wall of the chamber, is the sealed and hewn-out
chamber wherein lay the mummy of the temple's last priest.

"I broke into the crypt with not too much difficulty and
found the mummy exactly as is stated in the Black Book. Though
it was in a remarkable state of preservation, I was unable to
classify it. The withered features and general contour of the skull
suggested certain degraded and mongrel peoples of Lower Egypt,
and I feel certain that the priest was a member of a race more
akin to the Caucasian than the Indian. Beyond this, I can not
make any positive statement.

"But the jewel was there, the chain looped about the dried-up
neck."

From this point Tussmann's narrative became so vague that
I had some difficulty in following him and wondered if the tropic
sun had affected his mind. He had opened a hidden door in the
altar somehow with the jewel—just how, he did not plainly say,
and it struck me that he did not clearly understand himself the
action of the jewel-key. But the opening of the secret door had
had a bad effect on the hardy rogues in his employ. They had
refused point-blank to follow him through that gaping black
opening which had appeared so mysteriously when the gem was
touched to the altar.

Tussmann entered alone with his pistol and electric torch, finding a narrow stone stair that wound down into the bowels of the earth, apparently. He followed this and presently came into a broad corridor, in the blackness of which his tiny beam of light was almost engulfed. As he told this he spoke with strange annoyance of a toad which hopped ahead of him, just beyond the circle of light, all the time he was below ground.

Making his way along dank tunnels and stairways that were wells of solid blackness, he at last came to a heavy door fantastically carved, which he felt must be the crypt wherein was secreted the gold of the ancient worshippers. He pressed the toad-jewel against it at several places and finally the door gaped wide.

"And the treasure?" I broke in eagerly.

He laughed in savage self-mockery.

"There was no gold there, no precious gems—nothing"—he hesitated—"nothing that I could bring away."

Again his tale lapsed into vagueness. I gathered that he had left the temple rather hurriedly without searching any further for the supposed treasure. He had intended bringing the mummy away with him, he said, to present to some museum, but when he came up out of the pits, it could not be found and he believed that his men, in superstitious aversion to having such a companion on their road to the coast, had thrown it into some well or cavern.

"And so," he concluded, "I am in England again no richer than when I left."

"You have the jewel," I reminded him. "Surely it is valuable."

He eyed it without favor, but with a sort of fierce avidness almost obsessional.

"Would you say that it is a ruby?" he asked.

I shook my head. "I am unable to classify it."

"And I. But let me see the book."

He slowly turned the heavy pages, his lips moving as he read. Sometimes he shook his head as if puzzled, and I noticed him dwell long over a certain line.

"This man dipped so deeply into forbidden things," said he, "I can not wonder that his fate was so strange and mysterious. He must have had some foreboding of his end—here he warns men not to disturb sleeping things."

Tussmann seemed lost in thought for some moments.

"Aye, sleeping things," he muttered, "that seem dead, but only lie waiting for some blind fool to awake them—I should have read further in the Black Book—and I should have shut the door when I left the crypt—but I have the key and I'll keep it in spite of Hell."

He roused himself from his reveries and was about to speak when he stopped short. From somewhere upstairs had come a peculiar sound.

"What was that?" he glared at me. I shook my head and he ran to the door and shouted for a servant. The man entered a few moments later and he was rather pale.

"You were upstairs?" growled Tussmann.

"Yes, sir."

"Did you hear anything?" asked Tussmann harshly and in a manner almost threatening and accusing.

"I did, sir," the man answered with a puzzled look on his face.

"What did you hear?" The question was fairly snarled.

"Well, sir," the man laughed apologetically, "you'll say I'm a bit off, I fear, but to tell you the truth, sir, it sounded like a horse stamping around on the roof!"

A blaze of absolute madness leaped into Tussmann's eyes.

"You fool!" he screamed. "Get out of here!" The man shrank back in amazement and Tussmann snatched up the gleaming toad-carved jewel.

"I've been a fool!" he raved. "I didn't read far enough—and I should have shut the door—but by heaven, the key is mine and I'll keep it in spite of man or devil."

And with these strange words he turned and fled upstairs. A moment later his door slammed heavily and a servant, knocking timidly, brought forth only a blasphemous order to retire and a luridly worded threat to shoot anyone who tried to obtain entrance into the room.

Had it not been so late I would have left the house, for I was certain that Tussmann was stark mad. As it was, I retired to the room a frightened servant showed me, but I did not go to bed. I opened the pages of the Black Book at the place where Tussmann had been reading.

This much was evident, unless the man was utterly insane: he had stumbled upon something unexpected in the Temple of the Toad. Something unnatural about the opening of the altar door had frightened his men, and in the subterraneous crypt Tussmann had found *something* that he had not thought to find. And I believed that he had been followed from Central America, and that the reason for his persecution was the jewel he called the Key.

Seeking some clue in Von Junzt's volume, I read again of the Temple of the Toad, of the strange pre-Indian people who worshipped there, and of the huge, tittering, tentacled, hoofed monstrosity that they worshipped.

Tussmann had said that he had not read far enough when he had first seen the book. Puzzling over this cryptic phrase I came upon the line he had pored over—marked by his thumb nail. It seemed to me to be another of Von Junzt's many ambiguities, for it merely stated that a temple's god was the temple's treasure. Then the dark implication of the hint struck me and cold sweat beaded my forehead.

The Key to the Treasure! And the temple's treasure was the temple's god! And sleeping Things might awaken on the opening of their prison door! I sprang up, unnerved by the intolerable suggestion, and at that moment something crashed in the stillness and the death-scream of a human being burst upon my ears.

In an instant I was out of the room, and as I dashed up the stairs I heard sounds that have made me doubt my sanity ever since. At Tussmann's door I halted, essaying with shaking hand to turn the knob. The door was locked, and as I hesitated I heard from within a hideous high-pitched tittering and then the disgusting squashy sound as if a great, jelly-like bulk was being forced through the window. The sound ceased and I could have sworn I heard a faint swish of gigantic wings. Then silence.

Gathering my shattered nerves, I broke down the door. A foul and overpowering stench billowed out like a yellow mist. Gasping in nausea I entered. The room was in ruins, but nothing was missing except that crimson toad-carved jewel Tussmann called the Key, and that was never found. A foul, unspeakable slime smeared the windowsill, and in the center of the room lay Tussmann, his head crushed and flattened; and on the red ruin of skull and face, the plain print of an enormous hoof.

SEA CURSE

And some return by the failing light
And some in the waking dream.
For she hears the heels of the dripping ghosts
That ride the rough roofbeam.

—Kipling

THEY were the brawlers and braggarts, the loud boasters and hard drinkers, of Faring town, John Kulrek and his crony Lie-lip Canool. Many a time have I, a tousle-haired lad, stolen to the tavern door to listen to their curses, their profane arguments and wild sea songs; half fearful and half in admiration of these wild rovers. Aye, all the people of Faring town gazed on them with fear and admiration, for they were not like the rest of the Faring men; they were not content to ply their trade along the coasts and among the shark-teeth shoals. No yawls, no skiffs for them! They fared far, farther than any other man in the village, for they shipped on the great sailing-ships that went out on the white tides to brave the restless gray ocean and make ports in strange lands.

Ah, I mind it was swift times in the little sea-coast village of Faring when John Kulrek came home, with the furtive Lie-lip at his side, swaggering down the gang-plank, in his tarry sea-clothes, and the broad leather belt that held his ever-ready dagger; shouting condescending greeting to some favored acquaintance, kissing some maiden who ventured too near; then up the street, roaring some scarcely decent song of the sea. How the cringers and the idlers, the hangers-on, would swarm about the two desperate heroes, flattering and smirking, guffawing hilariously at each nasty jest. For to the tavern loafers and to some of the weaker among the straightforward villagers, these men with their wild talk and their brutal deeds, their tales of the Seven Seas and the far countries, these men, I say, were valiant knights, nature's noblemen who dared to be men of blood and brawn.

And all feared them, so that when a man was beaten or a woman insulted, the villagers muttered—and did nothing. And so when Moll Farrell's niece was put to shame by John Kulrek, none dared even to put into words what all thought. Moll had never married, and she and the girl lived alone in a little hut down close to the beach, so close that in high tide the waves came almost to the door.

The people of the village accounted old Moll something of a witch, and she was a grim, gaunt old dame who had little to say to anyone. But she minded her own business, and eked out a slim living by gathering clams, and picking up bits of driftwood.

The girl was a pretty, foolish little thing, vain and easily befooled, else she had never yielded to the shark-like blandishments of John Kulrek.

I mind the day was a cold winter day with a sharp breeze out of the east when the old dame came into the village street shrieking that the girl had vanished. All scattered over the beach and back among the bleak inland hills to search for her—all save John Kulrek and his cronies who sat in the tavern dicing and toping. All the while beyond the shoals, we heard the never-ceasing droning of the heaving, restless gray monster, and in the dim light of the ghostly dawn Moll Farrell's girl came home.

The tides bore her gently across the wet sands and laid her almost at her own door. Virgin-white she was, and her arms were folded across her still bosom; calm was her face, and the grey tides sighed about her slender limbs. Moll Farrell's eyes were stones, yet she stood above her dead girl and spoke no word till John Kulrek and his crony came reeling down from the tavern, their drinking-jacks still in their hands. Drunk was John Kulrek, and the people gave back for him, murder in their souls; so he came and laughed at Moll Farrell across the body of her girl.

"Zounds!" swore John Kulrek; "the wench has drowned herself, Lie-lip!"

Lie-lip laughed, with the twist of his thin mouth. He always hated Moll Farrell, for it was she that had given him the name of Lie-lip.

Then John Kulrek lifted his drinking-jack, swaying on his uncertain legs. "A health to the wench's ghost!" he bellowed, while all stood aghast.

Then Moll Farrell spoke, and the words broke from her in a scream which sent ripples of cold up and down the spines of the throng.

"The curse of the Foul Fiend upon you, John Kulrek!" she screamed. "The curse of God rest upon your vile soul throughout eternity! May you gaze on sights that shall sear the eyes of you and scorch the soul of you! May you die a bloody death and writhe in hell's flames for a million and a million and yet a million years! I curse you by sea and by land, by earth and by air, by the demons of the swamplands, the fiends of the forest and the goblins of the hills! And you"—her lean finger stabbed at Lie-lip Canool and he started backward, his face paling—"you shall be the death of John Kulrek and he shall be the death of you! You shall bring John Kulrek to the doors of hell and John Kulrek shall bring you to the gallows-tree! I set the seal of death upon your brow, John Kulrek! You shall live in terror and die in horror far out upon the cold gray sea! But the sea that took the soul of innocence to her bosom shall not take you, but shall fling forth your vile carcass to the sands! Aye, John Kulrek"—and she spoke with such a terrible intensity that the drunken mockery on the man's face changed to one of swinish stupidity—"the sea roars for the victim it will not keep! There is snow upon the hills, John Kulrek, and ere it melts your corpse will lie at my feet. And I shall spit upon it and be content."

Kulrek and his crony sailed at dawn for a long voyage, and Moll went back to her hut and her clam-gathering. She seemed to grow leaner and more grim than ever and her eyes smoldered with a light not sane. The days glided by and people whispered among themselves that Moll's days were numbered, for she faded to a ghost of a woman; but she went her way, refusing all aid.

That was a short, cold summer and the snow on the barren inland hills never melted; a thing very unusual, which caused much comment among the villagers. At dusk and at dawn Moll would come up on the beach, gaze up at the snow which glittered on the hills, then out to sea with a fierce intensity in her gaze.

Then the days grew shorter, the nights longer and darker, and the cold gray tides came sweeping along the bleak strands, bearing the rain and sleet of the sharp east breezes.

And upon a bleak day a trading-vessel sailed into the bay and anchored. And all the idlers and the wastrels flocked to the wharfs, for that was the ship upon which John Kulrek and Lie-lip Canool had sailed. Down the gang-plank came Lie-lip, more furtive than ever, but John Kulrek was not there.

To shouted queries, Canool shook his head. "Kulrek deserted ship at a port of Sumatra," said he. "He had a row with the skipper, lads; wanted me to desert, too, but no! I had to see you fine lads again, eh boys?"

Almost cringing was Lie-lip Canool, and suddenly he recoiled as Moll Farrell came through the throng. A moment they stood eyeing each other; then Moll's grim lips bent in a terrible smile.

"There's blood on your hand, Canool!" she lashed out suddenly—so suddenly that Lie-lip started and rubbed his right hand across his left sleeve.

"Stand aside, witch!" he snarled in sudden anger, striding through the crowd which gave back for him. His admirers followed him to the tavern.

Now, I mind that the next day was even colder; gray fogs came drifting out of the east and veiled the sea and the beaches. There would be no sailing that day, and so all the villagers were in their snug houses or matching tales at the tavern. So it came that Joe, my friend, a lad of my own age, and I, were the ones who saw the first of the strange things that happened.

Being harum-scarum lads of no wisdom, we were sitting in a small rowboat, floating at the end of the wharfs, each shivering and wishing the other would suggest leaving, there being no reason whatever for our being there, save that it was a good place to build air-castles undisturbed.

Suddenly Joe raised his hand. "Say," he said, "d'ye hear? Who can be out on the bay upon a day like this?"

"Nobody. What d'ye hear?"

"Oars. Or I'm a lubber. Listen."

There was no seeing anything in that fog, and I heard nothing. Yet Joe swore he did, and suddenly his face assumed a strange look.

"Somebody rowing out there, I tell you! The bay is alive with oars from the sound! A score of boats at the least! Ye dolt, can ye not hear?"

Then, as I shook my head, he leaped and began to undo the painter.

"I'm off to see. Name me liar if the bay is not full of boats, all together like a close fleet. Are you with me?"

Yes, I was with him, though I heard nothing. Then out in the grayness we went, and the fog closed behind and before so that we drifted in a vague world of smoke, seeing naught and hearing naught. We were lost in no time, and I cursed Joe for leading us upon a wild goose chase that was like to end with our being swept out to sea. I thought of Moll Farrell's girl and shuddered.

How long we drifted I know not. Minutes faded into hours, hours into centuries. Still Joe swore he heard the oars, now close at hand, now far away, and for hours we followed them, steering our course toward the sound, as the noise grew or receded. This I later thought of, and could not understand.

Then, when my hands were so numb that I could no longer hold the oar, and the forerunning drowsiness of cold and exhaustion was stealing over me, bleak white stars broke through the fog which glided suddenly away, fading like a ghost of smoke, and we found ourselves afloat just outside the mouth of the bay.

The waters lay smooth as a pond, all dark green and silver in the starlight, and the cold came crisper than ever. I was swinging the boat about, to put back into the bay, when Joe gave a shout, and for the first time I heard the clack of oar-locks. I glanced over my shoulder and my blood went cold.

A great beaked prow loomed above us, a weird, unfamiliar shape against the stars, and as I caught my breath, sheered sharply and swept by us, with a curious swishing I never heard any other craft make. Joe screamed and backed oars frantically, and the boat walled out of the way just in time; for though the prow missed us, still otherwise we had died. For from the sides of the ship stood long oars, bank upon bank which swept her along. Though I had never seen such a craft, I knew her for a galley. But what was she doing upon our coasts? They said, the far-farers, that such ships were still in use among the heathens of Barbary; but it was many a long, heaving mile to Barbary, and even so she did not resemble the ships described by those who had sailed far.

We started in pursuit, and this was strange, for though the waters broke about her prow, and she seemed fairly to fly through the waves, yet she was making little speed, and it was no time before we caught up with her. Making our painter fast to a chain far back beyond the reach of the swishing oars, we hailed those on deck. But there came no answer, and at last, conquering our fears, we clambered up the chain and found ourselves upon the strangest deck man has trod for many a long, roaring century.

"This is no Barbary rover!" Joe muttered fearsomely. "Look, how old it seems! Almost ready to fall to pieces. Why, 'tis fairly rotten!"

There was no one on deck, no one at the long sweep with which the craft was steered. We stole to the hold and looked down the stair. Then and there, if ever men were on the verge of insanity, it was we. For there were rowers there, it is true; they sat upon the rowers' benches and drove the creaking oars through the gray waters. *And they that rowed were skeletons!*

Shrieking, we plunged across the deck, to fling ourselves into the sea. But at the rail I tripped upon something and fell headlong, and as I lay, I saw a thing which vanquished my fear of the horrors below for an instant. The thing upon which I had tripped was a human body, and in the dim gray light that was beginning to steal across the eastern waves I saw a dagger hilt standing up between his shoulders. Joe was at the rail, urging me to haste, and together we slid down the chain and cut the painter.

Then we stood off into the bay. Straight on kept the grim galley, and we followed, slowly, wondering. She seemed to be heading straight for the beach beside the wharfs, and as we approached, we saw the wharfs thronged with people. They had missed us, no doubt, and now they stood, there in the early dawn light, struck dumb by the apparition which had come up out of the night and the grim ocean.

Straight on swept the galley, her oars a-swish; then ere she reached the shallow water—crash!—a terrific reverberation shook the bay. Before our eyes the grim craft seemed to melt away; then she vanished, and the green waters seethed where she had ridden, but there floated no driftwood there, nor did there ever float any ashore. Aye, something floated ashore, but it was grim driftwood!

We made the landing amid a hum of excited conversation that stopped suddenly. Moll Farrell stood before her hut, limned gauntly against the ghostly dawn, her lean hand pointing sea-ward. And across the sighing wet sands, borne by the gray tide, something came floating; something that the waves dropped at Moll Farrell's feet. And there looked up at us, as we crowded about, a pair of unseeing eyes set in a still, white face. John Kulrek had come home.

Still and grim he lay, rocked by the tide, and as he lurched sideways, all saw the dagger hilt that stood from his back—the dagger all of us had seen a thousand times at the belt of Lie-lip Canool.

"Aye, I killed him!" came Canool's shriek, as he writhed and groveled before our gaze. "At sea on a still night in a drunken brawl I slew him and hurled him overboard! And from the far seas he has followed me"—his voice sank to a hideous whisper—"because—of—the—curse—the—sea—would—not—keep—his—body!"

And the wretch sank down, trembling, the shadow of the gallows already in his eyes.

"Aye!" Strong, deep and exultant was Moll Farrell's voice. "From the hell of lost craft Satan sent a ship of bygone ages! A ship red with gore and stained with the memory of horrid crimes! None other would bear such a vile carcass! The sea has taken vengeance and has given me mine. See now, how I spit upon the face of John Kulrek."

And with a ghastly laugh, she pitched forward, the blood starting to her lips. And the sun came up across the restless sea.

THE TOMB'S SECRET

WHEN James Willoughby, millionaire philanthropist, realized that the dark, lightless car was deliberately crowding him into the curb, he acted with desperate decision. Snapping off his own lights, he threw open the door on the opposite side from the onrushing stranger, and leaped out, without stopping his own car. He landed sprawling on all fours, shredding the knees of his trousers and tearing the skin on his hands. An instant later his auto crashed cataclysmically into the curb, and the crunch of crumpled fenders and the tinkle of breaking glass mingled with the deafening reverberation of a sawed-off shotgun as the occupants of the mysterious car, not yet realizing that their intended victim had deserted his automobile, blasted the machine he had just left.

Before the echoes died away, Willoughby was up and running through the darkness with an energy remarkable for his years. He knew that his ruse was already discovered, but it takes longer to swing a big car around than for a desperately frightened man to burst through a hedge, and a flitting figure in the darkness is a poor target. So James Willoughby lived where others had died, and presently came on foot and in disheveled condition to his home, which adjoined the park beside which the murderous attempt had been made. The police, hastening to his call, found him in a condition of mingled fear and bewilderment. He had seen none of his attackers; he could give no reason for the attack. All that he seemed to know was that death had struck at him from the dark, suddenly, terribly and mysteriously.

It was only reasonable to suppose that death would strike again at its chosen victim, and that was why Brock Rollins, detective, kept a rendezvous the next evening with one Joey Glick, a nondescript character of the underworld who served his purpose in the tangled scheme of things.

Rollins bulked big in the dingy back-room appointed for the meeting. His massive shoulders and thick body dwarfed his height. His cold blue eyes contrasted with the thick black hair that crowned his low broad forehead, and his civilized garments could not conceal the almost savage muscularity of his hard frame.

Opposite him Joey Glick, never an impressive figure, looked even more insignificant than usual. And Joey's skin was a pasty gray, and Joey's fingers shook as he fumbled with a bit of paper on which was drawn a peculiar design.

"Somebody planted it on me," he chattered. "Right after I phoned you. In the jamb on the uptown train. Me, Joey Glick! They plant it on me and I don't even know it. Only one man in this burg handles dips that slick—even if I didn't know already.

"Look! It's the death-blossom! The symbol of the Sons of Erlik! They're after me! They've been shadowing me—tapping wires. They know I know too much—"

"Come to the point, will you?" grunted Rollins "You said you had a tip about the gorillas who tried to put the finger on Jim Willoughby. Quit shaking and spill it. And tell me, cold turkey—who was it?"

"The man behind it is Yarghouz Barolass."

Rollins grunted in some surprise.

"I didn't know murder was his racket."

"Wait!" Joey babbled, so scared he was scarcely coherent. His brain was addled, his speech disjointed. "He's head of the American branch of the Sons of Erlik—I know he is—"

"Chinese?"

"He's a Mongol. His racket is blackmailing nutty old dames who fall for his black magic. You know that. But this is bigger. Listen, you know about Richard Lynch?"

"Sure; got smashed up in an auto wreck by a hit-and-run speed maniac a week ago. Lay unidentified in a morgue all night before they discovered who he was. Some crazy loon tried to steal the corpse off the slab. What's that got to do with Willoughby?"

"It wasn't an accident." Joey was fumbling for a cigarette. "They meant to get him—Yarghouz's mob. It was them after the body that night—"

"Have you been hitting the pipe?" demanded Rollins harshly.

"No, damn it!" shrilled Joey. "I tell you, Yarghouz was after Richard Lynch's corpse, just like he's sending his mob after Job Hopkins' body tomorrow night—"

"What?" Rollins came erect, glaring incredulously.

"Don't rush me," begged Joey, striking a match. "Gimme time. That death-blossom has got me jumping sideways. I'm jittery—"

"I'll say you are," grunted Rollins. "You've been babbling a lot of stuff that don't mean anything, except it's Yarghouz Barolass who had Lynch bumped off, and now is after Willoughby. Why? That's what I want to know. Straighten it out and give me the low-down."

"Alright," promised Joey, sucking avidly at his cigarette. "Lemme have a drag. I been so upset I haven't even smoked since I reached into my pocket for a fag and found that damned death-flower. This is straight goods. I know why they want the bodies of Richard Lynch, Job Hopkins and James Willoughby—"

With appalling suddenness his hands shot to his throat, crushing the smoldering cigarette in his fingers. His eyes distended, his face purpled. Without a word he swayed upright, reeled and crashed to the floor. With a curse Rollins sprang up, bent over him, ran skilled hands over his body.

"Dead as Judas Iscariot," swore the detective. "What an infernal break! I knew his heart would get him some day, if he kept hitting the pipe—"

He halted suddenly. On the floor where it had fallen beside the dead man lay the bit of ornamented paper Joey had called the blossom of death, and beside it lay a crumpled package of cigarettes.

"When did he change his brand?" muttered Rollins. "He never smoked any kind but a special Egyptian make before; never saw him use this brand." He lifted the package, drew out a cigarette and broke it into his hand, smelling the contents gingerly. There was a faint but definite odor which was not part of the smell of the cheap tobacco.

"The fellow who slipped that death-blossom into his pocket could have shifted fags on him just as easy," muttered the detective. "They must have known he was coming here to talk to me. But the question is, how much do they know now? They can't know how much or how little he told me. They evidently didn't figure on him reaching me at all—thought he'd take a draw before he got here. Ordinarily he would have; but this time he was too scared even to remember to smoke. He needed dope, not tobacco, to steady his nerve."

Going to the door, he called softly. A stocky bald-headed man answered his call, wiping his hands on a dirty apron. At the sight of the crumpled body he recoiled, paling.

"Heart attack, Spike," grunted Rollins. "See that he gets what's needed." And the big dick thrust a handful of crumpled bills into Spike's fingers as he strode forth. A hard man, Rollins, but one mindful of his debts to the dead as well as the living.

A few minutes later he was crouched over a telephone.

"This you, Hoolihan?"

A voice booming back over the wires assured him that the chief of police was indeed at the other end.

"What killed Job Hopkins?" he asked abruptly.

"Why, heart attack, I understand." There was some surprise in the chief's voice. "Passed out suddenly, day before yesterday, while smoking his after-dinner cigar, according to the papers. Why?"

"Who's guarding Willoughby?" demanded Rollins without answering.

"Laveaux, Hanson, McFarlane and Harper. But I don't see—"

"Not enough," snapped Rollins. "Beat it over there yourself with three or four more men."

"Say, listen here, Rollins!" came back the irate bellow. "Are you telling *me* how to run my business?"

"Right now I am." Rollins' cold hard grin was almost tangible in his voice. "This happens to be in my particular domain. We're not fighting white men; it's a gang of River Street yellow-bellies who've put Willoughby on the spot. I won't say any more right now. There's been too damned much wire-tapping in this burg. But you beat it over to Willoughby's as fast as you can get there. Don't let him out of your sight. Don't let him smoke, eat or drink anything till I get there. I'll be right on over."

"Okay," came the answer over the wires. "You've been working the River Street quarter long enough to know what you're doing."

Rollins snapped the receiver back on its hook and strode out into the misty dimness of River Street, with its furtive hurrying forms—stooped alien figures which would have fitted less incongruously into the scheme of Canton, Bombay or Stamboul.

The big dick walked with a stride even springier than usual, a more aggressive lurch of his massive shoulders. That betokened unusual wariness, a tension of nerves. He knew that he was a marked man, since his talk with Joey Glick. He did not try to fool himself; it was certain that the spies of the man he was fighting knew that Joey had reached him before he died. The fact that they could not know just how much the fellow had told before he died, would make them all the more dangerous. He did not underestimate his own position. He knew that if there was one man in the city capable of dealing with Yarghouz Barolass, it was himself, with his experience gained from years of puzzling through the devious and often grisly mysteries of River Street, with its swarms of brown and yellow inhabitants.

"Taxi?" A cab drew purring up beside the curb, anticipating his summoning gesture. The driver did not lean out into the light of the street. His cap seemed to be drawn low, not unnaturally so, but, standing on the sidewalk, it was impossible for the detective to tell whether or not he was a white man.

"Sure," grunted Rollins, swinging open the door and climbing in. "540 Park Place, and step on it."

The taxi roared through the crawling traffic, down shadowy River Street, wheeled off onto 35th Avenue, crossed over, and sped down a narrow side street.

"Taking a short cut?" asked the detective.

"Yes, sir." The driver did not look back. His voice ended in a sudden hissing intake of breath. There was no partition between the front and back seats. Rollins was leaning forward, his gun jammed between the shoulders of the driver.

"Take the next right-hand turn and drive to the address I gave you," he said softly. "Think I can't tell the back of a yellow neck by the street lamp? You drive, but you drive careful. If you try to wreck us, I'll fill you full of lead before you can twist that wheel. No monkey business now; you wouldn't be the first man I've plugged in the course of duty."

The driver twisted his head about to stare briefly into the grim face of his captor; his wide thin mouth gaped, his coppery features were ashy. Not for nothing had Rollins established his reputation as a man-hunter among the sinister denizens of the Oriental quarter.

"Joey was right," muttered Rollins between his teeth. "I don't know your name, but I've seen you hanging around Yarghouz Barolass's joint when he had it over on Levant Street. You won't take me for a ride, not tonight. I know that trick, old copper-face. You'd have a flat, or run out of gas at some convenient spot. Any excuse for you to get out of the car and out of range while a hatchet-man hidden somewhere mows me down with a sawed-off. You better hope none of your friends see us and try anything, because this gat has a hair-trigger, and it's cocked. I couldn't die quick enough not to pull the trigger."

The rest of that grim ride was made in silence, until the reaches of South Park rose to view—darkened, except for a fringe of lights around the boundaries, because of municipal economy which sought to reduce the light bill.

"Swing into the park," ordered Rollins, as they drove along the street which passed the park, and, further on, James Willoughby's house. "Cut off your lights, and drive as I tell you. You can feel your way between the trees."

The darkened car glided into a dense grove and came to a halt. Rollins fumbled in his pockets with his left hand and drew out a small flashlight, and a pair of handcuffs. In climbing out, he was forced to remove his muzzle from close contact with his prisoner's back, but the gun menaced the Mongol in the small ring of light emanating from the flash.

"Climb out," ordered the detective. "That's right—slow and easy. You're going to have to stay here awhile. I didn't want to take you to the station right now, for several reasons. One of them is I didn't want your pals to know I turned the tables on you. I'm hoping they'll still be patiently waiting for you to bring me into range of their sawed-offs—ha, would you?"

The Mongol, with a desperate wrench, struck the flashlight from the detective's hand, plunging them into darkness.

Rollins' clutching fingers locked like a vise on his adversary's coat sleeve, and at the same instant he instinctively threw out his .45 before his belly, to parry the stroke he knew would instantly come. A knife clashed venomously against the blue steel cylinder, and Rollins hooked his foot about an ankle and jerked powerfully. The fighters went down together, and the knife sliced the detective's coat as they fell. Then his blindingly driven gun barrel crunched glancingly against a shaven skull, and the straining form went limp.

Panting and swearing beneath his breath, Rollins retrieved the flashlight and cuffs, and set to work securing his prisoner. The Mongol was completely out; it was no light matter to stop a full-arm swing from Brock Rollins. Had the blow landed solidly it would have caved in the skull like an egg-shell.

Handcuffed, gagged with strips torn from his coat, and his feet bound with the same material, the Mongol was placed in the car, and Rollins turned and strode through the shadows of the park, toward the eastern hedge beyond which lay James Willoughby's estate. He hoped that this affair would give him some slight advantage in this blind battle. While the Mongols waited for him to ride into the trap they had undoubtedly laid for him somewhere in the city, perhaps he could do a little scouting unmolested.

James Willoughby's estate adjoined South Park on the east. Only a high hedge separated the park from his grounds. The big three-storied house—disproportionately huge for a bachelor—towered among carefully trimmed trees and shrubbery, amidst a level, shaven lawn. There were lights in the two lower floors, none in the third. Rollins knew that Willoughby's study was a big room on the second floor, on the west side of the house. From that room no light issued between the heavy shutters. Evidently curtains and shades were drawn inside. The big dick grunted in approval as he stood looking through the hedge.

He knew that a plainclothes man was watching the house from each side, and he marked the bunch of shrubbery amidst which would be crouching the man detailed to guard the west side. Craning his neck, he saw a car in front of the house, which faced south, and he knew it to be that of Chief Hoolihan.

With the intention of taking a short cut across the lawn he wormed through the hedge, and, not wishing to be shot by mistake, he called softly: "Hey, Harper!"

There was no answer. Rollins strode toward the shrubbery.

"Asleep at the post?" he muttered angrily. "Eh, what's this?"

He had stumbled over something in the shadows of the shrubs. His hurriedly directed beam shone on the white, upturned face of a man. Blood dabbled the features, and a crumpled hat lay near by, an unfired pistol near the limp hand.

"Knocked stiff from behind!" muttered Rollins. "What—"

Parting the shrub he gazed toward the house. On that side an ornamental chimney rose tier by tier, until it towered above the roof. And his eyes became slits as they centered on a window on the third floor within easy reach of that chimney. On all other windows the shutters were closed; but these stood open.

With frantic haste he tore through the shrubbery and ran across the lawn, stooping like a bulky bear, amazingly fleet for one of his weight. As he rounded the corner of the house and rushed toward the steps, a man rose swiftly from among the hedges lining the walk, and covered him, only to lower his gun with an exclamation of recognition.

"Where's Hoolihan?" snapped the detective.

"Upstairs with old man Willoughby. What's up?"

"Harper's been slugged," snarled Rollins. "Beat it out there; you know where he was posted. Wait there until I call you. If you see anything you don't recognize trying to leave the house, plug it! I'll send out a man to take your place here."

He entered the front door and saw four men in plain clothes lounging about in the main hall.

"Jackson," he snapped, "take Hanson's place out in front. I sent him around to the west side. The rest of you stand by for anything."

Mounting the stair in haste, he entered the study on the second floor, breathing a sigh of relief as he found the occupants apparently undisturbed.

The curtains were closely drawn over the windows, and only the door letting into the hall was open. Willoughby was there, a tall spare man, with a scimitar sweep of nose and a bony aggressive chin. Chief Hoolihan, big, bear-like, rubicund, boomed a greeting.

"All your men downstairs?" asked Rollins.

"Sure; nothin' can get past 'em and I'm stayin' here with Mr. Willoughby—"

"And in a few minutes more you'd both have been scratching gravel in Hell," snapped Rollins. "Didn't I tell you we were dealing with Orientals? You concentrated all your force below, never thinking that death might slip in on you from above. But I haven't time to turn out that light. Mr. Willoughby, get over there in that alcove. Chief, stand in front of him, and watch that door that leads into the hall. I'm going to leave it open. Locking it would be useless, against what we're fighting. If anything you don't recognize comes through it, shoot to kill."

"What the devil are you driving at, Rollins?" demanded Hoolihan.

"I mean one of Yarghouz Barolass's killers is in this house!" snapped Rollins. "There may be more than one; anyway, he's somewhere upstairs. Is this the only stair, Mr. Willoughby? No back-stair?"

"This is the only one in the house," answered the millionaire. "There are only bedrooms on the third floor."

"Where's the light button for the hall on that floor?"

"At the head of the stairs, on the left; but you aren't—"

"Take your places and do as I say," grunted Rollins, gliding out into the hallway.

He stood glaring at the stair which wound up above him, its upper part masked in shadow. Somewhere up there lurked a soulless slayer—a Mongol killer, trained in the art of murder, who lived only to perform his master's will. Rollins started to call the men below, then changed his mind. To raise his voice would be to warn the lurking murderer above. Setting his teeth, he glided up the stair. Aware that he was limned in the light below, he realized the desperate recklessness of his action; but he had long ago learned that he could not match subtlety against the Orient. Direct action, however desperate, was always his best bet. He did not fear a bullet as he charged up; the Mongols preferred to slay in silence; but a thrown knife could kill as promptly as tearing lead. His one chance lay in the winding of the stair.

He took the last steps with a thundering rush, not daring to use his flash, plunged into the gloom of the upper hallway, frantically sweeping the wall for the light button. Even as he felt life and movement in the darkness beside him, his groping fingers found it. The scrape of a foot on the floor beside him galvanized him, and as he instinctively flinched back, something whined past his breast and thudded deep into the wall. Then under his frenzied fingers, light flooded the hall.

Almost touching him, half crouching, a copper-skinned giant with a shaven head wrenched at a curved knife which was sunk deep in the woodwork. He threw up his head, dazzled by the light, baring yellow fangs in a bestial snarl.

Rollins had just left a lighted area. His eyes accustomed themselves more swiftly to the sudden radiance. He threw his left like a hammer at the Mongol's jaw. The killer swayed and fell out cold.

Hoolihan was bellowing from below.

"Hold everything," answered Rollins. "Send one of the boys up here with the cuffs. I'm going through these bedrooms."

Which he did, switching on the lights, gun ready, but finding no other lurking slayer. Evidently Yarghouz Barolass considered one would be enough. And so it might have been, but for the big detective.

Having latched all the shutters and fastened the windows securely, he returned to the study, whither the prisoner had been taken. The man had recovered his senses and sat, handcuffed, on a divan. Only the eyes, black and snaky, seemed alive in the copperish face.

"Mongol alright," muttered Rollins. "No Chinaman."

"What is all this?" complained Hoolihan, still upset by the realization that an invader had slipped through his cordon.

"Easy enough. This fellow sneaked up on Harper and laid him cold. Some of these fellows could steal the teeth right out of your mouth. With all those shrubs and trees it was a cinch. Say, send out a couple of the boys to bring in Harper, will you? Then he climbed that fancy chimney. That was a cinch, too. I could do it myself. Nobody had thought to fasten the shutters on that floor, because nobody expected an attack from that direction.

"Mr. Willoughby, do you know anything about Yarghouz Barolass?"

"I never heard of him," declared the philanthropist, and though Rollins scanned him narrowly, he was impressed by the ring of sincerity in Willoughby's voice.

"Well, he's a mystic fakir," said Rollins. "Hangs around Levant Street and preys on old ladies with more money than sense—faddists. Gets them interested in Taoism and Lamaism and then plays on their superstitions and blackmails them. I know his racket, but I've never been able to put the finger on him, because his victims won't squeal. But he's behind these attacks on you."

"Then why don't we go grab him?" demanded Hoolihan.

"Because we don't know where he is. He knows that I know he's mixed up in this. Joey Glick spilled it to me, just before he croaked. Yes, Joey's dead—poison; more of Yarghouz's work. By this time Yarghouz will have deserted his usual hang-outs, and be hiding somewhere—probably in some secret underground dive that we couldn't find in a hundred years, now that Joey is dead."

"Let's sweat it out of this yellow-belly," suggested Hoolihan.

Rollins grinned coldly. "You'd sweat to death yourself before he'd talk. There's another tied up in a car out in the park. Send a couple of boys after him, and you can try your hand on both of them. But you'll get damned little out of them. Come here, Hoolihan."

Drawing him aside, he said: "I'm sure that Job Hopkins was poisoned in the same manner they got Joey Glick. Do you remember anything unusual about the death of Richard Lynch?"

"Well, not about his death; but that night somebody apparently tried to steal and mutilate his corpse—"

"What do you mean, mutilate?" demanded Rollins.

"Well, a watchman heard a noise and went into the room and found Lynch's body on the floor, as if somebody had tried to carry it off, and then maybe got scared off. And a lot of the *teeth* had been pulled or knocked out!"

"Well, I can't explain the teeth," grunted Rollins. "Maybe they were knocked out in the wreck that killed Lynch. But this is my hunch: Yarghouz Barolass is stealing the bodies of wealthy men, figuring on screwing a big price out of their families. When they don't die quick enough, he bumps them off."

Hoolihan cursed in shocked horror.

"But Willoughby hasn't any family."

"Well, I reckon they figure the executors of his estate will kick in. Now listen: I'm borrowing your car for a visit to Job

Hopkins' vault. I got a tip that they're going to lift his corpse tomorrow night. I believe they'll spring it tonight, on the chance that I might have gotten the tip. I believe they'll try to get ahead of me. They may have already, what with all this delay. I figured on being out there long before now.

"No, I don't want any help. Your flat-feet are more of a hindrance than a help in a job like this. You stay here with Willoughby. Keep men upstairs as well as down. Don't let Willoughby open any packages that might come, don't even let him answer a phone call. I'm going to Hopkins' vault, and I don't know when I'll be back; may roost out there all night. It just depends on when—or if—they come for the corpse."

A few minutes later he was speeding down the road on his grim errand. The graveyard which contained the tomb of Job Hopkins was small, exclusive, where only the bones of rich men were laid to rest. The wind moaned through the cypress trees which bent shadow-arms above the gleaming marble.

Rollins approached from the back side, up a narrow, tree-lined side street. He left the car, climbed the wall, and stole through the gloom, beneath the pallid shafts, under the cypress shadows. Ahead of him Job Hopkins' tomb glimmered whitely. And he stopped short, crouching low in the shadows. He saw a glow—a spark of light—it was extinguished, and through the open door of the tomb trooped half a dozen shadowy forms. His hunch had been right, but they had gotten there ahead of him. Fierce anger sweeping him at the ghoulish crime, he leaped forward, shouting a savage command.

They scattered like rats, and his crashing volley re-echoed futilely among the sepulchers. Rushing forward recklessly, swearing savagely, he came into the tomb, and turning his light into the interior, winced at what he saw. The coffin had been burst open, but the tomb itself was not empty. In a careless heap on the floor lay the embalmed corpse of Job Hopkins—*and the lower jawbone had been sawed away.*

"What the Hell!" Rollins stopped short, bewildered at the

sudden disruption of his theory. "They didn't want the body. What did they want? His teeth? And they got Richard Lynch's teeth—"

Lifting the body back into its resting place, he hurried forth, shutting the door of the tomb behind him. The wind whined through the cypress, and mingled with it was a low moaning sound. Thinking that one of his shots had gone home, after all, he followed the noise, warily, pistol and flash ready.

The sound seemed to emanate from a bunch of low cedars near the wall, and among them he found a man lying. The beam revealed the stocky figure, the square, now convulsed face of a Mongol. The slant eyes were glazed, the back of the coat soaked with blood. The man was gasping his last, but Rollins found no trace of a bullet wound on him. In his back, between his shoulders, stood up the hilt of a curious skewer-like knife. The fingers of his right hand had been horribly gashed, as if he had sought to retain his grasp on something which his slayers desired.

"Running from me he bumped into somebody hiding among these cedars," muttered Rollins. "But who? And why? By God, Willoughby hasn't told me everything."

He stared uneasily at the crowding shadows. No stealthy shuffling footfall disturbed the sepulchral quiet. Only the wind whimpered through the cypress and the cedars. The detective was alone with the dead—with the corpses of rich men in their ornate tombs, and with the staring yellow man whose flesh was not yet rigid.

"You're back in a hurry," said Hoolihan, as Rollins entered the Willoughby study. "Do any good?"

"Did the yellow boys talk?" countered Rollins.

"They did not," growled the chief. "They sat like pot-bellied idols. I sent 'em to the station, along with Harper. He was still in a daze."

"Mr. Willoughby," Rollins sank down rather wearily into an arm-chair and fixed his cold gaze on the philanthropist, "am I right in believing that you and Richard Lynch and Job Hopkins were at one time connected with each other in some way?"

"Why do you ask?" parried Willoughby.

"Because somehow the three of you are connected in this matter. Lynch's death was not accidental, and I'm pretty sure that Job Hopkins was poisoned. Now the same gang is after you. I thought it was a body-snatching racket, but an apparent attempt to steal Richard Lynch's corpse out of the morgue, now seems to resolve itself into what was in reality a successful attempt to get his teeth. Tonight a gang of Mongols entered the tomb of Job Hopkins, obviously for the same purpose—"

A choking cry interrupted him. Willoughby sank back, his face livid.

"My God, after all these years!"

Rollins stiffened.

"Then you do know Yarghouz Barolass? You know why he's after you?"

Willoughby shook his head. "I never heard of Yarghouz Barolass before. But I know why they killed Lynch and Hopkins."

"Then you'd better spill the works," advised Rollins. "We're working in the dark as it is."

"I will!" The philanthropist was visibly shaken. He mopped his brow with a shaking hand, and reposed himself with an effort.

"Twenty years ago," he said, "Lynch, Hopkins and myself, young men just out of college, were in China, in the employ of the war-lord Yuen Chin. We were chemical engineers. Yuen Chin was a far-sighted man—ahead of his time, scientifically speaking. He visioned the day when men would war with gases and deadly chemicals. He supplied us with a splendid laboratory, in which to discover or invent some such element of destruction for his use.

"He paid us well; the foundations of all of our fortunes were laid there. We were young, poor, unscrupulous.

"More by chance than skill we stumbled onto a deadly secret—the formula for a poisonous gas, a thousand times more deadly than anything yet dreamed of. That was what he was paying us to invent or discover for him, but the discovery sobered us. We realized that the man who possessed the secret of that gas, could easily conquer the world. We were willing to aid Yuen Chin against his Mongolian enemies; we were not willing to elevate a yellow mandarin to world empire, to see our hellish discovery directed against the lives of our own people.

"Yet we were not willing to destroy the formula, because we foresaw a time when America, with her back to the wall, might have a desperate need for such a weapon. So we wrote out the formula in code, but left out three symbols, without any of which the formula is meaningless and undecipherable. Each of us then, had a lower jaw tooth pulled out, and on the gold tooth put in its place, was carved one of the three symbols. Thus we took precautions against our own greed, as well as against the avarice of outsiders. One of us might conceivably fall so low as to sell the secret, but it would be useless without the other two symbols.

"Yuen Chin fell and was beheaded on the great execution ground at Peking. We escaped, Lynch, Hopkins and I, not only with our lives but with most of the money which had been paid us. But the formula, scrawled on parchment, we were obliged to leave, secreted among musty archives in an ancient temple.

"Only one man knew our secret: an old Chinese tooth-puller, who aided us in the matter of the teeth. He owed his life to Richard Lynch, and when he swore the oath of eternal silence, we knew we could trust him."

"Yet you think somebody is after the secret symbols?"

"What else could it be? I cannot understand it. The old tooth-puller must have died long ago. Who could have learned of it? Torture would not have dragged the secret from him. Yet it can be for no other reason that this fellow you call Yarghouz Barolass murdered and mutilated the bodies of my former companions, and now is after me.

"Why, I love life as well as any man, but my own peril shrinks into insignificance compared to the world-wide menace contained in those little carven symbols—two of which are now, according to what you say, in the hands of some ruthless foe of the western world.

"Somebody has found the formula we left hidden in the temple, and has learned somehow of its secret. Anything can come out of China. Just now the bandit war-lord Yah Lai is threatening to overthrow the National government—who knows what devilish concoction that Chinese caldron is brewing?

"The thought of the secret of that gas in the hands of some Oriental conqueror is appalling. My God, gentlemen, I fear you do not realize the full significance of the matter!"

"I've got a faint idea," grunted Rollins. "Ever see a dagger like this?" He presented the weapon that had killed the Mongol.

"Many of them, in China," answered Willoughby promptly.

"Then it isn't a Mongol weapon?"

"No; it's distinctly Chinese; there is a conventional Manchu inscription on the hilt."

"Ummmmmm!" Rollins sat scowling, chin on fist, idly tapping the blade against his shoe, lost in meditation. Admittedly, he was all at sea, lost in a bewildering tangle. To his companions he looked like a grim figure of retribution, brooding over the fate of the wicked. In reality he was cursing his luck.

"What are you going to do now?" demanded Hoolihan.

"Only one thing to do," responded Rollins. "I'm going to try to run down Yarghouz Barolass. I'm going to start with River Street—God knows, it'll be like looking for a rat in a swamp. I want you to contrive to let one of those Mongols escape, Hoolihan. I'll try to trail him back to Yarghouz's hangout—"

The phone tingled loudly.

Rollins reached it with a long stride.

"Who speaks, please?" Over the wire came a voice with a subtle but definite accent.

"Brock Rollins," grunted the big dick.

"A friend speaks, Detective," came the bland voice. "Before we progress further, let me warn you that it will be impossible to trace this call, and would do you no good to do so."

"Well?" Rollins was bristling like a big truculent dog.

"Mr. Willoughby," the suave voice continued, "is a doomed man. He is as good as dead already. Guards and guns will not save him, when the Sons of Erlik are ready to strike. But *you* can save him, without firing a shot!"

"Yeah?" It was a scarcely articulate snarl humming blood-thirstily from Rollins' bull-throat.

"If you were to come alone to the House of Dreams on Levant street, Yarghouz Barolass would speak to you, and a compromise might be arranged whereby Mr. Willoughby's life would be spared."

"Compromise, Hell!" roared the big dick, the skin over his knuckles showing white. "Who do you think you're talking to? Think I'd fall into a trap like that?"

"You have a hostage," came back the voice. "One of the men you hold is Yarghouz Barolass's brother. Let him suffer if there is treachery. I swear by the bones of my ancestors, no harm shall come to you!"

The voice ceased with a click at the other end of the wire.

Rollins wheeled.

"Yarghouz Barolass must be getting desperate to try such a child's trick as that!" he swore. Then he considered, and muttered, half to himself: "By the bones of his ancestors! Never heard of a Mongolian breaking *that* oath. All that stuff about Yarghouz's brother may be the bunk. Yet—well, maybe he's trying to outsmart me—draw me away from Willoughby—on the other hand, maybe he thinks that I'd never fall for a trick like that—aw, to Hell with thinking! I'm going to start acting!"

"What do you mean?" demanded Hoolihan.

"I mean I'm going to the House of Dreams, alone."

"You're crazy!" exclaimed Hoolihan. "Take a squad, surround the house, and raid it!"

"And find an empty rat-den," grunted Rollins, his peculiar obsession for working alone again asserting itself.

Dawn was not far away when Rollins entered the smoky den near the waterfront which was known to the Chinese as the House of Dreams, and whose dingy exterior masked a subterranean opium joint. Only a pudgy Chinaboy nodded behind the counter; he looked up with no apparent surprise. Without a word he led Rollins to a curtain in the back of the shop, pulled it aside, and revealed a door. The detective gripped his gun under his coat, nerves taut with excitement that must come to any man who has deliberately walked into what might prove to be a death-trap. The boy knocked, lifting a sing-song monotone, and a voice answered from within. Rollins started. He recognized that voice. The boy opened the door, bobbed his head and was gone. Rollins entered, pulling the door to behind him.

He was in a room heaped and strewn with divans and silk cushions. If there were other doors, they were masked by the black velvet hangings, which, worked with gilt dragons, covered the walls. On a divan near the further wall squatted a stocky, pot-bellied shape, in black silk, a close-fitting velvet cap on his shaven head.

"So you came, after all!" breathed the detective. "Don't move, Yarghouz Barolass. I've got you covered through my coat. Your gang can't get me quick enough to keep me from getting you first."

"Why do you threaten me, Detective?" Yarghouz Barolass's face was expressionless, the square, parchment-skinned face of a Mongol from the Gobi, with wide thin lips and glittering black eyes. His English was perfect.

"See, I trust you. I am here, alone. The boy who let you in said that you are alone. Good. You kept your word, I keep my promise. For the time there is truce between us, and I am ready to bargain, as you suggested."

"As *I* suggested?" demanded Rollins.

"I have no desire to harm Mr. Willoughby, any more than I wished to harm either of the other gentlemen," said Yarghouz Barolass. "But knowing them all as I did—from report and discreet observation—it never occurred to me that I could obtain what I wished while they lived. So I did not enter into negotiations with them."

"So you want Willoughby's tooth, too?"

"Not I," disclaimed Yarghouz Barolass. "It is an honorable person in China, the grandson of an old man who babbled in his dotage, as old men often do, drooling secrets torture could not have wrung from him in his soundness of mind. The grandson, Yah Lai, has risen from a mean position to that of war-lord. He listened to the mumblings of his grandfather, a tooth-puller. He found a formula, written in code, and learned of symbols on the teeth of old men. He sent a request to me, with promise of much reward. I have one tooth, procured from the unfortunate person, Richard Lynch. Now if you will hand over the other—that of Job Hopkins—as you promised, perhaps we may reach a compromise by which Mr. Willoughby will be allowed to keep his life, in return for a tooth, as you hinted."

"As *I* hinted?" exclaimed Rollins. "What are you driving at? I made no promise; and I certainly haven't Job Hopkins' tooth. You've got it, yourself."

"All this is unnecessary," objected Yarghouz, an edge to his tone. "You have a reputation for veracity, in spite of your violent nature. I was relying upon your reputation for honesty when I accepted this appointment. Of course, I already knew that you had Hopkins' tooth. When my blundering servants, having been frightened by you as they left the vaults, gathered at the appointed rendezvous, they discovered that he to whom was entrusted the jaw-bone containing the precious tooth, was not among them. They returned to the graveyard and found his body, but not the tooth. It was obvious that you had killed him and taken it from him."

Rollins was so thunderstruck by this new twist, that he remained speechless, his mind a tangled whirl of bewilderment.

Yarghouz Barolass continued tranquilly: "I was about to send my servants out in another attempt to secure you, when your agent phoned me—though how he located me on the telephone is still a mystery into which I must inquire—and announced that you were ready to meet me at the House of Dreams, and give me Job Hopkins' tooth, in return for an opportunity to bargain personally for Mr. Willoughby's life. Knowing you to be a man of honor, I agreed, trusting you—"

"This is madness!" exclaimed Rollins "I didn't call you, or have anybody call you. *You,* or rather, one of your men, called *me.*"

"I did not!" Yarghouz was on his feet, his stocky body under the rippling black silk quivering with rage and suspicion. His eyes narrowed to slits, his wide mouth knotted viciously.

"You deny that you promised to give me Job Hopkins' tooth?"

"Sure I do!" snapped Rollins. "I haven't got it, and what's more, I'm not 'compromising' as you call it—"

"Liar!" Yarghouz spat the epithet like a snake hissing. "You have tricked—betrayed me—used my trust in your blackened honor to dupe me—"

"Keep cool," advised Rollins. "Remember, I've got a Colt.45 trained on you."

"Shoot and die!" retorted Yarghouz. "I do not know what your game is, but I know that if you shoot me, we will fall together. Fool, do you think I would keep my promise to a barbarian dog? Behind this hanging is the entrance to a tunnel through which I can escape before any of your stupid police, if you have brought any with you, can enter this room. You have been covered since you came through that door, by a man hiding behind the tapestry. Try to stop me, and you die!"

"I believe you're telling the truth about not calling me," said Rollins slowly. "I believe somebody tricked us both, for some reason. You were called, in my name, and I was called, in yours."

Yarghouz halted short in some hissing tirade. His eyes were like black evil jewels in the lamplight.

"More lies?" he demanded uncertainly.

"No; I think somebody in your gang is double-crossing you. Now easy, I'm not pulling a gun. I'm just going to show you the knife that I found sticking in the back of the fellow you seem to think I killed."

He drew it from his coat-pocket with his left hand—his right still gripped his gun beneath the garment—and tossed it on the divan.

Yarghouz pounced on it. His slit eyes flared wide with a terrible light; his yellow skin went ashen. He cried out something in his own tongue, which Rollins did not understand.

In a torrent of hissing sibilances, he lapsed briefly into English: "I see it all now! This was too subtle for a barbarian! Death to them all!" Wheeling toward the tapestry behind the divan he shrieked: "Gutchluk!"

There was no answer, but Rollins thought he saw the black velvety expanse billow slightly. With his skin the color of old ashes, Yarghouz Barolass ran at the hanging, ignoring Rollins' order to halt, seized the tapestries, tore them aside—something flashed between them like a beam of white hot light. Yarghouz's scream broke in a ghastly gurgle. His head pitched forward, then his whole body swayed backward, and he fell heavily among the cushions, clutching at the hilt of a skewer-like dagger that quivered upright in his breast. The Mongol's yellow claw-like hands fell away from the crimsoned hilt, spread wide, clutching at the thick carpet; a convulsive spasm ran through his frame, and those taloned yellow fingers went limp.

Gun in hand, Rollins took a single stride toward the tapestries—then halted short, staring at the figure which moved imperturbably through them: a tall yellow man in the robes of a mandarin, who smiled and bowed, his hands hidden in his wide sleeves.

"You killed Yarghous Barolass!" accused the detective.

"The evil one indeed has been dispatched to join his ancestors by my hand," agreed the mandarin. "Be not afraid. The Mongol who covered you through a peep-hole with an abbreviated shotgun has likewise departed this uncertain life, suddenly and silently. My own people hold supreme in the House of Dreams this night. All that we ask is that you make no attempt to stay our departure."

"Who are you?" demanded Rollins.

"But a humble servant of Fang Yin, Lord of Peking. When it was learned that these unworthy ones sought a formula in America that might enable the upstart Yah Lai to overthrow the government of China, word was sent in haste to me. It was almost too late. Two men had already died. The third was menaced."

"I sent my servants instantly to intercept the evil Sons of Erlik at the vaults they desecrated. But for your appearance, frightening the Mongols to scattering in flight, before the trap could be sprung, my servants would have caught them all in ambush. As it was, they did manage to slay he who carried the relic Yarghouz sought, and this they brought to me."

"I took the liberty of impersonating a servant of the Mongol in my speech with you, and of pretending to be a Chinese agent of yours, while speaking with Yarghouz. All worked out as I wished. Lured by the thought of the tooth, at the loss of which he was maddened, Yarghouz came from his secret, well-guarded lair, and fell into my hands. I brought you here to witness his execution, so that you might realize that Mr. Willoughby is no longer in danger. Fang Yin has no ambitions for world empire; he wishes but to hold what is his. That he is well able to do, now that the threat of the devil-gas is lifted. And now I must be gone. Yarghouz had laid careful plans for his flight out of the country. I will take advantage of his preparations."

"Wait a minute!" exclaimed Rollins. "I've got to arrest you for the murder of this rat."

"I am sorry," murmured the mandarin. "I am in much haste. No need to lift your revolver. I swore that you would not be injured and I keep my word."

As he spoke, the light went suddenly out. Rollins sprang forward, cursing, fumbling at the tapestries which had swished in the darkness as if from the passing of a large body between them. His fingers met only solid walls, and when at last the light came on again, he was alone in the room, and behind the hangings a heavy door had been slid shut. On the divan lay something that glinted in the lamplight, and Rollins looked down on a curiously carven gold tooth.

THE HORROR FROM THE MOUND

STEVE BRILL did not believe in ghosts or demons. Juan Lopez did. But neither the caution of the one nor the sturdy skepticism of the other was shield against the horror that fell upon them—the horror forgotten by men for more than three hundred years—a screaming fear monstrously resurrected from the black lost ages.

Yet as Steve Brill sat on his sagging stoop that last evening, his thoughts were as far from uncanny menaces as the thoughts of man can be. His ruminations were bitter but materialistic. He surveyed his farmland and he swore. Brill was tall, rangy and tough as boot-leather—true son of the iron-bodied pioneers who wrenched West Texas from the wilderness. He was browned by the sun and strong as a longhorned steer. His lean legs and the boots on them showed his cowboy instincts, and now he cursed himself that he had ever climbed off the hurricane deck of his crankeyed mustang and turned to farming. He was no farmer, the young puncher admitted profanely.

Yet his failure had not all been his fault. Plentiful rain in the winter—so rare in West Texas—had given promise of good crops. But as usual, things had happened. A late blizzard had destroyed all the budding fruit. The grain which had looked so promising was ripped to shreds and battered into the ground by terrific hailstorms just as it was turning yellow. A period of intense dryness, followed by another hailstorm, finished the corn.

Then the cotton, which had somehow struggled through, fell before a swarm of grasshoppers which stripped Brill's field almost overnight. So Brill sat and swore that he would not renew his lease—he gave fervent thanks that he did not own the land on which he had wasted his sweat, and that there were still broad rolling ranges to the West where a strong young man could make his living riding and roping.

Now as Brill sat glumly, he was aware of the approaching form of his nearest neighbor, Juan Lopez, a taciturn old Mexican who lived in a hut just out of sight over the hill across the creek, and grubbed for a living. At present he was clearing a strip of land on an adjoining farm, and in returning to his hut he crossed a corner of Brill's pasture.

Brill idly watched him climb through the barbed-wire fence and trudge along the path he had worn in the short dry grass. He had been working at his present job for over a month now, chopping down tough gnarly mesquite trees and digging up their incredibly long roots, and Brill knew that he always followed the same path home. And watching, Brill noted him swerving far aside, seemingly to avoid a low rounded hillock which jutted above the level of the pasture. Lopez went far around this knoll and Brill remembered that the old Mexican always circled it at a distance. And another thing came into Brill's idle mind—Lopez always increased his gait when he was passing the knoll, and he always managed to get by it before sundown—yet Mexican laborers generally worked from the first light of dawn to the last glint of twilight, especially at these grubbing jobs, when they were paid by the acre and not by the day. Brill's curiosity was aroused.

He rose, and sauntering down the slight slope on the crown of which his shack sat, hailed the plodding Mexican.

"Hey, Lopez, wait a minute."

Lopez halted; looked about, and remained motionless but unenthusiastic as the white man approached.

"Lopez," said Brill lazily, "it ain't none of my business, but I just wanted to ask you—how come you always go so far around that old Indian mound?"

"No *sabe*," grunted Lopez shortly.

"You're a liar," responded Brill genially. "You savvy all right; you speak English as good as me. What's the matter—you think that mound's ha'nted or somethin'!"

Brill could speak Spanish himself and read it, too, but like most Anglo-Saxons he much preferred to speak his own language.

Lopez shrugged his shoulders.

"It is not a good place, *no bueno*," he muttered, avoiding Brill's eyes. "Let hidden things rest."

"I reckon you're scared of ghosts," Brill bantered. "Shucks, if that is an Indian mound, them Indians been dead so long their ghosts 'ud be plumb wore out by now."

Brill knew that the illiterate Mexicans looked with superstitious aversion on the mounds that are found here and there through the Southwest—relics of a past and forgotten age, containing the moldering bones of chiefs and warriors of a lost race.

"Best not to disturb what is hidden in the earth," grunted Lopez.

"Bosh," said Brill. "Me and some boys busted into one of them mounds over in the Palo Pinto country and dug up pieces of a skeleton with some beads and flint arrowheads and the like. I kept some of the teeth a long time till I lost 'em, and I ain't never been ha'nted."

"Indians?" snorted Lopez unexpectedly. "Who spoke of Indians? There have been more than Indians in this country. In the old times strange things happened here. I have heard the tales of my people, handed down from generation to generation. And my people were here long before yours, *Señor* Brill."

"Yeah, you're right," admitted Steve. "First white men in this country was Spaniards, of course. Coronado passed along not very far from here, I hear tell, and Hernando de Estrada's expedition came through here—away back yonder—I dunno how long ago."

"In 1545," said Lopez. "They pitched camp yonder where your corral stands now."

Brill turned to glance at his rail-fenced corral, inhabited now by his saddle-horse, a pair of workhorses and a scrawny cow.

"How come you know so much about it?" he asked curiously.

"One of my ancestors marched with de Estrada," answered Lopez. "A soldier, Porfirio Lopez; he told his son of that expedition, and he told his son, and so down the family line to me, who have no son to whom I can tell the tale."

"I didn't know you were so well connected," said Brill. "Maybe you know somethin' about the gold de Estrada was supposed to have hid around here, somewhere."

"There was no gold," growled Lopez. "De Estrada's soldiers bore only their arms, and they fought their way through hostile country—many left their bones along the trail. Later—many years later—a mule train from Santa Fe was attacked not many miles from here by Comanches and they hid their gold and escaped; so the legends got mixed up. But even their gold is not there now, because Gringo buffalo-hunters found it and dug it up."

Brill nodded abstractedly, hardly heeding. Of all the continent of North America there is no section so haunted by tales of lost or hidden treasure as is the Southwest. Uncounted wealth passed back and forth over the hills and plains of Texas and New Mexico in the old days when Spain owned the gold and silver mines of the New World and controlled the rich fur trade of the West, and echoes of that wealth linger on in tales of golden caches. Some such vagrant dream, born of failure and pressing poverty, rose in Brill's mind.

Aloud he spoke: "Well, anyway, I got nothin' else to do and I believe I'll dig into that old mound and see what I can find."

The effect of that simple statement on Lopez was nothing short of shocking. He recoiled and his swarthy brown face went ashy; his black eyes flared and he threw up his arms in a gesture of intense expostulation.

"*Dios, no!*" he cried. "Don't do that, *Señor* Brill! There is a curse—my grandfather told me—"

"Told you what?" asked Brill.

Lopez lapsed into sullen silence.

"I cannot speak," he muttered. "I am sworn to silence. Only to an eldest son could I open my heart. But believe me when I say better had you cut your throat than to break into that accursed mound."

"Well," said Brill, impatient of Mexican superstitions, "if it's so bad why don't you tell me about it? Gimme a logical reason for not bustin' into it."

"I cannot speak!" cried the Mexican desperately. "I know!—but I swore to silence on the Holy Crucifix, just as every man of my family has sworn. It is a thing so dark, it is to risk damnation even to speak of it! Were I to tell you, I would blast the soul from your body. But I have sworn—and I have no son, so my lips are sealed forever."

"Aw, well," said Brill sarcastically, "why don't you write it out?"

Lopez started, stared, and to Steve's surprise, caught at the suggestion.

"I will! *Dios* be thanked the good priest taught me to write when I was a child. My oath said nothing of writing. I only swore not to speak. I will write out the whole thing for you, if you will swear not to speak of it afterward, and to destroy the paper as soon as you have read it."

"Sure," said Brill, to humor him, and the old Mexican seemed much relieved.

"*Bueno*! I will go at once and write. Tomorrow as I go to work I will bring you the paper and you will understand why no one must open that accursed mound!"

And Lopez hurried along his homeward path, his stooped shoulders swaying with the effort of his unwonted haste. Steve grinned after him, shrugged his shoulders and turned back toward his own shack. Then he halted, gazing back at the low rounded mound with its grass-grown sides. It must be an Indian tomb, he decided, what with its symmetry and its similarity to other Indian mounds he had seen. He scowled as he tried to figure out the seeming connection between the mysterious knoll and the martial ancestor of Juan Lopez.

Brill gazed after the receding figure of the old Mexican. A shallow valley, cut by a half-dry creek, bordered with trees and underbrush, lay between Brill's pasture and the low sloping hill beyond which lay Lopez's shack. Among the trees along the creek bank the old Mexican was disappearing. And Brill came to a sudden decision.

Hurrying up the slight slope, he took a pick and a shovel from the tool shed built onto the back of his shack. The sun had not yet set and Brill believed he could open the mound deep enough to determine its nature before dark. If not, he could work by lantern light. Steve, like most of his breed, lived mostly by impulse, and his present urge was to tear into that mysterious hillock and find what, if anything, was concealed therein. The thought of treasure came again to his mind, piqued by the evasive attitude of Lopez.

What if, after all, that grassy heap of brown earth hid riches—virgin ore from forgotten mines, or the minted coinage of old Spain? Was it not possible that the musketeers of de Estrada had themselves reared that pile above a treasure they could not bear away, molding it in the likeness of an Indian mound to fool seekers? Did old Lopez know that? It would not be strange if, knowing of treasure there, the old Mexican refrained from disturbing it. Ridden with grisly superstitious fears, he might well live out a life of barren toil rather than risk the wrath of lurking ghosts or devils—for the Mexicans say that hidden gold is always accursed, and surely there was supposed to be some especial doom resting on this mound. Well, Brill meditated, Latin-Indian devils had no terrors for the Anglo-Saxon, tormented by the demons of drouth and storm and crop failure.

Steve set to work with the savage energy characteristic of his breed. The task was no light one; the soil, baked by the fierce sun, was iron-hard, and mixed with rocks and pebbles. Brill sweated profusely and grunted with his efforts, but the fire of the treasure-hunter was on him. He shook the sweat out of his eyes and drove in the pick with mighty strokes that ripped and crumbled the close-packed dirt.

The sun went down, and in the long dreamy summer twilight he worked on, almost oblivious of time or space. He began to be convinced that the mound was a genuine Indian tomb, as he found traces of charcoal in the soil. The ancient people which reared these sepulchers had kept fires burning upon them for days, at some point in the building. All the mounds Steve had ever opened had contained a solid stratum of charcoal a short distance below the surface: But the charcoal traces he found now were scattered about through the soil.

His idea of a Spanish-built treasure trove faded, but he persisted. Who knows? Perhaps that strange folk men now called Mound-Builders had treasure of their own which they laid away with the dead.

Then Steve yelped in exultation as his pick rang on a bit of metal. He snatched it up and held it close to his eyes, straining in the waning, light. It was caked and corroded with rust, worn almost paper-thin, but he knew it for what it was—a spur-rowel, unmistakably Spanish with its long cruel points. And he halted, completely bewildered. No Spaniard ever reared this mound, with its undeniable marks of aboriginal workmanship. Yet how came that relic of Spanish caballeros hidden deep in the packed soil?

Brill shook his head and set to work again. He knew that in the center of the mound, if it were indeed an aboriginal tomb, he would find a narrow chamber built of heavy stones, containing the bones of the chief for whom the mound had been reared and the victims sacrificed above it. And in the gathering darkness he felt his pick strike heavily against something granite-like and unyielding. Examination, by sense of feel as well as by sight, proved it to be a solid block of stone, roughly hewn. Doubtless it formed one of the ends of the deathchamber. Useless to try to shatter it. Brill chipped and pecked about it, scrapping the dirt and pebbles away from the corners until he felt that wrenching it out would be but a matter of sinking the pick-point underneath and levering it out.

But now he was suddenly aware that darkness had come on. In the young moon objects were dim and shadowy. His mustang nickered in the corral whence came the comfortable crunch of tired beasts' jaws on corn. A whippoorwill called eerily from the dark shadows of the narrow winding creek. Brill straightened reluctantly. Better get a lantern and continue his explorations by its light.

He felt in his pocket with some idea of wrenching out the stone and exploring the cavity by the aid of matches. Then he stiffened. Was it imagination that he heard a faint sinister rustling, which seemed to come from behind the blocking stone? Snakes! Doubtless they had holes somewhere about the base of the mound and there might be a dozen big diamond-backed rattlers coiled up in that cave-like interior waiting for him to put his hand among them. He shivered slightly at the thought and backed away out of the excavation he had made.

It wouldn't do to go poking about blindly into holes. And for the past few minutes, he realized, he had been aware of a faint foul odor exuding from interstices about the blocking stone—though he admitted that the smell suggested reptiles no more than it did any other menacing scent. It had a charnel-house reek about it—gases formed in the chamber of death, no doubt, and dangerous to the living.

Steve laid down his pick and returned to the house, impatient of the necessary delay. Entering the dark building, he struck a match and located his kerosene lantern hanging on its nail on the wall. Shaking it, he satisfied himself that it was nearly full of coal oil, and lighted it. Then he fared forth again, for his eagerness would not allow him to pause long enough for a bite of food. The mere opening of the mound intrigued him, as it must always intrigue a man of imagination, and the discovery of the Spanish spur had whetted his curiosity.

He hurried from his shack, the swinging lantern casting long distorted shadows ahead of him and behind. He chuckled as he visualized Lopez's thoughts and actions when he learned, on the morrow, that the forbidden mound had been pried into. A good thing he opened it that evening, Brill reflected; Lopez might even have tried to prevent him meddling with it, had he known.

In the dreamy hush of the summer night, Brill reached the mound—lifted his lantern—swore bewilderedly. The lantern revealed his excavations, his tools lying carelessly where he had dropped them—and a black gaping aperture! The great blocking stone lay in the bottom of the excavation he had made, as if thrust carelessly aside. Warily he thrust the lantern forward and peered into the small cave-like chamber, expecting to see he knew not what. Nothing met his eyes except the bare rock sides of a long narrow cell, large enough to receive a man's body, which had apparently been built up of roughly hewn square-cut stones, cunningly and strongly joined together.

"Lopez!" exclaimed Steve furiously. "The dirty coyote! He's been watchin' me work—and when I went after the lantern, he snuck up and pried the rock out and grabbed whatever was in there, I reckon. Blast his greasy hide, I'll fix him!"

Savagely he extinguished the lantern and glared across the shallow, brush-grown valley. And as he looked he stiffened. Over the corner of the hill, on the other side of which the shack of Lopez stood, a shadow moved. The slender moon was setting, the light dim and the play of the shadows baffling. But Steve's eyes were sharpened by the sun and winds of the wastelands, and he knew that it was some two-legged creature that was disappearing over the low shoulder of the mesquite-grown hill.

"Beatin' it to his shack," snarled Brill. "He's shore got somethin' or he wouldn't be travelin' at that speed."

Brill swallowed, wondering why a peculiar trembling had suddenly taken hold of him. What was there unusual about a thieving old greaser running home with his loot? Brill tried to drown the feeling that there was something peculiar about the gait of the dim shadow, which had seemed to move at a sort of slinking lope. There, must have been need for swiftness when stocky old Juan Lopez elected to travel at such a strange pace.

"Whatever he found is as much mine as his," swore Brill, trying to get his mind off the abnormal aspect of the figure's flight, "I got this land leased and I done all the work diggin'. A curse, heck! No wonder he told me that stuff. Wanted me to leave it alone so he could get it hisself. It's a wonder he ain't dug it up long before this. But you can't never tell about them spigs."

Brill, as he meditated thus, was striding down the gentle slope of the pasture which led down to the creek bed. He passed into the shadows of the trees and dense underbrush and walked across the dry creek bed, noting absently that neither whippoor-will nor hoot-owl called in the darkness. There was a waiting, listening tenseness in the night that he did not like. The shadows in the creek bed seemed too thick, too breathless. He wished he had not blown out the lantern, which he still carried, and was glad he had brought the pick, gripped like a battle-ax in his right hand. He had an impulse to whistle, just to break the silence, then swore and dismissed the thought. Yet he was glad when he clambered up the low opposite bank and emerged into the starlight.

He walked up the slope and onto the hill, and looked down on the mesquite flat wherein stood Lopez's squalid hut. A light showed at the one window.

"Packin' his things for a getaway, I reckon," grunted Steve. "Ow, what the—"

He staggered as from a physical impact as a frightful scream knifed the stillness. He wanted to clap his hands over his ears to shut out the horror of that cry, which rose unbearably and then broke in an abhorrent gurgle.

"Good God!" Steve felt the cold sweat spring out upon him. "Lopez—or somebody—"

Even as he gasped the words he was running down the hill as fast as his long legs could carry him. Some unspeakable horror was taking place in that lonely hut, but he was going to inves-tigate if it meant facing the Devil himself. He tightened his grip on his pick-handle as he ran. Wandering prowlers, murdering old Lopez for the loot he had taken from the mound, Steve thought, and forgot his wrath. It would go hard for anyone he caught molesting the old scoundrel, thief though he might be.

He hit the flat, running hard. And then the light in the hut went out and Steve staggered in full flight, bringing up against a mesquite tree with an impact that jolted a grunt out of him and tore his hands on the thorns. Rebounding with a sobbed curse, he rushed for the shack, nerving himself for what he might see—his hair still standing on end at what he had already seen.

Brill tried the one door of the hut and found it bolted. He shouted to Lopez and received no answer. Yet utter silence did not reign. From within came a curious muffled worrying sound that ceased as Brill swung his pick crashing against the door. The flimsy portal splintered and Brill leaped into the dark hut, eyes blazing, pick swung high for a desperate onslaught. But no sound ruffled the grisly silence, and in the darkness nothing stirred, though Brill's chaotic imagination peopled the shadowed corners of the hut with shapes of horror.

With a hand damp with perspiration he found a match and struck it. Besides himself only Lopez occupied the hut—old Lopez, stark dead on the dirt floor, arms spread wide like a crucifix, mouth sagging open in a semblance of idiocy, eyes wide and staring with a horror Brill found intolerable. The one window gaped open, showing the method of the slayer's exit—possibly his entrance as well. Brill went to that window and gazed out warily. He saw only the sloping hillside on one hand and the mesquite flat on the other. He stared—was that a hint of movement among the stunted shadows of the mesquites and chaparral—or had he but imagined he glimpsed a dim loping figure among the trees?

He turned back, as the match burned down to his fingers. He lit the old coal-oil lamp on the rude table, cursing as he burned his hand. The globe of the lamp was very hot, as if it had been burning for hours.

Reluctantly he turned to the corpse on the floor. Whatever sort of death had come to Lopez, it had been horrible, but Brill, gingerly examining the dead man, found no wound—no mark of knife or bludgeon on him. Wait. There was a thin smear of

blood on Brill's questing hand. Searching, he found the source—
three or four tiny punctures in Lopez's throat, from which blood
had oozed sluggishly. At first he thought they had been inflicted
with a stiletto—a thin round edgeless dagger then he shook his
head. He had seen stiletto wounds—he had the scar of one on
his own body. These wounds more resembled the bite of some
animal—they looked like the marks of pointed fangs.

Yet Brill did not believe they were deep enough to have
caused death, nor had much blood flowed from them. A belief,
abhorrent with grisly speculations, rose up in the dark corners
of his mind—that Lopez had died of fright and that the wounds
had been inflicted either simultaneously—with his death, or an
instant afterward.

And Steve noticed something else; scrawled about on the
floor lay a number of dingy leaves of paper, scrawled in the old
Mexican's crude hand—he would write of the curse of the
mound, he had said. There were the sheets on which he had
written, there was the stump of a pencil on the floor, there was
the hot lamp globe, all mute witnesses that the old Mexican had
been seated at the rough-hewn table writing for hours. Then it
was not he who opened the mound-chamber and stole the
contents—but who was it, in God's name? And who or what
was it that Brill had glimpsed loping over the shoulder of the
hill?

Well, there was but one thing to do—saddle his mustang and
ride the ten miles to Coyote Wells, the nearest town, and inform
the sheriff of the murder.

Brill gathered up the papers. The last was crumpled in the
old man's clutching hand and Brill secured it with some difficulty.
Then as he turned to extinguish the light, he hesitated, and
cursed himself for the crawling fear that lurked at the back of
his mind—fear of the shadowy thing he had seen cross the
window just before the light was extinguished in the hut. The
long arm of the murderer, he thought, reaching for the lamp to
put it out, no doubt. What had there been abnormal or inhuman

about that vision, distorted though it must have been in the dim lamplight and shadow? As a man strives to remember the details of a nightmare dream, Steve tried to define in his mind some clear reason that would explain, why that flying glimpse had unnerved him to the extent of blundering headlong into a tree, and why the mere vague remembrance of it now caused cold sweat to break out on him.

Cursing himself to keep up his courage, he lighted his lantern, blew out the lamp on the rough table, and resolutely set forth, grasping his pick like a weapon. After all, why should certain seemingly abnormal aspects about a sordid murder upset him? Such crimes were abhorrent, but common enough, especially among Mexicans, who cherished unguessed feuds.

Then as he stepped into the silent star-flecked night he brought up short. From across the creek sounded the sudden soul-shaking scream of a horse in deadly terror—then a mad drumming of hoofs that receded in the distance. And Brill swore in rage and dismay. Was it a panther lurking in the hills—had a monster cat slain old Lopez? Then why was not the victim marked with the scars of fierce hooked talons? *And who extinguished the light in the hut?*

As he wondered, Brill was running swiftly toward the dark creek. Not lightly does a cowpuncher regard the stampeding of his stock. As he passed into the darkness of the brush along the dry creek, Brill found his tongue strangely dry. He kept swallowing, and he held the lantern high. It made but faint impression in the gloom, but seemed to accentuate the blackness of the crowding shadows. For some strange reason, the thought entered Brill's chaotic mind that though the land was new to the Anglo-Saxon, it was in reality very old. That broken and desecrated tomb was mute evidence that the land was ancient to man, and suddenly the night and the hills and the shadows bore on Brill with a sense of hideous antiquity. Here had long, generations of men lived and died before Brill's ancestors ever heard of the land. In the night, in the shadows of this very creek, men had

no doubt given up their ghosts in grisly ways. With these reflec-
tions Brill hurried through the shadows of the thick trees.

He breathed deeply in relief when he emerged from the trees
on his own side. Hurrying up the gentle slope to the railed corral,
he held up his lantern, investigating. The corral was empty; not
even the placid cow was in sight. And the bars were down. That
pointed to human agency, and the affair took on a newly sinister
aspect. Someone did not intend that Brill should ride to Coyote
Wells that night. It meant that the murderer intended making
his getaway and wanted a good start on the law, or else—Brill
grinned wryly. Far away across a mesquite flat he believed he
could still catch the faint and faraway noise of running horses.
What in God's name had given them such a fright? A cold finger
of fear played shudderingly on Brill's spine.

Steve headed for the house. He did not enter boldly. He crept
clear around the shack, peering shudderingly into the dark
windows, listening with painful intensity for some sound to
betray the presence of the lurking killer. At last he ventured to
open the door and step in. He threw the door back against the
wall to find if anyone were hiding behind it, lifted the lantern
high and stepped in, heart pounding, pick gripped fiercely, his
feelings a mixture of fear and red rage. But no hidden assassin
leaped upon him, and a wary exploration of the shack revealed
nothing.

With a sigh of relief Brill locked the doors, made fast the
windows and lighted his old coal-oil lamp. The thought of old
Lopez lying, a glassy-eyed corpse alone in the hut across the
creek, made him wince and shiver, but he did not intend to start
for town on foot in the night.

He drew from its hiding-place his reliable old Colt.45, spun
the blue-steel cylinder, and grinned mirthlessly. Maybe the killer
did not intend to leave any witnesses to his crime alive. Well, let
him come! He—or they—would find a young cowpuncher with
a six-shooter less easy prey than an old unarmed Mexican. And
that reminded Brill of the papers he had brought from the hut.

Taking care that he was not in line with a window through which a sudden bullet might come, he settled himself to read, with one ear alert for stealthy sounds.

And as he read the crude laborious script, a slow cold horror grew in his soul. It was a tale of fear that the old Mexican had scrawled—a tale handed down from generation to generation—a tale of ancient times.

And Brill read of the wanderings of the *caballero* Hernando de Estrada and his armored pikemen, who dared the deserts of the Southwest when all was strange and unknown. There were some forty-odd soldiers, servants, and masters, at the beginning, the manuscript ran. There was the captain, de Estrada, and the priest, and young Juan Zavilla, and Don Santiago de Valdez—a mysterious nobleman who had been taken off a helplessly floating ship in the Caribbean Sea—all the others of the crew and passengers had died of plague, he had said and he had cast their bodies overboard. So de Estrada had taken him aboard the ship that was bearing the expedition from Spain, and de Valdez joined them in their explorations.

Brill read something of their wanderings, told in the crude style of old Lopez, as the old Mexican's ancestors had handed down the tale for over three hundred years. The bare written words dimly reflected the terrific hardships the explorers had encountered—drouth, thirst, floods, the desert sandstorms, the spears of hostile redskins. But it was of another peril that old Lopez told—a grisly lurking horror that fell upon the lonely caravan wandering through the immensity of the wild. Man by man they fell and no man knew the slayer. Fear and black suspicion ate at the heart of the expedition like a canker, and their leader knew not where to turn. This they all knew: among them was a fiend in human form.

Men began to draw apart from each other, to scatter along the line of march, and this mutual suspicion, that sought security in solitude, made it easier for the fiend. The skeleton of the expedition staggered through the wilderness, lost, dazed and helpless, and still the unseen horror hung on their flanks, dragging down the stragglers, preying on drowsing sentries and sleeping men. And on the throat of each was found the wounds of pointed fangs that bled the victim white; so that the living knew with what manner of evil they had to deal. Men reeled through the wild, calling on the saints, or blaspheming in their terror, fighting frenziedly against sleep, until they fell with exhaustion and sleep stole on them with horror and death.

Suspicion centered on a great black man, a cannibal slave from Calabar. And they put him in chains. But young Juan Zavilla went the way of the rest, and then the priest was taken. But the priest fought off his fiendish assailant and lived long enough to gasp the demon's name to de Estrada. And Brill, shuddering and wide-eyed, read:

"...And now it was evident to de Estrada that the good priest had spoken the truth, and the slayer was Don Santiago de Valdez, who was a vampire, an undead fiend, subsisting on the blood of the living. And de Estrada called to mind a certain foul nobleman who had lurked, in the mountains of Castile since the days of the Moors, feeding off the blood of helpless victims which lent him a ghastly immortality. This nobleman had been driven forth; none knew where he had fled but it was evident that he and Don Santiago were the same man: He had fled Spain by ship, and de Estrada knew that the people of that ship had died, not by plague as the fiend had represented, but by the fangs of the vampire."

"De Estrada and the black man and the few soldiers who still lived went searching for him and found him stretched in bestial sleep in a clump of chaparral; full-gorged he was with human blood from his last victim. Now it is well known that a vampire, like a great serpent, when well gorged, falls into a deep sleep and may be taken without peril. But de Estrada was at a loss as to how to dispose of the monster, for how may the dead be slain? For a vampire is a man who has died long ago, yet is quick with a certain foul unlife."

"The men urged that the Caballero drive a stake through the fiend's heart and cut off his head, uttering the holy words that would crumble the long-dead body into dust, but the priest was dead and de Estrada feared that in the act the monster might waken."

"So they took Don Santiago, lifting him softly, and bore him to an old Indian mound near by. This they opened, taking forth the bones they found there, and they placed the vampire within and sealed up the mound—*Dios* grant until Judgment Day."

"It is a place accursed, and I wish I had starved elsewhere before I came into this part of the country seeking work—for I have known of the land and the creek and the mound with its terrible secret, ever since childhood; so you see, *Señor* Brill, why you must not open the mound and wake the fiend—"

There the manuscript ended with an erratic scratch of the pencil that tore the crumpled leaf.

Brill rose, his heart pounding wildly, his face bloodless, his tongue cleaving to his palate. He gagged and found words.

"That's why the spur was in the mound—one of them Spaniards dropped it while they was diggin'—and I mighta knowed it's been dug into before, the way the charcoal was scattered out—but, good God—"

Aghast he shrank from the black visions—an undead monster stirring in the gloom of his tomb, thrusting from within to push aside the stone loosened by the pick of ignorance—a shadowy shape loping over the hill toward a light that betokened a human prey—a frightful long arm that crossed a dim-lighted window...

"It's madness!" he gasped. "Lopez was plumb loco! They ain't no such things as vampires! If they is, why didn't he get me first, instead of Lopez—unless he was scoutin' around, makin' sure of everything before he pounced? Aw, hell! It's all a pipe-dream—"

The words froze in his throat. At the window a face glared and gibbered soundlessly at him. Two icy eyes pierced his very soul. A shriek burst from his throat and that ghastly visage vanished. But the very air was permeated by the foul scent that had hung about the ancient mound. And now the door creaked—bent slowly inward. Brill backed up against the wall, his gun shaking in his hand: It did not occur to him to fire through the door; in his chaotic brain he had but one thought that only that thin portal of wood separated him from some horror born out of the womb of night and gloom and the black past. His eyes were distended as he saw the door give, as he heard the staples of the bolt groan.

The door burst inward. Brill did not scream. His tongue was frozen to the roof of his mouth. His fear-glazed eyes took in the tall, vulture-like form—the icy eyes, the long black fingernails—the moldering garb, hideously ancient—the long spurred boot—the slouch-hat with its crumbling feather—the flowing cloak that was falling to slow shreds. Framed in the black doorway crouched that abhorrent shape out of the past, and Brill's brain reeled. A savage cold radiated from the figure—the scent of moldering clay and charnel-house refuse. And then the undead came at the living like a swooping vulture.

Brill fired point-blank and saw a shred of rotten cloth fly from the Thing's breast. The vampire reeled beneath the impact of the heavy ball, then righted himself and came on with frightful speed. Brill reeled back against the wall with a choking cry, the gun falling from his nerveless hand. The black legends were true then—human weapons were powerless—for may a man kill one already dead for long centuries, as mortals die?

Then the clawlike hands at his throat roused the young cowpuncher to a frenzy of madness. As his pioneer ancestors fought hand to hand against brain-shattering odds, Steve Brill fought the cold dead crawling thing that sought his life and his soul.

Of that ghastly battle Brill never remembered much. It was a blind chaos in which he screamed beast-like, tore and slugged and hammered, where long black nails like the talons of a panther tore at him, and pointed teeth snapped again and again at his throat. Rolling and tumbling about the room, both half enveloped by the musty folds of that ancient rotting cloak, they smote and tore at each other among the ruins of the shattered furniture, and—the fury of the vampire was not more terrible than the fear-crazed desperation of his victim.

They crashed headlong, into the table, knocking it down upon its side, and the coal oil lamp splintered on the floor, spraying the walls with sudden flames. Brill felt the bite of the burning oil that spattered him, but in the red frenzy of the fight he gave no heed. The black talons were tearing at him, the inhuman eyes burning icily into his soul; between his frantic fingers the withered flesh of the monster was hard as dry wood. And wave after wave of blind madness swept over Steve Brill. Like a man battling a nightmare he screamed and smote, while all about them the fire leaped up and caught at the walls and roof.

Through darting jets and licking tongues of flames they reeled and rolled like a demon and a mortal warring on the firelanced floors of hell: And in the growing tumult of the flames, Brill gathered himself for one last volcanic burst of frenzied strength. Breaking away and staggering, up, gasping and bloody, he lunged blindly at the foul shape and caught it in a grip not even the vampire could break. And whirling his fiendish assailant bodily on high, he dashed him down across the uptilted edge of the fallen table as a man might break a stick of wood across his knee. Something cracked like a snapping branch and the vampire fell from Brill's grasp to writhe in a strange broken posture on the burning floor. Yet it was not dead, for its flaming eyes still burned on Brill with a ghastly hunger, and it strove to crawl toward him with its broken spine, as a dying snake crawls.

Brill, reeling and gasping, shook the blood from his eyes, and staggered blindly through the broken door. And as a man runs from the portals of hell, he ran stumblingly through, the mesquite and chaparral until he fell from utter exhaustion. Looking back he saw the flames of the burning house and thanked God that it would burn until the very bones of Don Santiago de Valdez were utterly consumed and destroyed from the knowledge of men.

THE CAIRN ON THE HEADLAND

*And the next instant this great red loon was
shaking me like a dog shaking a rat. "Where is
Meve MacDonnal?" he was screaming. By the
saints, it's a grisly thing to hear a madman in
a lonely place at midnight screaming the name
of a woman dead three hundred years.*

—**The Longshoreman's Tale.**

"This is the cairn you seek," I said, laying my hand gingerly
on one of the rough stones which composed the strangely
symmetrical heap.

An avid interest burned in Ortali's dark eyes. His gaze swept
the landscape and came back to rest on the great pile of massive
weather-worn boulders.

"What a wild, weird, desolate place!" he said. "Who would
have thought to find such a spot in this vicinity? Except for the
smoke rising yonder, one would scarcely dream that beyond that
headland lies a great city! Here there is scarcely even a fisher-
man's hut within sight."

"The people shun the cairn as they have shunned it for
centuries," I replied.

"Why?"

"You've asked me that before," I replied impatiently. "I can
only answer that they now avoid by habit what their ancestors
avoided through knowledge."

"Knowledge!" he laughed derisively. "Superstition!"

I looked at him sombrely with unveiled hate. Two men could
scarcely have been of more opposite types. He was slender,
self-possessed, unmistakably Latin with his dark eyes and sophis-
ticated air. I am massive, clumsy and bearlike, with cold blue
eyes and tousled red hair. We were countrymen in that we were

born in the same land; but the homelands of our ancestors were as far apart as South from North.

"Nordic superstition," he repeated. "It cannot imagine a Latin people allowing such a mystery as this to go unexplored all these years. The Latins are too practical—too prosaic, if you will. Are you sure of the date of this pile?"

"I find no mention of it in any manuscript prior to 1014 A.D.," I growled, "and I've read all such manuscripts extant, in the original. MacLiag, King Brian Boru's poet, speaks of the rearing of the cairn immediately after the battle, and there can be little doubt that this is the pile referred to. It is mentioned briefly in the later chronicles of the Four Masters, also in the Book of Leinster, compiled in the late 1150's, and again in the Book of Lecan, compiled by the MacFirbis about 1416. All connect it with the battle of Clontarf, without mentioning why it was built."

"Well, what is the mystery about it?" he queried. "What more natural than that the defeated Norsemen should rear a cairn above the body of some great chief who had fallen in the battle?"

"In the first place," I answered, "there is a mystery concerning the existence of it. The building of cairns above the dead was a Norse, not an Irish, custom. Yet according to the chroniclers, it was not Norsemen who reared this heap. How could they have built it immediately after the battle, in which they had been cut to pieces and driven in headlong flight through the gates of Dublin? Their chieftains lay where they had fallen and the ravens picked their bones. It was Irish hands that heaped these stones."

"Well, was that so strange?" persisted Ortali. "In old times the Irish heaped up stones before they went into battle, each man putting a stone in place; after the battle the living removed their stones, leaving in that manner a simple tally of the slain for any who wished to count the remaining stones."

I shook my head.

"That was in more ancient times; not in the battle of Clontarf. In the first place, there were more than twenty thousand warriors, and four thousand fell here; this cairn is not large enough to have served as a tally of the men killed in battle. And it is too symmetrically built. Hardly a stone has fallen away in all these centuries. No, it was reared to cover something."

"Nordic superstitions!" the man sneered again.

"Aye, superstitions if you will!" Fired by his scorn, I exclaimed so savagely that he involuntarily stepped back; his hand slipping inside his coat. "We of North Europe had gods and demons before which the pallid mythologies of the South fade to childishness. At a time when your ancestors were lolling on silken cushions among the crumbling marble pillars of a decaying civilization, my ancestors were building their own civilization in hardships and gigantic battles against foes human and inhuman.

"Here on this very plain the Dark Ages came to an end and the light of a new era dawned on the world of hate and anarchy. Here, as even you know, in the year 1014, Brian Boru and his Dalcassian ax wielders broke the power of the heathen Norsemen forever—those grim anarchistic plunderers who had held back the progress of civilization for centuries."

"It was more than a struggle between Gael and Dane for the crown of Ireland. It was a war between the White Christ and Odin, between Christian and pagan. It was the last stand of the heathen—of the people of the old, grim ways. For three hundred years the world had writhed beneath the heel of the Viking, and here on Clontarf that scourge was lifted forever.

"Then, as now, the importance of that battle was underestimated by polite Latin and Latinized writers and historians. The polished sophisticates of the civilized cities of the South were not interested in the battles of barbarians in the remote northwestern corner of the world—a place and peoples of whose very names they were only vaguely aware. They only knew that suddenly the terrible raids of the sea kings ceased to sweep along their coasts, and in another century the wild age of plunder and slaughter had almost been forgotten—all because a rude, half-civilized people who scantily covered their nakedness with wolf hides rose up against the conquerors."

"Here was Ragnarok, the fall of the Gods! Here in very truth Odin fell, for his religion was given its death blow. He was last of all the heathen gods to stand before Christianity, and it looked for a time as if his children might prevail and plunge the world back into darkness and savagery. Before Clontarf, legends say, he often appeared on earth to his worshippers, dimly seen in the smoke of the sacrifices where human victims died screaming, or riding the wind-torn clouds, his wild locks flying in the gale, or, appareled like a Norse warrior, dealing thunderous blows in the forefront of nameless battles. But after Clontarf he was seen no more; his worshippers called on him in vain with wild chants and grim sacrifices. They lost faith in him, who had failed them in their wildest hour; his altars crumbled, his priests turned gray and died, and men turned to his conqueror, the White Christ. The reign of blood and iron was forgotten; the age of the red-handed sea kings passed. The rising sun, slowly, dimly, lighted the night of the Dark Ages, and men forgot Odin, who came no more on earth."

"Aye, laugh if you will! But who knows what shapes of horror have had birth in the darkness, the cold gloom; and the whistling black gulfs of the North? In the southern lands the sun shines and flowers bloom; under the soft skies men laugh at demons. But in the North, who can say what elemental spirits of evil dwell in the fierce storms and the darkness? Well may it be that from such fiends of the night men evolved the worship of the grim ones, Odin and Thor, and their terrible kin."

Ortali was silent for an instant, as if taken aback by my vehemence; then he laughed. "Well said, my northern philosopher! We will argue these questions another time. I could hardly expect a descendant of Nordic barbarians to escape some trace of the dreams and mysticism of his race. But you cannot expect me to be moved by your imaginings, either. I still believe that this cairn covers no grimmer secret than a Norse chief who fell in the battle—and really your ravings concerning Nordic devils have no bearing on the matter. Will you help me tear into this cairn?"

"No," I answered shortly.

"A few hours' work will suffice to lay bare whatever it may hide," he continued as if he had not heard. "By the way, speaking of superstitions, is there not some wild tale concerning holly connected with this heap?"

"An old legend says that all trees bearing holly were cut down for a league in all directions, for some mysterious reason," I answered sullenly. "That's another mystery. Holly was an important part of Norse magic-making. The Four Masters tell of a Norseman—a white bearded ancient of wild aspect, and apparently a priest of Odin—who was slain by the natives while attempting to lay a branch of holly on the cairn, a year after the battle."

"Well," he laughed, "I have procured a sprig of holly—see?—and shall wear it in my lapel; perhaps it will protect me against your Nordic devils. I feel more certain than ever that the cairn covers a sea king—and they were always laid to rest with all their riches; golden cups and jewel-set sword hilts and silver corselets. I feel that this cairn holds wealth, wealth over which clumsy-footed Irish peasants have been stumbling for centuries, living in want and dying in hunger. Bah! We shall return here at midnight, when we may be fairly certain that we will not be interrupted—and you will aid me at the excavations."

The last sentence was rapped out in a tone that sent a red surge of blood-lust through my brain. Ortali turned and began examining the cairn as he spoke, and almost involuntarily my hand reached out stealthily and closed on a wicked bit of jagged stone that had become detached from one of the boulders. In that instant I was a potential murderer if ever one walked the earth. One blow, quick, silent and savage, and I would be free forever from a slavery bitter as my Celtic ancestors knew beneath the heels of the Vikings.

As if sensing my thoughts, Ortali wheeled to face me. I quickly slipped the stone into my pocket, not knowing whether he noted the action. But he must have seen the red killing instinct burning in my eyes, for again he recoiled and again his hand sought the hidden revolver.

But he only said: "I've changed my mind. We will not uncover the cairn tonight. Tomorrow night, perhaps. We may be spied upon. Just now I am going back to the hotel."

I made no reply, but turned my back upon him and stalked moodily away in the direction of the shore. He started up the slope of the headland beyond which lay the city, and when I turned to look at him, he was just crossing the ridge, etched, clearly against the hazy sky. If hate could kill, he would have dropped dead. I saw him in a red-tinged haze, and the pulses in my temples throbbed like hammers.

I turned back toward the shore, and stopped suddenly. Engrossed with my own dark thoughts, I had approached within a few feet of a woman before seeing her. She was tall and strongly made, with a strong stern face, deeply lined and weather-worn as the hills. She was dressed in a manner strange to me, but I thought little of it, knowing the curious styles of clothing worn by certain backward types of our people.

"What would you be doing at the cairn?" she asked in a deep, powerful voice. I looked at her in surprise; she spoke in Gaelic, which was not strange of itself, but the Gaelic she used I had supposed was extinct as a spoken language: it was the Gaelic of scholars, pure, and with a distinctly archaic flavor. A woman from some secluded hill country, I thought, where the people still spoke the unadulterated tongue of their ancestors.

"We were speculating on its mystery," I answered in the same tongue, hesitantly, however, for though skilled in the more modern form taught in the schools, to match her use of the language was a strain on my knowledge of it. She shook her head slowly. "I like not the dark man who was with you," she said sombrely. "Who are you?"

"I'm an American, though born and raised here," I answered. "My name is James O'Brien."

A strange light gleamed in her cold eyes.

"O'Brien—You are of my clan. I was born an O'Brien. I married a man of the MacDonnals, but my heart was ever with the folk of my blood."

"You live hereabouts?" I queried, my mind on her unusual accent.

"Aye, I lived here upon a time," she answered, "but I have been far away for a long time. All is changed—changed. I would not have returned, but I was drawn back by a call you would not understand. Tell me, would you open the cairn?"

I started and gazed at her closely, deciding that she had somehow overheard our conversation.

"It is not mine to say," I answered bitterly. "Ortali, my companion—he will doubtless open it and I am constrained to aid him. Of my own will I would not molest it."

Her cold eyes bored into my soul.

"Fools rush blind to their doom," she said sombrely. "What does this man know of the mysteries of this ancient land? Deeds have been done here whereof the world re-echoed. Yonder, in the long ago, when Tomar's Wood rose dark and rustling against the plain of Contarf, and the Danish walls of Dublin loomed south of the river Liffey, the ravens fed on the slain and the setting sun lighted lakes of crimson. There King Brian, your ancestor and mine, broke the spears of the North. From all lands they came, and from the isles of the sea; they came in gleaming mail and their horned helmets cast long shadows across the land. Their dragon-prows thronged the waves and the sound of their oars was as the beat of a storm.

"On yonder plain the heroes fell like ripe wheat before the reaper. There fell Jarl Sigurd of the Orkneys, and Brodir of Man, last of the sea kings, and all their chiefs. There fell, too, Prince Murrough and his son, Turlogh, and many chieftains of the Gael, and King Brian Boru himself, Erin's mightiest monarch."

"True!" My imagination was always fired by the epic tales of the land of my birth. "Blood of mine was spilled here, and, though I have passed the best part of my life in a far land, there are ties of blood to bind my soul to this shore."

She nodded slowly, and from beneath her robes drew forth something that sparkled dully in the setting sun.

"Take this," she said. "As a token of blood tie, I give it to you. I feel strange and monstrous happenings—but this will keep you safe from evil and the people of the night. Beyond reckoning of man, it is holy."

I took it, wonderingly. It was a crucifix of curiously, worked gold, set with tiny jewels. The workmanship was extremely achaic and unmistakably Celtic. And vaguely within me stirred a memory of a long-lost relic described by forgotten monks in dim manuscripts.

"Great heavens!" I exclaimed. "This is—this must be—this can be nothing less than the lost crucifix of Saint Brandon the Blessed!"

"Aye." She inclined her grim head. "Saint Brandon's cross, fashioned by the hands of the holy man in long ago, before the Norse barbarians made Erin a red hell—in the days when a golden peace and holiness ruled the land."

"But, woman!" I exclaimed wildly. "I cannot accept this as a gift from you! You cannot know its value! Its intrinsic worth alone is equal to a fortune; as a relic it is priceless—"

"Enough!" Her deep voice struck me suddenly silent. "Have done with such talk, which is sacrilege. The cross of Saint Brandon is beyond price. It was never stained with gold; only as a free gift has it ever changed hands. I give it to you to shield you against the powers of evil. Say no more."

"But it has been lost for three hundred years!" I exclaimed. "How—where...?"

"A holy man gave it to me long ago," she answered. "I hid it in my bosom—long it lay in my bosom. But now I give it to you; I have come from a far country to give it to you, for there are monstrous happening's in the wind, and it is sword and shield against the people of the night. An ancient evil stirs in its prison, which blind hands of folly may break open; but stronger than any evil is the cross of Saint Brandon, which has gathered power and strength through the long, long ages since that forgotten evil fell to the earth."

"But who are you?" I exclaimed.

"I am Meve MacDonnal," she answered.

Then, turning without a word, she strode away in the deepening twilight while I stood bewildered and watched her cross the headland and pass from sight, turning inland as she topped the ridge. Then I, too, shaking myself like a man waking from a dream, went slowly up the slope and across the headland. When I crossed the ridge it was as if I had passed out of one world into another: behind me lay the wilderness and desolation of a weird medieval age; before me pulsed the lights and the roar of modern Dublin. Only one archaic touch was lent to the scene before me: some distance inland loomed the straggling and broken lines of an ancient graveyard, long deserted and grown up in weeds, barely discernible in the dusk. As I looked I saw a tall figure moving ghostily among the crumbling tombs, and I shook my head bewilderedly. Surely Meve MacDonnal was touched with madness, living in the past, like one seeking to stir to flame the ashes of dead yesterday. I set out toward where, in the near distance, began the straggling window—gleams that grew into the swarming ocean of lights that was Dublin.

Back at the suburban hotel where Ortali and I had our rooms, I did not speak to him of the cross the woman had given me. In that, at least, he should not share: I intended keeping it until she requested its return, which I felt sure she, would do. Now as I recalled her appearance, the strangeness of her costume returned to me, with one item which had impressed itself on my subconscious mind at the time, but which I had not consciously realized. Meve MacDonnal had been wearing sandals of a type not worn in Ireland for centuries. Well, it was perhaps natural that with her retrospective nature she should imitate the apparel of the past ages which seemed to claim all her thoughts.

I turned the cross reverently in my hands. There was no doubt that it was the very cross for which antiquarians had searched so long in vain, and at last in despair had denied the existence of. The priestly scholar, Michael O'Rourke, in a treatise written about 1690, described the relic at length, chronicled its history exhaustively, and maintained that it was last heard of in the possession of Bishop Liam O'Brien, who, dying in 1595, gave it into the keeping of a kinswoman; but who this woman was, it was never known, and O'Rourke maintained that she kept her possession of the cross a secret, and that it was laid away with her in her tomb.

At another time my elation at discovering the relic would have been extreme, but, at the time, my mind was too filled with hate and smouldering fury. Replacing the cross in my pocket, I fell moodily to reviewing my connections with Ortali, connections which puzzled my friends, but which were simple enough.

Some years before I had been connected with a certain large university in a humble way. One of the professors with whom I worked—a man named Reynolds—was of intolerably overbearing disposition toward those whom he considered his inferiors. I was a poverty-ridden student striving for life in a system which makes the very existence of a scholar precarious. I bore Professor Reynolds' abuse as long as I could, but one day we clashed.

The reason does not matter; it was trivial enough in itself. Because I dared reply to his insults, Reynolds struck me and I knocked him senseless.

That very day he caused my dismissal from the university. Facing not only an abrupt termination of my work and studies, but actual starvation, I was reduced to desperation, and I went to Reynolds' study late that night intending to thrash him within an inch of his life. I found him alone in his study, but the moment I entered, he sprang up and rushed at me like a wild beast, with a dagger he used for a paperweight. I did not strike him; I did not even touch him. As I stepped aside to avoid his rush; a small rug slipped beneath his charging feet. He fell headlong, and, to my horror, in his fall the dagger in his hand was driven into his heart. He died instantly. I was at once aware of my position, I was known to have quarreled; and even exchanged blows with the man. I had every reason to hate him. If I were found in the study with the dead man, no jury in the world would believe that I had not murdered him. I hurriedly left by the way I had come, thinking that I had been unobserved. But Ortali, the dead man's secretary, had seen me. Returning from a dance, he had observed me entering the premises, and, following me, had seen the whole affair through the window. But this I did not know until later.

The body was found by the professor's housekeeper, and naturally there was a great stir. Suspicion pointed to me, but lack of evidence kept me from being indicted, and this same lack of evidence brought about a verdict of suicide. All this time Ortali had kept quiet. Now he came to me and disclosed what he knew. He knew, of course, that I had not killed Reynolds, but he could prove that I was in the study when the professor met his death, and I knew Ortali was capable of carrying out his threat of swearing that he had seen me murder Reynolds in cold blood. And thus began a systematic blackmail.

I venture to say that a stranger blackmail was never levied. I had no money then; Ortali was gambling on my future, for he was assured of my abilities. He advanced me money, and, by clever wire-pulling, got me an appointment in a large college. Then he sat back to reap the benefits of his scheming, and he reaped full fold of the seed he sowed. In my line I became eminently successful. I soon commanded an enormous salary in my regular work, and I received rich prizes and awards for researches of various difficult natures, and of these Ortali took the lion's share—in money at least. I seemed to have the Midas touch. Yet of the wine of my success I tasted only the dregs.

I scarcely had a cent to my name. The money that had flowed through my hands had gone to enrich my slaver, unknown to the world. A man of remarkable gifts, he could have gone to the heights in any line, but for a queer streak in him, which, coupled with an inordinately avaricious nature, made him a parasite, a blood-sucking leech.

This trip to Dublin had been in the nature of a vacation for me. I was worn out with study and labor. But he had somehow heard of Grimmin's Cairn, as it was called, and, like a vulture that scents dead flesh, he conceived himself on the track of hidden gold. A golden wine cup would have been, to him, sufficient reward for the labor of tearing into the pile, and reason enough for desecrating or even destroying the ancient landmark. He was a swine whose only god was gold.

Well, I thought grimly, as I disrobed for bed, all things end, both good and bad. Such a life as I had lived was unbearable. Ortali had dangled the gallows before my eyes until it had lost its terrors. I had staggered beneath the load I carried because of my love for my work. But all human endurance has its limits. My hands turned to iron as I thought of Ortali, working beside me at midnight at the lonely cairn. One stroke, with such a stone as I had caught up that day, and my agony would be ended. That life and hopes and career and ambition would be ended as well, could not be helped. Ah, what a sorry, sorry end to all my high dreams! When a rope and the long drop through the black trap should cut short an honorable career and a useful life! And all because of a human vampire who feasted his rotten lust on my soul, and drove me to murder and ruin.

But I knew my fate was written in the iron books of doom. Sooner or later I would turn on Ortali and kill him, be the consequences what they might. And I had reached the end of my road. Continual torture had rendered me, I believe, partly insane. I knew that at Grimmin's Cairn, when we toiled at midnight, Ortali's life would end beneath my hands, and my own life be cast away.

Something fell out of my pocket and I picked it up. It was the piece of sharp stone I had caught up off the cairn. Looking at it moodily, I wondered what strange hands had touched it in old times, and what grim secret it helped to hide on the

bare headland of Grimmin. I switched out the light and lay in
the darkness, the stone still in my hand, forgotten, occupied
with my own dark broodings. And I glided gradually into deep
slumber.

At first I was aware that I was dreaming, as people often are.
All was dim and vague, and connected in some strange way, I
realized, with the bit of stone still grasped in my sleeping hand.
Gigantic, chaotic scenes and landscapes and events shifted before
me, like clouds that rolled and tumbled before a gale. Slowly
these settled and crystallized into one distinct landscape, familiar
and yet wildly strange. I saw a broad bare plain, fringed by the
gray sea on one side, and a dark, rustling forest on the other; this
plain was cut by a winding river, and beyond this river I saw a
city—such a city as my waking eyes had never seen: bare, stark,
massive, with the grim architecture of an earlier, wilder age. On
the plain I saw, as in a mist, a mighty battle. Serried ranks rolled
backward and forward, steel flashed like a sunlit sea, and men
fell like ripe wheat beneath the blades. I saw men in wolfskins,
wild and shock-headed, wielding dripping axes, and tall men in
horned helmets, and glittering mail, whose eyes were cold and
blue as the sea. And I saw myself.

Yes, in my dream I saw and recognized, in a semi-detached
way, myself. I was tall and rangily powerful; I was shock-headed
and naked but for a wolf-hide girt about my loins. I ran among
the ranks yelling and smiting with a red ax, and blood ran down
my flanks from wounds I scarcely felt. My eyes were cold blue
and my shaggy hair and beard were red.

Now for an instant I was cognizant of my dual personality,
aware that I was at once the wild man who ran and smote with
the gory ax, and the man who slumbered and dreamed across
the centuries. But this sensation quickly faded. I was no longer
aware of any personality other than that of the barbarian who
ran and smote. James O'Brien had no existence; I was Red Cumal,
kern of Brian Boru, and my ax was dripping with the blood of
my foes.

The roar of conflict was dying away, though here and there struggling clumps of warriors still dotted the plain. Down along the river, half-naked tribesmen, waist-deep in reddening water, tore and slashed with helmeted warriors whose mail could not save them from the stroke of the Dalcassian ax. Across the river a bloody, disorderly horde was staggering through the gates of Dublin.

The sun was sinking low toward the horizon. All day I had fought beside the chiefs. I had seen Jarl Sigurd fall beneath Prince Murrough's sword. I had seen Murrough himself die in the moment of victory, by the hand of a grim mailed giant whose name none knew. I had seen, in the flight of the enemy, Brodir and King Brian fall together at the door of the great king's tent.

Aye, it had been a feasting of ravens, a red flood of slaughter, and I knew that no more would the dragon-prowed fleets sweep from the blue North with torch and destruction. Far and wide the Vikings lay in their glittering mail, as the ripe wheat lies after the reaping. Among them lay thousands of bodies clad in the wolf hides of the tribes, but the dead of the Northern people far outnumbered the dead of Erin. I was weary and sick of the stench of raw blood. I had glutted my soul with slaughter; now I sought plunder. And I found it—on the corpse of a richly-clad Norse chief which lay close to the seashore. I tore off the silver-scaled corselet, the horned helmet. They fitted as if made for me, and I swaggered among the dead, calling on my wild comrades to admire my appearance, though the harness felt strange to me, for the Gaels scorned armor and fought half-naked.

In my search for loot I had wandered far out on the plain, away from the river, but still the mail-clad bodies lay thickly strewn, for the bursting of the ranks had scattered fugitives and pursuers all over the countryside, from the dark waving Wood of Tomar, to the river and the seashore. And on the seaward slope of Drumna's headland, out of sight of the city and the plain of Clontarf, I came suddenly upon a dying warrior. He was tall and massive, clad in gray mail. He lay partly in the folds of a great dark cloak, and his sword lay broken near his mighty right hand. His horned helmet had fallen from his head and his elf-locks blew in the wind that swept out of the west.

Where one eye should have been was an empty socket, and the other eye glittered cold and grim as the North Sea, though it was glazing with approach of death. Blood oozed from a rent in his corselet. I approached him warily, a strange cold fear, that I could not understand, gripping me. Ax ready to dash out his brains, I bent over him, and recognized him as the chief who had slain Prince Murrough, and who had mown down the warriors of the Gael like a harvest. Wherever he had fought, the Norsemen had prevailed, but in all other parts of the field, the Gaels had been irresistible.

And now he spoke to me in Norse and I understood, for had I not toiled as slave among the sea people for long bitter years?

"The Christians have overcome," he gasped in a voice whose timbre, though low-pitched, sent a curious shiver of fear through me; there was in it an undertone as of icy waves sweeping along a Northern shore, as of freezing winds whispering among the pine trees. "Doom and shadows stalk on Asgaard and here has fallen Ragnarok. I could not be in all parts of the field at once, and now I am wounded unto death. A spear—a spear with a cross carved in the blade; no other weapon could wound me."

I realized that the chief, seeing mistily my red beard and the Norse armor I wore, supposed me to be one of his own race. But crawling horror surged darkly in the depths of my soul.

"White Christ, thou hast not yet conquered," he muttered deliriously. "Lift me up, man, and let me speak to you."

Now for some reason I complied, and, as I lifted him to a sitting posture, I shuddered and my flesh crawled at the feel of him, for his flesh was like ivory—smoother and harder than is natural for human flesh, and colder than even a dying man should be.

"I die as men die," he muttered. "Fool, to assume the attributes of mankind, even though it was to aid the people who deify me.

The gods are immortal, but flesh can perish, even when it clothes a god. Haste and bring a sprig of the magic plant—even holly—and lay it on my bosom. Aye, though it be no larger than a dagger point, it will free me from this fleshy prison I put on when I came to war with men with their own weapons. And I will shake off this flesh and stalk once more among the thundering clouds. Woe, then, to all men who bend not the knee to me! Haste; I will await your coming."

His lion-like head fell back, and feeling shudderingly under his corselet, I could distinguish no heartbeat. He was dead, as men die, but I knew that locked in that semblance of a human body, there but slumbered the spirit of a fiend of the frost and darkness.

Aye, I knew him: Odin, the Gray Man, the One-eyed, the god of the North who had taken the form of a warrior to fight for his people. Assuming the form of a human, he was subject to many of the limitations of humanity. All men knew this of the gods, who often walked the earth in the guise of men. Odin, clothed in human semblance, could be wounded by certain weapons, and even slain, but a touch of the mysterious holly, would rouse him in grisly resurrection. This task he had set me, not knowing me for an enemy; in human form he could only use human faculties, and these had been impaired by onstriding death.

My hair stood up and my flesh crawled. I tore from my body the Norse armor, and fought a wild panic that prompted me to run blind and screaming with terror across the plain. Nauseated with fear, I gathered boulders and heaped them for a rude couch, and on it, shaking with horror, I lifted the body of the Norse god. And as the sun set and the stars came silently out, I was working with fierce energy, piling huge rocks above the corpse. Other tribesmen came up and I told them of what I was sealing up—I hoped forever. And they, shivering with horror, fell to aiding me. No sprig of magic holly should be laid on Odin's terrible bosom. Beneath these rude stones the Northern demon should slumber until the thunder of Judgment Day, forgotten by the world which had once cried out beneath his iron heel. Yet not wholly forgotten, for, as we labored, one of my comrades said: "This shall be no longer Drumna's Headland, but the Headland of the Gray Man."

That phrase established a connection between my dream-self and my sleeping-self. I started up from sleep exclaiming: "Gray Man's Headland!"

I looked about dazedly, the furnishings of the room, faintly lighted by the starlight in the windows, seeming strange and unfamiliar until I slowly oriented myself with time and space.

"Gray Man's Headland," I repeated, "Gray Man—Graymin—Grimmin—*Grimmin's Headland!* Great God, the thing under the cairn!"

Shaken, I sprang up, and realized that I still gripped the piece of stone from the cairn. It is well known that inanimate objects retain psychic associations. A round stone from the plain of Jericho has been placed in the hand of a hypnotized medium, and she has at once reconstructed in her mind the battle and siege of the city, and the shattering fall of the walls. I did not doubt that this bit of stone had acted as a magnet to drag my modern mind through the mists of the centuries into a life I had known before.

I was more shaken than I can describe, for the whole fantastic affair fitted in too well with certain formless vague sensations concerning the cairn which had already lingered at the back of my mind, to be dismissed as an unusually vivid dream. I felt the need of a glass of wine, and remembered that Ortali always had wine in his room. I hurriedly donned my clothes, opened my door, crossed the corridor and was about to, knock at Ortali's door, when I noticed that it was partly open, as if someone had neglected to close it carefully. I entered, switching on a light. The room was empty.

I realized what had occurred. Ortali mistrusted me; he feared to risk himself alone with me in a lonely spot at midnight. He had postponed the visit to the cairn merely to trick me, to give himself a chance to slip away alone.

My hatred for Ortali was for the moment completely submerged by a wild panic of horror at the thought of what the opening of the cairn might result in. For I did not doubt the authenticity of my dream. It was no dream; it was a fragmentary bit of memory, in which I had relived that other life of mine. Gray Man's Headland—Grimmin's Headland, and under those rough stones that grisly corpse in its semblance of humanity. I could not hope that, imbued with the imperishable essence of an elemental spirit, that corpse had crumbled to dust in the ages.

Of my race out of the city and across those semi-desolate reaches, I remember little. The night was a cloak of horror through which peered red stars like the gloating eyes of uncanny beasts, and my footfalls echoed hollowly so that repeatedly I thought some monster loped at my heels.

The straggling lights fell away behind me and I entered the region of mystery and horror. No wonder that progress had passed to the right and to the left of this spot, leaving it untouched, a blind back-eddy given over to goblin-dreams and nightmare memories. Well that so few suspected its very existence.

Dimly I saw the headland, but fear gripped me and held me aloof. I had a vague, incoherent idea of finding the ancient woman; Meve MacDonnal. She was grown old in the mysteries and traditions of the mysterious land. She could aid me, if indeed the blind fool Ortali loosed on the world the forgotten demon men once worshipped in the North.

A figure loomed suddenly in the starlight and I caromed against him, almost upsetting him. A stammering voice in a thick brogue protested with the petulance of intoxication. It was a burly longshoreman returning to his cottage, no doubt, from some late revel in a tavern. I seized him and shook him, my eyes glaring wildly in the starlight.

"I am looking for Meve MacDonnal! Do you know her? Tell me, you fool! Do you know old Meve MacDonnal?"

It was as if my words sobered him as suddenly as a dash of icy water in his face. In the starlight I saw his face glimmer whitely and a catch of fear was at his throat. He sought to cross himself with an uncertain hand.

"Meve MacDonnal! Are ye mad? What would ye be doin' with *her?*"

"Tell me!" I shrieked, shaking him savagely. "Where is Meve MacDonnal—"

"There!" he gasped, pointing with a shaking hand, where dimly in the night something loomed against the shadows. "In the name of the holy saints, begone, be ye madman or devil, and I am an honest man alone! There, there ye'll find Meve MacDonnal—where they laid her, full three hundred years ago!"

Half heeding his words, I flung him aside with a fierce exclamation, and, as I raced across the weed-grown plain, I heard the sound of his lumbering flight. Half blind with panic, I came to the low structure the man had pointed out. And floundering deep in weeds, my feet sinking into the musty mould, I realized with a shock that I was in the ancient graveyard on the inland side of Grimmin's Headland, into which I had seen Meve MacDonnal disappear the evening before. I was close by the door of the largest tomb, and with an eerie premonition I leaned close, seeking to make out the deeply carven inscription. And partly by the dim light of the stars and partly by the touch of my tracing fingers, I made out the words and figures, in the half-forgotten Gaelic of three centuries ago: Meve MacDonnal—1565-1640.

With a cry of horror, I recoiled and, snatching out the crucifix she had given me, made to hurl it into the darkness—but it was as if an invisible hand caught my wrist. Madness and insanity—but I could not doubt: Meve MacDonnal had come to me from the tomb wherein she had rested for three hundred years to give me, the ancient, ancient relic entrusted to her so long ago by her priestly kin. The memory of her words came to me, and the memory of Ortali and the Gray Man. From a lesser horror I turned squarely to a greater, and ran swiftly toward the headland which loomed dimly against the stars toward the sea.

As I crossed the ridge I saw, in the starlight, the cairn, and the figure that toiled gnome-like above it. Ortali, with his accustomed, almost superhuman energy, had dislodged many of the boulders; and as I approached, shaking with horrified anticipation, I saw him tear aside the last layer, and I heard his savage cry of triumph that froze me in my tracks some yards behind him, looking down from the slope. An unholy radiance rose from the cairn, and I saw, in the north, the aurora came up suddenly with terrible beauty, paling the starlight. All about the cairn pulsed a weird light, turning the rough stones to a cold shimmering silver, and in this glow I saw Ortali, all heedless, cast aside his pick and lean gloatingly over the aperture he had made—and I saw there the helmeted head, reposing on the couch of stones where I, Red Cumal, had placed it so long ago. I saw the inhuman terror and beauty of that awesome carven face, in which was neither human weakness, pity nor mercy. I saw the soul-freezing glitter of the one eye, which stared wide open in a fearful semblance of life. All up and down the tall mailed figure shimmered and sparkled cold darts and gleams of icy light; like the northern lights that blazed in the shuddering skies. Aye, the Gray Man lay as I had left him more than nine hundred years before, without trace of rust or rot or decay.

And now as Ortali leaned forward to examine his find, a gasping cry broke from his lips—for the sprig of holly, worn in his lapel in defiance of "Nordic superstition," slipped from its place, and in the weird glow I plainly saw it fall upon the mighty mailed breast of the figure, where it blazed suddenly with a brightness too dazzling for human eyes. My cry was echoed by Ortali. The figure moved; the mighty limbs flexed, tumbling the shining stones aside. A new gleam lighted the terrible eye, and a tide of life flooded and animated the carven features.

Out of the cairn he rose, and the northern lights played terribly about him. And the Gray Man changed and altered in horrific transmutation. The human features faded like a fading mask; the armor fell from his body and crumbled to dust as it fell; and the fiendish spirit of ice and frost and darkness that the sons of the North deified as Odin, stood nakedly and terribly in the stars. About his grisly head played lightnings and the shuddering gleams of the aurora. His towering anthropomorphic form was dark as shadow and gleaming as ice; his horrible crest reared colossally against the vaulting arch of the sky.

Ortali cowered, screaming wordlessly, as the taloned, malformed hands reached for him. In the shadowy, indescribable features of the Thing, there was no tinge of gratitude toward the man who had released it—only a demoniac gloating and a demoniac hate for all the sons of men. I saw the shadowy arms shoot out and strike. I heard Ortali scream once—a single, unbearable screech that broke short at the shrillest pitch. A single instant a blinding blue glare burst about him, lighting his convulsed features and his upward-rolling eyes; then his body was dashed earthward as by an electric shock, so savagely that I distinctly heard the splintering of his bones. But Ortali was dead before he touched the ground—dead, shrivelled and blackened, exactly like a man blasted by a thunderbolt, to which cause, indeed, men later ascribed his death.

The slavering monster that had slain him lumbered now toward me, shadowy, tentacle-like arms outspread, the pale starlight making a luminous pool of his great inhuman eye, his frightful talons dripping with I know not what elemental forces to blast the bodies and souls of men.

But I flinched not, and in that instant I feared him not, neither the horror of his countenance nor the threat of his thunderbolt dooms. For in a blinding white flame had come to me the realization of why Meve MacDonnal had come from her tomb to bring me the ancient cross which had lain in her bosom for three hundred years, gathering unto itself unseen forces of good and light, which war forever against the shapes of lunacy and shadow.

As I plucked from my garments the ancient cross, I felt the play of gigantic unseen forces in the air about me. I was but a pawn in the game—merely the hand that held the relic of holiness, that was the symbol of the powers opposed forever against the fiends of darkness. As I held it high, from it shot a single shaft of white light, unbearably pure, unbearably white, as if all the awesome forces of Light were combined in the symbol and loosed in one concentrated arrow of wrath against the monster of darkness. And with a hideous shriek the demon reeled back, shrivelling before my eyes. Then, with a great rush of vulture-like wings, he soared into the stars, dwindling dwindling among the play of the flaming fires and the lights of the haunted skies, fleeing back into the dark limbo which gave him birth, God only knows how many grisly eons ago.

THE FIRE OF ASSHURBANIPAL

Yar Ali squinted carefully down the blue barrel of his Lee-Enfield, called devoutly on Allah and sent a bullet through the brain of a flying rider.

"Allaho akbar!"

The big Afghan shouted in glee, waving his weapon above his head, "God is great! By Allah, *sahib*, I have sent another one of the dogs to Hell!"

His companion peered cautiously over the rim of the sand-pit they had scooped with their hands. He was a lean and wiry American, Steve Clarney by name.

"Good work, old horse," said this person. "Four left. Look—they're drawing off."

The white-robed horsemen were indeed reining away, clustering together just out of accurate rifle-range, as if in council. There had been seven when they had first swooped down on the comrades, but the fire from the two rifles in the sand-pit had been deadly.

"Look, *sahib*—they abandon the fray!"

Yar Ali stood up boldly and shouted taunts at the departing riders, one of whom whirled and sent a bullet that kicked up sand thirty feet in front of the pit.

"They shoot like the sons of dogs," said Yar Ali in complacent self-esteem. "By Allah, did you see that rogue plunge from his saddle as my lead went home? Up, *sahib*; let us run after them and cut them down!"

Paying no attention to this outrageous proposal—for he knew it was but one of the gestures Afghan nature continually demands—Steve rose, dusted off his breeches and gazing after the riders, now white specks far out on the desert, said musingly: "Those fellows ride as if they had some set purpose in mind—not a bit like men running from a licking."

"Aye," agreed Yar Ali promptly and seeing nothing inconsistent with his present attitude and recent bloodthirsty suggestion, "they ride after more of their kind—they are hawks who give up their prey not quickly. We had best move our position quickly, Steve *sahib*. They will come back—maybe in a few hours, maybe in a few days—it all depends on how far away lies the oasis of their tribe. But they will be back. We have guns and lives—they want both. And behold."

The Afghan levered out the empty shell and slipped a single cartridge into the breech of his rifle.

"My last bullet, *sahib*."

Steve nodded. "I've got three left."

The raiders whom their bullets had knocked from the saddle had been looted by their own comrades. No use searching the bodies which lay in the sand for ammunition. Steve lifted his canteen and shook it. Not much water remained. He knew that Yar Ali had only a little more than he, though the big Afridi, bred in a barren land, had used and needed less water than did the American; although the latter, judged from a white man's standards, was hard and tough as a wolf. As Steve unscrewed the canteen cap and drank very sparingly, he mentally reviewed the chain of events that had led them to their present position.

Wanderers, soldiers of fortune, thrown together by chance and attracted to each other by mutual admiration, he and Yar Ali had wandered from India up through Turkistan and down through Persia, an oddly assorted but highly capable pair. Driven by the restless urge of inherent wanderlust, their avowed purpose—which they swore to and sometimes believed themselves—was the accumulation of some vague and undiscovered treasure, some pot of gold at the foot of some yet unborn rainbow.

Then in ancient Shiraz they had heard of the Fire of Asshurbanipal. From the lips of an ancient Persian trader, who only half believed what he repeated to them, they heard the tale that he in turn had heard from the babbling lips of delirium, in his distant youth. He had been a member of a caravan, fifty years before, which, wandering far on the southern shore of the Persian

Gulf trading for pearls, had followed the tale of a rare pearl far into the desert.

The pearl, rumored found by a diver and stolen by a shaykh of the interior, they did not find, but they did pick up a Turk who was dying of starvation, thirst and a bullet wound in the thigh. As, he died in delirium, he babbled a wild tale of a silent dead city of black stone set in the drifting sands of the desert far to the westward, and of a flaming gem clutched in the bony fingers of a skeleton on an ancient throne.

He had not dared bring it away with him, because of an overpowering brooding horror that haunted the place, and thirst had driven him into the desert again, where Bedouins had pursued and wounded him. Yet he had escaped, riding hard until his horse fell under him. He died without telling how he had reached the mythical city in the first place, but the old trader thought he must have come from the northwest—a deserter from the Turkish army, making a desperate attempt to reach the Gulf.

The men of the caravan had made no attempt to plunge still further into the desert in search of the city; for, said the old trader, they believed it to be the ancient, ancient City of Evil spoken of in the Necronomicon of the mad Arab Alhazred—the city of the dead on which an ancient curse rested. Legends named it vaguely: the Arabs called it *Beled-el-Djinn*, the City of Devils, and the Turks, *Kara-Shehr*, the Black City. And the gem was that ancient and accursed jewel belonging to a king of long ago, whom the Grecians called Sardanapalus and the Semitic peoples Asshurbanipal.

Steve had been fascinated by the tale. Admitting to himself that it was doubtless one of the ten thousand cock-and-bull myths booted about the East, still there was a possibility that he and Yar Ali had stumbled onto a trace of that pot, of rainbow gold for which they searched. And Yar Ali had heard hints before of a silent city of the sands; tales had followed the eastbound caravans over the high Persian uplands and across the sands of

Turkistan, into the mountain country and beyond—vague tales; whispers of a black city of the *djinn*, deep in the hazes of a haunted desert.

So, following the trail of the legend, the companions had come from Shiraz to a village on the Arabian shore of the Persian Gulf, and there had heard more from an old man who had been a pearl-driver in his youth. The loquacity of age was on him and he told tales repeated to him by wandering tribesmen who had them in turn from the wild nomads of the deep interior; and again Steve and Yar Ali heard of the still black city with giant beasts carved of stone, and the skeleton sultan who held the blazing gem.

And so, mentally swearing at himself for a fool, Steve had made the plunge, and Yar Ali, secure in the knowledge that all things lay on the lap of Allah, had come with him. Their scanty supply of money had been just sufficient to provide riding-camels and provisions for a bold flying invasion of the unknown. Their only chart had been the vague rumors that placed the supposed location of Kara-Shehr.

There had been days of hard travel, pushing the beasts and conserving water and food. Then, deep in the desert they invaded, they had encountered a blinding sand-wind in which they had lost the camels. After that came long miles of staggering through the sands, battered by a flaming sun, subsisting on rapidly dwindling water from their canteens, and food Yar Ali had in a pouch. No thought of finding the mythical city now. They pushed on blindly, in hope of stumbling upon a spring; they knew that behind them no oases lay within a distance they could hope to cover on foot. It was a desperate chance, but their only one.

Then white-clad hawks had swooped down on them, out of the haze of the skyline, and from a shallow and hastily scooped trench the adventurers had exchanged shots with the wild riders who circled them at top speed. The bullets of the Bedouins had skipped through their makeshift fortifications, knocking dust into their eyes and flicking bits of cloth from their garments, but by good chance neither had been hit.

Their one bit of luck, reflected Clarney, as he cursed himself for a fool. What a mad venture it had been, anyway! To think that two men could so dare the desert and live, much less wrest from its abysmal bosom the secrets of the ages! And that crazy tale of a skeleton hand gripping a flaming jewel in a dead city—bosh! What utter rot! He must have been crazy himself to credit it, the American decided with the clarity of view that suffering and danger bring.

"Well, old horse," said Steve, lifting his rifle, "let's get going. It's a toss-up if we die of thirst or get sniped off by the desert-brothers. Anyway, we're doin' no good here."

"God gives," agreed Yar Ali cheerfully. "The sun sinks westward. Soon the coolness of night will be upon us. Perhaps we shall find water yet, *sahib*. Look, the terrain changes to the south."

Clarney shaded his eyes against the dying sun. Beyond a level, barren expanse of several miles width, the land did indeed become more broken; aborted hills were in evidence. The American slung his rifle over his arm and sighed.

"Heave ahead; we're food for the buzzards anyhow."

The sun sank and the moon rose, flooding the desert with weird silver light. Drifted sand glimmered in long ripples, as if a sea had suddenly been frozen into immobility. Steve, parched fiercely by a thirst he dared not fully quench, cursed beneath his breath. The desert was beautiful beneath the moon, with the beauty of a cold marble lorelei to lure men to destruction. What a mad quest! his weary brain reiterated; the Fire of Asshurbanipal retreated into the mazes of unreality with each dragging step. The desert became not merely a material waste-land, but the gray mists of the lost eons, in whose depths dreamed sunken things.

Clarney stumbled and swore; was he failing already? Yar Ali swung along with the easy, tireless stride of the mountain man, and Steve set his teeth, nerving himself to greater effort. They were entering the broken country at last, and the going became harder. Shallow gullies and narrow ravines knifed the earth with wavering patterns. Most of them were nearly filled with sand, and there was no trace of water.

"This country was once oasis country," commented Yar Ali. "Allah knows how many centuries ago the sand took it, as the sand has taken so many cities in Turkistan."

They swung on like dead men in a gray land of death. The moon grew red and sinister as she sank, and shadowy darkness settled over the desert before they had reached a point where they could see what lay beyond the broken belt. Even the big Afghan's feet began to drag, and Steve kept himself erect only by a savage effort of will. At last they toiled up a sort of ridge, on the southern side of which the land sloped downward.

"We rest," declared Steve. "There's no water in this hellish country. No use in goin' on for ever. My legs are stiff as gun-barrels. I couldn't take another step to save my neck. Here's a kind of stunted cliff, about as high as a man's shoulder, facing south. We'll sleep in the lee of it."

"And shall we not keep watch, Steve *sahib*?"

"We don't," answered Steve. "If the Arabs cut our throats while we're asleep, so much the better. We're goners anyhow."

With which optimistic observation Clarney lay down stiffly in the deep sand. But Yar Ali stood, leaning forward, straining his eyes into the elusive darkness that turned the star-flecked horizons to murky wells of shadow.

"Something lies on the skyline to the south," he muttered uneasily. "A hill? I cannot tell, or even be sure that I see anything at all."

"You're seeing mirages already," said Steve irritably. "Lie down and sleep."

And so saying Steve slumbered.

The sun in his eyes awoke him. He sat up, yawning, and his first sensation was that of thirst. He lifted his canteen and wet his lips. One drink left. Yar Ali still slept. Steve's eyes wandered over the southern horizon and he started. He kicked the recumbent Afghan.

"Hey, wake up, Ali. I reckon you weren't seeing things after all. There's your hill—and a queer-lookin' one, too."

The Afridi woke as a wild thing wakes, instantly and completely, his hand leaping to his long knife as he glared about for enemies. His gaze followed Steve's pointing fingers and his eyes widened.

"By Allah and by Allah!" he swore. "We have come into a land of *djinn*! That is no hill—it is a city of stone in the midst of the sands!"

Steve bounded to his feet like a steel spring released. As he gazed with bated breath, a fierce shout escaped his lips. At his feet the slope of the ridge ran down into a wide and level expanse of sand that stretched away southward. And far away, across those sands, to his straining sight the 'hill' slowly took shape, like a mirage growing from the drifting sands.

He saw great uneven walls, massive battlements; all about crawled the sands like a living, sensate thing, drifted high about the walls, softening the rugged outlines. No wonder that at first glance the whole had appeared like a hill.

"*Kara-Shehr*!" Clarney exclaimed fiercely. "*Beled-el-Djinn*! The city of the dead! It wasn't a pipe-dream after all! We've found it—by Heaven, we've found it! Come on! Let's go!"

Yar Ali shook his head uncertainly and muttered something about evil *djinn* under his breath, but he followed. The sight of the ruins had swept from Steve his thirst and hunger, and the fatigue that a few hours' sleep had not fully overcome. He trudged on swiftly, oblivious to the rising heat, his eyes gleaming with the lust of the explorer. It was not altogether greed for the fabled gem that had prompted Steve Clarney to risk his life in that grim wilderness; deep in his soul lurked the age-old heritage of the white man, the urge to seek out the hidden places of the world, and that urge had been stirred to the depths by the ancient tales.

Now as they crossed the level wastes that separated the broken land from the city, they saw—the shattered walls take clearer form and shape, as if they grew out of the morning sky. The city seemed built of huge blocks of black stone, but how high the walls had been there was no telling because of the sand that drifted high about their base; in many places they had fallen away and the sand hid the fragments entirely.

The sun reached her zenith and thirst intruded itself in spite of zeal and enthusiasm, but Steve fiercely mastered his suffering. His lips were parched and swollen, but he would not take that last drink until he had reached the ruined city. Yar Ali wet his lips from his own canteen and tried to share the remainder with his friend. Steve shook his head and plodded on.

In the ferocious heat of the desert afternoon they reached the ruin, and passing through a wide breach in the crumbling wall, gazed on the dead city. Sand choked the ancient streets and lent fantastic form to huge, fallen and half-hidden columns. So crumbled into decay and so covered with sand was the whole that the explorers could make out little of the original plan of the city; now it was but a waste of drifted sand and crumbling stone over which brooded, like an invisible cloud, an aura of unspeakable antiquity.

But directly in front of them ran a broad avenue, the outline of which not even the ravaging sands and winds of time had been able to efface. On either side of the wide way were ranged huge columns, not unusually tall, even allowing for the sand that hid their bases, but incredibly massive. On the top of each column stood a figure carved from solid stone—great, somber images, half human, half bestial, partaking of the brooding brutishness of the whole city. Steve cried out in amazement.

"The winged bulls of Nineveh. The bulls with men's heads! By the saints, Ali, the old tales are true! The Assyrians did build this city! The whole tale's true! They must have come here when the Babylonians destroyed Assyria—why, this scene's a dead ringer for pictures I've seen—reconstructed scenes of old Nineveh! And look!"

He pointed down the broad street to the great building which reared at the other end, a colossal, brooding edifice whose columns and walls of solid black stone blocks defied the winds and sands of time. The drifting, obliterating sea washed about its foundations, overflowing into its doorways, but it would require a thousand years to inundate the whole structure.

"An abode of devils!" muttered Yar Ali, uneasily.

"The temple of Baal!" exclaimed Steve. "Come on!—I was afraid we'd find all the palaces and temples hidden by the sand and have to dig for the gem."

"Little good it will do us," muttered Yar Ali. "Here we die."

"I reckon so." Steve unscrewed the cap of his canteen. "Let's take our last drink. Anyway, we're safe from the Arabs. They'd never dare come here, with their superstitions. We'll drink and then we'll die, I reckon, but first we'll find the jewel. When I pass out, I want to have it in my hand. Maybe a few centuries later some lucky son-of-a-gun will find our skeletons—and the gem. Here's to him, whoever he is!"

With which grim jest Clarney drained his canteen and Yar Ali followed suit. They had played their last ace; the rest lay on the lap of Allah.

They strode up the broad way, and Yar Ali, utterly fearless in the face of human foci, glanced nervously to right and left, half expecting to see a horned and fantastic face leering at him from behind a column. Steve himself felt the somber antiquity of the place, and almost found himself fearing a rush of bronze war chariots down the forgotten streets, or to hear the sudden menacing flare of bronze trumpets. The silence in dead cities was so much more intense, he reflected, than that on the open desert.

They came to the portals of the great temple. Rows of immense columns flanked the wide doorway, which was ankle-deep in sand, and from which sagged massive bronze frameworks that had once braced mighty doors, whose polished woodwork had rotted away centuries ago. They passed into a mighty hall of misty twilight whose shadowy stone roof was upheld by columns like the trunks of forest trees. The whole effect of the architecture was one of awesome magnitude and sullen, breath-taking splendor, like a temple built by somber giants for the abode of dark gods.

Yar Ali walked fearfully, as if he expected to awake sleeping gods, and Steve, without the Afridi's superstitions, yet felt the gloomy majesty of the place lay somber hands on his soul.

No trace of a footprint showed in the deep dust on the floor; half a century had passed since the affrighted and devil-ridden Turk had fled these silent halls. As for the Bedouins, it was easy to see why those superstitious sons of the desert shunned this haunted city—and haunted it was, not by actual ghosts, perhaps, but by the shadows of lost splendors.

As they trod the sands of the hall, which seemed endless, Steve pondered many questions: How did these fugitives from the wrath of frenzied rebels build this city? How did they pass through the country of their foes—for Babylonia lay between Assyria and the Arabian desert. Yet there had been no other place for them to go; westward lay Syria and the sea, and north and east swarmed the 'dangerous Medes', those fierce Aryans whose aid had stiffened the arm of Babylon to smite her foe to the dust.

Possibly, thought Steve, Kara-Shehr—whatever its name had been in those dim days—had been built as an outpost border city before the fall of the Assyrian empire, whither survivals of that overthrow fled. At any rate it was possible that Kara-Shehr had outlasted Nineveh by some centuries—a strange, hermit city, no doubt, cut off from the rest of the world.

Surely, as Yar Ali had said, this was once fertile country, watered by oases; and doubtless in the broken country they had passed over the night before, there had been quarries that furnished the stone for the building of the city.

Then what caused its downfall? Did the encroachment of the sands and the filling up of the springs cause the people to abandon it, or was Kara-Shehr a city of silence before the sands crept over the walls? Did the downfall come from within or without? Did civil war blot out the inhabitants, or were they slaughtered by some powerful foe from the desert? Clarney shook his head in baffled chagrin. The answers to those questions were lost in the maze of forgotten ages.

"*Allaho akbar!*" They had traversed the great shadowy hall and at its further end they came upon a hideous black stone altar, behind which loomed an ancient god, bestial and horrific. Steve shrugged his shoulders as he recognized the monstrous aspect of the image—aye, that was Baal, on which black altar in other ages many a screaming, writhing, naked victim had offered up its naked soul. The idol embodied in its utter, abysmal and sullen bestiality the whole soul of this demoniac city. Surely, thought Steve, the builders of Nineveh and Kara-Shehr were cast in another mold from the people of today. Their art and culture were too ponderous, too grimly barren of the lighter aspects of humanity, to be wholly human, as modern man understands humanity. Their architecture was repellent; of high skill, yet so massive, sullen and brutish in effect as to be almost beyond the comprehension of moderns.

The adventurers passed through a narrow door which opened in the end of the hall close to the idol, and came into a series of wide, dim, dusty chambers connected by column-flanked corridors. Along these they strode in the gray ghostly light, and came at last to a wide stair, whose massive stone steps led upward and vanished in the gloom. Here Yar Ali halted.

"We have dared much, *sahib*," he muttered. "Is it wise to dare more?"

Steve, aquiver with eagerness, yet understood the Afghan's mind. "You mean we shouldn't go up those stairs?"

"They have an evil look. To what chambers of silence and horror may they lead? When *djinn* haunt deserted buildings, they lurk in the upper chambers. At any moment a demon may bite off our heads."

"We're dead men anyhow," grunted Steve. "But I tell you—you go on back through the hall and watch for the Arabs while I go upstairs."

"Watch for a wind on the horizon," responded the Afghan gloomily, shifting his rifle and loosening his long knife in its scabbard. "No Bedouin comes here. Lead on, *sahib*. Thou'rt mad after the manner of all Franks,—but I would not leave thee to face the *djinn* alone."

So the companions mounted the massive stairs, their feet sinking deep into the accumulated dust of centuries at each step. Up and up they went, to an incredible height until the depths below merged into a vague gloom.

"We walk blind to our doom, *sahib*," muttered Yar Ali. "*Allah il allah*—and Muhammad is his Prophet! Nevertheless, I feel the presence of slumbering Evil and never again shall I hear the wind blowing up the Khyber Pass."

Steve made no reply. He did not like the breathless silence that brooded over the ancient temple, nor the grisly gray light that filtered from some hidden source.

Now above them the gloom lightened somewhat and they emerged into a vast circular chamber, grayly illuminated by light that filtered in through the high, pierced ceiling. But another radiance lent itself to the illumination. A cry burst from Steve's lips, echoed by Yar Ali.

Standing on the top step of the broad stone stair, they looked directly across the broad chamber, with its dust-covered heavy tile floor and bare black stone walls. From about the center of the chamber, massive steps led up to a stone dais, and on this dais stood a marble throne. About this throne glowed and shimmered an uncanny light, and the awestruck adventurers gasped as they saw its source. On the throne slumped a human skeleton, an almost shapeless mass of moldering bones. A fleshless hand sagged outstretched upon the broad marble throne-arm, and in its grisly clasp there pulsed and throbbed like a living thing, a great crimson stone.

The Fire of Asshurbanipal! Even after they had found the lost city Steve had not really allowed himself to believe that they would find the gem, or that it even existed in reality. Yet he could not doubt the evidence of his eyes, dazzled by that evil, incredible glow. With a fierce shout he sprang across the chamber and up the steps. Yar Ali was at his heels, but when Steve would have seized the gem, the Afghan laid a hand on his arm.

"Wait!" exclaimed the big Muhammadan. "Touch it not yet, *sahib*! A curse lies on ancient things—and surely this is a thing triply accursed! Else why has it lain here untouched in a country of thieves for so many centuries? It is not well to disturb the possessions of the dead."

"Bosh!" snorted the American. "Superstitions! The Bedouins were scared by the tales that have come down to 'em from their ancestors. Being desert-dwellers they mistrust cities anyway, and no doubt this one had an evil reputation in its lifetime. And nobody except Bedouins have seen this place before, except that Turk, who was probably half demented with suffering.

"These bones may be those of the king mentioned in the legend—the dry desert air preserves such things indefinitely—but I doubt it. May be Assyrian—most likely Arab—some beggar that got the gem and then died on that throne for some reason or other."

The Afghan scarcely heard him. He was gazing in fearful fascination at the great stone, as a hypnotized bird stares into a serpent's eye.

"Look at it, *sahib*!" he whispered. "What is it? No such gem as this was ever cut by mortal hands! Look how it throbs and pulses like the heart of a cobra!"

Steve was looking, and he was aware of a strange undefined feeling of uneasiness. Well versed in the knowledge of precious stones, he had never seen a stone like this. At first glance he had supposed it to be a monster ruby, as told in the legends. Now he was not sure, and he had a nervous feeling that Yar Ali was right, that this was no natural, normal gem: He could not classify the style in which it was cut, and such was the power of its lurid radiance that he found it difficult to gaze at it closely for any length of time. The whole setting was not one calculated to soothe restless nerves. The deep dust on the floor suggested an unwholesome antiquity; the gray light evoked a sense of unreality, and the heavy black walls towered grimly, hinting at hidden things.

"Let's take the stone, and go!" muttered Steve, an unaccustomed panicky dread rising in his bosom.

"Wait!" Yar Ali's eyes were blazing, and he gazed, not at the gem, but at the sullen stone walls. "We are flies in the lair of the spider! *Sahib*, as Allah lives, it is more than the ghosts of old fears that lurk over this city of horror! I feel the presence of peril, as I have felt it before—as I felt it in a jungle cavern where a python lurked unseen in the darkness —as I felt it in the temple of Thuggee where the hidden stranglers of Siva crouched to spring upon us—as I feel it now, tenfold!"

Steve's hair prickled. He knew that Yar Ali was a grim veteran, not to be stampeded by silly fear or senseless panic; he well remembered the incidents referred to by the Afghan, as he remembered other occasions upon which Yar Ali's Oriental telepathic instinct had warned him of danger before that danger was seen or heard.

"What is it, Yar Ali?" he whispered.

The Afghan shook his head, his eyes filled with a weird mysterious light as he listened to the dim occult promptings of his subconsciousness.

"I know not; I know it is close to us, and that it is very ancient and very evil. I think—" Suddenly he halted and wheeled, the eery light vanishing from his eyes to be replaced by a glare of wolf-like fear and suspicion.

"Hark, *sahib*!" he snapped. "Ghosts or dead men mount the stair!"

Steve stiffened as the stealthy pad of soft sandals on stone reached his ear.

"By Judas, Ali!" he rapped; "something's out there—"

The ancient walls re-echoed to a chorus of wild yells as a horde of savage figures flooded the chamber. For one dazed insane instant Steve believed wildly that they were being attacked by re-embodied warriors of a vanished age; then the spiteful crack of a bullet past his ear and the acrid smell of powder told him that their foes were material enough. Clarney cursed; in their fancied security—they had been caught like rats in a trap by the pursuing Arabs.

Even as the American threw up his rifle, Yar Ali fired point-blank from the hip with deadly effect, hurled his empty rifle into the horde and went down the steps like a hurricane, his three-foot Khyber knife shimmering in his hairy hand. Into his gusto for battle went real relief that his foes were human. A bullet ripped the turban from his head, but an Arab went down with a split skull beneath the hillman's first, shearing stroke.

A tall Bedouin clapped his gun-muzzle to the Afghan's side, but before he could pull the trigger, Clarney's bullet scattered his brains. The very number of the attackers hindered their onslaught on the big Afridi, whose tigerish quickness made shooting as dangerous to themselves as to him. The bulk of them swarmed about him, striking with scimitar and rifle-stock while others charged up the steps after Steve. At that range there was no missing; the American simply thrust his rifle muzzle into a bearded face and blasted it into a ghastly ruin. The others came on, screaming like panthers.

And now as he prepared to expend his last cartridge, Clarney saw two things in one flashing instant—a wild warrior who, with froth on his beard and a heavy scimitar uplifted, was almost upon him, and another who knelt on the floor drawing a careful bead on the plunging Yar Ali. Steve made an instant choice and fired over the shoulder of the charging swordsman, killing the rifleman—and voluntarily offering his own life for his friend's; for the scimitar was swinging at his own head. But even as the Arab swung, grunting with the force of the blow, his sandaled foot slipped on the marble steps and the curved blade, veering erratically from its arc, clashed on Steve's rifle-barrel. In an instant the American clubbed his rifle, and as the Bedouin recovered his balance and again heaved up the scimitar, Clarney struck with all his rangy power, and stock and skull shattered together.

Then a heavy ball smacked into his shoulder, sickening him with the shock.

As he staggered dizzily, a Bedouin whipped a turban-cloth about his feet and jerked viciously. Clarney pitched headlong down the steps, to strike with stunning force. A gun-stock in a brown hand went up to dash out his brains, but an imperious command halted the blow.

"Slay him not, but bind him hand and foot."

As Steve struggled dazedly against many gripping hands, it seemed to him that somewhere he had heard that imperious voice before.

The American's downfall had occurred in a matter of seconds. Even as Steve's second shot had cracked, Yar Ali had half severed a raider's arm and himself received a numbing blow from a rifle-stock on his left shoulder. His sheepskin coat, worn despite the desert heat, saved his hide from half a dozen slashing knives. A rifle was discharged so close to his face that the powder burnt him fiercely, bringing a bloodthirsty yell from the maddened Afghan. As Yar Ali swung up his dripping blade the rifleman, ashy-faced, lifted his rifle above his head in both hands to parry the downward blow, whereat the Afridi, with a yelp of ferocious exultation, shifted as a jungle cat strikes and plunged his long knife into the Arab's belly. But at that instant a rifle-stock, swung with all the hearty ill-will its wielder could evoke, crashed against the giant's head, laying open the scalp and dashing him to his knees.

With the dogged and silent ferocity of his breed, Yar Ali staggered blindly up again, slashing at foes he could scarcely see, but a storm of blows battered him down again, nor did his attackers cease beating him until he lay still. They would have finished him in short order then, but for another peremptory order from their chief; whereupon they bound the senseless knife-man and flung him down alongside Steve, who was fully conscious and aware of the savage hurt of the bullet in his shoulder.

He glared up at the tall Arab who stood looking down at him.

"Well, *sahib*," said this one—and Steve saw he was no Bedouin—"do you not remember me?"

Steve scowled; a bullet-wound is no aid to concentration.

"You look familiar—by Judas!—you are! Nureddin El Mekru!"

"I am honored! The *sahib* remembers!" Nureddin salaamed mockingly. "And you remember, no doubt, the occasion on which you made me a present of—this!"

The dark eyes shadowed with bitter menace and the shaykh indicated a thin white scar on the angle of his jaw.

"I remember," snarled Clarney, whom pain and anger did not tend to make docile. "It was in Somaliland, years ago. You were in the slave-trade then. A wretch of a nigger escaped from you and took refuge with me. You walked into my camp one night in your high-handed way, started a row and in the ensuing scrap you got a butcher-knife across your face. I wish I'd cut your lousy throat."

"You had your chance," answered the Arab. "Now the tables are turned."

"I thought your stamping-ground lay west," growled Clarney; "Yemen and the Somali country."

"I quit the slave-trade long ago," answered the shaykh. "It is an outworn game. I led a band of thieves in Yemen for a time; then again I was forced to change my location. I came here with a few faithful followers, and by Allah, those wild men nearly slit my throat at first. But I overcame their suspicions, and now I lead more men than have followed me in years.

"They whom you fought off yesterday were my men—scouts I had sent out ahead. My oasis lies far to the west. We have ridden for many days, for I was on my way to this very city. When my scouts rode in and told me of two wanderers, I did not alter my course, for I had business first in Beled-el-Djinn. We rode into the city from the west and saw your tracks in the sand. We followed them, and you were blind buffalo who heard not our coming."

Steve snarled. "You wouldn't have caught us so easy, only we thought no Bedouin would dare come into Kara-Shehr."

Nureddin nodded. "But I am no Bedouin. I have traveled far and seen many lands and many races, and I have read many books. I know that fear is smoke, that the dead are dead, and that *djinn* and ghosts and curses are mists that the wind blows away. It was because of the tales of the red stone that I came into this forsaken desert. But it has taken months to persuade my men to ride with me here.

"But—I am here! And your presence is a delightful surprise. Doubtless you have guessed why I had you taken alive; I have more elaborate entertainment planned for you and that Pathan swine. Now—I take the Fire of Asshurbanipal and we will go."

He turned toward the dais, and one of his men, a bearded one-eyed giant, exclaimed, "Hold, my lord! Ancient evil reigned here before the days of Muhammad! The *djinn* howl through these halls when the winds blow, and men have seen ghosts dancing on the walls beneath the moon. No man of mortals has dared this black city for a thousand years—save one, half a century ago, who fled shrieking.

"You have come here from Yemen; you do not know the ancient curse on this foul city, and this evil stone, which pulses like the red heart of Satan! We have followed you here against our judgment, because you have proven yourself a strong man, and have said you hold a charm against all evil beings. You said you but wished to look on this mysterious gem, but now we see it is your intention to take it for yourself. Do not offend the *djinn*!"

"Nay, Nureddin, do not offend the *djinn*!" chorused the other Bedouins. The shaykh's own hard-bitten ruffians, standing in a compact group somewhat apart from the Bedouins, said nothing; hardened to crimes and deeds of impiety, they were less affected by the superstitions of the desert men, to whom the dread tale of the accursed city had been repeated for centuries. Steve, even while hating Nureddin with concentrated venom, realized the magnetic power of the man, the innate leadership that had enabled him to overcome thus far the fears and traditions of ages.

"The curse is laid on infidels who invade the city," answered Nureddin, "not on the Faithful. See, in this chamber have we overcome our *kafir* foes!"

A white-bearded desert hawk shook his head.

"The curse is more ancient than Muhammad, and recks not of race or creed. Evil men reared this black city in the dawn of the Beginnings of Days. They oppressed our ancestors of the black tents, and warred among themselves; aye, the black walls of this foul city were stained with blood, and echoed to the shouts of unholy revel and the whispers of dark intrigues.

"Thus came the stone to the city: there dwelt a magician at the court of Asshurbanipal, and the black wisdom of ages was not denied to him. To gain honor and power for himself, he dared the horrors of a nameless vast cavern in a dark, untraveled land, and from those fiend-haunted depths he brought that blazing gem, which is carved of the frozen flames of Hell! By reason of his fearful power in black magic, he put a spell on the demon which guarded the ancient gem, and so stole away the stone. And the demon slept in the cavern unknowing.

"So this magician—Xuthltan by name—dwelt in the court of the sultan Asshurbanipal and did magic and forecast events by scanning the lurid deeps of the stone, into which no eyes but his could look unblinded. And men called the stone the Fire of Asshurbanipal, in honor of the king.

"But evil came upon the kingdom and men cried out that it was the curse of the *djinn*, and the sultan in great fear bade Xuthltan take the gem and cast it into the cavern from which he had taken it, lest worse ill befall them.

"Yet it was not the magician's will to give up the gem wherein he read strange secrets of pre-Adamite days, and he fled to the rebel city of Kara-Shehr, where soon civil war broke out and men strove with one another to possess the gem. Then the king who ruled the city, coveting the stone, seized the magician and put him to death by torture, and in this very room he watched him die; with the gem in his hand the king sat upon the throne— even as he has sat upon the throne—even as he has sat throughout the centuries—even as now he sits!"

The Arab's finger stabbed at the moldering bones on the marble throne, and the wild desert men blenched; even Nureddin's own scoundrels recoiled, catching their breath, but the shaykh showed no sign of perturbation.

"As Xuthltan died," continued the old Bedouin, "he cursed the stone whose magic had not saved him, and he shrieked aloud the fearful words which undid the spell he had put upon the demon in the cavern, and set the monster free. And crying out on the forgotten gods, Cthulhu and Koth and Yog-Sothoth, and all the pre-Adamite Dwellers in the black cities under the sea and the caverns of the earth, he called upon them—to take back that which was theirs, and with his dying breath pronounced doom on the false king, and that doom was that the king should sit on his throne holding in his hand the Fire of Asshurbanipal until the thunder of judgment Day.

"Thereat the great stone cried out as a live thing cries, and the king and his soldiers saw a black cloud spinning up from the floor, and out of the cloud blew a fetid wind, and out of the wind came a grisly shape which stretched forth fearsome paws and laid them on the king, who shriveled and died at their touch. And the soldiers fled screaming, and all the people of the city ran forth wailing into the desert, where they perished or gained through the wastes to the far oasis towns. Kara-Shehr lay silent and deserted, the haunt of the lizard and the jackal. And when some of the desert-people ventured into the city they found the king dead on his throne, clutching the blazing gem, but they dared not lay hand upon it, for they knew the demon lurked near to guard it through all the ages—as he lurks near even as we stand here."

The warriors shuddered involuntarily and glanced about, and Nureddin said, "Why did he not come forth when the Franks entered the chamber? Is he deaf, that the sound of the combat has not awakened him?"

"We have not touched the gem," answered the old Bedouin, "nor had the Franks molested it. Men have looked on it and lived; but no mortal may touch it and survive."

Nureddin started to speak, gazed at the stubborn, uneasy faces and realized the futility of argument. His attitude changed abruptly.

"I am Master here," he snapped, dropping a hand to his holster. "I have not sweat and bled for this gem to be balked at the last by groundless fears! Stand back, all! Let any man cross me at the peril of his head!"

He faced them, his eyes blazing, and they fell back, cowed by the force of his ruthless personality. He strode boldly up the marble steps, and the Arabs caught their breath, recoiling toward the door; Yar Ali, conscious at last, groaned dismally. God! thought Steve, what a barbaric scene!—bound captives on the dust-heaped floor, wild warriors clustered about, gripping their weapons, the raw acrid scent of blood and burnt powder still fouling the air, corpses strewn in a horrid welter of blood, brains and entrails—and on the dais, the hawk-faced *shaykh*, oblivious to all except the evil crimson glow in the skeleton fingers that rested on the marble throne.

A tense silence gripped all as Nureddin stretched forth his hand slowly, as if hypnotized by the throbbing crimson light. And in Steve's subconsciousness there shuddered a dim echo, as of something vast and loathsome waking suddenly from an age-long slumber. The American's eyes moved instinctively toward the grim cyclopean walls. The jewel's glow had altered strangely; it burned a deeper, darker red, angry and menacing.

"Heart of all evil," murmured the *shaykh*, "how many princes died for thee in the Beginnings of Happenings? Surely the blood of kings throbs in thee. The sultans and the princesses and the generals who wore thee, they are dust and are forgotten, but thou blazest with majesty undimmed, fire of the world—"

Nureddin seized the stone. A shuddery wail broke from the Arabs, cut through by a sharp inhuman cry. To Steve it seemed, horribly, that the great jewel had cried out like a living thing! The stone slipped from the *shaykh's* hand. Nureddin might have dropped it; to Steve it looked as though it leaped convulsively, as a live thing might leap. It rolled from the dais, bounding from step to step, with Nureddin springing after it, cursing as his clutching hand missed it. It struck the floor, veered sharply, and despite the deep dust, rolled like a revolving ball of fire toward the back wall. Nureddin was close upon it—it struck the wall—the *shaykh's* hand reached for it.

A scream of mortal fear ripped the tense silence. Without warning the solid wall had opened. Out of the black wall that gaped there, a tentacle shot and gripped the *shaykh's* body as a python girdles its victim, and jerked him headlong into the darkness. And then the wall showed blank and solid once more; only from within sounded a hideous, high-pitched, muffled screaming that chilled the blood of the listeners. Howling wordlessly, the Arabs stampeded, jammed in a battling, screeching mass in the doorway, tore through and raced madly down the wide stairs.

Steve and Yar Ali, lying helplessly, heard the frenzied clamor of their flight fade away into the distance, and gazed in dumb horror at the grim wall. The shrieks had faded into a more horrific silence. Holding their breath, they heard suddenly a sound that froze the blood in their veins—the soft sliding of metal or stone in a groove. At the same time the hidden door began to open, and Steve caught a glimmer in the blackness that might have been the glitter of monstrous eyes. He closed his own eyes; he dared not look upon whatever horror slunk from that hideous black well. He knew that there are strains the human brain cannot stand, and every primitive instinct in his soul cried out to him that this thing was nightmare and lunacy. He sensed that Yar Ali likewise closed his eyes, and the two lay like dead men.

Clarney heard no sound, but he sensed the presence of a horrific evil too grisly for human comprehension—of an Invader from Outer Gulfs and far black reaches of cosmic being. A deadly cold pervaded the chamber, and Steve felt the glare of inhuman eyes sear through his closed lids and freeze his consciousness. If he looked, if he opened his eyes, he knew stark black madness would be his instant lot.

He felt a soul-shakingly foul breath against his face and knew that the monster was bending close above him, but he lay like a man frozen in a nightmare. He clung to one thought: neither he nor Yar Ali had touched the jewel this horror guarded.

Then he no longer smelled the foul odor, the coldness in the air grew appreciably less, and he heard again the secret door slide in its groove. The fiend was returning to its hiding-place. Not all the legions of Hell could have prevented Steve's eyes, from opening a trifle. He had only a glimpse as the hidden door slid to—and that one glimpse was enough to drive all consciousness from his brain. Steve Clarney, iron-nerved adventurer, fainted for the only time in his checkered life.

How long he lay there Steve never knew, but it could not have been long, for he was roused by Yar Ali's whisper, "Lie still, *sahib*, a little shifting of my body and I can reach thy cords with my teeth."

Steve felt the Afghan's powerful teeth at work on his bonds, and as he lay with his face jammed into the thick dust, and his wounded shoulder began to throb agonizingly—he had forgotten it until now—he began to gather the wandering threads of his consciousness, and it all came back to him. How much, he wondered dazedly, had been the nightmares of delirium, born from suffering and the thirst that caked his throat? The fight with the Arabs had been real—the bonds and the wounds showed that—but the grisly doom of the *shaykh*—the thing that had crept out of the black entrance in the wall—surely that had been a figment of delirium. Nureddin had fallen into a well or pit of some sort—Steve felt his hands were free and he rose to a sitting posture, fumbling for a pocket-knife the Arabs had overlooked. He did not look up or about the chamber as he slashed, the cords that bound his ankles, and then freed Yar Ali, working awkwardly because his left arm was stiff and useless.

"Where are the Bedouins?" he asked, as the Afghan rose, lifting him to his feet.

"Allah, *sahib*," whispered Yar Ali, "are you mad? Have you forgotten? Let us go quickly before the *djinn* returns!"

"It was a nightmare," muttered Steve. "Look—the jewel is back on the throne—" His voice died out. Again that red glow throbbed about the ancient throne, reflecting from the moldering skull; again in the outstretched finger-bones pulsed the Fire of Asshurbanipal. But at the foot of the throne lay another object that had not been there before—the severed head of Nureddin el Mekru stared sightlessly up at the gray light filtering through the stone ceiling. The bloodless lips were drawn back from the teeth in a ghastly grin, the staring eyes mirrored an intolerable horror. In the thick dust of the floor three spoors showed—one of the *shaykh's* where he had followed the red jewel as it rolled to the wall, and above it two other sets of tracks, coming to the throne and returning to the wall—vast, shapeless tracks, as of splayed feet, taloned and gigantic, neither human nor animal.

"My God!" choked Steve. "It was true—and the Thing—the Thing I saw—"

Steve remembered the flight from that chamber as a rushing nightmare, in which he and his companion hurtled headlong down an endless stair that was a gray well of fear, raced blindly through dusty silent chambers, past the glowering idol in the mighty hall and into the blazing light of the desert sun, where they fell slavering, fighting for breath.

Again Steve was roused by the Afridi's voice: "*Sahib, sahib*, in the Name of Allah the Compassionate, our luck has turned!"

Steve looked at his companion as a man might look in a trance: The big Afghan's garments were in tatters, and blood-soaked. He was stained with dust and caked with blood, and his voice was a croak. But his eyes were alight with hope and he pointed with a trembling finger.

"In the shade of yon ruined wall!" he croaked, striving to moisten his blackened lips. "*Allah il allah!* The horses of the men we killed! With canteens and food-pouches at the saddle-horns! Those dogs fled without halting for the steeds of their comrades!"

New life surged up into Steve's bosom and he rose, staggering.

"Out of here," he mumbled. "Out of here, quick!"

Like dying men they stumbled to the horses, tore them loose and climbed fumblingly into the saddles.

"We'll lead the spare mounts," croaked Steve, and Yar Ali nodded emphatic agreement.

"Belike we shall need them ere we sight the coast."

Though their tortured nerves screamed for the water that swung in canteens at the saddle-horns, they turned the mounts aside and, swaying in the saddle, rode like flying corpses down the long sandy street of Kara-Shehr, between the ruined palaces and the crumbling columns, crossed the fallen wall and swept out into the desert. Not once did either glance back toward that black pile of ancient horror, nor did either speak until the ruins faded into the hazy distance. Then and only then did they draw rein and ease their thirst.

"*Allah il allah!*" said Yar Ali piously. "Those dogs have beaten me until it is as though every bone in my body were broken. Dismount, I beg thee, *sahib*, and let me probe for that accursed bullet, and dress thy shoulder to the best of my meager ability."

While this was going on, Yar Ali spoke, avoiding his friend's eye, "You said, *sahib*, you said something about—about seeing? What saw ye, in Allah's name?"

A strong shudder shook the American's steely frame.

"You didn't look when—when the—the Thing put back the jewel in the skeleton's hand and left Nureddin's head on the dais?"

"By Allah, not I!" swore Yar Ali. "My eyes were as closed as if they had been welded together by the molten irons of Satan!"

Steve made no reply until the comrades had once more swung into the saddle and started on their long trek for the coast, which, with spare horses, food, water and weapons, they had a good chance to reach.

"I looked," the American said somberly. "I wish I had not; I know I'll dream about it for the rest of my life. I had only a glance; I couldn't describe it as a man describes an earthly thing. God help me, it wasn't earthly or sane either. Mankind isn't the first owner of the earth; there were Beings here before his coming—and now, survivals of hideously ancient epochs. Maybe spheres of alien dimensions press unseen on this material universe today. Sorcerers have called up sleeping devils before now and controlled them with magic. It is not unreasonable to suppose an Assyrian magician could invoke an elemental demon out of the earth to avenge him and guard something that must have come out of Hell in the first place."

"I'll try to tell you what I glimpsed; then we'll never speak of it again. It was gigantic and black and shadowy; it was a hulking monstrosity that walked upright like a man, but it was like a toad, too, and it was winged and tentacled. I saw only its back; if I'd seen the front of it—its face—I'd have undoubtedly lost my mind. The old Arab was right; God help us, it was the monster that Xuthltan called up out of the dark blind caverns of the earth to guard the Fire of Asshurbanipal!"

THE FEARSOME TOUCH OF DEATH

As long as midnight cloaks the earth
With shadows grim and stark,
God save us from the Judas kiss
Of a dead man in the dark.

Old Adam Farrel lay dead in the house wherein he had lived alone for the last twenty years. A silent, churlish recluse, in his life he had known no friends, and only two men had watched his passing.

Dr. Stein rose and glanced out the window into the gathering dusk.

"You think you can spend the night here, then?" he asked his companion.

This man, Falred by name, assented.

"Yes, certainly. I guess it's up to me."

"Rather a useless and primitive custom, sitting up with the dead," commented the doctor, preparing to depart, "but I suppose in common decency we will have to bow to precedence. Maybe I can find someone who'll come over here and help you with your vigil."

Falred shrugged his shoulders. "I doubt it. Farrel wasn't liked—wasn't known by many people. I scarcely knew him myself, but I don't mind sitting up with the corpse."

Dr. Stein was removing his rubber gloves and Falred watched the process with an interest that almost amounted to fascination. A slight, involuntary shudder shook him at the memory of touching these gloves—slick, cold, clammy things, like the touch of death.

"You may get lonely tonight, if I don't find anyone," the doctor remarked as he opened the door. "Not superstitious, are you?"

Falred laughed. "Scarcely. To tell the truth, from what I hear of Farrel's disposition, I'd rather be watching his corpse than have been his guest in life."

The door closed and Falred took up his vigil. He seated himself in the only chair the room boasted, glanced casually at the formless, sheeted bulk on the bed opposite him, and began to read by the light of the dim lamp which stood on the rough table.

Outside, the darkness gathered swiftly, and finally Falred laid down his magazine to rest his eyes. He looked again at the shape which had, in life, been the form of Adam Farrel, wondering what quirk in the human nature made the sight of a corpse not so unpleasant, but such an object of fear to man. Unthinking ignorance, seeing in dead things a reminder of death to come, he decided lazily, and began idly contemplating as to what life had held for this grim and crabbed old man, who had neither relatives nor friends, and who had seldom left the house wherein he had died. The usual tales of miser-hoarded wealth had accumulated, but Falred felt so little interest in the whole matter that it was not even necessary for him to overcome any temptation to prey about the house for possible hidden treasure.

He returned to his reading with a shrug. The task was more boresome than he had thought for. After a while he was aware that every time he looked up from his magazine and his eyes fell upon the bed with its grim occupant, he started involuntarily as if he had, for an instant, forgotten the presence of the dead man and was unpleasantly reminded of the fact. The start was slight and instinctive, but he felt almost angered at himself. He realized, for the first time, the utter and deadening silence which enwrapped the house—a silence apparently shared by the night, for no sound came through the window. Adam Farrel lived as far apart from his neighbors as possible, and there was no other house within hearing distance.

Falred shook himself as if to rid his mind of unsavory speculations, and went back to his reading. A sudden vagrant gust of wind whipped through the window, in which the light in the lamp flickered and went out suddenly. Falred, cursing softly, groped in the darkness for matches, burning his fingers on the lamp chimney. He struck a match, relighted the lamp, and glancing over at the bed, got a horrible mental jolt. Adam Farrel's face stared blindly at him, the dead eyes wide and blank, framed in the gnarled gray features. Even as Falred instinctively shuddered, his reason explained the apparent phenomenon: the sheet that covered the corpse had been carelessly thrown across the face and the sudden puff of wind had disarranged and flung it aside.

Yet there was something grisly about the thing, something fearsomely suggestive—as if, in the cloaking dark, a dead hand had flung aside the sheet, just as if the corpse were about to rise....

Falred, an imaginative man, shrugged his shoulders at these ghastly thoughts and crossed the room to replace the sheet. The dead eyes seemed to stare malevolently, with an evilness that transcended the dead man's churlishness in life. The workings of a vivid imagination, Falred knew, and he re-covered the gray face, shrinking as his hand chanced to touch the cold flesh—slick and clammy, the touch of death. He shuddered with the natural revulsion of the living for the dead, and went back to his chair and magazine.

At last, growing sleepy, he lay down upon a couch which, by some strange whim of the original owner, formed part of the room's scant furnishings, and composed himself for slumber. He decided to leave the light burning, telling himself that it was in accordance with the usual custom of leaving lights burning for the dead; for he was not willing to admit to himself that already he was conscious of a dislike for lying in the darkness with the corpse. He dozed, awoke with a start and looked at the sheeted form of the bed. Silence reigned over the house, and outside it was very dark.

The hour was approaching midnight, with its accompanying eerie domination over the human mind. Falred glanced again at the bed where the body lay and found the sight of the sheeted object most repellent. A fantastic idea had birth in his mind, and grew, that beneath the sheet, the mere lifeless body had become a strange, monstrous thing, a hideous, conscious being, that watched him with eyes which burned through the fabric of the cloth. This thought—a mere fantasy, of course—he explained to himself by the legends of vampires, undead ghosts and such like—the fearsome attributes with which the living have cloaked the dead for countless ages, since primitive man first recognized in death something horrid and apart from life. Man feared death, thought Falred, and some of this fear of death took hold on the dead so that they, too, were feared. And the sight of the dead engendered grisly thoughts, gave rise to dim fears of hereditary memory, lurking back in the dark corners of the brain.

At any rate, that silent, hidden thing was getting on his nerves. He thought of uncovering the face, on the principle that familiarity breeds contempt. The sight of the features, calm and still in death, would banish, he thought, all such wild conjectures as were haunting him in spite of himself. But the thought of those dead eyes staring in the lamplight was intolerable; so at last he blew out the light and lay down. This fear had been stealing upon him so insidiously and gradually that he had not been aware of its growth.

With the extinguishing of the light, however, and the blotting out of the sight of the corpse, things assumed their true character and proportions, and Falred fell asleep almost instantly, on his lips a faint smile for his previous folly.

He awakened suddenly. How long he had been asleep he did not know. He sat up, his pulse pounding frantically, the cold sweat beading his forehead. He knew instantly where he was, remembered the other occupant of the room. But what had awakened him? A dream—yes, now he remembered—a hideous dream in which the dead man had risen from the bed and stalked stiffly across the room with eyes of fire and a horrid leer frozen on his gray lips. Falred had seemed to lie motionless, helpless; then as the corpse reached a gnarled and horrible hand, he had awakened.

He strove to pierce the gloom, but the room was all blackness and all without was so dark that no gleam of light came through the window. He reached a shaking hand toward the lamp, then recoiled as if from a hidden serpent. Sitting here in the dark with a fiendish corpse was bad enough, but he dared not light the lamp, for fear that his reason would be snuffed out like a candle at what he might see. Horror, stark and unreasoning, had full possession of his soul; he no longer questioned the instinctive fears that rose in him. All those legends he had heard came back to him and brought a belief in them. Death was a hideous thing, a brain-shattering horror, imbuing lifeless men with a horrid malevolence. Adam Farrel in his life had been simply a churlish but harmless man; now he was a terror, a monster, a fiend lurking in the shadows of fear, ready to leap on mankind with talons dipped deep in death and insanity.

Falred sat there, his blood freezing, and fought out his silent battle. Faint glimmerings of reason had begun to touch his fright when a soft, stealthy sound again froze him. He did not recognize it as the whisper of the night wind across the windowsill. His frenzied fancy knew it only as the tread of death and horror. He sprang from the couch, then stood undecided. Escape was in his mind but he was too dazed to even try to formulate a plan of escape. Even his sense of direction was gone. Fear had so stultified his mind that he was not able to think consciously. The blackness spread in long waves about him and its darkness and void entered into his brain. His motions, such as they were, were instinctive. He seemed shackled with mighty chains and his limbs responded sluggishly, like an imbecile's.

A terrible horror grew up in him and reared its grisly shape, that the dead man was behind him, was stealing upon him from the rear. He no longer thought of lighting the lamp; he no longer thought of anything. Fear filled his whole being; there was room for nothing else.

He backed slowly away in the darkness, hands behind him, instinctively feeling the way. With a terrific effort he partly shook the clinging mists of horror from him, and, the cold sweat clammy upon his body, strove to orient himself. He could see nothing, but the bed was across the room, in front of him. He was backing away from it. There was where the dead man was lying, according to all rules of nature; if the thing were, as he felt, behind him, then the old tales were true: death did implant in lifeless bodies an unearthly animation, and dead men did roam the shadows to work their ghastly and evil will upon the sons of men. Then— great God!—what was man but a wailing infant, lost in the night and beset by frightful things from the black abysses and the terrible unknown voids of space and time? These conclusions he did not reach by any reasoning process; they leaped full-grown into his terror-dazed brain. He worked his way slowly backward, groping, clinging to the thought that the dead man must be in front of him.

Then his back-flung hands encountered something—something slick, cold and clammy—like the touch of death. A scream shook the echoes, followed by the crash of a falling body.

The next morning they who came to the house of death found two corpses in the room. Adam Farrel's sheeted body lay motionless upon the bed, and across the room lay the body of Falred, beneath the shelf where Dr. Stein had absent-mindedly left his gloves—rubber gloves, slick and clammy to the touch of a hand groping in the dark—a hand of one fleeing his own fear—rubber gloves, slick and clammy and cold, like the touch of death.

PEOPLE OF THE DARK

I came to Dagon's Cave to kill Richard Brent. I went down the dusky avenues made by the towering trees, and my mood well-matched the primitive grimness of the scene.

The approach to Dagon's Cave is always dark, for the mighty branches and thick leaves shut out the sun, and now the somberness of my own soul made the shadows seem more ominous and gloomy than was natural.

Not far away I heard the slow wash of the waves against the tall cliffs, but the sea itself was out of sight, masked by the dense oak forest. The darkness and the stark gloom of my surroundings gripped my shadowed soul as I passed beneath the ancient branches—as I came out into a narrow glade and saw the mouth of the ancient cavern before me. I paused, scanning the cavern's exterior and the dim reaches of the silent oaks.

The man I hated had not come before me! I was in time to carry out my grim intent. For a moment my resolution faltered, then like a wave there surged over me the fragrance of Eleanor Bland, a vision of wavy golden hair and deep gray eyes, changing and mystic as the sea. I clenched my hands until the knuckles showed white, and instinctively touched the wicked snub-nosed revolver whose weight sagged my coat pocket.

But for Richard Brent, I felt certain I had already won this woman, desire for whom made my waking hours a torment and my sleep a torture. Whom did she love? She would not say; I did not believe she knew. Let one of us go away, I thought, and she would turn to the other. And I was going to simplify matters for her—and for myself. By chance I had overheard my blond English rival remark that he intended coming to lonely Dagon's Cave on an idle exploring outing—alone.

I am not by nature criminal. I was born and raised in a hard country, and have lived most of my life on the raw edges of the world, where a man took what he wanted, if he could, and mercy was a virtue little known. But it was a torment that racked me day and night that sent me out to take the life of Richard Brent. I have lived hard, and violently, perhaps. When love overtook me, it also was fierce and violent. Perhaps I was not wholly sane, what with my love for Eleanor Bland and my hatred for Richard Brent. Under any other circumstances, I would have been glad to call him friend—a fine, rangy, upstanding young fellow, clear-eyed and strong. But he stood in the way of my desire and he must die.

I stepped into the dimness of the cavern and halted. I had never before visited Dagon's Cave, yet a vague sense of misplaced familiarity troubled me as I gazed on the high arching roof, the even stone walls and the dusty floor. I shrugged my shoulders, unable to place the elusive feeling; doubtless it was evoked by a similarity to caverns in the mountain country of the American Southwest where I was born and spent my childhood.

And yet I knew that I had never seen a cave like this one, whose regular aspect gave rise to myths that it was not a natural cavern, but had been hewn from the solid rock ages ago by the tiny hands of the mysterious Little People, the prehistoric beings of British legend. The whole countryside thereabouts was a haunt for ancient folk lore.

The country folk were predominantly Celtic; here the Saxon invaders had never prevailed, and the legends reached back, in that long-settled countryside, further than anywhere else in England—back beyond the coming of the Saxons, aye, and incredibly beyond that distant age, beyond the coming of the Romans, to those unbelievably ancient days when the native Britons warred with black-haired Irish pirates.

The Little People, of course, had their part in the lore. Legend said that this cavern was one of their last strongholds against the conquering Celts, and hinted at lost tunnels, long fallen in or blocked up, connecting the cave with a network of subterranean corridors which honeycombed the hills. With these chance meditations vying idly in my mind with grimmer speculations, I passed through the outer chamber of the cavern and entered a narrow tunnel, which, I knew by former descriptions, connected with a larger room.

It was dark in the tunnel, but not too dark for me to make out the vague, half-defaced outlines of mysterious etchings on the stone walls. I ventured to switch on my electric torch and examine them more closely. Even in their dimness I was repelled by their abnormal and revolting character. Surely no men cast in human mold as we know it, scratched those grotesque obscenities.

The Little People—I wondered if those anthropologists were correct in their theory of a squat Mongoloid aboriginal race, so low in the scale of evolution as to be scarcely human, yet possessing a distinct, though repulsive, culture of their own. They had vanished before the invading races, theory said, forming the base of all Aryan legends of trolls, elves, dwarfs and witches. Living in caves from the start, these aborigines had retreated farther and farther into the caverns of the hills, before the conquerors, vanishing at last entirely, though folklore fancy pictures their descendants still dwelling in the lost chasms far beneath the hills, loathsome survivors of an outworn age.

I snapped off the torch and passed through the tunnel, to come out into a sort of doorway which seemed entirely too symmetrical to have been the work of nature. I was looking into a vast dim cavern, at a somewhat lower level than the outer chamber, and again I shuddered with a strange alien sense of familiarity. A short flight of steps led down from the tunnel to the floor of the cavern—tiny steps, too small for normal human feet, carved into the solid stone. Their edges were greatly worn away, as if by ages of use. I started the descent—my foot slipped suddenly. I instinctively knew what was coming—it was all in part with that strange feeling of familiarity—but I could not catch myself. I fell headlong down the steps and struck the stone floor with a crash that blotted out my senses...

Slowly consciousness returned to me, with a throbbing of my head and a sensation of bewilderment. I lifted a hand to my head and found it caked with blood. I had received a blow, or had taken a fall, but so completely had my wits been knocked out of me that my mind was an absolute blank. Where I was, who I was, I did not know. I looked about, blinking in the dim light, and saw that I was in a wide, dusty cavern. I stood at the foot of a short flight of steps which led upward into some kind of tunnel. I ran my hand dazedly through my square-cut black mane, and my eyes wandered over my massive naked limbs and powerful torso. I was clad, I noticed absently, in a sort of loincloth, from the girdle of which swung an empty scabbard, and leathern sandals were on my feet.

Then I saw an object lying at my feet, and stooped and took it up. It was a heavy iron sword, whose broad blade was darkly stained. My fingers fitted instinctively about its hilt with the familiarity of long usage. Then suddenly I remembered and laughed to think that a fall on his head should render me, Conan of the reavers, so completely daft. Aye, it all came back to me now. It had been a raid on the Britons, on whose coasts we continually swooped with torch and sword, from the island called Eireann. That day we of the black-haired Gael had swept suddenly down on a coastal village in our long, low ships and in the hurricane of battle which followed, the Britons had at last given up the stubborn contest and retreated, warriors, women and bairns, into the deep shadows of the oak forests, whither we seldom dared follow.

But I had followed, for there was a girl of my foes whom I desired with a burning passion, a lithe, slim young creature with wavy golden hair and deep gray eyes, changing and mystic as the sea. Her name was Tamera—well I knew it, for there was trade between the races as well as war, and I had been in the villages of the Britons as a peaceful visitor, in times of rare truce.

I saw her white half-clad body flickering among the trees as she ran with the swiftness of a doe, and I followed, panting with fierce eagerness. Under the dark shadows of the gnarled oaks she fled, with me in close pursuit, while far away behind us died out the shouts of slaughter and the clashing of swords. Then we ran in silence, save for her quick labored panting, and I was so close behind her as we emerged into a narrow glade before a somber-mouthed cavern, that I caught her flying golden tresses with one mighty hand. She sank down with a despairing wail, and even so, a shout echoed her cry and I wheeled quickly to face a rangy young Briton who sprang from among the trees, the light of desperation in his eyes.

"Vertorix!" the girl wailed, her voice breaking in a sob, and fiercer rage welled up in me, for I knew the lad was her lover.

"Run for the forest, Tamera!" he shouted, and leaped at me as a panther leaps, his bronze ax whirling like a flashing wheel about his head. And then sounded the clangor of strife and the hard-drawn panting of combat.

The Briton was as tall as I, but he was lithe where I was massive. The advantage of sheer muscular power was mine, and soon he was on the defensive, striving desperately to parry my heavy strokes with his ax. Hammering on his guard like a smith on an anvil, I pressed him relentlessly, driving him irresistibly before me. His chest heaved, his breath came in labored gasps, his blood dripped from scalp, chest and thigh where my whistling blade had cut the skin, and all but gone home. As I redoubled my strokes and he bent and swayed beneath them like a sapling in a storm, I heard the girl cry: "Vertorix! Vertorix! The cave! Into the cave!"

I saw his face pale with a fear greater than that induced by my hacking sword.

"Not there!" he gasped. "Better a clean death! In Il-marenin's name, girl, run into the forest and save yourself!"

"I will not leave you!" she cried. "The cave! It is our one chance!"

I saw her flash past us like a flying wisp of white and vanish in the cavern, and with a despairing cry, the youth launched a wild desperate stroke that nigh cleft my skull. As I staggered beneath the blow I had barely parried, he sprang away, leaped into the cavern after the girl and vanished in the gloom.

With a maddened yell that invoked all my grim Gaelic gods, I sprang recklessly after them, not reckoning if the Briton lurked beside the entrance to brain me as I rushed in. But a quick glance showed the chamber empty and a wisp of white disappearing through a dark doorway in the back wall.

I raced across the cavern and came to a sudden halt as an ax licked out of the gloom of the entrance and whistled perilously close to my black-maned head. I gave back suddenly. Now the advantage was with Vertorix, who stood in the narrow mouth of the corridor where I could hardly come at him without exposing myself to the devastating stroke of his ax.

I was near frothing with fury and the sight of a slim white form among the deep shadows behind the warrior drove me into a frenzy. I attacked savagely but warily, thrusting venomously at my foe, and drawing back from his strokes. I wished to draw him out into a wide lunge, avoid it and run him through before he could recover his balance. In the open I could have beat him down by sheer power and heavy blows, but here I could only use the point and that at a disadvantage; I always preferred the edge. But I was stubborn; if I could not come at him with a finishing stroke, neither could he or the girl escape me while I kept him hemmed in the tunnel.

It must have been the realization of this fact that prompted the girl's action, for she said something to Vertorix about looking for a way leading out, and though he cried out fiercely forbidding her to venture away into the darkness, she turned and ran swiftly down the tunnel to vanish in the dimness. My wrath rose appallingly and I nearly got my head split in my eagerness to bring down my foe before she found a means for their escape.

Then the cavern echoed with a terrible scream and Vertorix cried out like a man death-stricken, his face ashy in the gloom. He whirled, as if he had forgotten me and my sword, and raced down the tunnel like a madman, shrieking Tamera's name. From far away, as if from the bowels of the earth, I seemed to hear her answering cry, mingled with a strange sibilant clamor that electrified me with nameless but instinctive horror. Then silence fell, broken only by Vertorix's frenzied cries, receding farther and farther into the earth.

Recovering myself I sprang into the tunnel and raced after the Briton as recklessly as he had run after the girl. And to give me my due, red-handed reaver though I was, cutting down my rival from behind was less in my mind than discovering what dread thing had Tamera in its clutches.

As I ran along I noted absently that the sides of the tunnel were scrawled with monstrous pictures, and realized suddenly and creepily that this must be the dread Cavern of the Children of the Night, tales of which had crossed the narrow sea to resound horrifically in the ears of the Gaels. Terror of me must have ridden Tamera hard to have driven her into the cavern shunned by her people, where it was said, lurked the survivors of that grisly race which inhabited the land before the coming of the Picts and Britons, and which had fled before them into the unknown caverns of the hills.

Ahead of me the tunnel opened into a wide chamber, and I saw the white form of Vertorix glimmer momentarily in the semidarkness and vanish in what appeared to be the entrance of a corridor opposite the mouth of the tunnel I had just traversed. Instantly there sounded a short, fierce shout and the crash of a hard-driven blow, mixed with the hysterical screams of a girl and a medley of serpentlike hissing that made my hair bristle. And at that instant I shot out of the tunnel, running at full speed, and realized too late the floor of the cavern lay several feet below the level of the tunnel. My flying feet missed the tiny steps and I crashed terrifically on the solid stone floor.

Now as I stood in the semidarkness, rubbing my aching head, all this came back to me, and I stared fearsomely across the vast chamber at that black cryptic corridor into which Tamera and her lover had disappeared, and over which silence lay like a pall. Gripping my sword, I warily crossed the great still cavern and peered into the corridor. Only a denser darkness met my eyes. I entered, striving to pierce the gloom, and as my foot slipped on a wide wet smear on the stone floor, the raw acrid scent of fresh-spilled blood met my nostrils. Someone or something had died there, either the young Briton or his unknown attacker.

I stood there uncertainly, all the supernatural fears that are the heritage of the Gael rising in my primitive soul. I could turn and stride out of these accursed mazes, into the clear sunlight and down to the clean blue sea where my comrades, no doubt, impatiently awaited me after the routing of the Britons. Why should I risk my life among these grisly rat dens? I was eaten with curiosity to know what manner of beings haunted the cavern, and who were called the Children of the Night by the Britons, but in it was my love for the yellow-haired girl which drove me down that dark tunnel—and love her I did, in my way, and would have been kind to her, had I carried her away to my island haunt.

I walked softly along the corridor, blade ready. What sort of creatures the Children of the Night were, I had no idea, but the tales of the Britons had lent them a distinctly inhuman nature.

The darkness closed around me as I advanced, until I was moving in utter blackness. My groping left hand encountered a strangely carven doorway, and at that instant something hissed like a viper beside me and slashed fiercely at my thigh. I struck back savagely and felt my blind stroke crunch home, and something fell at my feet and died. What thing I had slain in the dark I could not know, but it must have been at least partly human because the shallow gash in my thigh had been made with a blade of some sort, and not by fangs or talons. And I sweated with horror, for the gods know, the hissing voice of the Thing had resembled no human tongue I had ever heard.

And now in the darkness ahead of me I heard the sound repeated, mingled with horrible slitherings, as if numbers of reptilian creatures were approaching. I stepped quickly into the entrance my groping hand had discovered and came near repeating my headlong fall, for instead of letting into another level corridor, the entrance gave onto a flight of dwarfish steps on which I floundered wildly.

Recovering my balance I went on cautiously, groping along the sides of the shaft for support. I seemed to be descending into the very bowels of the earth, but I dared not turn back. Suddenly, far below me, I glimpsed a faint eerie light. I went on, perforce, and came to a spot where the shaft opened into another great vaulted chamber; and I shrank back, aghast.

In the center of the chamber stood a grim, black altar; it had been rubbed all over with a sort of phosphorous, so that it glowed dully, lending a semi-illumination to the shadowy cavern. Towering behind it on a pedestal of human skulls, lay a cryptic black object, carven with mysterious hieroglyphics. The Black Stone! The ancient, ancient Stone before which, the Britons said, the Children of the Night bowed in gruesome worship, and whose origin was lost in the black mists of a hideously distant past. Once, legend said, it had stood in that grim circle of monoliths called Stonehenge, before its votaries had been driven like chaff before the bows of the Picts.

But I gave it but a passing, shuddering glance. Two figures lay, bound with rawhide thongs, on the glowing black altar. One was Tamera; the other was Vertorix, bloodstained and disheveled. His bronze ax, crusted with clotted blood, lay near the altar. And before the glowing stone squatted Horror.

Though I had never seen one of those ghoulish aborigines, I knew this thing for what it was, and shuddered. It was a man of a sort, but so low in the stage of life that its distorted humanness was more horrible than its bestiality.

Erect, it could not have been five feet in height. Its body was scrawny and deformed, its head disproportionately large. Lank snaky hair fell over a square inhuman face with flabby writhing lips that bared yellow fangs, flat spreading nostrils and great yellow slant eyes. I knew the creature must be able to see in the dark as well as a cat. Centuries of skulking in dim caverns had lent the race terrible and inhuman attributes. But the most repellent feature was its skin: scaly, yellow and mottled, like the hide of a serpent. A loincloth made of a real snake's skin girt its lean loins, and its taloned hands gripped a short stone-tipped spear and a sinister-looking mallet of polished flint.

So intently was it gloating over its captives, it evidently had not heard my stealthy descent. As I hesitated in the shadows of the shaft, far above me I heard a soft sinister rustling that chilled the blood in my veins. The Children were creeping down the shaft behind me, and I was trapped. I saw other entrances opening on the chamber, and I acted, realizing that an alliance with Vertorix was our only hope. Enemies though we were, we were men, cast in the same mold, trapped in the lair of these indescribable monstrosities.

As I stepped from the shaft, the horror beside the altar jerked up his head and glared full at me. And as he sprang up, I leaped and he crumpled, blood spurting, as my heavy sword split his reptilian heart. But even as he died, he gave tongue in an abhorrent shriek which was echoed far up the shaft. In desperate haste I cut Vertorix's bonds and dragged him to his feet. And I turned to Tamera, who in that dire extremity did not shrink from me, but looked up at me with pleading, terror-dilated eyes. Vertorix wasted no time in words, realizing chance had made allies of us. He snatched up his ax as I freed the girl.

"We can't go up the shaft," he explained swiftly; "we'll have the whole pack upon us quickly. They caught Tamera as she sought for an exit, and overpowered me by sheer numbers when I followed. They dragged us hither and all but that carrion scattered—bearing word of the sacrifice through all their burrows, I doubt not. Il-marenin alone knows how many of my people, stolen in the night, have died on that altar. We must take our chance in one of these tunnels—all lead to Hell! Follow me!"

Seizing Tamera's hand he ran fleetly into the nearest tunnel and I followed. A glance back into the chamber before a turn in the corridor blotted it from view showed a revolting horde streaming out of the shaft. The tunnel slanted steeply upward, and suddenly ahead of us we saw a bar of gray light. But the next instant our cries of hope changed to curses of bitter disappointment. There was daylight, aye, drifting in through a cleft in the vaulted roof, but far, far above our reach. Behind us the pack gave tongue exultingly. And I halted.

"Save yourselves if you can," I growled. "Here I make my stand. They can see in the dark and I cannot. Here at least I can see them. Go!"

But Vertorix halted also. "Little use to be hunted like rats to our doom. There is no escape. Let us meet our fate like men."

Tamera cried out, wringing her hands, but she clung to her lover.

"Stand behind me with the girl," I grunted. "When I fall, dash out her brains with your ax lest they take her alive again. Then sell your own life as high as you may, for there is none to avenge us."

His keen eyes met mine squarely.

"We worship different gods, reaver," he said, "but all gods love brave men. Mayhap we shall meet again, beyond the Dark."

"Hail and farewell, Briton!" I growled, and our right hands gripped like steel.

"Hail and farewell, Gael!"

And I wheeled as a hideous horde swept up the tunnel and burst into the dim light, a flying nightmare of streaming snaky hair, foam-flecked lips and glaring eyes. Thundering my war-cry I sprang to meet them and my heavy sword sang and a head spun grinning from its shoulder on an arching fountain of blood. They came upon me like a wave and the fighting madness of my race was upon me. I fought as a maddened beast fights and at every stroke I clove through flesh and bone, and blood spattered in a crimson rain.

Then as they surged in and I went down beneath the sheer weight of their numbers, a fierce yell cut the din and Vertorix's ax sang above me, splattering blood and brains like water. The press slackened and I staggered up, trampling the writhing bodies beneath my feet.

"A stair behind us!" the Briton was screaming. "Half-hidden in an angle of the wall! It must lead to daylight! Up it, in the name of Il-marenin!"

So we fell back, fighting our way inch by inch. The vermin fought like blood-hungry devils, clambering over the bodies of the slain to screech and hack. Both of us were streaming blood at every step when we reached the mouth of the shaft, into which Tamera had preceded us.

Screaming like very fiends the Children surged in to drag us down. The shaft was not as light as had been the corridor, and it grew darker as we climbed, but our foes could only come at us from in front. By the gods, we slaughtered them till the stair was littered with mangled corpses and the Children frothed like mad wolves! Then suddenly they abandoned the fray and raced back down the steps.

"What portends this?" gasped Vertorix, shaking the bloody sweat from his eyes.

"Up the shaft, quick!" I panted. "They mean to mount some other stair and come at us from above!"

So we raced up those accursed steps, slipping and stumbling, and as we fled past a black tunnel that opened into the shaft, far down it we heard a frightful howling. An instant later we emerged from the shaft into a winding corridor, dimly illumined by a vague gray light filtering in from above, and somewhere in the bowels of the earth I seemed to hear the thunder of rushing water. We started down the corridor and as we did so, a heavy weight smashed on my shoulders, knocking me headlong, and a mallet crashed again and again on my head, sending dull red flashes of agony across my brain. With a volcanic wrench I dragged my attacker off and under me, and tore out his throat with my naked fingers. And his fangs met in my arm in his death-bite.

Reeling up, I saw that Tamera and Vertorix had passed out of sight. I had been somewhat behind them, and they had run on, knowing nothing of the fiend which had leaped on my shoulders. Doubtless they thought I was still close on their heels. A dozen steps I took, then halted. The corridor branched and I knew not which way my companions had taken. At blind venture I turned into the left-hand branch, and staggered on in the semidarkness. I was weak from fatigue and loss of blood, dizzy and sick from the blows I had received. Only the thought of Tamera kept me doggedly on my feet. Now distinctly I heard the sound of an unseen torrent.

That I was not far underground was evident by the dim light which filtered in from somewhere above, and I momentarily expected to come upon another stair. But when I did, I halted in black despair; instead of up, it led down. Somewhere far behind me I heard faintly the howls of the pack, and I went down, plunging into utter darkness. At last I struck a level and went along blindly. I had given up all hope of escape, and only hoped to find Tamera—if she and her lover had not found a way of escape—and die with her. The thunder of rushing water was above my head now, and the tunnel was slimy and dank. Drops of moisture fell on my head and I knew I was passing under the river.

Then I blundered again upon steps cut in the stone, and these led upward. I scrambled up as fast as my stiffening wounds would allow—and I had taken punishment enough to have killed an ordinary man. Up I went and up, and suddenly daylight burst on me through a cleft in the solid rock. I stepped into the blaze of the sun. I was standing on a ledge high above the rushing waters of a river which raced at awesome speed between towering cliffs. The ledge on which I stood was close to the top of the cliff; safety was within arm's length. But I hesitated and such was my love for the golden-haired girl that I was ready to retrace my steps through those black tunnels on the mad hope of finding her. Then I started.

Across the river I saw another cleft in the cliff-wall which fronted me, with a ledge similar to that on which I stood, but longer. In olden times, I doubt not, some sort of primitive bridge connected the two ledges—possibly before the tunnel was dug beneath the riverbed. Now as I watched, two figures emerged upon that other ledge—one gashed, dust-stained, limping, gripping a bloodstained ax; the other slim, white and girlish.

Vertorix and Tamera! They had taken the other branch of the corridor at the fork and had evidently followed the windows of the tunnel to emerge as I had done, except that I had taken the left turn and passed clear under the river. And now I saw that they were in a trap. On that side the cliffs rose half a hundred feet higher than on my side of the river, and so sheer a spider could scarce have scaled them. There were only two ways of escape from the ledge: back through the fiend-haunted tunnels, or straight down to the river which raved far beneath.

I saw Vertorix look up the sheer cliffs and then down, and shake his head in despair. Tamara put her arms about his neck, and though I could not hear their voices for the rush of the river, I saw them smile, and then they went together to the edge of the ledge. And out of the cleft swarmed a loathsome mob, as foul reptiles writhe up out of the darkness, and they stood blinking in the sunlight like the night-things they were. I gripped my sword-hilt in the agony of my helplessness until the blood trickled from under my fingernails. Why had not the pack followed me instead of my companions?

The Children hesitated an instant as the two Britons faced them, then with a laugh Vertorix hurled his ax far out into the rushing river, and turning, caught Tamera in a last embrace. Together they sprang far out, and still locked in each other's arms, hurtled downward, struck the madly foaming water that seemed to leap up to meet them, and vanished. And the wild river swept on like a blind, insensate monster, thundering along the echoing cliffs.

A moment I stood frozen, then like a man in a dream I turned, caught the edge of the cliff above me and wearily drew myself up and over, and stood on my feet above the cliffs, hearing like a dim dream the roar of the river far beneath.

I reeled up, dazedly clutching my throbbing head, on which dried blood was clotted. I glared wildly about me. I had clambered the cliffs—no, by the thunder of Crom, I was still in the cavern! I reached for my sword—

The mists faded and I stared about dizzily, orienting myself with space and time. I stood at the foot of the steps down which I had fallen. I who had been Conan the reaver, was John O'Brien. Was all that grotesque interlude a dream? Could a mere dream appear so vivid? Even in dreams, we often know we are dreaming, but Conan the reaver had no cognizance of any other existence. More, he remembered his own past life as a living man remembers, though in the waking mind of John O'Brien, that memory faded into dust and mist. But the adventures of Conan in the Cavern of the Children stood clear-etched in the mind of John O'Brien.

I glanced across the dim chamber toward the entrance of the tunnel into which Vertorix had followed the girl. But I looked in vain, seeing only the bare blank wall of the cavern. I crossed the chamber, switched on my electric torch—miraculously unbroken in my fall—and felt along the wall.

Ha! I started, as from an electric shock! Exactly where the entrance should have been, my fingers detected a difference in material, a section which was rougher than the rest of the wall. I was convinced that it was of comparatively modern workmanship; the tunnel had been walled up.

I thrust against it, exerting all my strength, and it seemed to me that the section was about to give. I drew back, and taking a deep breath, launched my full weight against it, backed by all the power of my giant muscles. The brittle, decaying wall gave way with a shattering crash and I catapulted through in a shower of stones and falling masonry.

I scrambled up, a sharp cry escaping me. I stood in a tunnel, and I could not mistake the feeling of similarity this time. Here Vertorix had first fallen foul of the Children, as they dragged Tamera away, and here where I now stood the floor had been awash with blood.

I walked down the corridor like a man in a trance. Soon I should come to the doorway on the left—aye, there it was, the strangely carven portal, at the mouth of which I had slain the unseen being which reared up in the dark beside me. I shivered momentarily. Could it be possible that remnants of that foul race still lurked hideously in these remote caverns?

I turned into the doorway and my light shone down a long, slanting shaft, with tiny steps cut into the solid stone. Down these had Conan the reaver gone groping and down them went I, John O'Brien, with memories of that other life filling my brain with vague phantasms. No light glimmered ahead of me but I came into the great dim chamber I had known of yore, and I shuddered as I saw the grim black altar etched in the gleam of my torch. Now no bound figures writhed there, no crouching horror gloated before it. Nor did the pyramid of skulls support the Black Stone before which unknown races had bowed before Egypt was born out of time's dawn. Only a littered heap of dust lay strewn where the skulls had upheld the hellish thing. No, that had been no dream: I was John O'Brien, but I had been Conan of the reavers in that other life, and that grim interlude a brief episode of reality which I had relived.

I entered the tunnel down which we had fled, shining a beam of light ahead, and saw the bar of gray light drifting down from above—just as in that other, lost age. Here the Briton and I, Conan, had turned at bay. I turned my eyes from the ancient cleft high up in the vaulted roof, and looked for the stair. There it was, half-concealed by an angle in the wall.

I mounted, remembering how hurriedly Vertorix and I had gone up so many ages before, with the horde hissing and frothing at our heels. I found myself tense with dread as I approached the dark, gaping entrance through which the pack had sought to cut us off. I had snapped off the light when I came into the dim-lit corridor below, and now I glanced into the well of blackness which opened on the stair. And with a cry I started back, nearly losing my footing on the worn steps. Sweating in the semidarkness I switched on the light and directed its beam into the cryptic opening, revolver in hand.

I saw only the bare rounded sides of a small shaftlike tunnel and I laughed nervously. My imagination was running riot; I could have sworn that hideous yellow eyes glared terribly at me from the darkness, and that a crawling something had scuttered away down the tunnel. I was foolish to let these imaginings upset me. The Children had long vanished from these caverns; a nameless and abhorrent race closer to the serpent than the man, they had centuries ago faded back into the oblivion from which they had crawled in the black dawn ages of the Earth.

I came out of the shaft into the winding corridor, which, as I remembered of old, was lighter. Here from the shadows a lurking thing had leaped on my back while my companions ran on, unknowing. What a brute of a man Conan had been, to keep going after receiving such savage wounds! Aye, in that age all men were iron.

I came to the place where the tunnel forked and as before I took the left-hand branch and came to the shaft that led down. Down this I went, listening for the roar of the river, but not hearing it. Again the darkness shut in about the shaft, so I was forced to have recourse to my electric torch again, lest I lose my footing and plunge to my death. Oh, I, John O'Brien, am not nearly so sure-footed as was I, Conan the reaver; no, nor as tiger-ishly powerful and quick, either.

I soon struck the dank lower level and felt again the dampness that denoted my position under the riverbed, but still I could not hear the rush of the water. And indeed I knew that whatever mighty river had rushed roaring to the sea in those ancient times, there was no such body of water among the hills today. I halted, flashing my light about. I was in a vast tunnel, not very high of roof, but broad. Other smaller tunnels branched off from it and I wondered at the network which apparently honeycombed the hills.

I cannot describe the grim, gloomy effect of those dark, low-roofed corridors far below the earth. Over all hung an over-powering sense of unspeakable antiquity. Why had the little people carved out these mysterious crypts, and in which black age? Were these caverns their last refuge from the onrushing tides of humanity, or their castles since time immemorial? I shook my head in bewilderment; the bestiality of the Children I had seen, yet somehow they had been able to carve these tunnels and chambers that might balk modern engineers. Even supposing they had but completed a task begun by nature, still it was a stupendous work for a race of dwarfish aborigines.

Then I realized with a start that I was spending more time in these gloomy tunnels than I cared for, and began to hunt for the steps by which Conan had ascended. I found them and, following them up, breathed again deeply in relief as the sudden glow of daylight filled the shaft. I came out upon the ledge, now worn away until it was little more than a bump on the face of the cliff. And I saw the great river, which had roared like a pris-oned monster between the sheer walls of its narrow canyon, had dwindled away with the passing eons until it was no more than a tiny stream, far beneath me, trickling soundlessly among the stones on its way to the sea.

Aye, the surface of the earth changes; the rivers swell or shrink, the mountains heave and topple, the lakes dry up, the continents alter; but under the earth the work of lost, mysterious hands slumbers untouched by the sweep of Time. Their work, aye, but what of the hands that reared that work? Did they, too, lurk beneath the bosoms of the hills?

How long I stood there, lost in dim speculations, I do not know, but suddenly, glancing across at the other ledge, crumbling and weathered, I shrank back into the entrance behind me. Two figures came out upon the ledge and I gasped to see that they were Richard Brent and Eleanor Bland. Now I remembered why I had come to the cavern and my hand instinctively sought the revolver in my pocket. They did not see me. But I could see them, and hear them plainly, too, since no roaring river now thundered between the ledges.

"By gad, Eleanor," Brent was saying, "I'm glad you decided to come with me. Who would have guessed there was anything to those old tales about hidden tunnels leading from the cavern? I wonder how that section of wall came to collapse? I thought I heard a crash just as we entered the outer cave. Do you suppose some beggar was in the cavern ahead of us, and broke it in?"

"I don't know," she answered. "I remember—oh, I don't know. It almost seems as if I'd been here before, or dreamed I had. I seem to faintly remember, like a far-off nightmare, running, running, running endlessly through these dark corridors with hideous creatures on my heels..."

"Was I there?" jokingly asked Brent.

"Yes, and John, too," she answered. "But you were not Richard Brent, and John was not John O'Brien. No, and I was not Eleanor Bland, either. Oh, it's so dim and far-off I can't describe it at all. It's hazy and misty and terrible."

"I understand, a little," he said unexpectedly. "Ever since we came to the place where the wall had fallen and revealed the old tunnel, I've had a sense of familiarity with the place. There was horror and danger and battle—and love, too."

He stepped nearer the edge to look down in the gorge, and Eleanor cried out sharply and suddenly, seizing him in a convulsive grasp.

"Don't, Richard, don't! Hold me, oh, hold me tight!"

He caught her in his arms. "Why, Eleanor, dear, what's the matter?"

"Nothing," she faltered, but she clung closer to him and I saw she was trembling. "Just a strange feeling—rushing dizziness and fright, just as if I were falling from a great height. Don't go near the edge, Dick; it scares me."

"I won't, dear," he answered, drawing her closer to him, and continuing hesitantly: "Eleanor, there's something I've wanted to ask you for a long time—well, I haven't the knack of putting things in an elegant way. I love you, Eleanor; always have. You know that. But if you don't love me, I'll take myself off and won't annoy you any more. Only please tell me one way or another, for I can't stand it any longer. Is it I or the American?"

"You, Dick," she answered, hiding her face on his shoulder. "It's always been you, though I didn't know it. I think a great deal of John O'Brien. I didn't know which of you I really loved. But today as we came through those terrible tunnels and climbed those fearful stairs, and just now, when I thought for some strange reason we were falling from the ledge, I realized it was you I loved—that I always loved you, through more lives than this one. Always!"

Their lips met and I saw her golden head cradled on his shoulder. My lips were dry, my heart cold, yet my soul was at peace. They belonged to each other. Eons ago they lived and loved, and because of that love they suffered and died. And I, Conan, had driven them to that doom.

I saw them turn toward the cleft, their arms about each other, then I heard Tamera—I mean Eleanor—shriek. I saw them both recoil. And out of the cleft a horror came writhing, a loathsome, brain-shattering thing that blinked in the clean sunlight. Aye, I knew it of old—vestige of a forgotten age, it came writhing its horrid shape up out of the darkness of the Earth and the lost past to claim its own.

What three thousand years of retrogression can do to a race hideous in the beginning, I saw, and shuddered. And instinctively I knew that in all the world it was the only one of its kind, a monster that had lived on, God alone knows how many centuries, wallowing in the slime of its dank subterranean lairs. Before the Children had vanished, the race must have lost all human semblance, living as they did the life of the reptile.

This thing was more like a giant serpent than anything else, but it had aborted legs and snaky arms with hooked talons. It crawled on its belly, writhing back mottled lips to bare needlelike fangs, which I felt must drip with venom. It hissed as it reared up its ghastly head on a horribly long neck, while its yellow slanted eyes glittered with all the horror that is spawned in the black lairs under the earth.

I knew those eyes had blazed at me from the dark tunnel opening on the stair. For some reason the creature had fled from me, possibly because it feared my light, and it stood to reason that it was the only one remaining in the caverns, else I had been set upon in the darkness. But for it, the tunnels could be traversed in safety.

Now the reptilian thing writhed toward the humans trapped on the ledge. Brent had thrust Eleanor behind him and stood, face ashy, to guard her as best he could. And I gave thanks silently that I, John O'Brien, could pay the debt I, Conan the reaver, owed these lovers since long ago.

The monster reared up and Brent, with cold courage, sprang to meet it with his naked hands. Taking quick aim, I fired once. The shot echoed like the crack of doom between the towering cliffs, and the Horror, with a hideously human scream, staggered wildly, swayed and pitched headlong, knotting and writhing like a wounded python, to tumble from the sloping ledge and fall plummetlike to the rocks far below.

DIG ME NO GRAVE

The thunder of my old-fashioned door-knocker, reverberating eerily through the house, roused me from a restless and nightmare-haunted sleep. I looked out the window. In the last light of the sinking moon, the white face of my friend John Conrad looked up at me.

"May I come up, Kirowan?" His voice was shaky and strained.

"Certainly!" I sprang out of bed and pulled on a bath-robe as I heard him enter the front door and ascend the stairs.

A moment later he stood before me, and in the light which I had turned on I saw his hands tremble and noticed the unnatural pallor of his face.

"Old John Grimlan died an hour ago," he said abruptly.

"Indeed? I had not known that he was ill."

"It was a sudden, virulent attack of peculiar nature, a sort of seizure somewhat akin to epilepsy. He has been subject to such spells of late years, you know."

I nodded. I knew something of the old hermit-like man who had lived in his great dark house on the hill; indeed, I had once witnessed one of his strange seizures, and I had been appalled at the writhings, howlings and yammerings of the wretch, who had groveled on the earth like a wounded snake, gibbering terrible curses and black blasphemies until his voice broke in a wordless screaming which spattered his lips with foam. Seeing this, I understood why people in old times looked on such victims as men possessed by demons.

"—some hereditary taint," Conrad was saying. "Old John doubtless fell heir to some ingrown weakness brought on by some loathsome disease, which was his heritage from perhaps a remote ancestor—such things occasionally happen. Or else—well, you know old John himself pried about in the mysterious parts of the earth, and wandered all over the East in his younger days. It is quite possible that he was infected with some obscure malady in his wanderings. There are still many unclassified diseases in Africa and the Orient."

"But," said I, "you have not told me the reason for this sudden visit at this unearthly hour—for I notice that it is past midnight."

My friend seemed rather confused.

"Well, the fact is that John Grimlan died alone, except for myself. He refused to receive any medical aid of any sort, and in the last few moments when it was evident that he was dying, and I was prepared to go for some sort of help in spite of him, he set up such a howling and screaming that I could not refuse his passionate pleas—which were that he should not be left to die alone.

"I have seen men die," added Conrad, wiping the perspiration from his pale brow, "but the death of John Grimlan was the most fearful I have ever seen."

"He suffered a great deal?"

"He appeared to be in much physical agony, but this was mostly submerged by some monstrous mental or psychic suffering. The fear in his distended eyes and his screams transcended any conceivable earthly terror. I tell you, Kirowan, Grimlan's fright was greater and deeper than the ordinary fear of the Beyond shown by a man of ordinarily evil life."

I shifted restlessly. The dark implications of this statement sent a chill of nameless apprehension trickling down my spine.

"I know the country people always claimed that in his youth he sold his soul to the Devil, and that his sudden epileptic attacks were merely a visible sign of the Fiend's power over him; but such talk is foolish, of course, and belongs in the Dark Ages. We all know that John Grimlan's life was a peculiarly evil and vicious one, even toward his last days. With good reason he was universally detested and feared, for I never heard of his doing a single good act. You were his only friend."

"And that was a strange friendship," said Conrad. "I was attracted to him by his unusual powers, for despite his bestial nature, John Grimlan was a highly educated man, a deeply cultured man. He had dipped deep into occult studies, and I first met him in this manner; for as you know, I have always been strongly interested in these lines of research myself.

"But, in this as in all other things, Grimlan was evil and perverse. He had ignored the white side of the occult and delved into the darker, grimmer phases of it—into devil-worship, and voodoo and Shintoism. His knowledge of these foul arts and sciences was immense and unholy. And to hear him tell of his researches and experiments was to know such horror and repulsion as a venomous reptile might inspire. For there had been no depths to which he had not sunk, and some things he only hinted at, even to me. I tell you, Kirowan, it is easy to laugh at tales of the black world of the unknown, when one is in pleasant company under the bright sunlight, but had you sat at ungodly hours in the silent bizarre library of John Grimlan and looked on the ancient musty volumes and listened to his grisly talk as I did, your tongue would have cloven to your palate with sheer horror as mine did, and the supernatural would have seemed very real and near to you—as it seemed to me!"

"But in God's name, man!" I cried, for the tension was growing unbearable; "come to the point and tell me what you want of me."

"I want you to come with me to John Grimlan's house and help carry out his outlandish instructions in regard to his body."

I had no liking for the adventure, but I dressed hurriedly, an occasional shudder of premonition shaking me. Once fully clad, I followed Conrad out of the house and up the silent road which led to the house of John Grimlan. The road wound uphill, and all the way, looking upward and forward, I could see that great grim house perched like a bird of evil on the crest of the hill, bulking black and stark against the stars. In the west pulsed a single dull red smear where the young moon had just sunk from view behind the low black hills. The whole night seemed full of brooding evil, and the persistent swishing of a bat's wings somewhere overhead caused my taut nerves to jerk and thrum. To drown the quick pounding of my own heart, I said:

"Do you share the belief so many hold, that John Grimlan was mad?"

We strode on several paces before Conrad answered, seemingly with a strange reluctance, "But for one incident, I would say no man was ever saner. But one night in his study, he seemed suddenly to break all bonds of reason.

"He had discoursed for hours on his favorite subject—black magic—when suddenly he cried, as his face lit with a weird unholy glow: 'Why should I sit here babbling such child's prattle to you? These voodoo rituals—these Shinto sacrifices—feathered snakes—goats without horns—black leopard cults—bah! Filth and dust that the wind blows away! Dregs of the real Unknown— the deep mysteries! Mere echoes from the Abyss!

"'I could tell you things that would shatter your paltry brain! I could breathe into your ear names that would wither you like a burnt weed! What do you know of Yog-Sothoth, of Kathulos and the sunken cities? None of these names is even included in your mythologies. Not even in your dreams have you glimpsed the black cyclopean walls of Koth, or shriveled before the noxious winds that blow from Yuggoth!

"'But I will not blast you lifeless with my black wisdom! I cannot expect your infantile brain to bear what mine holds. Were you as old as I—had you seen, as I have seen, kingdoms crumble and generations pass away—had you gathered as ripe grain the dark secrets of the centuries—'

"He was raving away, his wildly lit face scarcely human in appearance, and suddenly, noting my evident bewilderment, he burst into a horrible cackling laugh.

"'Gad!' he cried in a voice and accent strange to me, 'methinks I've frighted ye, and certes, it is not to be marveled at, sith ye be but a naked salvage in the arts of life, after all. Ye think I be old, eh? Why, ye gaping lout, ye'd drop dead were I to divulge the generations of men I've known—'

"But at this point such horror overcame me that I fled from him as from an adder, and his high-pitched, diabolical laughter followed me out of the shadowy house. Some days later I received a letter apologizing for his manner and ascribing it candidly—too candidly—to drugs. I did not believe it, but I renewed our relations, after some hesitation."

"It sounds like utter madness," I muttered.

"Yes," admitted Conrad, hesitantly. "But—Kirowan, have you ever seen anyone who knew John Grimlan in his youth?"

I shook my head.

"I have been at pains to inquire about him discreetly," said Conrad. "He has lived here—with the exception of mysterious absences often for months at a time—for twenty years. The older villagers remember distinctly when he first came and took over that old house on the hill, and they all say that in the intervening years he seems not to have aged perceptibly. When he came here he looked just as he does now—or did, up to the moment of his death—of the appearance of a man about fifty.

"I met old Von Boehnk in Vienna, who said he knew Grimlan when a very young man studying in Berlin, fifty years ago, and he expressed astonishment that the old man was still living; for he said at that time Grimlan seemed to be about fifty years of age."

I gave an incredulous exclamation, seeing the implication toward which the conversation was trending.

"Nonsense! Professor Von Boehnk is past eighty himself, and liable to the errors of extreme age. He confused this man with another." Yet as I spoke, my flesh crawled unpleasantly and the hairs on my neck prickled.

"Well," shrugged Conrad, "here we are at the house."

The huge pile reared up menacingly before us, and as we reached the front door a vagrant wind moaned through the near-by trees and I started foolishly as I again heard the ghostly beat of the bat's wings. Conrad turned a large key in the antique lock, and as we entered, a cold draft swept across us like a breath from the grave—moldy and cold. I shuddered.

We groped our way through a black hallway and into a study,

and here Conrad lighted a candle, for no gas lights or electric lights were to be found in the house. I looked about me, dreading what the light might disclose, but the room, heavily tapestried and bizarrely furnished, was empty save for us two.

"Where—where is—It?" I asked in a husky whisper, from a throat gone dry.

"Upstairs," answered Conrad in a low voice, showing that the silence and mystery of the house had laid a spell on him also. "Upstairs, in the library where he died."

I glanced up involuntarily. Somewhere above our head, the lone master of this grim house was stretched out in his last sleep—silent, his white face set in a grinning mask of death. Panic swept over me and I fought for control. After all, it was merely the corpse of a wicked old man, who was past harming anyone—this argument rang hollowly in my brain like the words of a frightened child who is trying to reassure himself.

I turned to Conrad. He had taken a time-yellowed envelope from an inside pocket.

"This," he said, removing from the envelope several pages of closely written, time-yellowed parchment, "is, in effect, the last word of John Grimlan, though God alone knows how many years ago it was written. He gave it to me ten years ago, immediately after his return from Mongolia. It was shortly after this that he had his first seizure.

"This envelope he gave me, sealed, and he made me swear that I would hide it carefully, and that I would not open it until he was dead, when I was to read the contents and follow their directions exactly. More, he made me swear that no matter what he said or did after giving me the envelope, I would go ahead as first directed. 'For,' he said with a fearful smile, 'the flesh is weak but I am a man of my word, and though I might, in a moment of weakness, wish to retract, it is far, far too late now. You may never understand the matter, but you are to do as I have said.'"

"Well?"

"Well," again Conrad wiped his brow, "tonight as he lay writhing in his death-agonies, his wordless howls were mingled with frantic admonitions to me to bring him the envelope and destroy it before his eyes! As he yammered this, he forced himself up on his elbows and with eyes staring and hair standing straight up on his head, he screamed at me in a manner to chill the blood. And he was shrieking for me to destroy the envelope, not to open it; and once he howled in his delirium for me to hew his body into pieces and scatter the bits to the four winds of heaven!"

An uncontrollable exclamation of horror escaped my dry lips.

"At last," went on Conrad, "I gave in. Remembering his commands ten years ago, I at first stood firm, but at last, as his screeches grew unbearably desperate, I turned to go for the envelope, even though that meant leaving him alone. But as I turned, with one last fearful convulsion in which blood-flecked foam flew from his writhing lips, the life went from his twisted body in a single great wrench."

He fumbled at the parchment.

"I am going to carry out my promise. The directions herein seem fantastic and may be the whims of a disordered mind, but I gave my word. They are, briefly, that I place his corpse on the great black ebony table in his library, with seven black candles burning about him. The doors and windows are to be firmly closed and fastened. Then, in the darkness which precedes dawn, I am to read the formula, charm or spell which is contained in a smaller, sealed envelope inside the first, and which I have not yet opened."

"But is that all?" I cried. "No provisions as to the disposition of his fortune, his estate—or his corpse?"

"Nothing. In his will, which I have seen elsewhere, he leaves estate and fortune to a certain Oriental gentleman named in the document as—Malik Tous!"

"What!" I cried, shaken to my soul. "Conrad, this is madness heaped on madness! Malik Tous—good God! No mortal man was ever so named! That is the title of the foul god worshipped by the mysterious Yezidees—they of Mount Alamout the Accursed—whose Eight Brazen Towers rise in the mysterious wastes of deep Asia. His idolatrous symbol is the brazen peacock. And the Muhammadans, who hate his demon-worshipping devotees, say he is the essence of the evil of all the universes—the Prince of Darkness—Ahriman—the old Serpent—the veritable Satan! And you say Grimlan names this mythical demon in his will?"

"It is the truth," Conrad's throat was dry. "And look—he has scribbled a strange line at the corner of this parchment: 'Dig me no grave; I shall not need one.'"

Again a chill wandered down my spine.

"In God's name," I cried in a kind of frenzy, "let us get this incredible business over with!"

"I think a drink might help," answered Conrad, moistening his lips. "It seems to me I've seen Grimlan go into this cabinet for wine—" He bent to the door of an ornately carved mahogany cabinet, and after some difficulty opened it.

"No wine here," he said disappointedly, "and if ever I felt the need of stimulants—what's this?"

He drew out a roll of parchment, dusty, yellowed and half covered with spiderwebs. Everything in that grim house seemed, to my nervously excited senses, fraught with mysterious meaning and import, and I leaned over his shoulder as he unrolled it.

"It's a record of peerage," he said, "such a chronicle of births, deaths and so forth, as the old families used to keep, in the Sixteenth Century and earlier."

"What's the name?" I asked.

He scowled over the dim scrawls, striving to master the faded, archaic script.

"G-r-y-m—I've got it—Grymlann, of course. It's the records of old John's family—the Grymlanns of Toad's-Heath Manor, Suffolk—what an outlandish name for an estate! Look at the last entry."

Together we read, "John Grymlann, borne, March 10, 1630."

And then we both cried out. Under this entry was freshly written, in a strange scrawling hand, "Died, March 10, 1930." Below this there was a seal of black wax, stamped with a strange design, something like a peacock with a spreading tail.

Conrad stared at me speechless, all the color ebbed from his face. I shook myself with the rage engendered by fear.

"It's the hoax of a madman!" I shouted. "The stage has been set with such great care that the actors have overstepped themselves. Whoever they are, they have heaped up so many incredible effects as to nullify them. It's all a very stupid, very dull drama of illusion."

And even as I spoke, icy sweat stood out on my body and I shook as with an ague. With a wordless motion Conrad turned toward the stairs, taking up a large candle from a mahogany table.

"It was understood, I suppose," he whispered, "that I should go through with this ghastly matter alone; but I had not the moral courage, and now I'm glad I had not."

A still horror brooded over the silent house as we went up the stairs. A faint breeze stole in from somewhere and set the heavy velvet hangings rustling, and I visualized stealthy taloned fingers drawing aside the tapestries, to fix red gloating eyes upon us. Once I thought I heard the indistinct clumping of monstrous feet somewhere above us, but it must have been the heavy pounding of my own heart.

The stairs debouched into a wide dark corridor, in which our feeble candle cast a faint gleam which but illuminated our pale faces and made the shadows seem darker by comparison. We stopped at a heavy door, and I heard Conrad's breath draw in sharply as a man's will when he braces himself physically or mentally. I involuntarily clenched my fists until the nails bit into the palms; then Conrad thrust the door open.

A sharp cry escaped his lips. The candle dropped from his nerveless fingers and went out. The library of John Grimlan was ablaze with light, though the whole house had been in darkness when we entered it.

This light came from seven black candles placed at regular intervals about the great ebony table. On this table, between the candles—I had braced myself against the sight. Now in the face of the mysterious illumination and the sight of the thing on the table, my resolution nearly gave way. John Grimlan had been unlovely in life; in death he was hideous. Yes, he was hideous even though his face was mercifully covered with the same curious silken robe, which, worked in fantastic bird-like designs, covered his whole body except the crooked claw-like hands and the bare withered feet.

A strangling sound came from Conrad. "My God!" he whispered; "what is this? I laid his body out on the table and placed the candles about it, but I did not light them, nor did I place that robe over the body! And there were bedroom slippers on his feet when I left—"

He halted suddenly. We were not alone in the death-room.

At first we had not seen him, as he sat in the great armchair in a farther nook of a corner, so still that he seemed a part of the shadows cast by the heavy tapestries. As my eyes fell upon him, a violent shuddering shook me and a feeling akin to nausea racked the pit of my stomach. My first impression was of vivid, oblique yellow eyes which gazed unwinkingly at us. Then the man rose and made a deep *salaam*, and we saw that he was an Oriental. Now when I strive to etch him clearly in my mind, I can resurrect no plain image of him. I only remember those piercing eyes and the yellow, fantastic robe he wore.

We returned his salute mechanically and he spoke in a low, refined voice, "Gentlemen, I crave your pardon! I have made so free as to light the candles—shall we not proceed with the business pertaining to our mutual friend."

He made a slight gesture toward the silent bulk on the table. Conrad nodded, evidently unable to speak. The thought flashed through our minds at the same time, that this man had also been given a sealed envelope—but how had he come to the Grimlan house so quickly? John Grimlan had been dead scarcely two hours and to the best of our knowledge no one knew of his demise but ourselves. And how had he got into the locked and bolted house?

The whole affair was grotesque and unreal in the extreme. We did not even introduce ourselves or ask the stranger his name. He took charge in a matter-of-fact way, and so under the spell of horror and illusion were we that we moved dazedly, involuntarily obeying his suggestions, given us in a low, respectful tone.

I found myself standing on the left side of the table, looking across its grisly burden at Conrad. The Oriental stood with arms folded and head bowed at the head of the table, nor did it then strike me as being strange that he should stand there, instead of Conrad who was to read what Grimlan had written. I found my gaze drawn to the figure worked on the breast of the stranger's robe, in black silk—a curious figure, somewhat resembling a peacock and somewhat resembling a bat, or a flying dragon. I noted with a start that the same design was worked on the robe covering the corpse.

The doors had been locked, the windows fastened down. Conrad, with a shaky hand, opened the inner envelope and fluttered open the parchment sheets contained therein. These sheets seemed much older than those containing the instructions to Conrad, in the larger envelope. Conrad began to read in a monotonous drone which had the effect of hypnosis on the hearer; so at times the candles grew dim in my gaze and the room and its occupants swam strange and monstrous, veiled and distorted like an hallucination. Most of what he read was gibberish; it meant nothing; yet the sound of it and the archaic style of it filled me with an intolerable horror.

"To ye contract elsewhere recorded, I, John Grymlann, herebye sweare by ye Name of ye Nameless One to keep goode faithe. Wherefore do I now write in blood these wordes spoken to me in thys grim & silent chamber in ye dedde citie of Koth, whereto no mortal manne hath attained but mee. These same wordes now writ down by mee to be rede over my bodie at ye appointed tyme to fulfill my parte of ye bargain which I entered intoe of mine own free will & knowledge beinge of rite mynd & fiftie years of age this yeare of 1680, A.D. Here begynneth ye incantation:

"Before manne was, ye Elder ones were, & even yet their lord dwelleth amonge ye shadows to which if a manne sette his foote he maye not turn vpon his track."

The words merged into a barbaric gibberish as Conrad stumbled through an unfamiliar language—a language faintly suggesting the Phoenician, but shuddery with the touch of a hideous antiquity beyond any remembered earthly tongue. One of the candles flickered and went out. I made a move to relight it, but a motion from the silent Oriental stayed me. His eyes burned into mine, then shifted back to the still form on the table.

The manuscript had shifted back into its archaic English.

"—And ye mortal which gaineth to ye black citadels of Koth & speaks with ye Darke Lord whose face is hidden, for a price maye he gain hys heartes desire, ryches & knowledge beyond countinge & lyffe beyond mortal span even two hundred and fiftie yeares."

Again Conrad's voice trailed off into unfamiliar gutturals. Another candle went out.

"—Let not ye mortal flynche as ye tyme draweth nigh for payement & ye fires of Hell laye hold vpon ye vytals as the sign of reckoninge. For ye Prince of Darkness taketh hys due in ye endde & he is not to bee cozened. What ye have promised, that shall ye deliver. Augantha ne shuba—"

At the first sound of those barbaric accents, a cold hand of terror locked about my throat. My frantic eyes shot to the candles and I was not surprised to see another flicker out. Yet there was no hint of any draft to stir the heavy black hangings. Conrad's voice wavered; he drew his hand across his throat, gagging momentarily. The eyes of the Oriental never altered.

"—Amonge ye sonnes of men glide strange shadows for ever. Men see ye tracks of ye talones but not ye feete that make them. Over ye souls of men spread great black wingges. There is but one Black Master though men calle hym Sathanas & Beelzebub & Apolleon & Ahriman & Malik Tous—"

Mists of horror engulfed me. I was dimly aware of Conrad's voice droning on and on, both in English and in that other fearsome tongue whose horrific import I scarcely dared try to guess. And with stark fear clutching at my heart, I saw the candles go out, one by one. And with each flicker, as the gathering gloom darkened about us, my horror mounted. I could not speak, I could not move; my distended eyes were fixed with agonized intensity on the remaining candle. The silent Oriental at the head of that ghastly table was included in my fear. He had not moved nor spoken, but under his drooping lids, his eyes burned with devilish triumph; I knew that beneath his inscrutable exterior he was gloating fiendishly—but why—why?

But I knew that the moment the extinguishing of the last candle plunged the room into utter darkness, some nameless, abominable thing would take place. Conrad was approaching the end. His voice rose to the climax in gathering crescendo.

"Approacheth now ye moment of payement. Ye ravens are flying. Ye bats winge against ye skye. There are skulls in ye starres. Ye soul & ye bodie are promised and shall bee delivered uppe. Not to ye dust agayne nor ye elements from which springe lyfe—"

The candle flickered slightly. I tried to scream, but my mouth gaped to a soundless yammering. I tried to flee, but I stood frozen, unable even to close my eyes.

"—Ye abysse yawns & ye debt is to paye. Ye light fayles, ye shadows gather. There is no god but evil; no lite but darkness; no hope but doom—"

A hollow groan resounded through the room. It seemed to come from the robe-covered thing on the table! That robe twitched fitfully.

"Oh winges in ye black darke!"

I started violently; a faint swish sounded in the gathering shadows. The stir of the dark hangings? It sounded like the rustle of gigantic wings.

"Oh redde eyes in ye shadows! What is promised, what is writ in bloode is fulfilled! Ye lite is gulfed in blackness! Ya—Koth!"

The last candle went out suddenly and a ghastly unhuman cry that came not from my lips or from Conrad's burst unbearably forth. Horror swept over me like a black icy wave; in the blind dark I heard myself screaming terribly. Then with a swirl and a great rush of wind something swept the room, flinging the hangings aloft and dashing chairs and tables crashing to the floor. For an instant an intolerable odor burned our nostrils, a low hideous tittering mocked us in the blackness; then silence fell like a shroud.

Somehow, Conrad found a candle and lighted it. The faint glow showed us the room in fearful disarray—showed us each other's ghastly faces—and showed us the black ebony table—empty! The doors and windows were locked as they had been, but the Oriental was gone—and so was the corpse of John Grimlan.

Shrieking like damned men we broke down the door and fled frenziedly down the well-like staircase where the darkness seemed to clutch at us with clammy black fingers. As we tumbled down into the lower hallway, a lurid glow cut the darkness and the scent of burning wood filled our nostrils.

The outer doorway held momentarily against our frantic assault, then gave way and we hurtled into the outer starlight. Behind us the flames leaped up with a crackling roar as we fled down the hill. Conrad, glancing over his shoulder, halted suddenly, wheeled and flung up his arms like a madman, and screamed:

"Soul and body he sold to Malik Tous, who is Satan, two hundred and fifty years ago! This was the night of payment—and my God—look! Look! The Fiend has claimed his own!"

I looked, frozen with horror. Flames had enveloped the whole house with appalling swiftness, and now the great mass was etched against the shadowed sky, a crimson inferno. And above the holocaust hovered a gigantic black shadow like a monstrous bat, and from its dark clutch dangled a small white thing, like the body of a man, dangling limply. Then, even as we cried out in horror, it was gone and our dazed gaze met only the shuddering walls and blazing roof which crumpled into the flames with an earth-shaking roar.